Truth and Lies

Marguerite Valentine

Published by Sideways On Publications 2017

www.margueritev.org

Printed by CreateSpace

Available on Amazon & Kindle

The primary purpose of literature is to tell us the truth about ourselves by telling us lies about people who never existed.

STEPHEN KING

Part 1

— 1 —

October 2008. Something was wrong. The economy was in deep trouble. The high octane energy of the City of London seemed to continue as it always did. Its workers still pitched up for work, but the trading floors in the Stock Exchange were quiet. Some knew what was coming, but to others, it came as a shock. The international money markets were in a state of collapse. Businesses, starved of funding, including the megalithic Lehmann Brothers, were slowly unfolding like a set of badly stacked dominoes.

Directors and CEOs were told to 'stand down' and those that remained had been informed, that for the interim, their bonuses would be curbed. The impact of this slow, lingering death soon spread to the high streets of Britain. Long, snaking queues of account holders were pictured, evidence that made even the smallest punter aware the financial situation was dire. Faces etched with anxiety, they forlornly waited outside the banks and the building societies, hoping to find somewhere safe to deposit their hard-earned money.

The Government meanwhile was treading water; ministers desperately trying to keep their head above the waves of criticisms and recriminations coming at them from all quarters. For a time, their response to the situation appeared dilatory, if not indifferent, but with the passing of each day, the outcry became more urgent, more vociferous, until it was blindingly obvious to everyone in the City of London that the Government must intervene, and soon. The question was, how?

The financial institutions of the City and the Western world, the factory owners of the UK, and the world's press, waited. Seb, a young City financier, cynical, and angry, also waited. Sitting in front of his state-of-the-art, wall-mounted television he tore open a bag of vegetable crisps, grabbed a handful, stuffed them into his mouth, and leaned back in his chair. The much-publicised Government press conference was about to begin. On the screen before him, standing behind two lecterns placed side by side, barricaded off, were the Prime Minister and the Chancellor of the Exchequer, and facing them, the press, tablets balanced on their knees, expressions of intense expectation written on their faces.

The Prime Minister glanced at his notes, then at the cameras arrayed round the room, and with a final look around the hall, began to speak. His words were measured, his tone authoritative.

'A global storm, a worldwide crisis in the money markets, caused by excessive risk-taking without sufficient underlying capitalisation, has created a grave economic situation. The financial markets are in a state of imminent collapse. This is not an abstraction, but an economic crisis. Restoring trust and confidence in the markets is essential. Urgent action is required.'

He paused and looked up. Only the sound of the assembled journalists tapping their electronic notebooks broke the silence. Taking a deep breath, he sketched out a raft of government measures. Designed to prop up the rapidly deteriorating money markets, the Government, he said, proposed to take more control of the banks, enforce a return to medium-term lending, and inject billions into the three banks most at risk of crashing, namely: The Royal Bank of Scotland, HBOS, and Lloyds TSB.

Seb chucked the empty crisp bag on the floor, pulled a chair close to him and, propping his feet on the arm, leant back. What a fucking mess. He'd been aware for months that the economy was not as it seemed. Like many in finance, he read the international as well as the national financial press, many of which had observed and commented on the huge amounts of debt piling up across the globe. The Government proposal, he thought, was interesting, but predictable. It was too little, too late. Even taking into account how little room for manoeuvre the Government had, anyone with half a brain knew if the banks collapsed, the consequences would be disastrous. The impact would travel like a tsunami across the world.

Along with the observations of the debts piling up, was the mood of hysteria which had slowly crept into the international money markets. While a minority of economists and financial journalists had predicted an imminent melt down, mostly they'd been ignored. Nobody wanted to know, or they didn't care, or things were moving so fast there seemed no possibility of stopping the conveyor belt of madness. Besides, there'd been too much money to be made and the British and American governments had, for whatever reason, turned a blind eye.

The camera moved to Eric Friedman, the BBC Business News Editor. He pointed firstly to the obvious: the financial sector was in meltdown. Secondly, that many economic historians saw the present panic as comparable to the debacle after the First World War. His third comment addressed the view that the bail out of the banks was a form of nationalisation and a betrayal of shareholders.

Dismissing these critiques, he argued that such opinions represented an outmoded neo-liberalism, and were no longer applicable to today's collapsing international financial sector. The UK banking system, he stressed, had been insufficiently regulated. Consequently the banks had built up too much power. While acknowledging there was some agreement on this, it all depended on who was doing the talking. He finished his analysis with a dramatic statement. 'Today,' he said, 'is a day of humiliation for the banks.'

The idea that bankers and financiers would feel humiliated by the present financial situation seemed impossibly naive and caused Seb to loudly guffaw. They might know the dictionary meaning of the word but, in practice, it would be an alien concept. Humiliated bankers were an unknown species. He knew the bankers and brokers in the City too well, and the government hadn't a hope in hell of controlling them. They wouldn't give a flying fuck whatever was said, whatever changes were made. They ducked, they dived, they employed accountants and lawyers with nerves of steel who knew the tax laws backward, exploited every loophole they could and invested any surplus, and there was lots of it, off-shore.

They were well used to sailing close to the wind. Deals were done with a nod and a wink, and with friends in high places, politicians could be bought off with large donations to their party. It was a system that had worked perfectly, until now. A balance between the aphrodisiac of political power and financial greed, with money as the go-between, it was a system made in heaven for those with a penchant for the creation of wealth, but made in hell for those with more immediate concerns on their mind.

It was Friday, early afternoon, and Seb had just worked out at the gym. He showered, wrapped a towel round his hips, stood before a mirror, and stared critically at himself. The work was paying off, the long hours running, the press ups, the weight lifting, the finger and hand exercises. He was tanned, toned, fit and his body looked good, but even so, despite his appearance, his father was right, he lacked the killer instinct. Not that he cared what his father thought. There wasn't much he did care about, but insofar as he was also aware of that, he didn't care about that either.

He took his time, got dressed, went to the bar, removed the nicotine chewing gum from his mouth, and ordered a carrot and orange juice. He glanced around, eyed up the women. No one he fancied. Anaemically pale or artificially tanned, beautiful bodies but intrinsically boring, the type turned on by the size of an expense account – he'd slept with more of them than he could remember, gone through the rituals of flirting, wooing, screwing, but in the end, he always moved on. None of them had had a hold on him, but, if he was honest with himself, and occasionally he could be, he regretted this. Something was missing from his life.

He pushed open the glass swing doors of the gym, took the lift to the ground floor, passed the ornate and beautiful bronze sculpture, noted but ignored the discreet security systems, walked down the steps into Canada Square straight into the middle of a noisy demonstration. The anti-capitalists, earnest, non-violent, but as irritating and as persistent as a cloud of midges, were, yet again, out in force. He began shoving a way through them, until forced to a stop. A young woman holding a bunch of leaflets stood directly in his path. He glanced at her – attractive, tanned, dressed in jeans and a tee shirt, dark hair cropped, challenging, light green eyes. She removed a leaflet from her pile, pushed it into his hand, looked at him, and waited for a response.

'Thanks, but no thanks,' he said.

She put her head on one side and smiled up at him. 'Why not?' she asked.

'Not my scene.' He took out another piece of chewing gum, pushed it into his mouth and stared at her.

'You haven't read it.'

'I don't need to.'

She sighed, keeping her eyes on him, but didn't move. He stopped chewing, and continuing to stare at her, paused, then said, 'Another day, maybe.'

'When?'

'I'll tell you when.'

'I'll hold you to that.'

She flashed him a smile. Her teeth were exceptionally white, almost perfect, except for the tiny gap between the front two, an imperfection which added to her charm, giving her the look of an urchin. He held her glance for a split second longer than necessary – his intention to make eye contact with her. It always worked. She looked away. He turned to walk towards the car park and immediately put her out of his mind, aware only of the rising level of noise surrounding him. Cordoned off by the police, the shouting, the catcalls and the whistles by the demonstrators were increasing minute by minute. The press and television were rolling in, and the atmosphere in the Square had become as taut as a tripwire

Thank Christ he was leaving for the weekend, not that he was looking forward to it. His parents' thirtieth anniversary, a party celebrating the fact they were still together despite everything, but money talks; an aphrodisiac, the glue for some couples, and cheaper and prettier than a divorce settlement. He reached his Audi, checked the presents for his parents were still in the boot, swung his brief case onto the back seat, pulled off his jacket, loosened his tie, undid the top button of his shirt and drove out, away from London, towards Lavenham in Suffolk.

He leant forward to play his current favourite music, a thrash metal band, but it didn't take long before a wave of irritation passed through him. It was too loud, too over the top, a mind fuck, it drowned out all thought, and right now, he just wasn't in that mood. He switched it off, and drove the rest of the way in silence.

The party was the weekend's big event. His mother had invited at least forty guests, all rich, all local, all in business. He wondered whether his parents' respective lovers had been invited and if so, how they'd play the game. The event could take their mind off the international money markets assuming, of course, they knew that the economy was on the brink of a free fall; but they'd be stupid if they didn't know. In any case, it would be amusing, watching how the bored and affluent made out in the face of the upcoming disaster. The rich at play – like Nero, they 'fiddled as Rome burned'. He put his foot hard down and overtook three cars at once; the party, at least, would be a distraction.

Not that the financial situation would affect

him, he was getting out of it, but even so, he'd be expected to socialise, make polite conversation, say what he was up to and talk about his career. That however was no longer possible. His upcoming new job was a no-go area. He flicked the steering wheel with one finger, pulled the gum out of his mouth, and pushed it out through the side window. Enough. A beer was in order. Before hitting home, he'd call into The Swan.

It was early evening when he arrived and he liked The Swan. He knew the landlord, but the best thing about it was, he'd be left alone. He greeted the landlord with a brief nod, ordered half a Bengal Lancer and moving well away from the bar, began watching the news on the large wall-mounted TV. The top story was the demo at Canary Wharf, and the usual suspects were all there.

The self-elected caring, sharing, groupies, the great and the good, all united by their common enemy: bankers, the new pariahs. Not that any of them would give a damn, considering boardroom bonuses were up by fifty per cent. A camera was shoved in the face of a protester. Ready with a speech, she was on a high. She reeled out a list of organisations opposing the banks and their attendant personnel, arguing passionately for a system based on people not profit. She kept her trump card till the last. The Archbishop of Canterbury supported them, she said. The camera moved away. Well, good for him, he thought.

She'd reminded him of an incident from school, when a member of the God squad at morning assembly had announced it was easier for a camel to go through the eye of a needle than the rich to enter the kingdom of God. The boys, seated in the pews facing him, including himself, sniggered. They were all from wealthy backgrounds, but that seemed to have escaped the speaker, but it hadn't them. They spent the next fifteen minutes making faces, gesturing and nudging each other until one of the masters noticed, and fixing them with his evil eye, had stopped them. Even now, the thought amused him. He turned away, put on his headphones to listen to music and watched the pub fill up.

The medieval village of Lavenham with its half-timbered houses, its self-conscious affluence and long history going back centuries had always attracted tourists, and tonight their numbers outweighed the regulars, but he was in no mood for talking. His aim was to keep himself to himself and psychologically prepare for the evening's entertainment. So, aware of his ambivalence in attending the planned party, and despite the influx of excitable, noisy tourists, he stayed as long as possible before reluctantly standing up to leave.

He'd reached the door when the landlord called over, 'Seb, I'll call a cab for you.'

He paused, smiled. 'Nah, I'll be alright. It's not far, but thanks. See you again.'

'Yeah. Enjoy, and be careful.'

It was gone nine and dusk as he approached his parents' house. An old manor farmhouse, down a remote country lane, and set in two acres, it was gated and electronically controlled which meant to open it he was forced to stop, retrieve and operate the zapper hidden in the glove compartment. Can't be too careful, his mother had said. He pushed the button and the gates swung open. The drive was gravelled; it wound under trees and past ornamental shrubs. His mother loved her house and she loved her garden. When they'd first moved there she'd employed two landscape gardeners. She'd had an affair with one of them. Nothing serious, she'd said. He'd been fourteen when she told him and back from school for the holidays. He was young and innocent then – it hadn't lasted long.

At the time he was close to her. He'd been telling her about the English teacher who had taken them through Lawrence's *Lady Chatterley's Lover*. The sex scenes between Lady Chatterley and Mellors had shocked him, but also fascinated him. But he didn't tell her that. His mother had laughed. Her laugh had irritated him, probably because she chose that moment to tell him she had her own 'Mellors'. She thought the coincidence amusing. He hadn't. He'd rather not have known about his mother's sex life, but that was his mother. Inappropriate. In his face. She'd never change.

He parked the car a little way from the house and walked up the drive. It was cluttered with sleek cars, the party was in full swing. The lights were on all over, the house lit up, the front door wide open. Nobody seemed to have heard of climate change or if they had, it was of sublime indifference. He walked into the hall and was greeted by a woman, he hadn't seen before. Probably employed for the occasion, she was fair, pale, with light blue eyes. She directed him towards the drawing room. 'From Poland?' he said. She coloured up. He smiled, 'I'm the son. Their one and only. Thanks. I know where to go.' She looked at the floor, frightened as a rabbit. He hesitated. Before venturing into the throng, he'd go to his bedroom, dump his holdall and chill out.

It was almost a year since he'd last visited. He walked upstairs and tried the door but it was locked. He knew the key would be hidden on the top of the wardrobe on the landing. He retrieved it, opened the door and looked around. There was a faint smell of perfume. It was familiar; it was one his mother wore. What she'd been doing there, he had no idea. Other than that, everything looked the same, and just as he liked it. The possessions and valuables of his childhood and youth, all kept in one room.

He walked over to the book shelves. Lines of school books, biology, physics, chemistry, exercise books, books from university on the economy, the political system, philosophy, a few paperbacks, mainly thrillers, pens, biros stuck in a pewter mug, a hockey stick lying under the hand basin. All where he'd last left them. His school blazer was still in the wardrobe. His mother had given away the rest of his uniform, but he'd wanted to hang onto that.

He picked up a photograph taken when they'd sailed round the Dodecanese Islands. It had been his favourite holiday. His father had charted a boat and for the duration of the holiday and for the first time ever, his parents hadn't quarrelled. In the photograph, he was standing between them. All three were smiling. A farce. Everything appeared normal, but it wasn't and never had been. There were other photographs, some faded, some of his school friends, many he'd lost touch with, but the framed photo of Helen, his first girlfriend, he still hung onto. Blonde, pretty, straight talking, she wanted to be a lawyer. He'd thought he'd love her forever, but after she got to university, she'd dumped him. Too uncommunicative, she'd said. He'd been devastated. For a long time he thought he'd never meet anyone like her again and he'd been right, he hadn't. She was a one-off, but there were always others. Not the same, but in their different ways, they amused him, even if only temporarily.

He lay back on the bed, his arms under his head and stared at the ceiling. He was in no rush to go downstairs. The chatter and laughter from the party downstairs filtered through the door, and he was about to drift off when there was a tap on the door. It had to be his mother. She walked straight in. He sat up and with a hint of sarcasm in his voice, said, 'Do come in.'

'Seb, your father saw you skulk upstairs. Why didn't you stop to say hello?'

She had a little girl's voice which didn't quite match how she looked; a slim, middle-aged, stylish woman. She was wearing a black straight dress with very high heels, holding a drink in one hand. She was elegant and classy, but she'd always drunk too much and as a child he'd found that an embarrassment.

'You're drunk.'

'Why do you say that?'

'Because you are and I should know. You sound petulant, you're swaying and I can smell the alcohol from here, plus the fact your eyes are glassy.'

'It's a party, Seb. Don't you have anything nice to say?'

'Happy anniversary.'

'What are you doing?'

'What's it look like I'm doing?'

'I can tell you're in a bad mood. I'm going.'

'Please do. Where's the old man?'

'Downstairs. Talking business.'

'Surprise, surprise.' His mother continued staring at him as if she couldn't quite focus.

'Please go, Mother. I'll be down later. By the way, did you invite Carole?'

'Carole? Of course I did. She knows you're coming. I'll tell her you're here. She was asking after you, and she wanted to know when you'd arrive. She... ' Her voice dropped conspiratorially.

'Mother, spare me.'

'I was going to say... '

He lay back on the bed, turned away, waited for her to leave the room and the door to close, then he got up, turned the key in the lock and fell asleep.

Ten minutes later, he was woken again. Someone was standing outside the door and softly calling his name. Through the blur of sleep, he recognised the voice: Carole, his mother's best friend and his first lover.

'Yes?'

'Seb, it's me, open the door. I have some bubbly for you.'

He got up, walked across and pulled open the door. 'Christ, can't I be left in peace!' He stood looking at her. Fifteen years older, she was a dark blonde with sleepy green eyes and a permanently fixed mocking smile. Aged fifteen, he'd been crazy about her and he couldn't get enough of her, but those times had gone. Now he reserved his infatuations for younger women. She was holding two glasses of champagne. She placed one of them on the floor and looked at him from under her long lashes.

'I've brought this for you.' He didn't reply. 'Well, aren't you going to invite me in?' He shrugged, turned and walked back to his bed. 'I'll take that as a yes. Let me get your drink.' She retrieved the glass from where she'd left it on the floor and tottered into his room, placing the drink on his bedside table.

He leaned against the headboard. She was wearing a bright blue dress with a full skirt, a halter neck and very high heels. The dress suited her. She wasn't bad for her age. He picked up the glass she'd brought him, took a sip, and watched her as she walked across to the window. She pulled the curtains across, put on the side lamp and sat down. She carefully hitched up her skirt, crossed her legs and sat, slipping her shoe on and off the one foot. It drew attention to her legs.

'How are you Seb? How's life treating you?'

'Fine, and you?'

'I'm fine too.'

'Your husband?'

'Just the same, fornicating around, but basically fine.'

'The horse? No, don't answer, let me guess. He's fine too.'

'He's a she.'

'Who cares. A horse is a horse.'

'Why did you come tonight?'

'For their anniversary, no other reason. It's the right thing to do.' He paused. 'Not to see you, if that's what you wanted me to say.'

She put her hands behind her head, lifted her hair away from her neck, and let it down again. 'Flattery's never been your bag, has it, Seb? But that's your attraction. No sweet talk. Straight. You tell it like it is.' Seb raised his eyebrows.

She stood up, walked over to him. 'It's two years since... '

'Yes, I can count too. You're standing too close. Back off.'

'You didn't used to say that to me.'

'Probably not. Times change.'

'You've changed.'

'You think so?'

She looked coy. 'Come on, Seb. How about it? It's been a while. They're all downstairs. No one will know.'

Seb sighed and looked away. 'What's with your husband?'

'He's screwing a new girl at the stables. No time

for me.' She came across the room, sat on his bed, undid his shirt and ran one finger down his chest. 'Come on, Seb. No one will know.'

He paused. 'Okay. If that's what you want. Go down and choose a bottle or two of whatever, and lock the door behind you.'

She smiled. 'Then what? '

'You know what. That's why you're here, isn't it.' He eyeballed her, unsmiling.

'You're a cynic.'

He stared intensely at her, 'Do you know the definition of a cynic?' He paused. 'Probably not and furthermore, you couldn't care less.'

She made no reply, shrugging in response. 'You still like older women then?'

'They make fewer demands. Usually.'

'I taught you everything you know.'

'You're boring me and I'm about to fall asleep. Take the key, get some more drink, and like I said, lock the door behind you.'

She walked out. He got up, stripped off, lay back on the bed and promptly fell asleep. When he woke, she was sitting reading, and drinking champagne. She wore a skimpy white lace bra and pants, which showed off her tan. She was slim with a taut, toned body, not because she went to a gym but because she regularly rode. She wasn't particularly desirable, but she knew how to work him, and they shared a history, and she could keep her mouth shut.

She looked up, saw he was awake, 'I didn't know you were interested in politics.'

'What are you reading?'

'A leaflet, it's about the anti-globalisation movements.'

'They were scattered around Canary Wharf. I'm not interested. I picked one up, read it, and stuck it in my pocket, end of story. Are you planning to spend the night sitting in that chair?'

'Don't you want another drink?'

'I was waiting for you to bring me one.'

She got up, filled his glass, put the glass on his bedside table and stood looking down at him. She smiled. He knew the routine. He sat up and pulled her pants off. She turned round. He undid her bra. She got onto his bed and against the background of music, laughter, and shouting, they had sex. It didn't take long. Afterwards, she got dressed and turned to speak to him before she left, but he was already asleep.

— 2 —

He woke early, in his line of business, early starts were compulsory. At eight the markets opened and the bidding started. The house was quiet except for the muffled sound of a vacuum cleaner in the living room. He went downstairs, put his head round the door and glancing at the litter of empty glasses, introduced himself to the cleaner, before walking into the breakfast room. It hadn't been his intention to miss the party. After Carole, he'd fallen into a deep sleep and consequently failed to wake and give the anniversary presents to his parents. He felt bad about that. His father was sure to have something to say. He let himself out of the house and walked down the drive towards his car, intending to retrieve their presents before starting his breakfast.

He'd chosen the presents with care, and as part of the store's service, he'd asked for them to be wrapped. Each was a small work of art. For his mother, her favourite perfume, Gucci Premiere; for his father, a range of six single-malt whiskies; and for them both, tickets to the Royal Opera House. He placed the perfume and the tickets on the table, the whisky on the floor by his father's usual chair, and began his breakfast – freshly squeezed orange juice, sugar and salt-free muesli, two slices of toast, thickly buttered, finished off with strong coffee. He stood up and stretched, reflecting as he did, that their dining room was like an upmarket boutique hotel.

He glanced at his watch, it was still only nine

and predictably, there was no sign of his parents. Hanging around and waiting for them had always made him feel edgy. He had no idea when the party had finished last night, but it could be hours before they put in an appearance and they were sure to be hung over.

He walked across to the window and looked out over the lawns. The trees were on the turn, leaves were already falling and until the sun was higher, the air would feel cold. A familiar feeling of impatience, irritability, and argumentativeness swept over him. Seeing his parents had that effect on him. Invariably the atmosphere was oppressive and reminded him of his childhood and every time he visited, he'd vowed he'd never come again. But he always did.

He had to do something. Drive some place until lunchtime, so with luck, by the time he got back, his parents would be up and their hangovers would partially have worked through their system. His father with a hangover was even nastier than usual. He picked up his car keys, walked outside and climbed into his car. He put the keys in the ignition but didn't drive off. Maybe he'd ring Ben and suggest an early game of squash.

He decided against it. He wasn't in the right mood. He had to be in the right state of mind to play squash. He felt in a limbo, hovering between two worlds, each with a very different set of values and rules of engagement. He sat for a moment with the engine running, aware his life was about to change, and that he needed time and space to think through what he was about to get into. He wanted to drive away, go somewhere he wasn't known.

Aldeburgh was near enough, he'd been taken there as a child and he'd liked it. At the very least, it would pass the time. He pulled out of the drive, put his foot down and taking the A12, drove his car hard until he reached the coast. He parked the car as near to the sea as he could get.

The weather was good that morning, the air warm, with only the faint stirring of wind. He took a deep breath. The smell of the sea had always evoked freedom and space. Lying ahead was the vast expanse of the North Sea, the water flat calm under a pale blue sky, streaked with long wisps of clouds. An empty beach, devoid of people, stretched out across the horizon. He began walking, his feet crunching in the shingle. He was conscious only of the sound of the ocean. It seemed to sigh, rhythmically, hypnotically, slowly, as it moved back and forth across the pebbles. Raising a hand as protection from the daylight's glare, he walked along the shoreline, until he came to a halt in front of a sculpture.

It was incongruous. It stood alone, as if in opposition to the destructive force of the elements. Shaped like an open scallop shell, it seemed to hold strength, resistance and resilience; its presence demanding attention. Beaten by the waves, the wind and the sea, and made of steel, it was taller and wider than him Deep, uneven, indentations like irregular, rough scars had formed along its edges and written along the jagged edge were the words, 'I hear those voices that will not be drowned.' He read them twice. He closed his eyes, and running his hands along the surface, felt the hard contours of the metal holding the warmth of the sun. He leant his back against it and, closing his eyes, imagined he could absorb its power.

'Do you like it?'

The voice of a child – disconcerted, he opened his eyes.

A young girl stood watching him. A couple of metres away, she was brown in the way children go brown, evenly and naturally. Eleven or twelve years of age, dressed in jeans, with a striped orange and navy tee shirt, serious, unsmiling, strands of hair straggling round her face from an untidy pony tail.

He smiled. 'I didn't see you.'

'I was following you.'

'Well, I didn't see you… You're up early.'

'It's not that early. I come earlier than this sometimes.' She continued gazing at him.

'Are you on your own?'

'Yes. I come here when I'm fed up. The shell makes me feel better. It's always here.'

'It's beautiful.'

'You can sit on it, if you like. Would you like to sit on it?'

'Maybe.'

'Well, you have to go round to the other side to do that.'

'Is that what you do?'

'Yes, then I look at the sea and think. Is that what you were doing? Your eyes were closed. Were you thinking?' He smiled. She continued, 'I know the person who made it. Her name's Maggie. She went to art school and that's where I want to go. But it costs too much money. That's what my mum said.'

'So you like art?'

'Yes, I'm good at it. My mum told me that. We used to colour in together. That was before… what's your name?'

'Seb, short for Sebastian. What's yours?'

'Imogen. I haven't seen you before. You don't

live round here, do you?'

'No.'

'I can tell that. You don't talk like people round here. You sound posh.'

'Really?'

'It doesn't matter. I don't mind. But I can see you like the shell. Some people don't. If we walk along the beach, and look back at it, then it's different.'

'You seem to have studied it.'

'Yes, I have studied it. That's because it's nice. Do you want to see what I mean?' She stood waiting. He didn't move. She said, 'Are you coming?'

'Where to?'

'Along there, where you'll see it's different.' She pointed her finger along the shoreline.

'Okay.'

'Come on then.'

He paused, disconcerted by her friendliness, but he had nothing better to do. They walked in silence. Every now and again she looked up at him as if to make sure he was still with her. Eventually, she came to a stop. She said, 'Now look round. See what I mean? It's different.' She waited for his response.

He paused. 'It looks different, but it's still the same. It's a different angle. It's the same and different. You know, like people can be. Sometimes they're sad, sometimes they're angry and they seem different, but inside they're the still the same person.'

She stared at him. 'That's like my dad. Sometimes he changes into someone different.'

'Is that bad?'

'I don't like it and my mum didn't either. But why does he do that?'

'Well, I'm not sure. Maybe... maybe it's the stresses of life, wearing away what they were like when they were first born. Look at this shell. Once it was new and shiny, but now the weather, the winds, rain, salt water have changed it.'

'Oh. But I still like it, because it is the same, to me it is.' She looked away and over towards the sea and seemed to drift away, before she turned her attention back to him. 'What shall we do now?'

'I have to go back.'

'But I don't want you to go back. I thought you'd stay longer.'

There was a slight tone of peevishness in her voice. 'I have to. I don't live here.'

He looked intently at her. She was old beyond her years. He found her curious, even strange. He looked at his watch, caught between two minds; he wasn't sure what to do.

'Are you hungry?'

'I am. Shall we have some breakfast? I know somewhere good.'

'I've had breakfast.'

'I'd like fish and chips. I can show you where we can buy some.'

'Fish and chips... they're not breakfast.'

'My dad lets me have fish and chips. I can have them whenever I want.' She stared at him. She looked serious. 'Come on then. Shall we go? I know where your car is.'

'Do you now?'

'Yes, I do. It's black and it looks new.'

'What else do you know?'

She tilted her head back defiantly. 'Lots.'

Seb laughed.

'What are you laughing at?'

'You. You're funny.' She looked so determined, he said, 'Okay. Show me where to go and I'll buy you some fish and chips.'

She laughed, and spinning round, she held her arms away from her body, and ran ahead, calling over her shoulder, 'Follow me. I'm thistledown, and the wind blows me all over the place.'

He followed, puzzled. She behaved as if she'd known him for years. When they reached the car park, she ran to his car and standing by it, waited for him, then she said, 'This is yours, isn't it? Come on, slow coach, be quick, open it and drive to the fish and chips. I'm starving.'

Seb hesitated. He felt deeply uneasy. What must it look like? A young man with a girl he didn't know aged about eleven or twelve, taking her into his car. He tentatively opened the door, was about to say he hadn't the time after all, but wasn't quick enough. She'd jumped into the front passenger seat. Reluctantly he got in. The situation was strange. He glanced again at her. Why did she have no qualms about sitting in a car with a total stranger? It didn't feel right. Maybe he shouldn't have talked to her, but he'd gone so far, to withdraw at this point would feel as if he was rejecting her. He glanced at her. He had to go through with it.

Oblivious to his thoughts, she said, 'Can you drive really fast?'

He hesitated. Her face was lit up with a childlike excitement. He smiled, and said, 'Okay, I'll show you how fast I can go, if that's what you really want. Let's check the safety belt.'

He leant across to pull her safety belt tight, and headed for the A12. Parts of the road were long and straight, perfect for speeding, as long as no police mobile speed vans were parked on the slipways. He couldn't see any. He accelerated up to ninety. Imogen was silent. He glanced at her. She was tense, holding fast onto the seatbelt. He noticed how small her hands were and felt a wave of protectiveness for her.

'You're frightened. I'm going too fast.'

'No. I like it.'

You don't. You're scared.' He slowed right down and keeping within the speed limits, drove aimlessly around before returning to Aldeburgh. She'd become quiet. He wondered what was going on in her head. Eventually she spoke, giving him instructions on how to get to her favourite fish-and-chip shop in Aldeburgh. He stopped outside, and turned towards her.

'Okay, what do you want?'

'Cod with chips, with vinegar and lots of red sauce on them, please.'

He hauled himself out of the car, keenly aware he wanted to get away from her, not because he disliked her, but because the situation was bizarre. He walked into the shop and looked around. There was a small framed notice on the counter, stating they had top marks for hygiene and on the wall a large blackboard with a list of the fish supplied.

'Cod with chips, please.'

'Small or large?'

'Small will be fine.'

He caught sight of the man closely scrutinising him. 'Is that Imogen sitting in your car?'

'Yeah, why?'

The man avoided his eyes, 'Just wondered.'

'She's hungry.'

He didn't reply, but silently fried the fish, then placed it with a portion of chips in a large, flat box and handed them over. 'She usually has large.'

He shrugged. 'How was I to know?'

'Knowing Imogen, she's not backward in coming forward.'

'Thanks, I'll bear that in mind.'

Back in the car, he handed over the fish and chips and watched as she shovelled the food into her mouth.

'You seem hungry.'

'I said I was. That's why I usually have large.'

'You should have said… It looks a soggy mess with all that sauce. Is it good?'

She glanced up. 'Yes, it's delicious. Want some?' She speared a chip onto the plastic fork and pushed it towards his mouth.

'No thanks. I'm not hungry. I've had breakfast.'

'I've had no breakfast. That's why I'm hungry.'

In between mouthfuls, she chatted. About anything and everything that came to her mind: school, Ruth, her best friend with a bad limp and who couldn't run. Born with some problem with her hips, Imogen didn't know what it was, but she helped her with her homework. She could do her own home work easily, and said with some pride, she never had to ask for help. Her favourite lessons were painting and drawing. Seb listened; but made no comment, thinking she was too friendly, too trusting, too unworldly and too open. He felt he should say something to her about that, but he had no idea how to go about it. She was in full flow when he realised it was almost lunchtime.

'Imogen, I have to go now. I have to get back.'

She stared. She looked shocked, as if she was about to cry. She tried to clamber out of the car. He took hold of her arm. He couldn't just let her go. Suddenly he knew why she'd attached herself to him. She was a neglected and lonely child and she had no sense of what was appropriate and what wasn't. When she'd said she was like thistledown, that had been and maybe still was her experience of life. She was blown about by circumstance over which she had no control. She'd been about to walk on the beach, had seen him arrive in his car and watched him, as he, like her, walked on his own. She was as curious about him, as he was about her. She'd made those comments about people changing. The shell was always there, she'd said. Maybe there was nobody who cared about her. Nobody who realised she was alone on the beach and had had no breakfast.

He had to say something. That she shouldn't be so trusting, that she should be more suspicious, that she should learn how to protect herself, because no one else had.

'Imogen, I've been thinking. I need to tell you something.' A couple walked past. They looked curious. The whole scene, a man sitting with a prepubescent girl in an expensive car, must have looked suspicious. He waited until they'd walked on to the end of the road and had turned the corner. 'Listen to me.'

She stared at him. She looked frightened. 'I probably won't see you again, but I've been thinking and I want you to promise me something. Never, ever go with anyone you don't know for a walk or a ride. Some people are bad. They might harm you when you're on your own with them, but you won't know they're like that until it's too late. You know, just because they look nice and are kind to you, doesn't mean they are.'

She took a quick look at him, her eyes full of tears, but said nothing,

'Will you remember? I want you to look after yourself. Do you promise me?'

She bit her lower lip, looked down at her hands in her lap and spoke without looking at him. 'That's not right. You haven't been bad and I didn't know you. You're saying that to get away from me.'

He sighed. 'No, I'm not. That's not true. But that's my point. You didn't know me. You took a risk... I have to go now, but I want you to look after yourself. Do you understand me?'

She nodded, stared straight ahead. She said, 'Are you going home?'

'Yes, I have to. I've liked being with you, but I have to go, and so must you. Go home, see your mum. She'll be worried about you.'

She looked away. 'I haven't got a mum. Not anymore. I don't know where she is.'

He did a double take, remembering how she'd referred to her mum but then had stopped herself.

'So who looks after you?'

'My dad and his girlfriend. They fight, that's when I go out.'

He paused. He felt bad. 'I'm sorry, Imogen, but I still have to go.'

'Will you come and see the shell with me again?'

'Maybe, and if I do, I'll look out for you. That's a promise.'

'Are we friends?'

'Yes. We're friends.'

She climbed out of the car and stood looking at him. Her face was expressionless, as she waited for him to drive away. He put the car into gear, drove to the end of the road, decided to do a 'u' turn. Sweeping past, he slowed right down, honked his horn and flashed his lights. She waved, a small child alone by the side of the road and missing her mum. He drove in silence back towards Lavenham.

— 3 —

His parents were eating lunch by the time he arrived; his father hiding behind the Financial Times, his mother reading a fashion magazine, but there was no sign of the presents he'd left out for them.

'Hi,' he said and, pulling out a chair, sat down.

His mother gave a thin smile. 'Would you like some soup, Sebastian? It's carrot and coriander.'

'Please.' She disappeared into the kitchen.

Seb picked up the neatly ironed napkin, shook it out, placed it on his lap and, glancing at his father, said in a conversational tone, 'Much mess to clear up from last night?'

His father, sitting opposite him, put down the newspaper he was reading and looked at him. 'Ah,' he said. 'The return of the prodigal son.' He picked up the paper again, sighed loudly, noisily straightened it out, and placed it directly in front of him. It was so effective; he couldn't see or be seen.

Seb began humming, 'When the saints come marching in' accompanying himself by drumming his fingers lightly on the table. His father ignored him and continued to read.

Five minutes later, his mother returned with a bowl of soup which she placed in front of Seb.

'Thanks,' he said and began eating, then looking directly at his mother, he said, 'Has father lost his voice?' The sarcasm in the question was obvious. His mother smiled nervously, but said nothing. Seb continued, 'I was asking, whether there was much mess left last night? Could anybody answer? One or other of you. I don't mind who, it's a simple question, after all. '

His father spoke from behind the paper. 'No, not much, only what you'd expect.'

'Sorry I didn't make it. Exhaustion. Hard day and all that, fell asleep and didn't wake up till this morning.'

His father put the paper down, eyeballed him, and said, 'Why don't you tell the truth? Just this once.'

Seb glanced at him and returning his hard stare, said, with a slight smile, 'The truth? Since you know what that is, and apparently I don't, perhaps you could tell me?'

'You had a woman in your room.'

'Ah, a spy is in our midst. A spy and a grand inquisitor.'

'Stop talking bullshit.'

His mother stood up. 'I'm going if you two are going to start.'

'Sit down, Annabelle. Just a game we play.' He turned to his son. 'Sebastian, it would have been common courtesy if you'd graced us with your presence when you first came in, even if for a few minutes, that's all that was required. Instead of which you went up to your room, and sent Carole down to forage for drinks.'

Seb laughed humourlessly. 'Forage. What a stupid word.' His father glared. 'Well, I'm sorry. I had no idea my presence was so important, but why didn't you come up? You could have checked out how I was?'

'Hardly, and interrupt your nocturnal activities?'

His mother stood up, folded up her napkin. 'I've had enough. It might amuse you two to carry on in this way, but it certainly doesn't me.' She walked out, her lips pursed in disapproval.

There was silence before his father spoke again. 'How long do you intend to stay?'

'Possibly until tomorrow. It depends.'

'On what?'

'On how welcome I'm made to feel.'

'That's your call,' he said, and returned to reading the paper.

'I presume you got my presents?'

'Yes. I did. Thank you.' He paused, 'How did you know the whisky I like?'

'Bob told me. Then it was a question of tracking down who sold them.'

'It must have set you back a bit.'

Seb sighed. 'Did mother like her present?'

His mother returned and began clearing the table. 'I heard that, Seb. Yes, I did like the perfume. It was thoughtful of you. Too expensive for every day, but thank you.'

'Glad I got something right.'

'I'll put some on later, since you gave it to me.' She smiled at him, then after rearranging the flowers in the vase on the sideboard, watched by Seb, she left the room for the kitchen, carrying the tray of dirty plates. The rest of the meal was eaten in silence.

Seb stood up. 'Right, I'll be off to my room.'

His father put his paper aside and looked across the table at him. 'If you're here tomorrow, we could go to church. It must be a long time since you last attended, then we could have lunch at The Swan.'

'I was at The Swan last night, but as for church, thanks but no thanks. I don't do church. I've told you that numerous times. I had enough of it at school.'

'Well, that's that then.' His father hesitated.

'You're impossible to please.'

'Just like you are. It must run in the family,' Seb said, but observing his father's face gradually turning puce, he added, 'Anyway, enough of this jocularity? How are the markets?'

'Flat, but that's to be expected. Too many people expecting something for nothing. There's no money in the system.'

'You have to be joking. Lavenham's awash with money – and you're not exactly cutting back either.'

His father's voice was cold. 'We deserve it. I earned mine and with no help, which is more than can be said about you.'

'Thanks. I wondered how long before you'd bring that up. If your half brother takes a shine to me, and doles out the readies, over and above the miserly contributions you used to give why should I complain? Or you, for that matter?' His father was silent. 'Well, here's some good news – as from next Monday, I start a new project and it's got a decent salary.'

'Doing what?'

'Financial compliance for an organisation in the City. I'll be trained, probably in the States so...' He stared at his father. He'd made no response but his face had become redder. 'What's wrong, aren't you pleased? Is it beyond you to offer any congratulations? ... By the way, you should have your blood pressure checked. Or perhaps it's your temper? Hard to know, but you do have a high colour.'

'Cut the sarcasm, I'm sure you don't give a jot about my health.'

Seb sighed. 'The implications are, because of this new post, I can pay you back for the hand outs. I never actually did need them, but there you are, we're taught never to look a gift horse in the mouth.' Still there was no response. 'And secondly, I'm going to be tied up while training so it might be difficult, if not impossible, to get hold of me.'

'Who are you working for?'

'Can't say exactly. I'm employed as a kind of a financial free wheeler, bouncing around wherever I'm needed.' There was a long silence. 'Well, glad you're pleased... Like I said, I'll be off. Maybe give Ben a bell, check out if he fancies a game of squash. I'll see you later. Tell mother I'll be back for supper but I'll shoot off tomorrow morning, first thing. Oh, and if you or mother see Carole and John, do you mind telling them, I'll be in the Swan about seven. If they're free, that is.'

His father gave him an acid look and returned to reading his paper. Seb left the room. Invariably after talking with his father, he was left feeling depressed. He had no intention of hanging around. He walked outside to his car, wishing he could escape. His mind returned to Imogen and what she'd said about her father. It must be tough for her and he'd liked to have helped in some way, but it wasn't possible, they lived in different worlds. He took off in his car, drove randomly for several miles, until he arrived in Sudbury and noticing an attractive-looking pub, he pulled in for a drink.

No one knew him, so he could keep himself to himself and the weather was good enough to sit outside. He chose an empty table, and sat alone, staring into his beer, contemplating his future and what he was about to take up. It was a challenge, an unknown quantity, and once he'd started, there'd be no turning back. He'd be on his own. But, it was something his father couldn't or never would do, and that pleased him. For once, his father couldn't compete with him.

He returned to his car and began the drive back. He was three miles away from the house when, on a whim, he decided to see Carol. He felt at a loose end. Maybe it was because she was part of his past, and he was about to separate from that. He turned down the side road leading towards her stables, parked his car down the narrow lane running past her house and walked the rest of the way. The kitchen door had been left open, but there was no sign of either her or her husband. Maybe they were with the horses. He wandered across the courtyard toward the stables. If she was anywhere, she'd be in one of the stalls where the horses were kept.

She was in the end stall talking to her horse as she groomed her. He stood by the door, silently watching until she became aware of his presence. She glanced up and, showing no surprise, stopped what she was doing. Sounding slightly challenging, she said, 'I was told you'd be at the Swan.'

'I was just passing, and thought I'd drop by to see if you were still here – aren't you going to the Swan?'

'Not after last night. My liver needs a break.' She turned her attention back to her horse.

'Where's your hubby?'

'In the Swan, probably waiting for you and the others.'

'Well, I've changed my mind.'

'You're not going then?'

'Nope.'

'Not sure then why you're here. Your mum said you'd be at the Swan, but whatever.' She looked over her shoulder at him and gave him a half smile.

'You look different. Your dress, last night, I liked it. I didn't have a chance to tell you.' He caught hold of her and pulled her round. 'Put the brush down. You won't need that.' She bent down, placed it on the floor and stood facing him as he slowly undid the buttons on her shirt and pulling it open exposed her breasts.

He lightly ran his hands over them. 'Why no bra?'

She shrugged. 'I don't always. Maybe I had a premonition.'

'Of what?

'That I'd have a visitor.' She took off her shirt, hung it on a nearby hook and, putting her hands on her hips, smiled provocatively. 'Is there something you want?'

'I gather by that question, you're up for it?'

'Do we have enough time?'

'There's enough time.'

'Is that why you dropped by? For a quick fuck?'

'It wasn't, but seeing you standing like that, it is now. What about you?'

'What do you think? ... But not here. Not in front of Mitzy.'

Seb laughed. 'What difference will your horse make?'

'None at all. I just prefer we're totally alone.' Leaving her shirt on the hook, she led him to an empty stall, and shut the door behind them. They stood in the half light. She leant back against the wall and looked questioningly at him. 'So, why now? For two years nothing, now twice in twenty-four hours, isn't that pushing it?'

'Do you need a reason? I'm starting a new job. Besides I want a woman.'

'And I'm conveniently around... Should I be flattered? No, I don't think so. You didn't exactly make me feel welcome last night.'

'You know the score. Besides I was exhausted... I'm not now, so what about it?'

She made no reply. She pulled him roughly towards her. It was sex the way it had always been between them; quick, urgent, a physical act which lacked tenderness, romance or affection. No questions asked, nothing was expected, other than the obvious. All either wanted was the occasional fuck, and that suited them both. She was still pulling on her clothes as he pulled open the door to return to his car. 'Thanks,' she said, to his disappearing back.

He turned round. 'My pleasure. It was just what I needed.'

She walked across to him and, putting her face up to his, she said, 'If you're going away, why don't you kiss me?'

He took a step back, distancing himself from her upturned face. 'Kiss you. Are you joking? No, I don't kiss. I'm not into it. Neither you or anyone else.'

'Why not?

'Because I don't, I just don't. It's not my bag. I'll see you sometime.'

He walked rapidly down the lane, flung himself into the car and accelerated off. He got to the end of the lane when it occurred to him that he rarely kissed any woman. The realisation had shocked him. He leant forward, fumbled in the glove department for his gum, pushed it into his mouth and drove at speed back to Lavenham.

— 4 —

Mid morning and Seb was about to meet his handler at a coffee shop in Stoke Newington, Hackney. The handler liaised between the Met, and the corporate and private investigation firm which employed him. He'd never met him before. All he knew was his name, Gimp. Neither did he know Hackney, other than it bordered the largely affluent Borough of Islington as well as the ethnically diverse Haringey. Both had a mixed population which included the cool hipster, the urban literati, some professionals, and what was euphemistically called, the materially deprived.

Before he'd been taken on as an undercover agent, he'd been given a number of tests and passed them all: the physical, the mental, the psychometric and the psychological. He'd even role-played, something he hated, but gritting his teeth, he'd got through and was now officially classified as 'fit for purpose'. He felt a sense of achievement. One up on his father, he wouldn't have had the balls.

He had no idea how ultimately things would pan out, but he'd go with the flow. That was all he could do. His task was to infiltrate the anti-globalisation movements, feed back information on their members, their policies, their aims, their plans to resist and disrupt. He didn't care who funded who or what their beliefs were, quite simply he saw it as an interesting opportunity. From now on he could seduce, lie, manipulate, blackmail, betray – all the things some City traders did on a day-to-day basis, but without the consequences. Its secrecy appealed, and he had no strong feelings about what he would be called to do.

He'd been surprised and more than suspicious when he'd been first contacted. He'd been told there was the possibility of a new post, one which could include a large element of 'compliance' in the financial sector. It was for a good cause, protecting the State, and would be well paid and independent of market fluctuations. He'd assumed this meant monitoring the errant, those who didn't follow the rules and regulations of the market place and there were plenty of them. But he'd been wrong, they weren't interested in them.

What they wanted was as much information as he could gather on what they called the anarchic riff raff. The anarchists were seen as the principal threat. They were unorganised, angry, well-read and worse, sought to destroy the foundations of the financial system itself. It was they who made the most noise about the present failures in the international money markets, and their message was having an impact. Support for the cause was growing.

He'd been told that they wanted someone who was aggressive, someone who could work independently, play both sides at once, take risks, talk the talk, and had a cool head; qualities he'd used regularly as a financier. He hadn't asked whether it would be within the law. It was immaterial, he didn't care if it was or wasn't, he'd do what was necessary. It was an opportunity, a challenge and one he thought he was well up to.

As an Investment Fund Manager he'd become used to taking risks, playing the market, watching the political economies around the world, waiting for the assassinations, the coups, the crashes, the bad harvests; then he'd move in, mop up, buy up. He was merciless, thoughtless to the harm he might cause. He'd made thousands for his clients, but he'd been looking for greater challenges and was at the point of moving into Hedge Fund Management when he received the call. Someone had been watching him, had seen him as a good bet.

The irony hadn't and didn't escape him. At one of the many interviews he'd been put through, he'd told them his motivation was purely personal and that he viewed with contempt the anti-globalisation protesters who seemed to haunt the City and Canada Square. But he was also curious. He wanted to know how they operated, who they were, and if money didn't motivate them, what did? Their motivations were unknown to him, but he looked forward to the work. He'd get under their skin, get one over them, beat them at their own game and on their home ground. But the element that really appealed was becoming somebody else. That's what he wanted.

He'd been told to wait inside the Fat Cat coffee shop in Stoke Newington Church Street, and he'd be contacted. He had no idea what his handler looked like or even whether the handler was a man or woman. The name, Gimp, was totally neutral, although he assumed it would be a man.

He'd parked his car down a side street, walked to the Fat Cat, and after ordering a coffee, sat down, and picked up one of the free papers scattered on the tables. His usual daily paper had been the Telegraph or the Financial Times but since the orientation programmes he'd started reading the Guardian. This was the paper of choice for the bleeding-hearted liberal, or that's how he saw it.

He'd been told he had to live the lie. Not so difficult he'd thought, it was something he'd been practising most of his life.

Twenty minutes later, as he was about to order his second coffee, someone walked in and caught his attention. He didn't quite fit into the cafe dress code, young, sharp, and urban. This guy had thinning grey hair, wore old baggy cord trousers, a check shirt, no tie, and an anorak. None of these fitted him. He stood briefly just inside the door, his gaze taking in the occupants of the cafe. His eyes were sharp, cold and grey, like granite. It would have been hard to place in terms of his occupation. The nearest description might be that he was an eccentric, with little regard for his surroundings or of fitting in, alternatively an intellectual down on his luck. Evidently having identified Seb, he walked across, drew up a chair opposite and sat down at the table.

He leant back in his chair scrutinising him, then leaned towards him and lowering his voice said, 'Seb? Right? ' Seb nodded, held out his hand, which the man ignored. 'I'm Gimp, so you can call me Gimp. We've business to do. They've told you the basics; I'll tell you our expectations.' He paused. 'I'll see you down the street' and then he left.

Seb paid the bill, walked outside, and for a moment, he thought Gimp had disappeared but then he caught sight of him. He was looking in an upmarket junk shop window, a few minutes walk away.

He glanced up, saw Seb and said, 'I was about to say, before the chappie at the next table showed an unusual interest in our conversation, for the moment you have to contact me regularly – daily preferably, any problem, any time, day or night.'

He scrutinised Seb, watching him closely for any reaction, then said, 'Let's go,' and set off at a fast pace towards Clissold Park. He talked as he walked, occasionally throwing quick glances at Seb, presumably checking he was still paying attention.

'You need to get up to speed. Your clothes have to go. Dress charity shop. If you have to buy new, go to an outdoor shop; choose middle range, nothing flash. Don't attract attention. Ordinary poor, that's the look.

'Shoes; trainers, fell boots, look scruffy, down at heel, dress the way they dress. It's function, not style.' He stopped and stared at him. 'You look like a nob. You'd stick out a mile looking like that. You've got to merge in. Right? Do you get what I'm saying?

'Second. Lingo. Talk the talk. You've got to get into a different mindset, see the world a different way, their way, so listen, pick up the jargon. You're reading the Guardian. A good start, but it's only one of their papers. Read the Independent and the financial press, then there's the anarchist propaganda. Half of them are comics. They're all crap anyway. But they're not stupid. They use the net, twitter, facebook. Keep on top of the game. Watch what you say and who you're speaking to, and keep looking over your shoulder... This should be revision for you. Any questions? '

'What about my car?'

'What about it? It's an Audi, isn't it? Or was.' For the first time, he smiled. 'As we speak, it's being towed away, but we're not cruel. You need wheels. So we've left a van in its place. It's a nice one, red, appropriately, and straight from the public sector auction. An old post office van. You'll like it.'

'Is it okay to drive straightaway?'

'Yes, but not back to Shoreditch. You should have been told that. You're moving to Seven Sisters. Very salubrious. It's all arranged, including your rent on both properties. You don't have to do a thing, except pitch up there. Here's the address. I'll see you there. Tomorrow, ten a.m. Anything else?'

Seb shook his head.

'Good. Enough. For the time being.' He stopped, handed Seb two lots of keys, one for the van, the other for the flat, and strode off.

Seb looked at his vanishing back. A man of few words but an arsehole of the first order. He walked back to where he'd parked his Audi and as Gimp had said, it had gone. In its place a red, old post office van, clean inside and big enough to carry any gear he might need. Inside the glove compartment, were insurance papers and a log book, both were registered in the name of Seb William Harvey. The date of birth was the same as his own. His new identity. He turned the key in the ignition and drove to the address he'd been given.

It was a small, ground-floor flat in an old Victorian house. The street was dismal looking, not far from the tube and well placed for the City. Inside the furnishings were minimal. There was a strong smell of disinfectant as if it had been cleaned recently. Seb took a look round. It didn't take long. One bedroom with a single bed, one bathroom, one living room, one tiny kitchen, and every floor covered with a cheap wood laminate. No pictures, except for a reproduction of Constable's The Hay Wain. He took it down and pushed it under the bed. Apart from that, a table, a small bookcase, two chairs, a sofa, a worn rug, lace curtains in the window that looked out over the street, and heavier ones to pull across when it was dark.

The only thing new was a television with internet access. He opened one of the kitchen cupboards, found a packet of unopened teabags, made himself a mug of tea without milk, and sat down. It was time to get a feel for the area and check out the charity shops for the type of clothes Gimp had advocated. Wood Green was the nearest shopping centre and within walking distance.

He stopped outside the first charity shop he came across, and stood outside for a moment before he swung inside. He knew such places existed but he'd never set foot inside one, until now. Even Lavenham had them. His mother, amongst other moneyed members of the community, sent her cast-offs to them. There, they were smart, expensive and looked more like boutiques, but the same couldn't be said here. The clothes were well worn, cheap, made of manmade fibre, and a contrast to what he was used to: natural fibres, sweaters made of cashmere, alpaca wool, shirts of the finest cotton. He felt distaste, even revulsion as he fingered the outworn garments but he forced himself to pick through them. He finally bought a selection of tee shirts, sundry trousers and two pairs of worn trainers.

He handed them over to the shop assistant. She was sitting behind a counter and looking bored, as she stared down at her mobile.

'Do you have any fleeces?' he asked.

She glanced up. 'They fly off the shelves as soon as they come in,' she said. 'Try the market or T K Max.' He must have looked blank. 'It's down the road, in the shopping centre, but you'll have to buy new.'

It didn't take long. He returned to the flat, emptied the plastic bags carrying his new gear, bundled the charity-shop clothes into the washing machine and stood looking out of the window. All he could see was a constant stream of cars, with a few passers-by. He was bored. He put on the television, flicked through the channels, idly watched the Parliamentary debates, and the lists of market fluctuations in the City. The rates were still falling. The hysteria still rising. He reflected on the fact he was now an ordinary member of the public, an observer of the economy and not part of it, and that without the buzz of the City and clinching a deal, for the moment he felt at a dead end. He wanted some excitement. He wondered who else lived in the house. He idly picked up a book he'd brought with him, called Profits before People; he'd been told it was essential reading.

He heard the front door slam; someone ran up the stairs and walked heavily across the floor in the flat above. He read only a few pages, before falling asleep and when he woke it was dark and the street lights were flooding into the flat. He pulled the curtains across, crawled into bed and slept deeply. He woke just before nine, breakfasted, watched the news and sat waiting for his meeting with Gimp.

Gimp was on time. He greeted Seb cursorily, sat down on the threadbare sofa and asked how he was, but true to form, didn't wait for an answer. There were no niceties. He was on transmission, no reception. He had a direct stare, almost as if spearing Seb with his eyes. It was intimidating. He refused Seb's offer of tea or coffee.

'Okay, let's go. First, get to know the local groups. You attend their meetings. Mix with them. Talk the talk. Go to demos. You pitch up to anything and everything. Your role is to find the most vocal, the most organised, the most committed, the ones with the most followers. Then you begin infiltrating, forming alliances, making contacts. Get your face known.'

'I need my cover story for that.'

'Yeah, well, you've got one. But you got to know it backwards, forwards, inside out, so, no matter what, you never think about it.'

'I'll be okay. Some of it's true.'

'Like what?'

'Affluent background. Disillusionment. No brothers, no sisters.'

'That's part of it.' He paused, fixing Seb with his penetrating stare and, slowing his staccato speech right down, he said, 'Okay, let's practice. I'm gonna take you through it. Give you a hard time. See how good you are at blagging it. See how you operate under pressure.'

'Now?'

'Yeah, right now. Sit over there.' He pointed to the table.

Seb moved across. Gimp placed his chair opposite and gave him one of his specials, the Gimp death stare.

'Okay. Your name?'

'Seb, Seb Harvey.'

'Age? Date of birth?'

'Twenty five, born 3rd Feb 1983.'

'Which university did you go to?'

'Buckingham.'

'Why?'

'What do you mean, why?'

'Why Buckingham. It's self-funding, isn't it?'

'My father chose it. He knew people there.'

'You can't stand up to your father.'

Seb paused. 'Is that a question or a statement? '

'Just answer.'

'Don't know what to say.'

'How about he's a bastard, and look at me straight in the eye when you say it.'

'It's difficult.'

'Go on, say it. Loud, with passion.'

'I reserve that for women.'

'Is that supposed to be funny... let's hope your interrogator also has a sense of humour... So... returning to the chase, what course did you do?'

'Business with Computer Security and Economics. Joint honours and I got a first.'

'Big deal. So you're a swot. And then?'

'Didn't want to work in finance, but my father insisted, got me a job in the City. I didn't stay long, I dropped out.'

'Why, when you had a good job.'

'Didn't like it. Didn't like the people. They got up my nose. Greedy, ruthless. I began questioning what it was all about.'

'Good. That's good. Think up an example, one where they screwed someone, and let them know all about it.'

For two hours Seb was faced with a battery of hostile questions. He answered all of them without blinking. He'd put himself in the mindset of how he'd felt as a child when his father used to harangue him for not having done something that he should have done. He'd developed a technique of switching off from him so nothing could get through. He'd transformed into an automaton. Nothing fazed him, because he'd become devoid of emotion.

Gimp suddenly stopped. 'Not bad, not bad at all but we'll have another session. I'll drop by, catch you when you're least expecting it, focus on your childhood, your past. I know a bit about it. Some crazy snatched you from your cot, didn't she?'

Seb didn't answer. 'Well, isn't that true? That's what I've been told.'

'I have no memories of it.' He looked away from Gimp's prying eyes, thinking he had no intention of telling him.

Gimp leant towards him. 'Really? Maybe you don't have any memories of it, but I know now how to rattle your cage. Next time, look at me straight. Tell me it's none of my business. Pressure. You gotter get used to it. Once they know your weak point, they'll go for it, until you crack.' He stood up. 'Any questions?'

Seb looked him straight in the eye. 'Yeah, women. How far can I go?'

Gimp laughed. 'The question that's always asked. Women. They're useful, they're a way in, they talk, they fall in love, but don't bring your women here. Keep your address to yourself. It's work. You're not on holiday looking for the next screw. So don't go for your usual type. Avoid especially older married women who ride to the hounds.'

'How do you know about her?'

Gimp didn't answer. 'And don't get any of them pregnant. It's messy and we don't like paying for abortions, not only that, it makes working undercover difficult. They start pressurising, want you to meet the family. So don't go there. Keep to the straight and narrow. Keep it easy.'

He stared at Seb. 'Right. Next. Your induction starts next week. It's an overview of how these people operate, their belief systems, typical backgrounds, and all the rest. You'll have several of these before we let the reins go, then you're on your own, except for keeping in touch with me.' He paused. 'I see you're in your new gear, good, you're coming on. Oh, and check out this book. Just published. I'll leave it with you. Interesting. Learn from it.'

He left, slamming the door behind him. Seb walked to the window and watched him walk down the street. He had a slight limp, but despite that, he walked fast, probably ex-Met, Seb thought, or the army.

He turned and gazed round his flat. The thought of bringing a woman here didn't do it for him. It would be the last place on earth he'd show anyone. He'd been used to wining and dining, before the big seduction scene. Who'd be interested in him if they saw this shit-hole? Certainly not the kind he was used to, the city types he used to score with. But the fact Gimp knew about Carole, could only mean one thing. He was under surveillance. That was obvious. Maybe it was part of the ongoing selection process but even so, he didn't like it. His life was no longer his own.

He picked up the book Gimp had left and began reading. It was about a cop who'd gone in deep. He'd worked undercover for years, and had lived and worked with an environmental activist, then he'd been busted along with others when they'd tried to sabotage a power plant. They'd been charged and it had all come out. The press had got hold of it. It hit the headlines. He was an infiltrator working for the police. He'd lost everything; his wife, his family, his job.

The following week, the day of his induction, Seb and five others were sitting in a room on the top floor of a high rise block located along Tottenham Court Road. Offices that looked ordinary from the outside, but evidently wasn't. Security was tight at the headquarters of Corporate Security and Information Systems UK and Worldwide. He'd been filmed, fingerprinted and frisked before he'd even sat down. He'd been issued with a code to travel through the card readers allowing access to certain areas of the office. Biometric 'touch and go' systems were in use, and cameras were placed at strategic points along the corridors, monitoring and logging every step he took. It stood to reason that someone, somewhere, must be observing and tracking every move he made.

Nobody was speaking. Maybe because they hadn't been introduced to each other and because casual friendships between agents wasn't encouraged. There were no social niceties. The only name they'd been given was Bill, the man standing in front of them.

Probably from MI5, he was giving a rundown of the anti-globalisation movements across the Western world, with a special focus on the UK. Dressed casually but expensively, he spoke in a clipped, military manner. There were no jokes, just a stream of information with the occasional sarcastic aside. He knew his stuff. Ultimately he was a performer, a dramatist who spoke apocalyptically about the rise of the internet, and the unholy alliance between the godly and the godless, whom, he maintained were fighting for the demise of capitalism. His version of events placed some of the blame for the present economic mess squarely on the shoulders of the anarchists.

'The aim of this rabble,' he said, 'is to undermine and destroy the economic system, not with weapons,' he paused dramatically, 'but covertly, using propaganda and industrial sabotage. Hacking, flooding the internet with spam to bring it down, subverting legitimate governmental and corporate systems, manipulating it for their own purposes, bombarding the public and the press with a stream of misinformation. They're young, angry, educated, with friends in high places, and they have to be stopped... and that's your job. You'll supply the counter intelligence and we'll act on it.'

'What drives them?' someone asked. He was older, with a double chin, carrying too much weight, and had heavily nicotine-stained fingers. Seb couldn't imagine him on a demo, but they must employ all sorts.

'They hate capitalism. In particular, the globalisation of capital and the power of the large corporations. If you want to know more, read No Logo or Affluenza. It's all there. Just like the anti-consumerists, they're envious of wealth and jealous of success. Infantile, if you ask me. Spoilt kids who can't make the grades, but, if it wasn't for them, we'd be out of a job.'

'Yes, but how does their argument stack up?'

'You want me to spoon feed you?' Bill sounded exasperated. 'In a nutshell, they believe consumerism corrupts humanity, it's based on greed and envy, creates false needs, exploits people, animals, and desecrates the environment, causes global warming and blah de blah-blah; get it, want me to continue?'

'Maybe they have a point.' Whoever he was, spoke with a slight but mocking smile on his face.

The comment didn't go down well. Bill paused, walked across the room and glowered at the questioner. 'Do you think that's funny? What's your name. Christian name?'

'Nigel.'

'I'll see you later, Nigel, but while you're here, perhaps you'd like to share with the rest of us, as an example of affluent consumerism, how much that very expensive watch cost. The one you're wearing. Take that off for a start, it won't go down well on the next demo.'

Seb looked down at his notes and wrote a reminder to himself, that when he got back to his flat, to remove his TAG Heuer watch, and replace it with something cheap.

He stared down at his notes, was this man for real? He felt bombarded, as if he was back at school again or at home. It was like listening to his father after he'd drunk one too many. He could rant for the devil. He was fond of saying that all the ills of Great Britain could be laid at the doors of the unemployed. They were all work shy, they lacked talent, they were paid too much by the state, they should be made to work. His mind drifted away to the charity shops in Wood Green, to the cheapness of the clothes and the poverty of the customers. He knew from his student days at Buckingham it was a tad more complex than that. Perhaps the anti-consumerists were onto something. He switched his attention back to Bill.

'We'll stop for coffee. Stay where you are. It'll be brought in. Any questions?'

Yes, I have one, Seb thought, but I'll keep to myself. It's about liberal democracy but I don't want my head bitten off. You may believe in what you're advocating, but others don't.

A middle-aged woman brought in a trolley and placed a cup of weak coffee in front of each of them. Seb glanced at the others. They had their heads down and were typing into their laptops. No one looked up, including the overweight guy who'd spoken out. He looked a loser. He couldn't be one of them. He was a stooge. A plant, placed amongst them to flush out those who disagreed with the views

Bill was advocating. He finished his coffee, stood up and wandered over to the window, and gazed out at the lines of traffic stopping at the traffic lights before taking off at speed.

A woman dressed in a tight black suit and in high heels stepped into the road and waved down a cab. Her spare figure and gestures reminded him of Carole. His mind drifted back to when he'd last had sex with her. Born and bred in Lavenham, she lived in another world in comparison with what he'd observed from his forays into the charity shops of Wood Green. What would she make of them? Probably not a lot. She was indifferent to how other people lived, happy enough with what she had, including the occasional sex with him, and probably others who came across her path.

Her concept of free enterprise was based on the freedom to put herself about. She'd said to him on one occasion, if her husband could play the field, why shouldn't she? He'd been fifteen, when she'd first come onto him, but despite several fumbling attempts, he hadn't actually made out with anyone. She'd been his first.

She'd called in to see his mother, but as she was out, Carole invited him over to the stables. With hindsight, it had probably been a put up. He'd already guessed she fancied him by her tight and often revealing clothes, plus the fact she had a way of looking at him – always direct and straight into his eyes. Then she'd smile. She was seductive, exciting and he'd been a willing partner. At the time, it hadn't been something he'd thought about. His mind had gone into overdrive about what could happen. But he'd been up for it. He was curious. Having illicit sex with an older married woman was a major turn on, especially as she was friends with his parents.

It was something he knew and they didn't. It was a way of breaking the norms of convention, and a way of getting back at them, especially his father. Having sex with her, he'd proved to himself he was a man and no longer a child. He'd boasted about what they did to his friends but now, ten years on, she was still ready and available, whenever he went back home, but for him, the excitement had long worn off. He'd become tired of her.

He heard his name called. He looked back into the room. All eyes were turned on him. He'd forgotten where he was. Bill was saying, 'In your own time,' and eyeballing him. The others were waiting for him. Maybe thinking about sex right now wasn't such a good idea. He smiled, apologised and made his way to his seat. There was silence as he sat down.

'Do you have any questions?' The question was directed at him.

'No, sorry. I haven't. It's all very interesting, what you're saying. I'll keep my questions until the end.'

'So... moving on, you have to familiarise yourselves with the opposition groups.' He passed round leaflets.

'As you can see, Dash for Gas has become Dash for Cash and then there's UK Uncut. Both groups oppose Government cuts, and names and shames those individuals and corporations who practice the fine art of tax avoidance. Then there's a bunch, a large bunch, it has to be said, opposing the G8, the IMF, the World Trade Organisation, and last but not least, comes the alternatives; the life-style organisations. They have a different ideology, or that's what they say. Take a look at Free Cycle, Fuel Poverty Action, Grass Roots, and that's just the beginning. There's others, for those really interested.'

'Do we have to know all of them?' The questioner was tall, gangly, with a face like a fox, cold, close-set eyes and a pointy nose.

'Look,' Bill said, 'there's something for everybody and you have to choose, because it'll be one or more of these you have to get into. If you're interested, the easier it'll be to dish the dirt and the deeper you go, the more you'll find out, and the more useful you'll be.'

'Yes, I understand that, but what if going deeper means we get compromised. I mean emotionally speaking, or because we're working closely with them, we find their arguments persuasive, isn't there a risk of being brainwashed?'

'I'm glad you raised that. One of the problems with going undercover and living and working with this bunch, is you might find yourself impressed by their arguments. But don't go there. Look at it this way, you've been chosen for your intellect and courage. What they're advocating is bull shit, as well as being illegal. You're the elite, so just make sure it's not going to happen.'

'That's all very well, but we work in isolation. It must be easier said than done.'

An expression of irritation passed over Bill's face. He stared at the questioner and leant over his table towards him. 'You know about your handler, don't you? You should have met him or, her. So… ' He slowed down his speech as if talking to a difficult child. 'You take it to your handler. But never forget, and this is addressed to you all – the politicos, they might sound convincing, but never forget, they're out to destabilise the system. But worst of all are, in my opinion, the anarchists. They don't believe in law and order, or private property.'

He held up a book, it was the same one Gimp had left for him. 'This is about a cop who worked undercover. He's been outed. Consequences? It's harder for our agents to get in. They're on the lookout for informers, so watch your back and read it. It's an object lesson in how not to do it. Keep away from women. Screwing an attractive bird may be just what you think you need, but you could be heading for a downfall. These birds are trained to set traps especially for the sad and lonely. Not that any of you come in that category.' He picked up his papers and left the room.

— 5 —

It was the following year and the ongoing crisis in the world markets continued. Furious with the bank bail outs and the size of bankers' bonuses, the economic crisis well and truly angered the opposition. Protesters, united by the opportunity to undermine the political system and observing the evident iniquities of the system, were out for a fight, Seb, meanwhile had spent months poring over the literature of the various radical national and international opposition groups and armed now with the most up-to-date information, was confident he now knew enough about the various political groups to put this knowledge into practice.

Working on his own for the first time, he planned to attend what was forecast as the biggest demo ever to be held in the City of London; a socialist coalition of anti-capitalists, environmentalists, and non-aligned protesters. His intention was to observe, get his face known, make contacts, merge in and move amongst what his employers called the riff raff; the politicos, the god squad, the anarchists. For this he had to look the part.

As he left his flat, he took a final look at himself in the mirror. He'd changed. He hardly recognised himself. The cool, smooth, well-heeled image of his Canary Wharf days had gone, and in its place was a scruffily dressed male in his mid-twenties with longish hair and the beginnings of a beard. He took a closer look. He felt pleased. He looked interesting, attractive, a bit like, an actor in a Hollywood film.

Maybe today he'd be lucky and pick up a woman. Celibacy, he'd discovered, didn't come easily to him. And there could be an added bonus, because if he did make out with one of the leftie politicos, she'd be a source of information. He couldn't lose. It was a 'win win' situation.

Closing his flat door, he walked to Seven Sisters tube. From there he caught the Piccadilly Line to Holborn, then changed to the Northern Line for Bank, arriving finally at the Bank of England on Threadneedle Street. The noise. Before he got there, he could hear it. The sounds of protest; the chanting, the whistling, the shouting, and the closer he got, the louder it was. Down the side streets, the police presence was immense. Lines of vans parked up ready for trouble, sliding side doors left open for a rapid exit, windscreens protected by grilles. He walked past, glanced quickly at the riot police inside, they were playing cards, chatting, smoking, laughing, generally joshing, waiting for, it seemed, the expected clash.

Outside the bank, the crowds were gathering. A solid wall of sound, the place heaving with a waving sea of placards: 'Need not Greed', 'Mobilise for Global Justice', 'Occupy'. The drumming, the bugles, the whistles, the shouting, the chanting: 'People before Profit', 'You say banking, we say wanking'; melodic refrains taken up and passing like a vocal Mexican wave through the crowd. The energy, the excitement of the crowds crackled through the air; the majority out for a good time – a minority, out for trouble – but who were they and where were they?

He moved round the crowd observing the demographics: more men than women, intense, serious-looking students, middle-aged hippies, jugglers balancing on unicycles, the old, the world weary, the poor, the office workers, the curious, the apprehensive, the angry, the suburbanites from the provinces. A party atmosphere with musicians and the expectations of a jolly time; hard to believe the economy was in deep trouble. Leaflets were pushed into his hands, but it wasn't the time or the place to read them, or to get into conversation. The noise, the shouting, the pushing and the shoving was too great, and on the side lines, out in force, the press. They stood near to the television cameras, positioned to move in close, film the first sign of trouble.

Forming a barrier outside the Bank of England, and the first line of defence between the protesters pushing and shoving outside and the bank employees inside, stood the police. Standing shoulder to shoulder in a tight line, tense, impassive, chewing gum, but all with their eyes fixed on an unseen midpoint. That way they could avoid the anger and hostility in the eyes of the protesters. Seb looked back over his shoulder. Some of the protesters were wearing scarves or balaclavas to cover their faces.

But the odds were stacking up. It was obvious. Trouble lay ahead. A riot was imminent. He pushed his way to the front of the demonstrators.He was prepared, physically and mentally. It was an opportunity to see how they operated. He had no strong feelings either way. He wasn't involved. He could be neutral. He looked up at the bank building. Above the police lines, he could see distant faces staring down at the protesters, some serious, some scared, some contemptuous.

The Square fell silent. It was uncanny. The silence came from nowhere. It seemed to last forever. The crowds were waiting, but for what? The anger, the fear, the contempt, the hostility and the disgust, swirled back and forth between the protesters, the city workers and the police, the forces of the State. A standoff – waiting for the trigger. And it came. From within the building, someone pressed their fingers hard against the window, smirked, mouthed an obscenity and gave the universal sign of triumphal contempt – the V sign. That was it. That was all that was required.

A roar broke out from the crowd; loud, defiant, strong. Seb felt himself pushed nearer and nearer to the building; an irresistible force of bodies pressing against him until he was so close, he was staring the police in the face. The police held the line. The drumming was louder, faster, more energetic, the whistles, the chanting, more and more insistent. 'Where's all the money gone?', 'Jail not bail', 'Give us our money'.

But then again, silence. Ominous, threatening, menacing; the police and protesters stared at each other, waiting for the inevitable clash. A helicopter hovered above, the clack, clack, clack of its rotor blades breaking the stillness, adding to the atmosphere of menace.

A missile was thrown from the back of the crowd. It caught a police officer in the face. Bleeding, he was pulled out of the line. That was the signal for the fight. More and more missiles rained through the air, stones, bricks, anything and everything that could be picked up and thrown, winged over the heads of the crowd. The chanting got louder, the pushing greater.

An order rang out. The police drew their batons. A further order. From the side streets ran the riot police, in a line, straight towards the protesters, a phalanx of force, advancing shoulder to shoulder, shouting, pushing, shoving, banging riot shields with batons, faces concealed by visors.

The crowd scattered, attempting to avoid the police; but they were unstoppable. They kept coming. Trained to intimidate, they came into the crowd, violently shoving a way through with batons, randomly hitting out, separating them, pushing the protesters back. The screams, the whistles, the shouting, the rhythmic chanting from the crowd, the drumming, the noise, had reached a crescendo.

Seb looked for an escape route. He glanced down a side street, saw the mounted police. The horses were powerful, large, unsettled, agitated, tossing their heads, pawing the ground, their ears pinned back. The police were holding hard on their reins, barely able to control them.

In that moment, he realised he was caught in a pincer movement; horses on one side, lines of police on the other. There was nowhere safe to go. He was trapped. A second later, the horses were cantering towards the demonstrators. He ran for his life. The crowd split in two, the protesters running in all directions, to avoid falling under the horses' hooves.

Crush barriers were grabbed, passed over the heads of the demonstrators, and thrown at the police. Then, 'shame on you' over and over. The police struck out men and women with their batons, at both, anywhere over the body, anyone in the way, anyone shouting, anyone running, anyone standing. It was random, indiscriminate, and brutal.

Seb pushed his way through the crowds. He had to get out. He'd seen enough, he'd had enough. He reached a side street, looked back, and noticed a young woman running from the crowd. A second later, she fell. In the panic and the crush of crowd, no one stopped. She lay directly in the line of the horses, terrified, coiled up, covering her head with her arms. A moment longer, she'd be trampled.

Without thinking, he ran over, yanked her to her feet, and holding her by the arm, half pushing, half dragging her, pulled her into a quiet passage way.

He glanced at her. She looked out of it, pale, breathing shallowly, in a state of shock. 'Breathe deeply. You're okay. I'll get you out of this.' She didn't respond, looked at him, her eyes huge with fear. He put his arm round her. 'Let's go, we'll find somewhere for you to sit down.' They walked until they reached a cafe. 'Have a seat here. Are you okay?' he said. She nodded. 'Thanks. My friend will find me. I'll wait for her here.'

He walked rapidly away, aiming for Cannon Street Station. All the major side roads were blocked with police cordons. He double backed, eventually found a long and circuitous route down the back streets; and only then did he slow down. He took out his gum, thrust it into his mouth and kept walking until he was far enough away to feel safe and stop in a coffee shop.

He'd made it. It was a Starbucks, part of a global chain and crowded, but right now, he couldn't have cared less. Placards from the demonstration were piled outside and inside the place was full of angry and upset protesters. He took his place in the queue for coffee, and looked around. It was noisy and full. He picked up his coffee, carried it outside and sat down at an empty table, his mind going over what he'd just been through. The rapid disintegration into chaos, the police loss of control, the brutality, the general mayhem had disturbed him. Without thinking, he poured sugar into his coffee. He didn't like it, but he couldn't be bothered to queue for a fresh cup.

He'd been there fifteen minutes when he noticed the two women. Neither was looking in his direction, but he recognised one as the woman he'd pulled away from the horses. She put her backpack on one of the tables, opened it, drew out her purse and emptied the contents on the table. She looked exasperated. Her friend glanced across at him, caught his eye and smiled. She said something to her friend, and stood up.

He knew who she was; she was the girl with the gap between her teeth, the one who'd been at the Canary Wharf demo. It had been his last day and he'd had to pass through the protesters to get to the car park before driving to Lavenham to attend his parents' anniversary party. He remembered her distinctly because she'd pushed a leaflet into his hand –and her smile.

She was walking towards him and looking as if she knew him. Would she recognise him from Canary Wharf? Then he'd been a financier, now he was passing off as a demonstrator. His cover could be blown. It was a coincidence, but coincidences happen and he'd been trained for this. He'd been told to deny everything and play it cool. She may think she'd met him before, but he had to convince her she was wrong. She came to a halt at his table and stood looking at him. He waited for her to speak, took a sip of his almost cold coffee and glanced up at her.

'Hi. You been to the demo?'

'Yeah.' He tipped his chair back, leant forward with his elbows on the table, and looked at her with a serious expression. 'Bad, really bad,' he said, 'but they're rattled. It's the markets… they're in a state of collapse and they have to maintain order… not that I'm making excuses.'

She didn't appear to hear what he was saying, but seemed to be studying him. 'Well, thanks anyway.'

'Thanks? For what?'

'For helping my friend. Pulling her away from the horses. She could have been killed.'

'I couldn't leave her there.'

'Some would.'

'She's okay then?'

'Yeah. She noticed you, so I said I'd thank you – on her behalf. She's still shaky.' She was looking intently at him. 'I've seen you before, but where that was, I have no idea.'

He smiled. 'I have one of those faces, you know, the type where people say, I've seen you before. Or, I have a double.'

'Yes, you must have. Well, everyone has a double, that's what they say, don't they?"

He shrugged, raised his hands as if he were French. He'd got away with it. She hadn't recognised him.

'Anyway', he said, 'you didn't come over just to tell me this, is there a problem?'

'No problem, just wanted to thank you.'

'Like I said, think nothing of it.'

She continued scrutinising him, then turned to make her way back to her friend.

'Just a minute. Before you go, what's your name?'

'Nixie.'

'Nixie. Nice name.'

She stared down at him, 'Where are you from?'

'Not far from Seven Sisters. I've only just moved there. This is my first demo, but after all that shit I've just seen, I want to get involved. Any ideas, you know, what opposition groups are there?'

'There's Grassroots.'

'Grassroots. I think I've heard of them. Environmentalists and anti-globalisation, aren't they? Where do they hold meetings?'

'A pub, it's called The Bricklayers. It's not far from Tottenham, by Wood Green tube, and along the High Road. We meet every Wednesday in the top room.' She paused, as if thinking. 'If you like, I could meet you there.'

'Okay, great, I'll see you, Nixie, and since you haven't asked, I'm Seb.' She laughed, and he noticed again the tiny gap between her teeth.

'You look like a Seb, I think,' she said.

He looked at her closely. That was personal, a chat-up line. Was it deliberate? He'd find out. 'In what way do I look a Seb?'

'You're a bit posh. I'm not sure why, but you look like a Seb. Is it short for Sebastian?'

'Yep. So your name, Nixie. It's unusual. Where's that from?'

'My mum, she's got a kind of romantic approach to life. She chose it. It means water sprite.'

'And are you? Are you a water sprite?'

'You could say that, because I do love the sea. I was conceived on a Scottish Island, that's what she said, but brought up in Pembrokeshire, by the sea, and now I live here. No sea.'

'Sounds good, and what do you do? '

'This and that. I went to uni here, but I've been kind of drifting, not sure what I want. I work for an agency, a social work agency, as a carer. What about you?'

Seb stood up. 'Out of work. But sorry, I gotta go, promised to see a mate. Nixie, I'll be seeing you, and look after your friend. It was good meeting you.'

For a brief moment, their eyes met. She looked disconcerted, maybe she expected him to hang around but the words of Gimp still rang in his ears. Be careful not to get set up. Could he trust her?

Was he being set up? He glanced at her quickly. She seemed straight but how could he tell? She was attractive, but not his usual type. The 'au natural' look wasn't what he usually went for. She wore no makeup and she wasn't glamorous. But then, his taste in women could change and, he'd been celibate for weeks and he didn't like being celibate. She was a 'politico' and she'd be a contact. What would she be like in bed?

'What are you thinking?'

He felt as if she'd caught him out. 'Nothing much,' he said. 'I'll see you. Next week.' He gave her a smile and left. Hours later, he went over what she'd said. Conceived on a Scottish island? Something didn't sound right about that, but whatever that was, he couldn't make sense of why he was so preoccupied with her, and told himself to forget it.

— 6 —

It was one of those depressed, dark terraced houses in the back streets and the type of house which untouched by gentrification, and where poverty left neither the time nor the inclination to know your neighbours. Seb glanced around. The room was tiny. The curtains were drawn and a cheap light shade hung at an angle in the middle of the ceiling. The light bulb had burnt through the plastic.

True to style, Gimp got straight to the point. 'This demo has hit the press big time and calls for an official Inquiry.'

'Yeah.'

'So you were there, what did you make of it?'

'I survived. It was an eye opener. Things blow up fast.'

'Take me through it.'

'The rioters kicked off first. I was standing in front of the bank. I got pushed by the crowds towards the police until I was so close, I could smell the hostility, the fear, the tension. It was all around, like waiting for a bomb to go off. Then it did go. The crowd exploded. Missiles came from the back of the crowd aimed at the police and at the bank buildings. All fucking hell broke loose. Stones, bricks, whatever they could get their hands on. Guaranteed to cause trouble and injury, and it did… but, whatever the rights and wrongs; law and order had to be maintained… by any means necessary.'

'Cut the moralising, Seb.' He eyeballed him. 'You got too close. Keep away from the front line.

Keep a low profile. Don't put yourself in a position where you could be called as a witness. If that happens, your cover could be blown.' Seb was silent as he took that in. 'That USB, I gave you, anything of interest on it?'

'Yeah, four or five of them were wearing scarves or balaclavas to hide their faces, and they worked as a group. But one of them stood out. He'd got tattoos along his right arm and I'm pretty sure the stone throwing started with him. But when the fighting kicked off, he disappeared. Either that, or he'd changed his appearance and melted into the fray.'

'Interesting. Write it up in as much detail as you can and I'll pass it on to the Met. We'll try and get a match with known agitators. Anything else I need to know?'

'Yeah, I've made a contact. A woman called Nixie. I met her after the demo in Starbucks. We got talking, so... I'm going to my first meeting of Grassroots and if luck's on my side, I'll get an opening.'

'Good, well keep me in the picture.' He stood up. 'Got to go, I'll have more time when we meet next time. You're doing well so I can let you off the leash now. See you, if not before, in a fortnight, same day, same time, unless of course, you contact me before then.' He walked over to the door, turned the handle and then looked back. 'Make sure you do as much background research as you can before you pitch up at that meeting. You'll be under scrutiny, extreme scrutiny. It'll be a test.'

Wednesday, and it was the day of the Grassroots meeting. To prepare for it, Seb read voraciously. The politics of the anti-consumerists bored him, but reading took his mind off things – like the occasional loneliness he experienced. Once he'd had an identity, now he had none. He lived on the margins of society, with no attachments, pretending to be what he wasn't, colluding with a deception, but for what? Was it some sort of truth? But whatever that might be, he had no idea.

He'd become introspective. Maybe he had too much time on his hands or his reading made him question himself and his life. His thoughts inevitably returned to his last visit home and how meeting his father had inevitably disintegrated into a quarrel. He'd tried to make sense of it, by getting out of the house, and driving to Aldeburgh, it hadn't really worked. The young girl he'd met on the beach, she'd been strange. How lonely, trusting and innocent she seemed. Would she still be there, visiting the Shell?

He brought himself back to the present. Enough. He had a job to do. He caught the bus to Tottenham High Road and walked the rest of the way. The pub was on the corner, huge, red brick, ugly, and by the look of it, probably Victorian. Inside it was noisy, crowded and after asking a barman where the meeting was, he threaded his way through the bar to a side door, climbed the stairs and walked along a dimly lit corridor until he reached a half-open door.

He looked inside and stood for a moment in the doorway. A small group of people sat in a circle, chatting to each other. One of them glanced up, saw him, sprang up from the group, and walked rapidly over to him. He wasn't exactly friendly. He stood barring his way, stretching his tattooed arm across the doorway. Seb took a step back. Hard looking with a mean face, the man's hair was so short it clung to his skull, his eyes cold behind old-fashioned, round, steel-rimmed glasses. He wore jeans and a tight black tee shirt. It carried the logo in red, 'Eat the rich'.

Eyeballing Seb, he said, 'Just a minute, mate, where do you think you're going?'

'A meeting. I've been told Grassroots meets here.'

'It's private. Members only.'

He was about to say he was a newcomer when he noticed Nixie. She'd been chatting but once she'd seen him, she stood up, walked across the room, and put her hand on the man's arm. 'Mike, he's okay. I invited him. We met at the demo, he's just moved here.' His eyes narrowed. He looked at Nixie, then back again at Seb. 'I've checked him out,' she added.

Mike paused, then he said, 'Okay, but he can't just barge in.' He gave Seb a hard look and said, 'Wait here, while I check out with the others whether you can join us.' He shut the door in Seb's face.

Seb took his chewing gum out and pushed it in his mouth. He'd give them ten minutes. Any longer and he'd go. He wasn't used to being treated like that. The hostility from the guy at the door peed him off. He felt like walking out, but he had to go through with it. While he waited, he'd have a quick drink downstairs in the bar. It was even busier than when he'd arrived. He pushed his way to the bar, but had to wait five minutes before he was served.

He stared into his drink. The pub smelt of stale beer and his feet stuck to the filthy carpet. He almost walked out there and then. He spoke to no one and no one spoke to him. He was anonymous. An image of the champagne bars he used to frequent around Canary Wharf floated into his mind. The only thing this place shared with them, apart from the numbers of people getting trollied, was the noise. It was an equal match as far as the decibel level went, but the accents were different. In the City the estuary English of London traders, the classy careful articulations of the Home Counties, the transatlantic nasal drawl of the international traders. All he could hear in this pub was the effing and blinding of north Londoners. He stood drinking, then threw back his beer and sprinted up the stairs. If they weren't ready for him, it was time to go. He wasn't used to being treated like a spare part.

Mike was standing by the door. 'You can stay, but we need to know more about you.'

All eyes were on him as he took his seat. Nixie flashed him a quick smile; she seemed the only friendly face, the rest of the group stared at him, as if he'd come off another planet, which was exactly how he felt right then. The questioning started as soon he'd sat down.

'We need to know why you are here.'

He didn't answer, taken aback by the speed and directness of the woman's question.

Mike glanced at Seb. 'That's a straight enough question, isn't it? Why are you here?

Nixie spoke then, 'Mike's right. Sorry, I should have told you. We can't be too careful about who joins us.' She gave Seb an encouraging smile.

That was when he realised the meeting was going to be difficult. Naively, he'd assumed he could just walk in, but the vibes weren't exactly inviting. He tried to look nonchalant. He looked round the group. 'Fair enough, but what do you want to know?'

'Before we start, have you got a mobile on you?'

'Yeah. Why?'

'Give it to me.' Mike put out his hand and Seb passed it over. Mike removed the cover and prised out the exposed SIM card and battery, and placed them on the table. Leaning back in his chair, he folded his arms and said, 'Okay, tell us about yourself, your name for a start, and then anything relevant about you, like your background.'

At that point, Seb thought he'd rather be anywhere than where he was right then, but the long hours of training and preparation kicked in. 'My name? Seb, Seb Harvey.' He paused. 'The demo at the bank was my first demo. I knew what had been going on in the world markets, because for the last two years I've been working in the financial sector, but I left. I was sickened by the risk taking, the exploitation of the naive and gullible, and the worship of money.'

'So how come you were working there in the first place?'

'My father's in business and... '

Mike cut across him, 'Don't tell me, he wanted you to follow in his footsteps. You've had it easy. I'm right, aren't I?'

'I'm not responsible for that, just as you're not. '

'What do you mean?' There was a long silence. He'd put his foot in it. He tried backtracking. 'Well, all I meant to say was, what our parents do, and who they are, we have no control over. So, I'm not like him. He's a self-made successful, businessman, a bastard basically, greedy and ruthless.'

Still no comment. Mike broke the silence and said, 'Okay, we get that, so what made you leave your work?'

'The whole thing. The people. The system. It's sickening, the differences between the haves and the have-nots. And it can only get worse. A lot worse. They're going to want to recoup their losses, which can only mean one thing, an attack on the public sector and since the public sector employs the ordinary people, they'll be paying the price.

They have no power, no status, no clout to fight back, because Thatcher destroyed the unions. I want things to be different.'

He glanced round, he'd got their attention. He continued; there were no interruptions. He spoke fluently about his background, his work, his gradual disillusionment. It had built up over time, he said, until he reached the point where he couldn't continue. He'd dropped out, he didn't know what he wanted, but he did know what he didn't want. He was looking for a purpose in life, something that would engage him.

'So apart from your personal stuff, at what point, did you make that decision – to get out?'

'I was working in Canary Wharf. It's like the Vatican, only the worship of money has replaced the worship of God. The wealth of the shops, the bars, the buildings, it's like a gilded cage. One day I reread Orwell's *Down and Out in London and Paris* – that had been a school book, so I ventured outside Canary Wharf and I had a shock. I saw the poverty, the food banks, the rough sleepers, the drug users. I hadn't known and I hadn't understood that their lives are about survival.'

'Where did you go?'

'Central London, parts of Islington, Peckham, Camberwell…'

Mike spoke again, 'Okay. We get it, but why Grassroots?'

Seb looked quickly at Nixie. She smiled at him.

'The Bank of England demo, like I said, that was my first experience. I was shocked, seeing innocent people kicked and batoned. The police brutality was a wakeup call. I had to get involved. It was a chance meeting at Starbucks. Nixie was there with a friend and we got talking.'

Nixie laughed. 'Yeah, what he hasn't said, is that he pulled my mate, Andrea, from under the hooves of the police horses. She'd have been trampled to death, but for him.'

'Anyone would have done that,' Seb said.

Mike was staring at him. 'Returning to the matter in hand,' he said.

'We began chatting and she told me about Grassroots.'

Silence. Seb considered whether he should say more about the personal life of the traders, the financiers he'd worked with and the politicians, how they'd had their own way for too long and how the police protect the status quo, but decided he'd said enough.

'So what can you bring to the table?'

'I want to join others in opposition.'

'Yeah, yeah, be more specific.'

'I've got a degree in business and computer security, and an insider's knowledge in how the financial sector works. I can make sense of company accounts and I have a rough idea of who's who in the system. I know who to watch in the City, the ones who hang out with the politicians, talk the talk, and do the deals under the table.'

All eyes were fixed on him. Mike continued eyeballing him. He didn't trust him and that made him feel uneasy.

'So where did you go to school?' The question was from Nixie.

'My father worked for an international company with business interests in the Far East. I went to a load of different schools, including the International School in Singapore, mixed with kids like myself, privileged but starved of a proper family life. We moved every few years. I'm a bit of a nomad really,

I don't belong anywhere.'

'And where do you live now?'

'In a flat. It's cheap but I'm on my own. I prefer to keep myself to myself. I don't want anyone poking their nose in my business.'

There was another silence. Mike was studying his face intently. Then he spoke, 'Okay, step outside. We'll have a chat. We'll be ten minutes, give or take.'

Seb stood up. He hadn't liked the attitude of Mike and being interrogated. He left the room and went downstairs to the bar. Had he been over the top, given too much away, stuff they could check up on? The barman pushed across his beer, and without looking at him, silently held out his hand for the money. He felt so pissed off, again he almost walked out, but he drank his beer and dragged himself back.

Mike was waiting. He put his hand out in greeting. 'Okay mate, you're on. Here's your mobile and Nixie'll show you the ropes, take a seat.' He pushed a chair towards him. Seb wondered if he ever smiled. He sat down and glanced at Nixie. She smiled warmly at him, mouthed 'welcome' and the meeting began.

He only half listened to what was said; an analysis of the demo and the brutality of the police. He'd heard it all before. It bored him. He wanted some action, something significant, something he could report back to Gimp but there was nothing that grabbed his attention.

He waited for the meeting to end, and then sauntered over to Nixie. 'Greetings,' he said, smiling.

'Well, what do you think?' she asked.

'Interesting, if not fascinating. Thanks for the support. Drink?'

She smiled at him. 'Yeah, why not. Here?'

'Too noisy. Is there somewhere quieter?'

'There's a smaller pub, nearby, The Lamb and Lion.'

It was a few streets away. It was quieter but only marginally so. He bought the drinks and they found somewhere less crowded to retreat to.

'So tell me more, how do you think it went?'

'A bit heavy, but to be expected.'

'We haven't had anyone new for a while but we have to be careful. Since that guy was busted as a police informer, we don't know who's a friend and who's an enemy. That's why Mike took your mobile. Meetings have been recorded and everyone can get rounded up just before a big demo. By the way, how old did you say you were?'

'I didn't say. Why do you want to know?'

'Personal. Just interested.'

'Part of the inquiry?'

'Yeah, you could say that.'

'Well, I'm twenty five.' There was a silence. 'Mike seems to be on top of the game.'

'He is, he's been an activist ever since he could walk.' She laughed. 'He knows his stuff, he specialises in communication.'

'So what's that mean?'

'Social media, he knows his way round, so when some group plans an event and wants support, he's your man. Knows everybody there is to know. He gets the people out and on the streets. He was behind the bank demo.'

'Impressive. How well do you know him?'

'We were at uni together, but on different courses, so we never bumped into each other, then I met him at a demo and we took off from there.'

'We? Are you an item?'

'Off and on, but he's too intense for me, sleeps,

eats and breathes the cause. A man on a mission.'

'You like your men to lighten up a bit then?'

'I wouldn't say that. I like men, particularly men who want to change society. I take after my dad in that way.'

'Tell me more.'

'Not right now, I only just met you.'

She laughed, and looked away across the room to avoid eye contact, but she must have seen someone she knew because she waved. She stood up. 'I won't be long, just got to say hello to a friend.' She walked over to a group of women.

He watched her as she talked. She was animated, listening closely to what her friends were saying, occasionally nodding her head encouragingly. He took a good look at her. She was attractive. Her Levis and tee shirt were tight enough to show off her figure and her body looked good. Compared with Carole, she was serious, politically and socially concerned, so definitely not his usual type. He turned his attention back to Nixie and tried to imagine her dressed in a tight short skirt with heels, but it wasn't possible. His imagination failed him. She just wasn't like that. With her short crop, her jeans and tee shirt she was more the outdoor or gamine type, sporty, fit, and she had that gap in her teeth. The imperfection appealed to him.

She was walking back across to him, and sat down. 'Sorry about that.'

'No worries,' he said. 'Fellow conspirators?'

'What? You mean... well yes, I guess so.'

'Everyone seems to have a role, so what's yours?'

'You're looking at it. I look after the newbies, encourage them, support them.'

'Ah, and report on them?'

She gave him a look. He could see she wasn't

amused. He changed tack, reverted to his usual chat-up line, 'So, when you saw me across a crowded Starbucks, did you accost me not because you fancied me, but because you saw me as a prospective member of Grassroots?'

'What are you talking about? Do you carry on like this all the time?'

'You mean flirting. No, only with attractive women.' He grinned. 'Just kidding. So what's next? Given the shit going on, what plans are there?'

'I can't tell you much, except have you heard of the Occupy movement?'

'A little, tell me more.'

'Well, it started in the States. It's about fighting globalisation and the lack of democracy so a group of us are getting together for a sit in. We want to bring the City to its knees. That's all I know right now.'

Seb looked at her. If that was the best they could do, what was basically a propaganda stunt, his employers had nothing to fear. But he kept his mouth shut and was just about to ask another question, before he decided against it. He'd asked enough and she might get suspicious. He'd work on his friendship with her, get to know her better, see how she operated. Once he knew that, he'd have the advantage. Job done. He finished his drink.

'Got to go, Nixie, any plans for the rest of the evening?'

'No, not really.'

A hint of disappointment passed over her face. He trusted his observations. It was a skill he'd developed at school. There'd always been something going on between the boys and he'd learnt how to be one step ahead. Ages ago, he'd realised whoever wrote *Lord of the Flies* had got it right. It was a dog eat dog situation. The aggression in the City was less in your face than at school, but working with traders was like conducting a game of poker. The mouth said one thing, the eyes another. But if you watched and listened, you could keep ahead of the game. As far as Nixie went, what he was tuning into was a certain vulnerability and if he was right about that, if and when he did get involved with her, she'd be a pushover.

He said, 'I'll walk you home.' It was a try-on. He'd expected her to play hard to get, tell him to get lost but she didn't play that game. She said nothing other than, 'If you're going that way.' He hadn't been, but he was now.

Fifteen minutes later they arrived outside a block of council flats. It was one of many and part of the Broadwater Farm estate. High, gaunt and built in concrete, it reminded him of a prison. She stood at the bottom of one of the stairwells, looking as if she didn't know what to say or what she should do. 'Do you want to come up? I live on the second floor. There's no lifts.'

It wasn't exactly welcoming but he took up the invitation.

She shared her flat with one other, a woman by the look of the clothes scattered around, but whoever she was, she was out. It was the first time he'd been inside a council flat and he was curious to see what they were like inside.

He'd been oblivious to them once but since he'd taken up this work he'd become aware of the differences between the haves and the have-nots, especially when it came to the housing market. Some had money, and some hadn't, but he had no conscience or guilt about this inequality. His attitude and interest was neutral, if not anthropological. It was just the way it was. Interesting, but different.

She offered him tea which he accepted and while she was in the kitchen, he took a look around. The decor was, he observed, an object lesson in how to be creative on next to nothing – anti-consumerism in action. Whoever put the room together had made the best of a few possessions. Most things looked second-hand, and had probably been picked up in a charity warehouse or on Freecycle. The walls were red and covered with posters. Piles of leaflets were stacked neatly on the floor. A navy patterned Indian throw was draped over an old sofa. The bookshelves were made from reclaimed wood balanced on bricks. There were the usual books critiquing capitalism and consumerism globalisation; the advocates of different values and life styles by the authors they all read and admired, Noam Chomsky, Naomi Klein, Oliver James, Vance Packard.

His eye was drawn to an unframed photograph of Nixie propped against some books. Taken from above, she was climbing a sea cliff and smiling up at the camera. Below her could be seen the sea, the water swirling, surging, foaming on the rocks. She must have nerves of steel. He was impressed.

'I see you go sea cliff climbing.'

She put down the mugs of tea, and sat down. 'Yeah, whenever I can.'

'Where do you go? I'm a climber but I've never tried sea cliffs. I'd like to.'

'Really? Slab climbing gives me a buzz. The photo was taken by my mum not far from Porth Clais in Pembrokeshire. That's where I was brought up. It's great. I've been climbing since I was eleven. My dad taught me first, now I climb with my mates. Where do you usually go?'

'The Lake District or the Isle of Skye, but they're

too far. I need to get in some practice, somewhere closer.'

She looked at him as if considering what she was about to say. 'Don't you know the Castle in Stoke Newington? It's got a climbing wall. '

He considered whether to invite himself when she went next, but decided against it. He was getting her measure. He'd wait for an invitation. He didn't have to wait long,

'No, never heard of it. I'll check it out.'

'I go Sunday mornings, do you want to come along?'

He smiled. 'You're on. Ten thirty?'

'No, early is better. Say nine thirty. Is that okay? There's fewer people Sunday mornings... so where did you learn climbing?'

For a split second he almost told the truth, that one of the masters at his school climbed and he'd taken a few boys, including himself, to the Dales over the weekends, but then he remembered his story.

'When my dad worked in the States, I used to climb in the Yosemite National Park, I started with Go Climb a Rock. It was for beginners and it took off from there.'

'Wow, I'd love to go there.' She paused, looked hard at him. 'You really have had a privileged background. But I still don't get it. Why you've joined us?'

He looked straight at her.'I've told you. You heard in the Bricklayers. The system sickens me. Maybe it's to do with my father. He's part and parcel of it.'

'Maybe so, but look at it this way, because of him, you've had loads of opportunities the rest of us haven't.'

'So what. You wouldn't say that if you knew my father. I've had to live with him.'

'Don't lose your cool. I'm only asking.'

'Does it matter anyway – what my motivation is?'

'Maybe not, but it's interesting, you know, what drives people.'

'So what about you? What's pushing your button?'

'I've been brought up that way.It's all I've known. My dad's an environmental activist, he used to work for Greenpeace, not so much now. My mum's a forensic psychologist. She's doing research.'

'Forensic? Is she interested in criminals?'

'Yes and no. She's researching the psychopathic personality.'

'What's that?'

'I'm quoting my mum now. It's a set of personality factors that some traders and politicians have.'

'Like what?'

'Like superficial charm, grandiosity, pathological lying and manipulation, no guilt, no empathy. The list goes on.'

'Very attractive. Sounds like me.'

Nixie laughed. 'We all think that. But it's a question of degree and how we operate.'

'So how did your mother get into that?'

She gave him an intense stare, then looked away, avoiding his eyes.

'What's going on? Why so upset?'

'Do I look upset?'

'You look something. But until you tell me, I don't know.'

'It's a long story.'

She put her tea down, got up, walked across the room and stood with her back to the wall, her arms folded across her chest, as if to protect herself. She looked intently at him as if considering whether to tell him. Seb sensed something catastrophic had happened. He waited for her to speak. The expression on her face reminded him of his mother on one of the occasions she'd become very upset – usually because of his father.

'Nixie, you look distressed. I'm sorry. Is it my questions?'

'No, not really. It's not your fault.'

'So tell me, tell me what it is. It's okay. Whatever it is, it's over.'

'Look, I've only just met you, and I don't know you.'

'Well. You know more about me than I do you. Don't you?'

'Like what?'

'Like I didn't like my work and my father's a bastard. That's all pretty personal stuff.'

'I guess so, but I feel ashamed.'

'I'm intrigued but I'm not about to judge you. Please tell me what's going on for you, because holding back is making it worse for you. Trust me.'

There was a long silence, then she said, 'Okay. Not sure whether I can trust you but I will tell you... My mum got in trouble when she was young. She did something wrong. I won't say what, but she got help. For a while she helped other women and she became a forensic psychotherapist. Recently she's become involved with a research project. It's about psychopathy in different occupations.'

'What did she do that was so wrong?'

'You really want to know?'

'Yes, I do. I want to know the whole story.'

Avoiding his eyes, she blurted out, 'She stole someone's baby.'

Seb took a deep breath while it registered. Despite his shock, he had to know more. Keeping his voice well modulated, he said, 'Stole a baby? From where?'

'Don't sound like that. It was ages ago. She's changed. It was from a flat in Earl's Court. She wasn't in her right mind. She never harmed him.'

'And...?' She didn't reply. He continued. 'You say "him". It was a boy then.'

'Yes, she kept him for over two months. She ran off with him to a Scottish island but they tracked her down.'

The conversation in Starbucks after the demo was returning to him. She'd said she was conceived on a Scottish Island. It had stuck in his mind but he hadn't known why. Now it was beginning to make sense.

'What did the parents do?'

'They worked in the City.'

'I mean after the baby was returned?'

'No idea, from what I gathered they were pretty unpleasant. They worked in finance; one was a trader... funnily enough. Are you okay? You look as if you've seen a ghost.'

'I'm fine.' He stood up, he had to get out. 'I have to be off. It's been a long day.'

'Why so fast? Has it put you off?'

'No, no, it hasn't. It all makes sense Weird. What your mother did, is not your fault.'

'I sometimes wonder how the baby got on, and what he might be doing now.'

'Well, he recovered. Look, I must go, Nixie. I really am tired.'

'What about Sunday? Will I see you Sunday?' She looked anxious.

'I'll be there.'

He glanced at Nixie. He had considered making a pass, but he couldn't do that now. Not after what he'd just heard. He stared at her. She seemed to change in front of him. Her hair was a rich brown, shoulder length, thick and glossy. She had a half smile on her face. She was no longer Nixie. The person standing in front of him, was her mother. He felt as if he knew her. She was taking a step towards him, her arms outstretched. The walls were closing in on him. He felt more and more disorientated, as if he might pass out.

'I have to go.'

Nixie put out her hand. He looked mindlessly at her hand and then her face. He left abruptly.

— 7 —

He was preoccupied as if he wasn't part of everyday life, but existing in another time and place. Of his early life he knew little, other than what his mother, in a rare moment of intimacy, had told him. It had been the night before he was due to start prep school. He'd gone to bed early and been woken by his father bellowing at his mother.

He'd lain, unsuccessfully trying to get back to sleep. Eventually he'd crept out from his bedroom and, pressing his face between the balusters, had sat listening from the top of the stairs. The door had been left open to the lounge and he could hear everything; his father yelling, his mother crying. He was brutal, roaring at her to shut up and toughen up, but this caused her to cry even more until all he could hear was great, gasping sobs.

His father shouted, 'You don't get it, do you? He's too close to you. Do you want a son like a big girl's blouse?'

The phrase stuck with him. It had taken time before he understood it, but when he had, from that moment on he felt pure hatred for his father.

'I don't want him to go, Rupert. It's cruel. Can't you understand? When he's not with me, it brings it all back – he was only two months old. Snatched. The agony of not knowing whether he was alive, of not being able to see him, of not being able to hold him in my arms. It was torture and I vowed then I would always have him near me.'

'Shut up.' There was a long silence.

'Don't make him go. Please. It'll be torture for me.'

'I said, shut up.' His father had been silent. Then he heard him say, 'Oh, grow up, woman,' and he'd left the room, banging the door behind him.

When Seb had been sure he'd gone, he'd crept downstairs. He wanted to comfort her, put his arms round her. He'd told her he loved her, but that had made her cry even more, until eventually his father heard them, had come back into the room, and dragged him away. He'd sobbed as he was carried upstairs, but his father was unmoved. He pushed him into his bedroom and slammed the door behind him. He'd been seven years old then, and that was the first and last time he cried in front of his father. The next day, he was taken to prep school.

Several times he'd tried to get his mother to tell him more. He'd asked what she'd meant when she'd said 'snatched' and that he'd only been two months old, but she'd always clammed up. She said it was too upsetting, that his father had forbidden her to talk about it. She'd said what had happened was in the past and it was unhealthy wallowing in negative feelings and endlessly going over things.

But he hadn't forgotten the row and the phrase 'a big girl's blouse'. It continued to haunt him. He hated it and because of that, he knew he had to eventually pull away from his mother. He began to see her through his father's eyes. He began to associate her with being soft and feminine, qualities he came to despise and to see as weak.

He tried to win his father's affection and attention by imitating him, but it hadn't worked and as he got older, it dawned upon him that his father was indifferent to him. He was a bully and realising this made him critical of everything about him; his views, his politics, his attitudes, even the way he dressed and spoke. Something had been switched off inside himself. It was as if he'd grown a shell around himself, and the shell protected him from being hurt ever again. He felt nothing – other than that he despised his father.

Still he remained curious. He wanted to know about his early life and what his mother was referring to when she said that she didn't know whether he was alive. He knew he couldn't ask or confront her, because she wouldn't answer. He'd tried and it hadn't worked. Besides he didn't want her disintegrating into a sobbing wreck all over again. There had to be another way. If he had been snatched, it would have been reported.

Two weeks later, armed with the relevant dates, addresses, and using his real name, Albert Sebastian Melbury, Seb visited the Newspaper National Archives. Bertie, short for Albert, had been his first name. He'd been named after his great grandfather, but when he got to prep school, finding he was the object of ridicule, he'd refused to be known as Bertie. Instead, he insisted on being called Seb, the shortened version of his middle name, Sebastian. He planned to focus his research on the national newspapers of the time, when he was two months old. The national press of the time had been put on microfiche and everything he wanted to know was there.

He read slowly, starting with the Daily Telegraph. It had made the front page, with the headline, 'Baby Snatched from Cot as Parents Sleep'. It described how in the early hours of a morning, someone, probably a woman, had crept up a fire escape running up outside a block of mansion flats in West London and entered one of the flats through an open window. It was believed she'd hidden behind the floor-length curtains in the sitting room, waited until the baby's parents had gone to bed, and had then snatched him.

He read on. All the newspapers covered the developing story. That 'someone' was Flori, and she'd been helped by a friend called Rose. She'd taken him to a Scottish island and he'd been with her for two months before she was caught. A recording of a Crime Watch programme showed an appeal for further information. The clip showed an interview with his parents. He watched it and grimly noticed that whereas his mother was visibly distraught; his father seemed indifferent to her distress.

Nothing has changed, Seb thought. It brought home to him how totally alienated from his feelings his father was. But he felt the same. Reading about what had happened seemed to have little effect on him. He was empty of emotion, even when the interviewer revealed he'd been conceived via IVF. That was something he hadn't known, but he didn't feel any identification with himself as a tiny baby. It was as if this baby was a stranger and had nothing to do with him. He saw his parents' distress as a charade, an act, a lie, a show for the world they'd created of themselves as the happy couple.

On his second visit, he came across a later article in the Saturday Guardian. It was about Rose, the woman's accomplice, and written four years after he'd been snatched. She now worked as an anthropologist and had just returned from Northern Canada where, motivated by her friend's tragic history, she'd researched Post-natal Depression among the Inuit. She had opened up to the journalist and described her relationship with Flori. They'd met when they'd worked at Harrods.

Rose had initially found her fascinating, but now she recognised they'd been far too close.

'Do you think there was some sexual attraction between the two of you?' the journalist had asked.

'No, not at all. It was more about us standing together against the world. We were like sisters, although we'd had totally different backgrounds. She always knew what she wanted, and she could make me laugh. I'd become too dependent on her, that was the problem.'

'The psychiatrist's report said you both shared the same delusions and desires. Did you agree with that?'

'Not at the time, but now I do. He said we thought and behaved as if we were one. It's a rare psychiatric condition known as "folie a deux".'

'So what happened then?'

'We were banned from further contact with each other and Flori was given a compulsory treatment order. She had to attend sessions with a therapist.'

'Have you seen her, since then?'

'No. At first, being banned from seeing her was devastating, but in the long run, it was a good thing. I had to separate from her…'

'And what about the baby?'

'The baby was beautiful. She called him Owain. That wasn't his real name. Flori told me she'd chosen it while she was in some kind of trance. She loved him. She really cared about him. When she took him, he had a little fat giraffe in his crib lying beside him and she always insisted that the giraffe should be kept for him.'

'There was a lot of hostility from the public directed at her for what she did. She became a hate figure to many…'

'Yes, but that wasn't fair. They didn't know her.

She wasn't like that. She used to read a poem to him, one she was very fond of, by Pablo Neruda. When she was forced to abandon Owain on Jura, she left the giraffe, the poem and a note with him. Did you know about that?'

'It came out in Court.'

'Well, she'd asked that they be kept for him. Whether that happened, I have no idea. But she'd told me she'd always love him.'

He turned away. He'd had enough, read enough. He had no conscious memory of her, of the island, of returning to his parents. He looked around the room. He was alone, isolated in the world with his thoughts. Fragments, images, incidents, like snapshots, invaded his mind. None of them made sense. He was slipping away. The feelings of claustrophobia were returning. Feelings he'd had when Nixie had told him about her mother. The walls were closing in on him. How and why had that happened? Was there some unknown force impelling the two of them to meet?

He stared at his hands as if they were a reminder he was real. Before meeting Nixie he would have thought the chances of ever coming across the woman who'd snatched him would be infinitesimal. Although theoretically possible, he would have thought it was improbable. Was it just bad luck then that he'd met the woman's daughter? But the coincidence was so mind blowing, it had to mean something. The questions kept coming. He was on overdrive, trying to make some sort of sense of his life. Maybe it was a stitch-up? Someone who knew about his history and had organised his meeting Nixie? But what would be the motivation? He could ask Gimp, but he'd probably say life is full of bizarre coincidences, that he had a job to do, and investigating his own past was not part of it, or what he was paid for.

But whatever it did mean, he wanted to know more. More about his past, more about what had exactly happened, and more about his snatcher, Nixie's mother. It was possible that his parents had kept those items Rose had referred to; the poem, and the giraffe. There was only one way to find out, and that was to search his parents' house.

He'd use the breaking and entering techniques he'd been taught during his induction and in the meantime, he'd continue cultivating Nixie. It was now even more important. She was the link with his snatcher and she was a source of vital information for his work. He'd win her over. It was only a matter of time.

That's what he had hoped, but weeks later it was obvious; his usual charm wasn't working. She didn't operate like the women he'd hung around with before. He could no longer flash his cash or show off his car, and it dawned upon him that, as far as these tactics went, his powers of influence were limited. This annoyed him, particularly as his previous, preferred way with women had been to 'wine and dine' them. There had to be some other way.

He consulted with Gimp, told him of his frustrations. Gimp reassured him, said he must be patient, and to bear in mind, 'When one technique fails, it's time to try another. Get involved in other ways. An opportunity will present itself soon enough.'

Gimp was right; he didn't have to wait long. One Sunday, he was with Nixie at the climbing wall in Stoke Newington, when she mentioned she was going to Pembrokeshire.

'Who are you going with?' he'd asked.

'A couple of climbing friends. We're staying at my parents' farmhouse in Caefai.'

'Carfai, where's that?'

'Near St David's.'

'Sounds good. A spring holiday along the Welsh coast?'

'Yes and no, it's to get in some practice at Porth Clais, on the sea cliffs.'

'Practice? What's that about? What's the plan?'

She laughed and said, 'Well, wouldn't you like to know?'

Her answer annoyed him, but it also made him suspicious. Why hadn't she asked him? She knew he wanted to try sea-cliff climbing. Was she involved with some kind of project; one that involved climbing that she didn't want him to know about?

It was time to change tactics. He'd make her jealous. He'd make it personal. As an undercover agent, he saw himself as representing the forces of law and order, fighting the saboteurs and those seeking to destroy the status quo. Lying in that context was legitimate and necessary. It justified his employment and it was necessary to preserve the stability of society.

Seen in this way, he could justify anything he did, but lying for his own purposes, even on a small scale, was to go into new territory. By now he knew Nixie well enough to know how to get under her skin and he was prepared to manipulate her and any situation if it suited him. 'That's strange,' he said. 'I was planning to visit St David's the same week with a friend called Jane. She's a member of UK Uncut. She's not a climber, but she loves coasteering. She took it up in Cornwall and she's keen to try the cliffs and waters off Pembrokeshire.'

Nixie's eyes widened. 'I've never tried coasteering. It doesn't appeal. Too scary, throwing yourself off a cliff into deep water.'

'Yes, it's not for everyone. But she says it sharpens her reaction times and it's good preparation for more risky operations as an activist. Have you ever come across her?'

'Yes,' she said. 'Maybe. Does she have blonde hair and live in Ealing?'

'That's her,' he said. 'Her hair's long. She's very pretty. Funny thing is, when I asked if she knew you, she said she didn't, but she said she'd like to meet you.' He laughed as he said this.

Nixie digested this piece of information then, looking closely at Seb, she said, 'So where will you stay?'

'In a tent, not sure where. Any ideas?'

'There's loads of camping sites between Newgale and St David's.' She looked at him quizzically. 'How well do you know her?'

'I'd say very well.' He looked straight at her. She was so naive. She hadn't got it; that he was trying, and succeeding, to make her jealous.

'I didn't know you were involved with Uncut.'

'I attend their meetings now and again. They're interesting. They've got some projects they're planning, but I'm sure Mike will know of them already. Maybe Jane and I could meet up with you in St David's.' He felt safe saying this because he knew she'd refuse. He was right.

'That won't be possible. We have a full on week.'

'Doing what? Tell me more.'

She paused, then she said, 'Training sessions. Something's coming up.'

'At Porth Clais? Why there?'

'Climbing. There's an event planned in two

months. There's three of us but we need to train, climb and get to know how we work together.'

'If I can be of any help…'

'I'll let you know.'

'No worries, if we come across each other…' He didn't finish his sentence. She'd gone quiet. Nothing more was said. She clammed up.

He was hardly any further in knowing more. Some of what he'd said was true. He did know a Jane but she wasn't in Uncut and she wasn't an activist. He'd known her when he worked in the City and had had a fling with but he didn't approve of her recreational drug use. He'd tried it but hadn't liked it. Coke wasn't his bag.

Apart from that, Nixie may not have issued an invite to him, but that wasn't about to stop him. He bought an Ordinance Survey map of Pembrokeshire and began tracing the outlines of the jagged coast path which followed the deeply indented coastline. By putting together all that Nixie had told him and by a process of elimination, before long he'd located her parents' farmhouse. It was close to Caefai and surrounded by fields and remotely situated.

He pitched his tent in a farmer's field a mile away from the coast. It was off a lane which led to the farmhouse, but far enough away not to bump into Nixie by mistake and close enough for him to walk to it. He worked out the best way to reach the farmhouse and practised the route, walking down the old drovers' paths alongside the fields and through the scatter of farm outbuildings. He got to know which fields to bypass, and how to avoid the bullocks that ran at him and the farm dogs that barked and growled as he passed.

Two nights later he made his first visit. It was almost midnight and there was no moon. Standing in a small copse some distance away from the building, he kept well away from the front of the house. Security lights had been installed. On the ground floor a light from inside the house shone out into the darkness. He stood for ten minutes, before moving nearer. He was standing outside a large kitchen. The curtains were open. A woman was sitting at the kitchen table reading. She must have heard something or had the sixth sense of an animal because she stood up, walked over to the window and pulled the curtains across.

He moved back into the shadows and waited. There was a tiny gap between the curtains where they didn't meet. Unwittingly, she'd made it easier for him to watch her, so if he stood right outside the window he could still see her. She'd moved to a large armchair. A reading light shone over her. This had to be Nixie's mother. She was the right age.

His mind went blank. He'd been so focused on finding out about Nixie, it hadn't occurred to him he might see her mother. In her early fifties, she was still attractive. Her hair was dark, longish, going grey and she'd pulled it up each side of her face tethering it with a clasp on the top of her head. What was she reading? Whatever it was held her attention. Then he remembered what Nixie had told him, that she was researching psychopathy.

He walked back into the shadows, his mind going back to what he knew about being snatched. This was the woman his parents refused to talk about; a woman who looked normal, but with a terrible history. What had driven her? Who was she? He knew very little about her, yet she was part of his history. Seeing her unexpectedly disturbed him. For one mad moment, he almost threw a stone at the window. But then, his attention was caught by the headlights of a car moving slowly along the lane towards the farmhouse.

He moved rapidly away and returned to his original place, standing some distance away in the darkness amongst the trees. It was far enough away not to be seen, but it wasn't a good vantage point. He could hear but not see what was going on. The car pulled onto the concrete drive and Nixie's voice rang out. A moment later, her mother came out to meet them and they went inside.

He'd take another look, see who was there. Her mother was making tea, offering sandwiches to Nixie and her two friends – none he recognised, but by the way they greeted each other, they knew each other well. They sat together at the table, laughing and talking. The only person missing was Nixie's father. There was no sign of him. He continued watching until they disappeared upstairs.

He walked back to his tent, his torch lighting up the path between and over the fields. Mission accomplished; he knew now where the farmhouse was, what the security was like, what her mother looked like and that Nixie was there as she had said she would be. He'd use this knowledge at some point, as and when an opportunity presented itself.

Sunday, mid-morning, a few clouds scudded across the bright blue sky. Seb parked his van, not in one of the designated car parks, but off road in an isolated spot. Hoping he might come across Nixie climbing, he began walking along the coast path towards Porth Clais. There was a strong wind, the sea rolling in steadily, the occasional huge wave slapping against the rocks, sending plumes of foam and spray high into the air. This hadn't stopped the climbers. They were already out. Clinging to the rock, their fingers searched for tiny crevices, their feet finely balanced on slight indentations or protrusions in the rock. He stood watching as they clung to near vertical slabs of sandstone rising straight from the sea. Slowly making their way up the rock face, they occasionally stopped to dip their hands into the chalk bags hanging from their harnesses. This is what he'd come for, or at least, that's what he'd told Nixie, but so far, there was no sign of her.

He turned abruptly round, walked the half mile or so back to his van, and collected his swimming gear. By the time he'd arrived in Porth Clais, there were even more climbers, swimmers, jumpers, and divers. He struggled down an overgrown path towards the water, clambered across the rocks and, balancing on a small, flat rock, pulled on his swimming trunks and a wet suit. Then he waited for the big waves to subside, and lowered himself into the water.

It was cold, but he'd been in colder. The water was so clear he could see the rocks way below the surface, but as he was surrounded by coasteers jumping in all around him, he pulled away from them, and began swimming parallel to the cliffs. As he swam, he looked up at the climbers, hoping he might see Nixie. He'd reached the cliff face, the one the climbing books called, 'Dream Boat Annie', when he stopped, and treading water, looked up at the rock. Classified as between difficult and severe, only a few were climbing that morning, but one of them was Nixie. He recognised her immediately. It was her bright gear; the tight, pink tank top and the black climbing shorts that caught his attention. She was soloing, slowly making her way up the rock face.

He watched her stretch her arm across a deep

fissure in the cliff, her hand grasping to grab a protruding rock. She was leaning further over, when it happened. She'd reached too far and within a fraction of a second, she'd lost her balance, missed her footing, and was falling in a straight line towards the water, the rope dangling behind her.

It happened so fast he didn't have time to think about his response. His arms cleaving through the waves, he swam to where she'd entered the water. The impact had either concussed or shocked her. She was floating head down. He pulled her face up, flipped her over onto her back, pulled her across his body and, holding her in that position, swam to the nearest horizontal piece of rock, and dragged her out of the water.

She was breathing. She opened her eyes, looked briefly at him. 'Nixie, it's me. Are you okay?' Her eyes closed again. She hadn't recognised him. He glanced up; people were scrambling down the rocks and crowding round her inert body. Someone had called for an ambulance and within a short space of time one arrived. A paramedic briefly examined her, he said she was shocked but she'd be okay, they'd take her to hospital for a check up. He gave the ambulance men his mobile number and asked to be kept informed.

He slowly swam back to the cove where he'd left his clothes. He was cold. Although the sun was up, it wasn't warm. He stripped off his wet suit, stuffed it into a plastic bag, dressed and began the walk back along the coast path. He was glad she was okay but, it also had occurred to him, he couldn't have wished for a better opportunity if he'd planned it. He'd been in the right place at the right time but what she was doing there, and why, he still didn't know. He'd give her three days and if he'd heard nothing, he'd go back to London and try alternative measures. Patience had never been one of his virtues.

A day later she called. She'd been discharged from hospital and wanted to thank him. With that came an invite.

'Seb, how about coming to the farmhouse? My mum wants to meet you and she does a good line in cakes. You can stay for tea.'

He answered immediately. 'Sounds good to me,' he said.

The possibility of actually setting foot in her house put him on a high. He rang Gimp to let him know. 'This is the break I've been waiting for.'

'It's good, but don't get too excited, this is a long game, so assume nothing. Keep cool. You've got a way in, but don't blow it. The meeting could be crucial. Find out as much as possible, but say as little as possible. Anything else you think I should know?'

He hesitated. Should he tell him about Nixie's mother? He decided against it. Why would he tell him? Gimp didn't need to know. He was interested only in information to do with Seb's work as an undercover agent. So he'd pass on any information relevant to that, and nothing more. The rest belonged to him.

— 8 —

Seb took the back off his watch and inserted the tiny receiver. It was neat. At the right moment, he'd switch it on. He crawled out of his tent, zipped it up behind him, paused to make sure he'd left no incriminating evidence, then began the walk across the fields towards the farmhouse. The day was downcast, the sky grey but it was close, humid, almost oppressive, as if a storm was due.

It took twenty minutes to reach the farm but before knocking on the front door, he paused, checking for any external cameras he hadn't noticed on his first visit. There were none, only the security light he'd noticed previously. He was apprehensive. Not because he was there to find out as much as he could about Grassroots, but because it would be his first face to face with the woman who'd snatched him. He wanted to observe her, how she talked, how she laughed, how she gestured, hoping that way, he might understand her.

Two cars and a Land Rover were parked outside. He recognised the cars, one belonged to Nixie, one to her mother, but the land rover was new. He knocked, and while he waited for the door to be opened, he looked up. There was a hanging glass porch light and he could just see a tiny wire, protruding from the top of the lamp. It was an ideal place to conceal a camera. So, he was under some sort of surveillance. He took care to act nonchalantly.

The door was opened by a tallish, fit-looking, middle-aged man with sandy coloured hair. He looked straight at him, as if he was sizing him up. Then smiling, he held out his hand and shaking Seb's hand firmly, said, 'You must be Seb. I'm Matt. I've heard about you from my daughter. Come in. She's been baking with her mother and they're not quite ready, but they won't be long.'

He had a slight Scottish accent. He led him down a hall way and then gestured to a side room. It looked like a study, 'Take a seat, I'm in the middle of a phone call but I won't be long.' He left.

It was all a little formal. Seb glanced around. Plenty of books on the shelves, but the room was set up for meetings. Seb felt suspicious. Given the security lights and the concealed camera, it was highly probable there was some sort of a bugging device amongst the books. He walked across to the window, and with his back to the room, stared out, pretending to adjust his sleeves. He switched on his wire. Then he took a seat in one of the chairs placed round the table and glanced around.

On the wall, a black-and-white framed photograph of a man. It was taken from behind, so his face was hidden. Probably, Seb thought, Nixie's father. He was looking out to sea, and written underneath was a line of poetry, 'I must go down to the seas again, to the lonely sea and the sky.' It reminded him of the shell at Aldeburgh. He stood up and looked along the bookshelves. Books were always a giveaway. They tell a story about their owner and these were no exception. Matt, it was obvious, was a marine biologist, an environmentalist, an activist. None of the books were familiar to Seb. He picked one off the shelf at random and flicked open the pages. He read the opening paragraph. It was about the impact of oil spills on the oceanic eco-system and too technical for him to browse. He replaced it and pulled out another.

This one described the grounding of the massive oil tanker, called the Sea Empress and the subsequent oil spillage off the rocks of Pembrokeshire. He read that in 1996 one of the largest and most environmentally damaging oil spills in European history occurred. The Sea Empress, Norwegian owned, crewed by Russians hit the mid-channel rocks as they entered Milford harbour. Subsequent violent gales and falling tides meant 72,000 tonnes of crude oil were released into the sea around the coast, a region renowned for the beauty and diversity of its coastline. Marine birds were hit particularly hard during the early weeks of the spill, resulting in thousands of casualties... seals were little affected but shore seaweeds and invertebrates were killed in large quantities.

He paused. Now he understood why Nixie loved the sea, and why she'd become an activist. She'd said she'd learnt it at her father's knee, so like father, like daughter. It also explained why there was so much security on the outside of the house. It wasn't only because, as he'd originally thought, the farmhouse was remote but because Matt, as well as Nixie, probably had something to hide. He looked up from the book. Matt was standing in the doorway, silently watching him. It disconcerted him.

'So what do you think?' Matt said.

'About the oil spills? Shocking. I had no idea.'

'It's going on all the time and all over the world. They're taken to court, given massive fines, but they never pay up. They get away with it. It's a waste of time.'

'I have read about the Nigerian oil spillage... maybe direct action is the only response.'

'It was one of the worst. Devastating to the eco-system, the mangrove swamps, marine life, and public health, it's sickening.'

'You seem to know what you're talking about. Are you a marine biologist?'

Matt hesitated, then laughed. 'You could say that... but tea's ready, so we'd better go.'

Nixie was standing with her mother by the long kitchen table. She'd inherited her mother's dark eyes and the shape of her mouth. She looked shy when she saw him, and quickly introduced her mother.

'Seb, this is my mother, Flori.'

Seb walked across and shook Flori's outstretched hand. He looked closely at her. So this was Flori. Flori, the baby snatcher, the woman he'd spent the first two months of his life with. She was serious looking, tense, and spoke rapidly and nervously. Did she have some idea of who he was?

'Thank you so much for rescuing Nixie. I don't like her soloing, but she takes no notice of me. Well, she can thank her lucky stars you were there.'

He smiled at Nixie. 'No problem. Have you recovered?'

'I have. And thanks to you, I'm still alive. It's the second time.'

'Second time?'

'It's happened before. Falling.'

'Hmm. A cat has nine lives, they say. So two down, seven to go. Maybe it's time to give the sea cliffs a miss, don't you think?'

Her mother spoke, 'That's what I say, but it's like talking to the deaf. I've told her over and over... but she takes no notice.'

'It's necessary, Mum. I told you. It's practice. For the project.'

Seb spoke, 'Project? What project is that?'

Her mother answered, 'Oh, some foolhardy project. Climbing Big Ben. She takes after her father. He was the same, drawn to danger, and big publicity stunts.'

Seb silently thanked her. He noticed Nixie glance towards her father. He was looking tight lipped. Her mother laughed awkwardly, then seeming to realise the implications of what she'd just said, tried to cover up with the comment, 'Oh dear, I shouldn't have said that. Forget you heard it. Won't you sit down Seb and have some tea?'

'Sure.' He looked across at Nixie, 'Is that why you have two friends with you – to practise climbing?'

'They're still here, but they've gone to explore the coastline. I would have gone with them, but Mum insisted I took time off, and we wanted to thank you.'

Seb looked at Flori. 'I agree with you. Nixie should take more care and give herself a break.'

Flori smiled. 'You see, Seb agrees with me.'

She gestured towards a chair, poured out the tea and passed across a plate of homemade cakes. He picked one at random.

'Great location, your farmhouse, how long have you lived here?'

Matt answered, 'Oh a long time. We've lived in Pembrokeshire for years. It's the sea we love.' He paused, before asking, 'Where are you from? I can't quite place your accent.' He looked at Seb curiously.

'Lived mainly abroad as a child, and my father's work meant I went to a series of International Schools. After uni, I worked in the City.'

'And then you had a change of heart, Nixie tells me. What brought that on?'

'Events, experience, the people. I couldn't stand the greed and corruption, so eventually I dropped out, went to the bank demo and the rest is history.'

'Isn't that where you met Nixie?'

'Yes, we met after the demo, in Starbucks. She'd told me about Grassroots so I went to one of their meetings.'

There was a long silence. He felt as if he was under scrutiny, and being interrogated again.

'So how do you think you'll be able to help?'

The question seemed innocent enough, but it was the kind of question Mike had asked in 'The Bricklayers'.

'Well, give me a balance sheet, tell me which politician or financier you're interested in and I'll dish the dirt. I've got contacts and I can talk the talk.'

Suddenly he felt anxious, as if that sounded arrogant, but there was no immediate response from Matt. But his next question confirmed his suspicions. Nixie must have told her father he wasn't involved with the project and that he hadn't been invited to Pembrokeshire.

'So how come you're here at Porth Clais, the same time as Nixie?'

He glanced at Flori. He had to come up with something, something plausible. He thought quickly. He'd use the fact they already had a connection, that he admired her and found her attractive.

Smiling, he looked at Nixie, he spoke as if he was joking, but he wasn't. He was serious. 'Nixie and I had been to the climbing wall in Stoke Newington, and she mentioned she was off to Pembrokeshire. I'd hoped to get an invite, but none was forthcoming. So what's a man to do, but follow his heart.' He smiled again. 'She'd told me she'd be at Porth Clais, and I wanted to see her. So that's why I was there.'

Nixie said, 'But you said you were coming with Jane.'

'True, I did ask Jane. I don't like being on my own, but she cancelled at the last minute, which, I have to admit, suited me just fine. It left the way clear to see you, which is what I really wanted.' He continued, 'But I know now why I didn't get an invite. The climbing practice was work.'

Nixie paused and then she said, 'I can tell you more, if you want, but it's not definite.'

'Yes, tell me, Nixie, put me out of my misery.'

'I meant about the climb' She looked at her mother and grinned. 'Mum, Seb's such a flirt. He's an embarrassment.'

Her mother smiled, 'Enjoy it while you can, it doesn't last.'

'You see, Nixie, listen to your mother.' Seb sighed. 'It's tough being rejected.'

'See what I mean? He's shameless.'

Her mother laughed, but although his charm might be working with her mother, Matt continued to watch him. It wasn't obvious, but enough to make him feel uncomfortable. He decided to leave as soon as the conversation lagged. He'd wait for the right moment.

Fifteen minutes later, he glanced out of the window, and noticing what looked like oncoming rain, he used this as an excuse to make his departure. Thanking them profusely, he set off back over the fields. It had been difficult, especially when Nixie brought up Jane, but he'd managed to blag his way through that. However, right now, he wanted to be on his own.

He'd crossed over the first field when he heard Nixie calling his name. He turned and waited for her to catch up. She was out of breath from running. 'Seb, I fancy a walk. Mind if I accompany you?'

'No, of course not, but it does look like rain, so

you might get wet.'

'No worries, I've got a cagoule in my rucksack,' she said. 'I'd also like to see where you're staying.'

'I'm in a tent.'

'Are you really? I'd assumed you'd be in some posh bed and breakfast.'

'Listen, I'm a reformed character and that means staying close to the ground near to the people.'

'Staying close to the ground. Like being in a tent? Are you having me on?'

'I mean it.'

She laughed, and then looking serious, she said, 'Did you mean what you said just now?'

'What was that? You'll have to tell me more, which bit?'

'You know, about following your heart.'

He hadn't realised she'd take him seriously. He stopped and looked at her closely. 'Does it matter to you?'

She looked down at the ground and said in a low voice, 'Actually it does.' He laughed. 'Don't laugh at me, Seb.'

'I'm not laughing at you. It's just... oh, I dunno, you surprise me. I guess I'm not used to women who care about what I think.' The truth was, he liked it. So much so, he took a step closer, pulled her towards him, as if to kiss her, but then seemed to change his mind. He abruptly let her go. 'I'm off,' he said and walked away quickly. Turning to speak to her over his shoulder, he said, 'We're nearly there, but if you want to come any further, it's up to you.'

She ran to catch him up. 'What's wrong with you? You've suddenly become unfriendly.'

'I'm not unfriendly. I'm not sure what to make of you.'

'How do you mean?'

'It doesn't matter. But thanks for the tea, your parents are very sociable.' He continued at the same fast pace.

'I can't keep up with you.'

'Sorry, I'll slow down.'

They walked in silence until Nixie said, 'You seem to know your way around.'

He said curtly, 'I read maps.'

They reached the camp site. Since he'd first arrived, more tents had been pitched, but his tent was still well away from the others. It was dark green, a two-person, double-skinned dome, pitched at the bottom of an incline near a stream dividing two fields. A hedge of hawthorn, willow and crab apple grew along the opposite side.

He said, 'So this is it. Now what?' He crossed his arms and looked at her quizzically.

Nixie walked across to the stream, bent down, and dipping her hand into the water, she looked up at him. 'It's pretty here. Shame Jane cancelled.'

'Well, that's the way she is – unreliable.'

'I'm sorry.'

He looked at her thoughtfully, 'I'm not. It's not a problem… you're here. Ever been inside a tent?'

'Of course I have.'

'But not my tent.'

'That's true, but why would I want to come inside your tent?' She was smiling.

'That's what I'm wondering. I assumed there was a reason why you came back with me, other than making pleasant conversation.' He looked into her eyes. His gaze was neutral. 'It's up to you. You're a big girl now.'

'I take that as an invite, of sorts. It could still rain, so in case it does, I'll stop off here, that is, if you have no objection.' She swung her rucksack off her back, bent down to undo the tent's zip, crawled inside and peeked out at him. 'Come on Seb, it is going to rain.'

He looked down at her. 'You're surprising me.'

'Why would I surprise you? I'm not a child.'

'That's becoming increasingly obvious, Nixie.'

He bent down and followed her into the tent. There was a separate area for storage and just enough space for two people to sleep side by side. With difficulty, he unzipped and opened up his sleeping bag, and spread it out so it was flat and big enough for them both to sit on. It was cramped. They sat side by side in awkward silence.

He said, 'Shall I make tea? I can do it outside.'

'No. No thanks, I've had enough tea. What about a lager? I can see you've got some stashed away in the corner.'

'Sure.'

He leant forward to retrieve a can, pulled the tab up at the top of the can, passed it across to her, and then opened one for himself. She took a sip. 'I'm really grateful to you…you know, when I climb, I'm hardly aware of the risks… I've climbed there before. the rock must have been slippery. Everything was so fast. The last thing I remember was missing my footing, overbalancing, then pitching forward and falling. When I hit the water it was like hitting a wall. I must have passed out. After you'd dragged me to the rock, that's when I realised I could have died.'

He lay back. 'But you didn't die. You need to be more careful.'

'I was careful.'

'Not careful enough, it seems. Accidents can happen. Life's full of unknown dangers.'

'I like climbing. I'm not giving it up.'

'So even though you plummeted like a stone

into the water, you're still up for it?'

She glanced quickly at him, brought the can of beer up to her mouth and, tipping it back, drained its contents and said, 'I've had some training on falling into water, about how to fall, and anyway it wasn't too high, but I think you're talking about something else?'

'Your mother mentioned Big Ben. What's that about?'

She looked at him thoughtfully. 'I'm wondering whether I should tell you.'

'Why shouldn't you?'

'You haven't been around long enough, not really.'

'You know enough, what more is there to know?'

'There's something about you, something unknown. I'm not sure what it is.' She continued gazing at him. 'Are you frightened of women?'

He laughed. 'Why do you say that? Do you think I might be? Nobody has ever said that before, that I'm frightened of women. If anything, the opposite is true.'

'Do you mean you're a game player and put yourself about?'

'Well, I wouldn't say that either. Is that what you believe? Here, you need a top-up.'

'Thanks.' She pulled the tag off and tipped the can to her mouth. 'Tell me more about yourself. The personal stuff.'

'What do you want to know?'

'What it was like working in big financial companies.'

He took the lager out of her hands and pulled her down so she was lying beside him and, leaning on his side, studied her face. 'You know, I find you attractive, very attractive.' He tentatively put his hand under her tee shirt.

She was unfazed. 'Don't distract me, Seb. I want to know about your work.'

He removed his hand, sat up, and thought for a minute before he spoke.

'Okay. Canary Wharf, it's another planet. It's a private estate owned by a consortium of billionaires, protected by security firms with all the latest technological paraphernalia. Smart restaurants, cocktail bars, privately owned sculpture, fountains with all kinds of water features, yet at the time I hardly noticed. I took it for granted, as if it was God given. I had no idea, about what was really going on.'

He leant forward, took another lager. The drink was beginning to get to him. He was silent, wary of saying too much, and incriminating himself. Nixie's eyes were fixed on him. 'You want to know more?'

'Yeah, it sounds like la-la land.'

'It is, it's unreal. The people are unreal. Everything is unreal. A concentration camp of wealth, a system based on the haves and the have-nots. But, since I've left, I've noticed another side. The rough sleepers in doorways, the ever-present violence, the druggies, the poverty, the shit housing – and it pisses me off.' He lay back down. 'I've said enough, now you talk to me.'

'I've got nothing to say.'

'I'm sure you have.'

'I could talk about the economy… the five per cent fall in energy consumption, the eight per cent reduction in the UK's trade deficit, the collapse of the money markets, but that can wait… I have other things on my mind.' She looked sideways at him.

He didn't respond straightaway. Then with studied indifference, he said, 'Like what?' Holding his gaze, she sat up, pulled off her tee shirt, undid and removed her bra. He looked away, to avoid looking at her breasts. Then glancing at her, he said, 'You're drunk.'

'So what, Seb. Any objections?'

'No, it's just that... well...'

'I fancy you. Alright?'

Before he could reply, she leant over and kissed him. Her mouth tasted of beer.

'Did you like that?'

'Maybe.'

'You're playing cool.'

'I take some convincing. Try harder.' He smiled and closed his eyes. She pulled off her clothes, and lay back. He'd been celibate for too long. She was beautiful.

'Seb,' she said.

'What?'

'Now get your kit off or...'

'Or what?'

'I'll take them off.'

He removed his watch, placed it in a safe place, stripped and leaned over her. She was about to speak and got as far as saying, 'So, you know what...' but she never finished.

It was dark and raining when he woke. He lay silently beside her until she sat up suddenly and asked him the time. He glanced at his watch, 'Eleven,' he said, 'We've been asleep hours.'

'Christ. I'll have to go. They'll been wondering where I am.'

'They'll guess, I should think.'

'Maybe.'

'Are you alright?'

'Of course, why do you ask?'

'You were muttering in your sleep.'

'In my sleep? What was I saying?'

'Couldn't make it out, you mentioned Big Ben and something about falling.'

'No, really? If you were Mike, you'd say I wasn't to be trusted.'

He felt a flash of jealousy. 'Mike, the one I've met, in Grassroots?'

'Yeah, him.'

'Well, lesson one: don't sleep with strange men, because you talk in your sleep.'

'Strange men…like you?'

'Yeah, strange like me, so what's your concern about the project?'

'Oh, I don't know. Maybe I am scared I'll fall. It would make sense, wouldn't it? But I'm going ahead. I want to do it.'

'Why? Why risk your life?'

'Don't exaggerate. Why do you think? We'll get max publicity. It's a demo. Against the iniquities of capitalism and all that.'

'You must be mad.'

'You think so?' She pulled on her clothes, rummaged through her rucksack and passed over a crumpled leaflet. 'Here's a draft of a leaflet we're working on. Read it when you have time. I have to go now.'

'Thanks. Like some tea before you go?'

'No time, but thanks.'

'I'll walk you back.' He pulled on his jeans and a tee shirt. 'I'm ready when you are. Tell me a bit more about the project.'

'Well, we've got a really helpful Member of Parliament supporting us. She represents Somerset.'

'What's her name?'

'Freda Arnsberg. She's great. There's not that much more to say, actually. It's still at the planning stage, but I'll tell you more when it's firmed up. Are you really coming back with me?'

'Of course. It's dark and you shouldn't go back on your own.'

Nixie laughed. 'I'm not scared. I'd just like your company.'

'Really?'

'Yes, really, why the surprise?'

'Dunno. Not used to anyone telling me that.'

'Oh, come on, Seb.' She grinned at him.

They walked back in virtual silence and having arrived, he stood awkwardly by the farm gate, as if unsure what to say.

Nixie spoke first. 'You seem to know your way across the fields in the dark.'

'I've got cat's eyes.' He laughed. 'Check them out. Can you see them? Are they green?'

'You're taking the piss out of me… Shall we meet again?'

'Yeah, why not… okay, I'll be off.'

He observed a look of disappointment cross her face, but she said nothing. He'd almost crossed the first field, when on an impulse, he turned to look over his shoulder. She was standing watching him. He walked back quickly, then drawing her close, he kissed her. It was long and slow. 'I like you,' he said, 'and I mean that.' Then he left to walk back.

It had all gone well, he thought, in every way. But it wasn't the information about the planned demo that was uppermost in his mind, it was Nixie. Her commitment, her indifference to money, her ideals, her drive to change the system, intrigued him. She was different from any other woman he'd slept with and above all, she excited him. But despite trying to push these feelings away, it hadn't worked. He hardly slept that night.

— 9 —

He was to meet Gimp in a safe house in the London Borough of Hackney. The houses were large, terraced and converted into flats or bedsitters and, it would be safe to assume, no one had the time or the inclination to notice who their neighbours were, or what they might be up to. The locality was ethnically mixed, with a constantly shifting residential population, but still not gentrified, even though close to the City, and sharing a border with its comparatively affluent neighbour, the London Borough of Islington. Seb had handed over his wire a week earlier. He'd felt awkward, aware of its content and avoided Gimp's eyes as he'd handed it over. 'It's all there...everything.'

It was his second visit since the demo. Gimp spoke straightaway. 'Well, well, well. Congratulations. So you made it. You laid her. So... feeling better.' He laughed.

'I'm glad you find it amusing.' It was the type of male banter familiar to Seb. 'So, what did I think? I get paid for this and it can't be bad.'

'A good fuck then?'

That grated. 'I wouldn't put it like that.'

'How would you put it?'

'She's...well, she's okay. Good looking, lovely actually, affectionate, and conveniently talks in her sleep. '

Gimp paused. 'So job done. A kind of quid pro quo situation. That's one reason we employed you. You like women and they like you.'

'Maybe.'

'What's that mean? "Maybe". You're useful. And she's useful.'

Seb shrugged.

Gimp eyeballed him. 'But... I'm suspicious.'

'What about?'

'I'll tell you what about. I've been here before with someone else, so I'm looking at you and I'm thinking you're new to this, but you're not asking yourself what's going on. And that rings alarm bells. She seduced you. That's what it sounds like and then she talks. Why? There's some sort of game going on. I'm getting bad vibes. Not sure why but... I'm thinking you've fallen for her, and if that's true, you've just broken rule number one. '

'Which is?'

'Don't fall for the enemy. Sex is okay. Love and affection isn't. Remember? It's work.'

Seb paused, then he said, 'Look, I slept with her to get her to talk and she did. I got loads of info. So I succeeded. End of.'

'Maybe you did, but I think there's more going on...and whatever that is, you're not telling me. I may look stupid...'

'I've told you, she serves a purpose. She's not my type. I'm neutral about her.'

Gimp shook his head 'Sorry, mate, but I'm not buying it. From what I heard, I wouldn't say either of you were neutral, as you put it, but if that's what you want to believe, so be it. But watch it.' He stared at Seb.

'Okay. I'll think about it, but look at this. Nixie gave it me to read.'

'When?'

'Just as we parted.'

Seb passed over a draft leaflet. Headed with

'The Truth behind the Lies', it began with 'What caused the Economic Collapse?' followed by a series of questions, ending with 'What You Can Do.' The answer given was simple and straightforward; 'Stop Buying Crap.'

Gimp rapidly skimmed the leaflet and looked up. 'So what did you say?'

'Nothing at the time. It was late so I read it later, and when I'd had time to think about it, I tried arguing with her. I said business collapse means rising unemployment and escalating poverty, but I got nowhere. She said there was enough wealth in this country for fair redistribution. She argued growth had to be curbed and the value system changed. The rich should be forced to pay their taxes and the government should stop spending on projects like Langhithe Marshes Nuclear Power Station, and concentrate on renewable sources of energy.'

'Well, a word of caution. You're a bit too word perfect. Know what I mean? As if you've done your homework? Don't forget, you'll still be under scrutiny... it's likely you're still not trusted, and maybe never will be... Think about it... So what's with the this protest? What's the deal?'

'Three of them plan to climb Big Ben, and unfurl a banner at the top.'

'Saying what?'

'The best things in life are free.'

'Fucking hell. What a nerve. Is Nixie one of them?'

'Yep, and her mates. That's why they were in Pembrokeshire. Climbing practice, she'd said.'

'I doubt they'll get through security.'

'It's all planned. She's got a contact inside the Commons. An MP for Somerset, by the name of Freda Arnsberg. She's introducing the Private Member's Bill opposing advertisements directed at children, and she's a member of a group opposed to Langhithe Marshes Power Plant.'

'They haven't a snowball's chance in hell of getting that through.'

'They know that. That's not the point. What they want is publicity.'

'I've heard of this woman, but I didn't know she's involved with Grassroots.'

'I've looked her up. She's married to a Brit, was brought up in Germany and her parents were involved in the seventies with the Green Movement.'

'Mmm...I'll tip off the Met. Ultimately it's harmless, but we need to protect your identity. If they go in heavy handed, Nixie could get suspicious. You've just screwed her, she tells you about a publicity stunt, and it's busted.' He was silent for a while and then staring at Seb, he said, 'Like I say, this could be a trap. It doesn't need an Einstein to put two and two together.'

'And make five. I've said... that's not how it was.'

'Don't be so bleeding naive. I told you about the women. They're used as decoys. What makes you think you're special? You think she fell in love with you? Grow up.'

'Look, she came onto me. Big time.'

'That's my point. Of course she did, you're the business. You've got a bit of je ne sais quoi, or putting it another way, you know how to play the field when it comes to women. You want to screw her, but she takes the initiative. You fall for it. She's got the hots for you but my guess is she's playing you at your own game.'

Seb was silent. His mind went back to the

evening with Nixie. Maybe Gimp was right, she was entrapping him and it was all a put on. His mind veered away from the implications. He heard Gimp say, 'Are you listening?'

'Yeah, yeah, carry on.'

'Okay. Big Ben, we tip off security, but advise a light-handed approach. Right?'

'And I do what?'

'Same as you're doing now, keep your eyes and ears open and report back.'

'Fine, I'll keep you posted.'

Gimp's comments had got to him. Whether true or not, again he'd sown the seeds of suspicion in Seb's mind and that made him uneasy. Was Nixie really playing a game? Could he trust her? He hadn't made out with anyone like her before. She was a one-off, a woman with her own mind, and she knew what she wanted. He would have liked to wine and dine her. He'd have liked to give her a good time in the champagne bars around Canary Wharf the way he used to with the women he'd eventually taken to bed, even though it was probable it wouldn't have impressed her.

The visit to Pembrokeshire, meeting Nixie's father, with his history of activism, and his views on the environment and inequality had raised his curiosity. And her mother hadn't been what he'd expected. She seemed normal, but she couldn't have been – not when she snatched him. It was the action of somebody deranged, even though, it had been said, she cared for him when she'd been alone on the island.

As for his own research, the newspapers had raised even more questions. Questions which, if he asked his parents for more info, they'd never answer. They never had opened up to him, and it would be a waste of time to try again.Maybe it was time to implement his plan; go home and do a search. He'd start with his father's office; go through the boxes and cases dumped in the attic. He'd look for newspaper clippings, hidden away or forgotten. He'd do it. Having made that decision, he felt more focused. He had a plan, a purpose in life. It ran parallel to his undercover work, but it felt strangely similar.

Two days later, he phoned his parents. He told them he was back from the States for a week and that he'd make a flying visit over the weekend. Apparently they were due to leave Saturday for a cruise around Iceland and the Norwegian fjords. That's fine, he said, there's still time for a visit, and I'd like to see you. The timing couldn't have been better. After they'd left, he'd be alone in the house.

He told Grassroots he was visiting an elderly relative. Then he rang Islington Car Hire and arranged to pick up an Audi; his car was something he'd missed. He shaved off his beard, had his hair cut and bought some new clothes from American Apparel in Hoxton. He retrieved the TAG Heuer watch given to him by his parents for his eighteenth birthday. It had been expensive and one of his favourite possessions, but after the sessions with Bill, he'd realised he couldn't wear it and placed it in a drawer. Now he could.

He went over his cover story. He had to be word perfect, fluent, able to reel off where he lived, what his work was – it was all secret, an alliance between the Met and the FBI concerning serious financial fraud – but regretfully, he could say no more. And yes, he was enjoying it, he was proud of his work, but it meant he had to disappear frequently.He planned to wait for the Friday before he left for Lavenham.

Freda Arnsberg in Parliament was to ask a series of awkward questions under the time allocated to a Private Member's Bill, and while this was going on, Nixie and two others would begin climbing Big Ben. He sat watching the television, flicking impatiently between the twenty-four-hour news channel and Parliament Today, waiting for a news report. Nothing happened. The silence puzzled him. Was there a news blackout?

He continued waiting but by midday, there was still nothing. He wondered if there had been an embargo on news reporting. Had he got the time and day wrong? Two hours later, he came to the conclusion it had to have been pulled. But why and by whom?

Perhaps Gimp was right, Nixie did suspect him. She didn't trust him and Grassroots' operations group had recommended some other time, a date unknown to him. Or the alternative, that the Met had flooded the place with cops and the protesters had been frightened off. Whatever it was, he wanted to know. It was playing on his mind.

He rang Nixie. 'What's happened to the protest?'

'Pulled.'

'Why?'

There was a long silence. 'Not sure.'

'A tip off?'

'Maybe.'

'What's wrong?'

'Nothing, why do you ask?'

'You're not saying much.'

'Nothing much to say.'

She was blocking him, that's how it felt. 'When shall we meet up? .I'm missing you.' It was a try-on, a test, to see how she'd respond.

'It's difficult right now. I'm really busy. My

mum's coming up soon. It's her birthday. But after that, I'll have more free time.'

'Okay, let me know.'

It felt like a brush off, and he was disappointed. But it wasn't his style to wait around for women; anger rapidly took over from the disappointment. He picked up his bag, slammed the flat door behind him, caught a cab to Islington, picked up the Audi, and drove out at speed out of London. He put his foot down for Lavenham.

— 10 —

'Darling, it's been so long.' He avoided his mother's gaze. 'Sorry, couldn't get here earlier. How's it going?'She didn't answer but taking his overnight bag out of his hand, smiled. He continued, 'Well, here I am, your long lost boy.' As soon as the words were out of his mouth, he wished he hadn't said that. Why he'd said it, he had no idea. He glanced at her. The comment seemed to have stopped her in her tracks.

Her eyes shifted nervously towards him, but then she looked away. 'Shall I take your bag up?'

'No, I'll do it. Thanks.'

He took the bag from her, walked upstairs to his room, unpacked, and stood staring out of the window. His father was talking to the gardener. He was animated, gesturing towards a triangular bed of newly planted roses, probably giving him instructions of some sort. They moved on to the next bed. His father continued gesturing, with wide expansive hand and arm movements.

He returned downstairs, walked into the kitchen and sat down. He felt edgy, preoccupied with what might lie ahead and what he might find; even a little distant from his surroundings and his mother. She gave him a coffee, and began to talk. Perhaps she was nervous and had picked up something from his mood. She asked nothing about his life, but presented him with the minutiae of her daily life: who she'd seen, who they'd had dinner with, and the prospective cruise round Norway. He switched off, letting the avalanche of words wash over him, the trivia of everyday life that preoccupied her but which even at the best of times, bored him rigid. After a decent interval he apologised and taking his coffee went to the garden room.

Returning home had reminded him of his past involvement with Carole. He began to think about her, how the last time he'd seen her, they'd had sex. He wondered whether she'd heard about his visit and whether she knew his parents were away and whether she planned to drop in on him. If so, it wouldn't stop there. For certain, she'd want more than a conversation from him. That was the usual routine and up to now he'd complied.

But this time, he wanted it to be different. He wasn't prepared to play that game any longer. His eyes narrowed as he thought of her. All she'd ever wanted from him was a quick fuck. That was then. But now? He'd had enough. In the past, he'd tried to finish with her, but each time she'd inveigled her way back. This time he wasn't going to give in. She treated him as her possession, as her plaything, as if he was her gigolo. It had worked once because he was young and inexperienced and he'd found sex exciting. But those times were past. He realised, he disliked her. He felt used by her. He wanted more than sex. He wanted a relationship with someone – someone like Nixie.

His mind returned to Pembrokeshire and when he'd slept with Nixie. She'd been slightly tipsy and as she'd lain by him, they'd listened to the sounds of the evening; the wind, the birdsong, the rain, the sound of the water in the stream close by as it tumbled over the rocks. He'd stroked her warm skin and when he kissed her, her mouth tasted of beer. She'd looked him straight in the eye and smiled.

‘Seb.’ He looked up, dragged himself back to the present. His father was standing in the doorway, looking pleased with himself. The markets must be doing well. He stood up, walked towards his father and shook his hand. ‘Dad, good to see you. You’re looking better.’

‘Thanks, son, things are picking up, and that always cheers me, as you know. How’s the job going?’

‘Well. It’s going well.’

‘Like it?’

‘Yeah, a challenge, but with plenty of opportunities.’

‘Well, good, tell me more later. I thought we’d go out for supper tonight. The Great House Hotel. Heard of it? There’s a new chef. Supposed to be superb. Great reviews.’

His mother came and stood beaming by his side. Evidently, they were pleased by his visit, but as he listened to their conversation, it struck him how bizarre it all was, that an event so traumatic, as being snatched from his crib, so soon after his birth, was never alluded to. It was as if it had never happened. It was crazy.

But for the sake of appearances, this time, he’d make an effort to be pleasant. He’d ignore his mother’s empty tittle-tattle and his father’s malicious asides, and focus on the purpose of his visit. Until they left for Norway, he’d play the role of the dutiful son and try his best to make sure the evening would be enjoyable.

It had gone well. Even his father had been amusing with his malicious yet witty tales of working in the City. The thing is, he’d said, no one can tell the difference between truth and lies but it doesn’t matter, because everyone is the same. They all share the same purpose, to make money by manipulating the markets, and hang the consequences. It's just one big game, he'd said, and the rules change every day. Seb made no comment, but it crossed his mind how different his father's values were compared with those in Grassroots, but he kept his mouth shut, and listened and observed.

They left early for Norway the next day and after waving them off, he made himself a coffee. He could breathe now. He took his coffee to the garden room, put on his headphones and leant back in a sun lounger, intending to relax for a while before beginning his search. He was conscious he was putting off the moment before he began. He wasn't looking forward to it. Maybe he'd find nothing, or alternatively, that the information he did find, would disturb him. He couldn't forget that moment when he'd realised that Nixie was the daughter of the woman who'd snatched him. It had made him feel strange and he didn't want a repeat of that.

Half an hour later, as he was about to drift off to sleep he heard a loud tapping on the window. He glanced up. Carole was standing outside in the garden. He wasn't pleased. He stood up and reluctantly let her in. 'I was just going out,' he said.

She was smiling broadly and dressed in her riding gear. She ignored what he said. 'I rang the front door but you couldn't have heard. Your mother told me you'd be here for the weekend. Can I come in, have a quick coffee.'

'I'm going out soon.'

'Fine, just wanted to see how you were.'

'I'm well, thanks. I haven't much time.'

She looked uncomfortable. 'You seem preoccupied,' she said.

'Yes, I am. I was listening to my music.'

'Well, I didn't want to interrupt you.'

'You have already.'

He drummed his fingers on the side table, and stared out of the window.

'You've got a new car. The number plate's different.'

'What about it?'

'Just commenting...'

'Look, I've got things to do. Is there anything in particular you've come to see me about?'

'Just wondered...' She glanced at him from under her eyelashes and looked coyly at the floor.

Her facial expression irritated him. A wave of dislike passed through him. For the first time ever, he thought she looked old. She'd been round the block too often to carry off the coquette look.

'Wondered what? If it's what I think it is, the answer's no. Look, I've been thinking.' The words he used were spontaneous and unplanned. 'Time's up for you and me, Carole.' She appeared not to hear and continued smiling. He repeated, 'I said it's over.'

Still no response. 'Did you hear me?'

She heard him that time. She looked taken aback. She pursed her lips in annoyance, turned away for a moment then, looking him straight in the eye, she said, 'You're ditching me? Just like that. After all this time? You're brutal.'

'I have to be, otherwise you don't get it.'

'We've known each other for so long.'

'Exactly right. So long is too long.'

She stood glaring at him. He stood his ground, watching her closely, waiting for her next move. She came towards him, pressed her body against his and draped her arms round his neck, holding her face up as if she was about to kiss him. He took a step back and pushed her away. 'Don't... do... that. I've told you. It's over.'

'But what about me?'

He let out an exasperated laugh, 'What about you? You'll find someone else. There's always someone else.'

'Are you jealous?'

'Me? Jealous? Of you, and your other lovers? Give me a break. '

'You've met another woman.'

'Carole, I'm busy. I have a schedule to keep, and satisfying your sexual needs isn't on it. Try your husband for a change.'

'You've fallen for someone younger.'

'And prettier.'

It was provocative and he knew it. She brought up her hand to strike him across the face but he caught hold of it, twisted it and held it briefly, before letting it go. He looked at her, his eyes cold. 'I don't hit women and I won't say this again. Piss off.'

They stood eye balling each other. She was furious, breathing fast, her face red, her eyes hard, her mouth drawn in a tight line. She turned and stalked across the room. When she reached the door, she paused, and said in a low voice, 'Fuck you. You're a bastard. Like your father. Always have been and always will be.'

She left, leaving the door wide open behind her. He made no reply. He stood impassively, his arms folded, waiting for her to drive off. Until she'd gone, he couldn't relax. For five minutes there was silence, she must have been sitting in her car, thinking what her next move could be, but then he heard her car engine revving up, and she accelerated off.

He walked over to the door, pulled it shut, locked it and went into the sitting room to get himself a drink. He was about to pour himself a whisky when his mobile went off. He glanced at it. Predictably, it was Carole, but he didn't answer.

He'd changed. Perhaps it was since he'd become involved with Nixie, or perhaps he'd grown up and wanted more than just sex. He put down the whisky he'd been about to drink, and began to pace back and forth, stopped, thrust a piece of chewing gum into his mouth and stood slowly chewing. His mind returned to the past and how Carole used to turn him on. Not anymore. If anything, her assumption that he was always ready to attend to her sexual needs, whenever or wherever, he saw now as demeaning, if not exploitative. He deleted her number, switched off his mobile, and returned to listening to his music.

He waited until almost lunchtime before starting his investigation. He wanted to be absolutely sure his parents had gone and weren't about to return because they'd forgotten something. Standing in the doorway of his father's office, he glanced around. His father had always been tidy, perhaps obsessively so. His shelves, lined with files, were all arranged alphabetically, each one pertaining to a different investment. He pulled on a pair of latex gloves to avoid leaving fingerprints and systematically began working through the files.

His father's computer would be password protected but he knew how to bypass that and hack into the system — if he wanted. That was one of the many useful bits of information he'd gleaned from his computer security course, but since he was looking for a file at least twenty years old, and therefore much earlier than this computer, there'd be no point. The files weren't in date order, but they were what they said they were; accounts and information about various types of business – nothing personal. He turned his attention to his father's desk, pulled at the first drawer. All four drawers to the desk were locked. But that was no problem, unpicking desk locks was usually easy.

He pulled out his collection of tools. It included a strong bent paper clip which he pushed into the lock and within a minute the drawers slid open. Letters, memos and accounts had been placed in various folders, all of them relating to companies he'd heard of, when he'd worked in finance. He flicked through them, until he came to one that caught his attention.

Marked 'Confidential' it contained copies of recent emails and letters exchanged between his father and a certain John Fortescue. He'd heard of John Fortescue through Grassroots. He was a well-known and respected Tory Member of Parliament for Faring, but he also chaired the Energy and Climate Change Committee. Seb pulled up a chair, sat down, and began reading.

His father and Fortescue were on first name terms. It was also obvious they knew each other well, very well. The emails indicated that some deal was underway, but whatever that was, the contents indicated that it was to be a closely guarded secret. One letter in particular stood out. It was undated and from Fortescue to his father. Seb read it with increasing interest.

> My dear Rupert,
>
> Re Langhithe: Transportation Costs.
>
> I very much appreciate your input. As you say, it is important we use known and reliable suppliers for the conveyance of goods and materials. That you have access to several such companies, is fortunate, but you will be aware that any contract will be subject to open tender. Given this, it is most important that due process is seen to be followed; that is, to all intents and purposes.

I note you recommend one company in particular and that a prominent member on the board of this company is also a Member of Parliament. As you point out, he is in a position to provide any information we might require as to costs.

Inevitably there will be a difference between the actual and projected costs, this difference giving, to those of us with a leaning towards the entrepreneurial, opportunities for maximising profit – at the Government's expense.

In order to achieve the desired outcome, we will, of course, require some recompense. Primarily this will be financial, but you may also be in a position to assist in less conventional ways. I am referring to the procurement of what euphemistically may be called, 'ladies of pleasure'. However, referring to the said MP, who for the moment shall be nameless, he has particular interests above and beyond the usual which, for obvious reasons, I think it preferable to meet face to face to discuss these matters more fully.

Also it is of the utmost importance these developments remain strictly confidential, so it would be wise to destroy this letter once you have read it. I look forward to your response.

Sincerely,

John

Seb placed the letter aside. This was dynamite. He was shocked, but not too shocked. He knew that mixing politics with business was often questionable and what he'd just read was no exception. Tip offs and 'sweeteners' were common in the business world, frequently to the detriment of the consumer. The emails and letters he'd just read made clear a game plan – a case of deal breaking, with his father as master of ceremonies negotiating between an unidentified MP and Fortescue. A triangular trail of tip offs relating to the construction of Langhithe Nuclear Energy Plant.

Government backing of buying and selling of goods and services provided the potential; the covert if not overt opportunities for those driven by greed. This particular development had however an added bonus; that of 'sweeteners' all round. For Fortescue, the aphrodisiac of power and influence, for his father, a possible peerage, for them both advance information on government contracts and, for the source of information, the unidentified MP, the hint of an illicit 'sweetener'. It was 'Cash for Access' with all the pigs' snouts well and truly in the financial trough. The stink of corruption had spread so far and so wide, he could smell it from where he stood.

He laid the folder out on the desk and stared across the room. He had to decide what, if anything, he should do with this information. He had to use it in some way. It was too good to ignore. He walked back and forth across the room working through the possible options. He was employed to infiltrate the anti-capitalist movements, but, ironically this trio of thieves were anything but that. Ostensibly, they were part of it. They supported the system but they used and abused it, exploiting every loophole for their own advantage. They were both inside and outside the system.

He knew the arguments. Operating in the grey area between legitimate and illegitimate business activity, their defence would be they were merely identifying and making use of the legal and organisational weaknesses of the system. What they wouldn't say, nor would many others, was that they were exploiting individual gullibility and stupidity, a skill which would earn them the reputation of being clever. The reality was they had no moral compass, no sense of social justice and like the cowboys of the old Wild West were travelling along the unregulated frontiers. In this instance those of the money markets. So the truth was, in the last analysis, they were oiling the wheels of capitalism, so why should he or anyone bother? Was he surprised? Not really. He also had little concern for the failings of the system and like his father, he took an amoral approach, because, albeit reluctantly, he recognised so far, he'd benefited from the system.

But something else drove him. He burned with an impotent anger, a visceral resentment which cut through his guts. It had developed in childhood, and was borne of a thousand petty asides and putdowns, leaving him stranded with feelings of powerlessness and rage. He'd always dreamt of revenge. Now here was the opportunity, handed to him on a plate, and he could use it, if he so desired.

His decision didn't take long. He smiled; it was payback time for his father's years of denigration towards himself and his mother as he'd grown up. He picked out the letter from Fortescue, walked across to his father's photocopier conveniently kept in the corner of his office, and made three copies. He took out three A4 brown envelopes, placed a copy of the letter inside each of them, together with his father's compliment slip. He addressed one to the Business Editor of the Guardian, one to the Finance and Business Editor of the Telegraph, and the remaining one to the Business Editor of the BBC. One or all three would pick this up. As an exposé implicating the City, Parliament, and the murky sex lives of certain Members of Parliament, it was an opportunity too good to miss and, with any luck, it would create enough noise to keep the media busy for days. He smiled again. A useful morning's work; he'd post them in Central London on his way back.

It was time to eat. He returned to the kitchen, opened the fridge and pulled out the salmon quiche with the Waldorf salad his mother had left for him. He removed a bottle of white wine from a stash left in the chiller, hardly looking at the label, except to notice, as he poured himself a large glass, it was a Sauvignon Blanc. He sat down. He was pleased, on a high. He leant back on the chair and reviewed his actions, tilting the chair so it balanced on its back two legs.

Although he'd interfered with the locking mechanism of his father's desk, he was relying on his father's lack of mechanical skill not to see it had been broken into. He'd assume there was a malfunction, but even if he was suspicious, he could hardly contact the police or challenge his own son. For one thing, he'd have to say it had been locked, and any complaint would be followed by a police investigation, and this would bring down the whole pack of cards.

Perhaps he should leave a note on his father's computer saying 'Invest in better locks next time', but despite finding this thought amusing, he decided against it. For one thing, it would warn his father somebody was on his case. No, he'd make do with anticipating the uproar once the press got hold of the emails. He wished there was some other person he could tell but, other than Nixie, there was nobody and he'd be a fool to tell her. He finished his lunch and the last of the wine, but hit by waves of exhaustion he dragged himself to his bedroom, and fell into a deep asleep. An hour later disturbed by bad dreams of his father's anger, he woke in a state of mild panic. He still had work to do.

He climbed the stairs to the top of the house, entered the attic and glanced around. It had been years since he'd last been there but as a child he remembered it had always smelt musty and strange. And it still did. There was something about its atmosphere, a kind of stillness, an unsettling sense of something unknown, which disturbed him. An anxiety so strong took him over, to the point he had to take a step back to gather his thoughts, and force himself to be logical and to think rationally.

Sunlight streamed through the gabled windows lighting up the dust on the piles of boxes and old trunks stacked against the wall. He walked across. He ignored the ones with his father's and grandfather's initials printed on them. He was looking for a comparatively new trunk, one used when he'd been sent away. A large trunk made from maroon leather had been pushed against a wall. It was stamped with Sebastian Melbury, the Christian name he'd discarded when he'd first been sent to prep school. He roughly pulled open the brass clasp holding down the lid.

Inside were piles of documents; reports and letters from school, programmes of plays, information about sports days, but bizarrely, lying amongst them was a giraffe wrapped in a plastic bag. He stared at it. This must be the toy that Rose had spoken of in her interview with the journalist. His initial reaction was mild curiosity. He removed the giraffe from the bag and turned it around in his hand. Some of the fur had worn away on the horns. He placed it on the floor, and continued looking through the trunk, unsure of what he might find or what he was looking for. Glancing quickly through the piles of random documents, he noticed something that stood out from the official-looking documents. A hand-written note, written on ordinary paper. It was folded over and on the outside in large handwriting were the words 'To whoever finds Baby Owain'.

He held it in his hands and stared into space. His mind returned to the journalist's account that he had seen at the Newspaper Archives. Rose told her that Flori had called the baby Owain. She'd also said the baby's favourite toy was a giraffe, and that when she'd tried to escape from the police, she'd left a note with him. This had to be that note. It could only have been written by her.

He slowly opened it. It was on lined paper as if torn out of an exercise book. Steeling himself, he began reading. He was barely able to take it in, and had to read it three times before the words made any sense. It had been written by Flori in her actual handwriting – and it made clear what was going on.

Flori must have written this when she was being hunted down. She was alone on Jura, knew the police were after her and in an attempt to save herself, she abandoned him. But she was filled with guilt and remorse. The note was detailed; how he loved being taken out, the food he liked, and how he clung to his toy giraffe, his only possession. She wanted it saved for him. She referred to the poems she read to him, and one in particular, by Pablo Neruda. This must be the poem Rose had mentioned, the one she couldn't remember the name of, when she'd been talking to the journalist. It was here.

He tried to read it, but he couldn't get past the first line. The words were too much. It felt as if a knife was being twisted in his gut.

'I love you as certain dark things are to be loved, in secret, between the shadow and the soul', followed by and 'I'm sorry for all the trouble I've caused everybody, and I especially want Rose to know that.' It finished with, 'With all my love to Owain.'

It was like a knife twisting in his guts. He felt dizzy, as if he was about to pass out. He sat down. The words and the phrases she'd chosen spinning round and round inside his head. Everything was true. It had happened. It was real. Real, but crazy. So crazy he couldn't get his head round it. It was mad, she must have been mad. Questions, questions, questions, crowded in on him, until he felt like screaming. How did she get away with it for so long? How could she have taken him from his cot while his parents lay asleep in the next room? Had they had so much to drink? Were they so flat out, they were oblivious to what was going on?

Now he understood why his mother had refused to talk about it. It must have torn her apart. She'd been forced to endure two months of not knowing where he might be or whether he was dead or alive. It must have been unbearable. But how had he been snatched from under their noses? Were they so neglectful and so wrapped up in their own world, they'd been deaf to his cries? No wonder they were secretive about what had happened.

And what of Flori? How could that be understood? A woman who looked so normal and was now a mother herself. What had been going on for her? How could she snatch someone's baby in the first months of his life? When he was only two months old, and had no speech, no understanding, and was totally dependent on others. He'd been treated like a parcel, a thing, a pet, as if he were her plaything. She'd said she loved him, but how could she? He hadn't been hers to love.

He'd hoped that finding out more about how he'd been snatched would settle him but, instead, it had raised even more questions. Someone other than Rose, must have helped her. She would have had to leave London with him, and travel hundreds of miles before she reached Jura. It couldn't have been Rose, because her involvement had been thoroughly investigated.

That left only one person. Matt. Had it ever crossed the minds of the police to put the thumbscrews on him, to find out what he was up to at the time? He had a history of environment activism and law breaking, he'd virtually admitted that, and given he'd known Flori for years, it would make him a strong candidate for assisting her. Yet, somehow, he'd got away with it. Why had Matt had never been implicated and as far as he knew, never been investigated. There was only one conclusion possible. Matt must have been of some use to the police. Matt had been a police informer.

Conflicting emotions surged through him. The principal one, hate, but then rage. He felt sickened. The sour taste of bile filled his mouth. He began to heave. He sprinted downstairs to the bathroom and with his head over the toilet bowl, retched until he vomited. He stood up, but the heaving began again. His body convulsing, he leant over, spraying the remains of his lunch around the inside of the toilet. He felt as if he was inhabited by a malign force. He could trust nobody or anything. Everything was a potential lie. He walked over to the basin, threw water on his face, wiped clean his mouth and, forced himself to return to the attic.

He stared out of the window onto the garden, trying to clear his mind of the conflicting feelings and thoughts coursing through his head. Gradually a sense of normality returned. He turned away, was about to leave the attic, when he caught sight of the giraffe, lying on the floor where he'd left it.

A second wave of monumental anger passed through him. He grabbed hold of it and flung it across the room with such force, it hit the wall. It lay slumped against the skirting board. He picked up the note, the one Flori had left with him all those years ago, and was about to tear it up, when an idea came to him. He'd keep them both, the note and the giraffe. He'd find some way to use them and take revenge. He'd made a start with his father.

It was now time to turn his attention to Flori and Matt. They were implicated and he would punish them. He'd wipe that self-satisfied smile off their faces. He wasn't sure how, but he'd find a way. It was a matter of time until an opportunity would present itself, and he'd be ready.

— 11 —

The day was humid, the sky downcast, the sea as flat and grey as the sky. He parked his car in the same place as before, and walked across the shingle towards the Shell. He'd slept badly and after breakfast, his mind in turmoil, he'd drifted around the garden. His thoughts returned to when he'd first met Imogen on the beach at Aldeburgh. Although it was unlikely she'd be there now, walking by the sea and coming across the Shell had calmed him before. He remembered her innocence, her seriousness and how she'd distracted him from his own problems.

He'd had to get out of the oppressive atmosphere of the house. Little by little he was unravelling his early history. The missing pieces of his life; the experiences denied or never articulated – it was these that had made him into a persona non grata. He didn't belong. He was different, an outsider to conventional society.

He hadn't been able to stop thinking about the note in the attic. Even its heading, 'Whoever Finds Baby Owain' caused waves of frustrated anger to wash over him. He felt bitter, obsessively and keenly aware; he'd been made a victim by the neglect of his parents and the craziness of Flori. He gazed out over the sea. Picking up a flat stone he walked to the water's edge and skimming the stone, watched it bounce over the still surface until it sank. He'd played this game as a boy and it had distracted him then, as it did now. Over and over, he repeated this action, trying to increase the length of time the stone bounced before it disappeared under water.

He looked along the beach towards Thorpeness. In the distance a small boat with an outboard motor was heading towards the shore. A young girl who reminded him of Imogen was running towards it, waving. He stopped to watch. The man at the controls brought the boat into the shallow water, jumped out, and began pulling the boat up onto the foreshore. The girl reached the boat. It was Imogen. When he'd first met her she'd been very much the child. Her hair had been tied back. Now it was loose.

She wore a startling, white floppy shirt and a tight short skirt which showed off her brown legs. She'd grown taller, had filled out. She had the look of a young adolescent about to enter womanhood. He paused, curious to see what was happening. She took off her sandals and waded into the water to help the man pull the boat up onto the beach. She was laughing, talking, playfully splashing him and clearly pleased to see him. He looked middle aged, Who could he be? Maybe an uncle?

But the scene struck him as odd. Why would a middle-aged man, wearing old jeans rolled up to his knees, a scruffy, blue shirt with short sleeves, choose an isolated area of the beach to bring his boat ashore to meet a child? Apart from himself there was no one around. He hung back and watched as the man bent down and put on well-worn boat shoes. Imogen seemed to be chatting to him nonstop, so much so that neither of them looked back or noticed him. Something wasn't right.

They began walking away in the opposite direction. After a moment's hesitation, he decided to follow them. Keeping a good distance away but close to the sand dunes, he planned to disappear into the long Marram grass if they looked back.

They came to a stop. Imogen was circling round the man laughing, than she ran off along the beach. It was a 'catch-up' game. The man ran after her until he caught up and grabbing her round her waist, threw her on the sand. It looked as if he was tickling her but it was a mock game; the real aim being, Seb realised, was for the man to get his hands on Imogen's body.

He pulled her back on her feet and they walked together to where the shingle stopped and huge tufts of Marram grass grew. They disappeared. The wind had created perfect hiding places in the sand, the tall Marram grass acting as a shelter from the wind and from prying eyes.

His suspicions about the man's intentions were growing by the minute. The sand between the shingle and the dunes forced him to walk slowly, but it also enabled him to be silent. He walked for several minutes until he heard voices. A man's low voice, the other Imogen's. He stopped. He could hear her but not see her. She was talking. She sounded anxious, almost as if she was pleading.

'You're hurting me. Don't do that.'

He couldn't hear the man's reply but he could hear the tone. It was low and reassuring. It was enough. He'd heard enough. He moved towards them. They lay in one of the sand hollows. He stood for a split second, looking down at them. Imogen was on her back, her shirt open, her breasts exposed. The man was partially lying on her, his hand up her skirt. She looked past the man and saw Seb.

He was close, only a few feet away. Her eyes widened. He didn't think. He acted. He moved towards the man. He took hold of the back of his shirt. He pulled him violently off her and onto his feet. The man was shorter but stockier than him.

Seb twisted him round so they were face to face. He noticed his eyes; faded, blue, watery. The man looked astonished, opened his mouth to speak. Seb hit him hard. The blow was hard, brutal, and in his face. He reeled away and fell to the ground.

Seb glanced at Imogen. She was struggling to sit up. Putting out his hand, he roughly pulled her up. Glaring at her, he shouted, 'Do yourself up.' She was frightened, her eyes fixed on Seb, her hands trembled as she did up her shirt buttons.

The man staggered to his feet, and lurched towards Seb as if to attack him. Seb didn't wait. He pulled his fist back and hit him again. The man fell to the floor. Seb kicked him twice, violently, as he lay on the sand. He bellowed, 'You fucking wood louse,' and brought his fist up ready to hit him again. The man curled into a ball, and lay still, covering his head with his hands. Seb watched, ready with his fists, if he attempted to get up and attack him.

Through his rage, he heard Imogen screaming, 'Stop it, stop it.' She was crying.

Her distress brought him to his senses. He took hold of her and, pulling her away, he shouted at the man, 'Keep your fucking hands off her, you fucking pervert.'

Turning to Imogen, he said, 'Let's go. I'm taking you home.' He pushed her ahead of him, 'Go on, run.'

He looked back over his shoulder. The man was lying on his side, his legs drawn up as if in extreme pain, his face covered in blood.

Imogen ran ahead, half running, half walking. He caught up with her and breathing hard, took hold of her shoulder to stop her. She continued crying, wiping her runny nose with her shirt. He gave her a paper handkerchief and waited for her to calm down.

Her face full of resentment, she said, 'Why did you do that? Why did you hit him?'

'Didn't I tell you? When I saw you before? I said don't go with strange men.'

'He's a friend.'

'Are you mad? A friend. How can he be?'

'He gives me presents.'

'Oh, does he? What kind of presents?'

'Clothes. He gave me these, what I'm wearing, and he takes me in his boat.'

'Very nice, and what does he want you to do? What do you do in exchange?'

'Nothing. I do nothing.'

'You're lying, Imogen. Tell me the truth.'

She looked down and away to avoid his gaze.

'I'm waiting. Tell me.'

'He wants...'

'Yes.'

'I can't say.'

'Well let me say it for you, because I saw what he was doing and I heard you. He was hurting you. He was interfering with your body, wasn't he, and do you know what comes next?' She didn't answer, but shifted her gaze away from his eyes. 'I think you do, Imogen. I told you to look after yourself and you're not. He's not your friend and he doesn't care about you. He's dirty and old and a pervert, which means he wants sex with very young girls, the younger the better.'

'Don't you know who he is?'

'I have no idea who he is and furthermore, I don't give a shit who he is, except he's a creepy old man.'

'He's an MP and his name is Makepeace.'

'He told you that?'

'No. He calls himself Barry but I found out. I

saw a picture of him.. At school we were looking at Parliament and their committees; and he's on one called Energy and Climate Change. He looked different from how he looks when he sees me. He had on a suit.'

'And have you told him, you know who he was?'

'No, I've never told him or anyone. He said we're friends, and what we do is our secret.'

'For fuck's sake, Imogen, they all say that, don't you know?' Seb paused and then said, 'How many times have you've met him?'

'I dunno, maybe five or six. He brings his boat up on the beach to see me.'

'And… what else?' She was looking blank. 'Does he give you money?'

She shook her head and looked away. 'I want to go home.'

'He's touched you where he shouldn't, hasn't he?'

She shrugged, 'Maybe… once or twice.'

'And how old are you? You're about twelve, aren't you… that's just the beginning. Have you heard about rape?'

She looked at the ground.

'Do you know what it is?'

'I'll be thirteen soon.'

Seb didn't respond. He stood staring at her before he spoke. 'You're still a child Imogen… I'm taking you home. Tell me where you live.' Neither spoke any further.

She lived in a house on a scruffy estate. The type where police cars patrol at night and where baby buggies are left outside in the rain and discarded mattresses are left propped against walls until the council gets round to removing them. She didn't want him to park his car outside. He ignored her.

He said he wasn't leaving until he knew she was home.

They walked up the path. She took out her key and opened the door. A group of youths stood watching. Drinking cider from a shared plastic bottle, they were passing round a roll-up and leaning against a garden wall a few doors away. One of them shouted out, 'Hey, Gen, did yer get yer tits out for him?' There was a burst of crude laughter.

Seb stopped, walked back, took hold of one of them by the throat and said, 'Say that again, and my fist meets your face, and that applies to you all. Right. Fuck off.' They stood staring. 'D'you hear? Move on. You fucking bunch of wankers.' They began shuffling away, 'And if any one of you touches my car, I'll kick your asses till you beg for mercy. So fuck off.'

He waited until they reached the street corner and returned to Imogen. She was standing by the door, her mouth open with astonishment. She looked at him, but said nothing other than asking him to wait in the hall. A strong smell of chips pervaded the atmosphere. She peeked in the back room and then shouted up the stairs. 'Dad, I'm home.'

A man in his thirties appeared at the top of the stairs. He had an unhealthy pallor, a cigarette hung out of his mouth. He wore a grey vest, baggy chinos, and flip flops on his feet. He was unsmiling. He didn't look friendly. He stared at Seb and turning to his daughter, he said, 'Who's this?'

Imogen looked at Seb and then her father, 'A friend.'

'A friend? What kind of friend?' he sneered.

He slowly walked down the stairs until he stood level with Seb, and came to a stop. He folded his arms as if to protect himself, and waited.

Seb said, 'Your daughter...' then he stopped, unsure what he should say. 'Okay, let me put it this way, I came across her on the beach.'

Her father cut across him. 'What about it?

'A man was with her. An older man.'

'So what, she speaks to anyone.' His tone was challenging, arrogant, unfriendly.

Seb felt a familiar flash of anger, 'You don't want to know, do you? You stupid fucker. In fact, you don't give a shit about your daughter.'

Imogen turned her face to the wall and began to cry. Seb looked at her in exasperation. 'Tell him. Imogen, tell him what you told me.' She didn't look up, her cries turning rapidly to sobs. Her father ignored her, but continued staring at Seb, an expression of contemptuous disbelief in his eyes.

'Okay then, I'll tell you, since she won't. A man was interfering with her. His hand was up her skirt. He buys her, gives her presents.' Her father still didn't react. 'She sees him regularly. She needs protecting.' He said nothing. 'You still don't get it, do you? Do you want me to spell it out? Are you stupid or something?'

'Who are you to give me advice?'

They were standing face to face. Seb eyeballed him. 'Just a concerned passer-by. Nothing more, nothing less.' He turned, walked back to the front door, paused, and said. 'Sort it out. You're her dad, aren't you? '

'I'm on my own. My girlfriend just left me.'

Seb stopped. 'Really? Shame. My heart bleeds for you, but to use your words, "So what?" It happens. You're an adult. She's not. You can look after yourself. She can't. I'm going now.'

He looked at Imogen. 'I'll tell you again, Imogen. Keep away from that man. Don't take his presents, and don't believe anything he says. You told me once you wanted to go to art school, so go for it. Talk to someone who can help you... the woman who made the Shell, you said you liked her. Clothes and presents don't matter. Your safety and happiness does.'

He pulled open the door and left the house. He half expected his car to have been trashed, but it was still where he'd left it. The youths had grouped further down the street and watched him sullenly as he made a point of walking round his car examining it for signs of damage. There was none. He felt bad about leaving Imogen, but he could do no more. He'd have liked to have gone to the police with her, expose the bastard and push her father to be more responsible but he couldn't. His undercover work prevented that. He drove back to Lavenham.

He went to the kitchen, took a beer from the fridge, sat down in the sitting room to watch television and immediately fell asleep. When he woke the national news had finished, and the local news was showing.

He watched impassively as the newsreader reported that the MP for Suffolk Coastal, Paul Makepeace, had been walking through the sand dunes at Aldeburgh when he was randomly and violently attacked. The cause of the attack was unknown. The police had been given a description of the assailant. The search was on for a dark-haired, well-built, well-spoken man, in his twenties.

An image of the MP's face appeared staring sullenly at the camera. Bloodied and bruised, it had been stitched above the left eyebrow. Seb stood up and switched the TV off. His first thought was to disappear, go undercover a.s.a.p. His second, this incident, if it came out, could be awkward. How much, if anything, should he tell Gimp? Overall, he felt profoundly indifferent to the possible consequences. He'd got the bastard and that made him feel good. He'd keep his mouth shut.

Then he remembered something significant; Imogen had said the man buying her gifts was an MP and he was on the Energy and Climate Change Committee. Fortescue's letter to his father also had referred to someone as having useful connections on the Board and that the man had, what he'd euphemistically referred to, as 'particular interests'. Putting two and two together, he now had some idea what these 'particular interests' were – sex with prepubescent girls. This could mean only one thing – his father, with Makepeace, and Fortescue all had some connection with an illicit business deal. But worse, it was possible young girls were part of these transactions.

His father's involvement didn't surprise him too much. No wonder he was so pleased with himself and talked about the success of his business ventures. No wonder too, he could afford to take his mother off on a luxury cruise. It was at someone else's expense. How much was he and others siphoning off from government contracts, and how much were they swindling HMRC, and how many more were involved in insider trading? He'd check out the lot of them, and see what, if any, apart from committee work, was their precise connection, and also, while he was at it, he'd get that repulsive bastard, Makepeace. One way or another, he'd find a way to screw them all.

— 12 —

He left Lavenham early, stopping first to post the incriminating correspondence close to Mount Pleasant, in Farringdon. Mount Pleasant was London's main sorting office and at regular intervals, day and night, mail was collected and sent out. From there, the letter would hit the relevant news desks and imagining the uproar and trouble it would create pleased him no end. He had no conscience about dropping 'the band of thieves', which included his father, well and truly in it. Revenge was the name of the game and his father had it coming to him for the years he'd given him grief.

He returned the hired Audi and headed back to his flat to change into his usual working undercover gear. He texted Nixie, suggesting they meet up but after opening his backpack, he wasn't quite sure what to do with the letter and giraffe he'd found in the attic. He left them out on the table, thinking a plan would come to him eventually.

An hour later his mobile rang. It was Nixie. Her mother was visiting and they were planning to see a film at the Renoir in Brunswick Square before going on for a meal somewhere close by. She asked whether he'd like to come. Even though his head was still full with the weekend's discoveries and events, he agreed. It was only later, he realised that it would have been wiser to stay away until he got his head sorted, but at the time he didn't think about that.

For one thing, he was curious why the Big

Ben demo had been pulled. But apart from that, it seemed a long time since he'd last seen her and the memories of them in the tent and having sex, still pleased him. They arranged to meet at seven in Giovanni's, an Italian taverna, just off Tottenham Court Road. He knew it. It was an ordinary restaurant, used by the locals, with mid-range prices, and good plain Italian food.

He arrived early, ordered a bottle of the house red, and sat at a table at the back of the restaurant, and began thinking about what might lie ahead. The reality of spending time with Nixie's mother for the next hour or two and acting normally after seeing the pathetic letter she'd left on Jura all those years ago, didn't exactly fill him with enthusiasm. Worse, if he thought about it in detail, it enraged him.

He'd have to cover up, blag it, but he was good at that, and if they were late, that would suit him just fine. It would give him time to prepare. In fact, the later, the better, as far he was concerned. He was on his third glass when they entered the restaurant. Nixie smiled and walked across to him, followed by her mother who excused herself to go to the loo. Nixie didn't sit down but stood gazing at him. Her intensity made him feel uncomfortable.

'Anything wrong?' he said.

'You look different; you've shaved off your beard and you're more spruced up. What have you been up to?'

'Nothing special,' he said. 'But since I was seeing you, I made an effort.'

He smiled and, looking straight into her eyes, leant forward to kiss her, but she took a step back, so instead, he squeezed her hand. Their eyes locked, as if each was trying to read the other's mind, before she sat down. She was wearing a tight black tee shirt with her usual straight-cut jeans, and an expensive-looking leather belt. Even if her clothes were routine, she managed to look classy. He poured her a glass of wine, conscious of the atmosphere of awkwardness as they waited for her mother to return, and a further moment as they shuffled round the table, while her mother decided where to sit.

He glanced again at Nixie. She was sitting opposite him and his mind went back to when they'd first had sex. It seemed a long time ago. He began mentally undressing her, but stopped when he noticed her mother watching him. Did she know what he was thinking? She looked the same as when he'd first seen her in the farmhouse: a middle-aged woman who, like her daughter, must have been a stunner in her youth.

But she seemed to be studying him. Was it his imagination or could she mind read? He tried avoiding her eyes, but decided that might look as if he was covering something up, which actually, he was. He felt increasingly uncomfortable, and so ill at ease he had to speak. He had to act as if everything was totally normal and not dwell on the fact how much he knew about her history.

'What film did you see?'

'Nixie chose it. It's called The Cove. It's old, a documentary made about the annual killing of dolphins in Taji, Japan.'

'Doesn't sound much fun. Why see that?'

'Nixie takes after her father; she has a big interest in marine conservation.'

Nixie spoke then. 'I'm interested in Japan. I have a half sister who lives there. That's where dad is now, visiting Nami.'

'I didn't know you had a half sister. Where does she live in Japan?'

'Well, how would you know? It's a place called Tokai, not far from Tokyo. She takes after Dad, as well as her mum. She teaches marine ecology, and comes over here about once a year to visit him. They alternate visits.'

Seb was silent, wondering how Matt came to father a Japanese child. He decided against asking any questions. He said, 'It seems to run in the family, an interest in the sea.'

Nixie said, 'An interest? More than that, it's an obsession. That's one of the reasons I'm involved with the proposal at Langhithe. Ever wondered why nuclear power stations are built by the sea?'

'Can't say I have.'

'It's because the reactors need water for cooling, but when the water is discharged into the sea, the ecological systems are messed up, big time.'

'Really?'

Nixie's mention of Langhithe distracted him. His mind returned to the weekend in Lavenham – images of breaking into his father's office, the emails, to the beach at Aldeburgh, the fear on Imogen's face, Makepeace's bloodied face. How long would he have to wait until the emails he'd posted hit the news?

Nixie picked up something in the tone of his voice. 'Why do you sound so surprised?'

He side-stepped her question. 'No surprise.' Turning to Flori, he said, 'So, Flori, what are the plans for the rest of your stay?'

'Tomorrow I'm seeing Rose, she's a friend and goes back to when I worked in London. I haven't seen her for years and I'm looking forward to seeing her again.'

'Was that when you were at Harrods?'

There was a silence.

'How did you know my mother worked at Harrods?'

'You told me.'

Nixie looked sharply at him. 'No, I didn't. I've never said my mother worked at Harrods.'

Seb paused, she hadn't. She was right. He only knew because of his newspaper research. He had to blag it, cover up fast. 'I'm sure you did, Nixie. When I saw you in Wales, you were talking about your mum, and that's when you mentioned it.'

'Well, I don't remember that. I'm sure I didn't.' She seemed suspicious.

'Well, how else would I know? But don't let's argue. Does it really matter? Let's agree to differ.' He smiled at Flori. 'Don't you agree, Flori?' He knew Flori would respond to his flirtatious manner as she had before, and it would work this time as it had before.

Flori said, 'Well, Seb, who ever did tell you, was right. I worked there with Rose.'

'Mum, I wish you wouldn't keep going on about the past, does it matter... let's talk about something else. I'm sure Seb isn't interested.' She glared at her mother. 'We haven't even eaten yet. Let's order.' She glanced down at the menu and passed it to her mother.

The conversation may have irritated Nixie, but her irritation was nothing compared to how Seb felt. Inside, he was seething. Sitting in front of Flori, knowing now what he did, how she'd come to snatch him; the help she'd had from Rose and an unknown other, the note, the giraffe she'd left with him when she'd been on the run, was so awful he felt he couldn't bear to sit with her mother any longer.

But it was the giraffe which enraged him more than anything. The giraffe was pathetic, a symbol of his dependence and vulnerability and he hated it; its softness, its stupidity, its simplicity. It was only a toy but he couldn't get it out of his head. It was part of his past, and he wanted to destroy that.

He glanced at Flori. She was smiling, complacent, unconcerned, and still ready to chat about her past. The woman had no conscience. How else could she meet up with Rose, her accomplice in the crime? He felt like walking out, but this would make things worse. Instead, he withdrew. He made little effort to engage in the conversation. He sat, half listening to their conversation, his mind taken over with how he might take revenge. He wanted to do something, something that would disturb Flori; something extreme, something unpredictable, something that would destroy her complacency – an idea came.

Ten minutes later, he stood up, excused himself and went to the loo. It was empty. He went into one of the cubicles and locked the door. He set the alarm on his watch to ring in half an hour, and then returned to the table.

Flori was talking about an ecological house which had just been built along the coast from her parents' farmhouse, a mile or two from St David's. He forced himself to join in the conversation. It was interesting but irrelevant. He was waiting for his watch to ring.

It rang, right on time. He brought his wrist up and glanced at his watch. 'Christ, Nixie. I forgot that I've made an arrangement to meet my mate. I'm really sorry but I have to go.' He stood up. She seemed to have forgotten about the dispute.

'Do you have to? Can't you say you're otherwise engaged?'

'I can't. He needs help with his computer. It's some kind of glitch. I'm sorry. I promised. How about if I give you a ring tomorrow?'

'Promise?'

'First thing. Trust me.' He bent down, kissed her briefly and shook hands with her mother. 'Good to see you again, Flori. Enjoy the rest of the time here. Here's my share of the bill.' He put down three ten-pound notes, walked out onto Tottenham Road and caught a cab back to his flat. Pretending everything was hunky-dory stuck in his gullet, but it was just about bearable because he had a plan. He was about to get his own back.

He didn't have much time. He unlocked the door to his flat and moving quickly changed his clothing. He picked out a pair of trainers, packed a head torch, a small- and medium-sized jemmy, a screwdriver and some protective gloves into his rucksack. He took the letter, the toy giraffe and placed them in the glove compartment of his van. Heading out to the M4, he drove out of London. Luck was on his side, the roads were clear that night and he could drive fast.

By the time he arrived in Pembrokeshire, it was the early hours. He drove towards the isolated country lane near Caefai. It was where he'd camped previously and he pulled off the road into the field beyond. Parked where he couldn't be seen by passing vehicles then, changing his shoes for trainers, put the giraffe and the note in his rucksack, put on his head torch and made his way across the fields to the farmhouse.

There were no cars in the drive. The place was in darkness. Nixie's mother must have forgotten to switch the security light on when she left for London and Nixie's comment that Matt was in Japan was helpful, very helpful. He smiled to himself. Knowing that he was away made his project easier. He was about to play his own version of mind games. She had to understand. Have a dose of her own medicine; know how it felt to be the victim, to be powerless, to be the object of someone else's craziness. She was too complacent, too pleased with herself. She had to feel threatened, confused, destabilised, frightened, as he had been.

He pulled on his latex gloves and walked slowly round the outside of the house, looking for a way in. Nixie had said it was safe living round here. There was no crime, she'd said, we leave our doors unlocked, even when we go out. She'd failed to mention the security system, which he avoided by trying a door at the back of the house. It was locked, but the downstairs toilet window had been partially left open and it was the work of a moment to apply his jemmy and prise it open further.

He climbed in, switched on his head torch. He had to be fast. He had a job to do and the sooner he did it, the sooner he'd get away. He walked upstairs looking for the main bedroom, opening every door until he came to the largest one. It contained a double bed and the curtains were still drawn. This had to be their bedroom. His head torch lit up the room. Clothes were draped across a chair. The bed was unmade. A bra hung from the corner of the wardrobe door. The linen basket was almost full. Books were piled sideways along the bookshelf, and on the floor, along each side of the bed lay a book. He picked one up, glanced at the cover. *Psychometric Testing: A Critique.* That had to be one of hers. The other, *Marine Conservation and the Global Crisis*, one of Matt's.

He pulled the rucksack off his back. He'd

planned the next step. He took out the giraffe. He walked over to her side of the bed, pulled the bedclothes up, and placed the giraffe underneath so it was concealed. When she got into bed, and pulled the duvet back, she'd see it.

The giraffe would be lying there. It would stare. Its eyes would accuse her of the crime of theft. She'd be reminded of the time she took a defenceless baby. How would she react? Disbelief? Hysteria? Terror? Would she scream? She'd get the message. In her absence, someone, someone unknown, had got inside the house, had been in her bedroom, knew who she was, where she lived, what she'd done, and they wanted her to know that they knew.

He smiled. It was a version of what she'd done all those years ago. Then it was a mansion flat in Earls Court, now it was a farmhouse in Pembrokeshire. History repeats itself, the first time a tragedy, the second time a farce.

He slung his rucksack on his shoulder and ran back downstairs to the kitchen. One more thing left to do. He took out the letter she'd written, the one he'd found in the attic, the one she'd left with him on the mountain at night. He read it one more time.

'He likes going out, either being pushed in his buggy or in a car. He likes it if you sing to him. His loves his fat giraffe and on no account must this be lost. It's his only possession and has been with him forever. It's precious to him.'

He paused. Fuck. Something had changed. The first time he'd read it, he was enraged, but now he wasn't so sure. There was something poignant, almost sad about it. He stood tapping the note against his hand, wondering whether to leave it. It was after all, a copy, and he still had the original. That's what decided him. He placed the copy, open and unfolded, on the table, where it couldn't be missed. Revenge, he'd keep to his plan.

Exalted with success and high on an adrenalin rush, he left the way he'd come, through the downstairs window. He sprinted back along the fields to his van, removed his trainers and drove back to London without stopping. He arrived in the middle of morning rush hour. The stop-go of London's traffic delayed him an hour but his overwhelming feeling, apart from exhaustion, was an enormous sense of achievement. His anger after the previous evening's meeting with Nixie's mother had been channelled. He'd made sure she'd had her comeuppance. His aim had been to freak her and he was fairly sure it would.

But how would he know? Only if Nixie mentioned it. Not that that mattered. The thought of her mother's possible reaction was enough. He glanced at his watch. It was almost eight thirty. He'd promised to contact Nixie. It wasn't too early. He texted her, asking when they could meet. Within a minute she'd replied. I'm at home, come any time after eleven. My mum will have gone by then. He took off his watch, set his alarm for ten thirty, flung himself on the bed and was asleep within seconds.

It was after eleven when he woke. He was late, but there was still time to take a quick shower to wake up. He arrived at her flat just before twelve. He rang the bell and stared along the long corridor running outside the flats. He was exhausted, despite his sleep. He didn't wait long. Nixie opened the door and stood smiling in a white bathrobe, her wet hair wrapped in a towel.

'I'm just out of the shower,' she said.

'So I see. Sorry I'm late.'

'No worries. You've come at the right time.

Mum's just left.'

'Sure it's okay? I can come back later.'

'No, it's fine.' She stood aside to let him in. 'Want a coffee?'

They walked into the kitchen. He sat down and watched as she took out two mugs.

'I've only got instant, is that okay?'

'Instant will do. It's you I've come to see.'

She turned round, smiled, looked straight into his eyes and walked across to him.

It was invitation, one he accepted. He slowly undid her bathrobe, and unwrapped the towel from round her hair, 'You're beautiful, but you know I think that, don't you?' He pulled her towards him. 'And you smell good.' He kissed her, 'You see,' he said, 'I've missed you.'

He was alone when he woke, and as he sat up, for a split second he feared she'd left him, but then he heard the clatter of crockery in the kitchen and the radio. He called out but she couldn't have heard, so he lay back, and waited for her. She was carrying two coffees and still wearing her bathrobe when she appeared. She placed the coffees on a side table and sat next to him on the side of the bed.

'How did you know I was awake?'

'I didn't, but I thought it was time for you to get up.'

'What's the time?'

'Three. But listen. Something interesting has happened. The press have been tipped off by an anonymous whistleblower. Financial stuff. An MP called Fortescue, and another with the name of Makepeace. Did he make that name up? It's stupid. But I've heard of him. He's on the Energy committee. They're both involved with some kind of wheeling, dealing financier.'

'Who's the financier?'

'It didn't say. Some rich bastard, no doubt. You know what they say – much makes more.'

He sat up, so there'd been a response already. Great. He couldn't ask for anything better. So far, so good, but he had to play his cards right, which meant keeping his mouth shut.

'You know what? I don't give a shit. We can talk about it later. Like you once said to me, if you remember, don't talk politics, there's a time and a place for that. Right now. I've got other things on my mind.' He pulled her towards him. 'What time does your mother get back?'

'Round about four, she said.'

'Good, we have enough time, then.'

— 13 —

A series of images flashed across the screen; a girl's face, 'pixelated' to protect her identity, a long, shingle, beach, the bruised face of Makepeace. The place was Aldeburgh, the girl, Imogen, and the police were asking for anyone who'd been in the vicinity on that morning and who may have seen the possible attacker, to get in touch. The police hadn't mentioned, or even implied, a possible motive why Makepeace was attacked and, it seemed, he wasn't being held for questioning. A destructive burst of energy coursed through Seb's body. Hitting the arm of the chair he was sitting in, he leapt up, punched one hand into the other and, lurching towards the television, snapped it off.

So Makepeace had lied to the police. He'd presented the assault as a random attack. Hadn't it occurred to anybody, how strange it was that he was alone in the dunes with a young girl and she wasn't a relative?

But wouldn't the police have called round on her father? But even if they had, how would he have responded? Defensively, most probably. He could write the script. He'd deny all knowledge of what his daughter got up to, where she was, or who she was with. He'd say at the time he was in bed with his girlfriend and he could offer no further information. The truth was Imogen's father didn't give a damn about his daughter's welfare. He was indifferent, neglectful, and had no interest in protecting her. Which meant it was highly likely Imogen was still being groomed by that bastard Makepeace. He was the type of bloke that didn't give up easily and had little or no respect for the laws that governed the 'ordinary' members of society. He was above all that, laws didn't apply to him.

In frustration, Seb kicked open the kitchen door, walked across to the fridge, and pulled out a beer. He sat down, breathing heavily, contemplating what, if anything, he could do. It would give him the greatest of pleasure to tell the police what he'd seen in the dunes, but that was impossible. He couldn't do it. He couldn't tell them anything. More questions would be asked and his undercover work would be blown apart.

But why the police weren't suspicious, continued to puzzle him. Was it possible that the police did know something, but were waiting to get enough evidence? He'd kicked the shit out of Makepeace, so maybe it was a matter of time until everything came out. He had to be patient and with luck, what would come out, wouldn't just be about Makepeace, but about the whole fucking lot of them. Moodily he walked across to the window and gazed out though the net curtains. It was almost dark. The street was quiet with few cars.

Someone caught his attention. A man, standing on the other side of the road, staring intently at his flat. He moved away from the window. Casually dressed, in his mid-thirties and wearing a cross-body messenger bag, he seemed to be monitoring his flat, but strangely, made no attempt to hide his presence.

Unsettled, he returned to watching the television. Ten minutes later he went again to the window to check whether the man was still there. He'd moved further away down the road and was looking at his mobile phone, the light from the mobile's screen glowing as he held it to his face. Evidently speaking into the phone, he glanced again towards Seb's flat, before walking rapidly away.

On three further occasions in the same month, Seb saw him. Each time he made little effort to hide himself. Once, he followed him to the tube, sat down in the same carriage and, avoiding Seb's eyes, studied his mobile. Another time, he walked behind him along Seven Sisters Road, and later the same day, as Seb was about to enter his favourite coffee shop, he saw he was inside reading the *Telegraph*.

He was getting under Seb's skin. By now, he could recognise him a mile off. He was tall, in his thirties, with sandy coloured hair cut short, and eyes set close together, like a fox, but other than that, he was unremarkable in every way. Casually but well dressed, with his cross-body messenger bag, he could have passed as a North London architect, a designer, or someone in the media. Maybe it was coincidental that this man kept cropping up, but whether it was or not, he was rattled.

It felt like harassment and Seb was becoming increasingly paranoid. He took to glancing over his shoulder and changing his routes to meetings. Once on his way to Nixie he'd stopped to look in a shop window and glimpsed him some way behind. He waited for him to catch up, thinking he might confront him, but the man took off in the opposite direction.

He told Gimp, who said it came with the territory. He seemed unconcerned, but advised Seb to continue monitoring when and where he was followed. Seb said nothing to him of his double game, of his role as a whistleblower, or of beating up Makepeace. He couldn't. For one, he was acting well out of his professional remit which, if it came to Gimp's attention, wouldn't go down too well. Knowing he'd tipped off the press about his father, beaten up Makepeace, and played head games with Nixie's mother: any one of these could result in the end of his career and he wasn't ready for that. Besides it would have implications for his relationship with Nixie, which for the moment, both on a professional and personal level, preoccupied and amused him. Somehow he had to deal with it himself.

His mind ranged over who could have set this up. It was a form of psychological warfare, with an unknown enemy. Was it his mind playing tricks? His father, Makepeace, even Nixie's mother; any one of them would have a motive, although Nixie's mother was less likely to be in the frame. He didn't know her reaction to the giraffe and the letter he'd left in the farmhouse and 'not knowing' how she'd responded, and thinking about that only added to his sense of being hunted by a person or persons unknown. He could also have come to the attention of other undercover agents working for the Met or MI5, and they might assume that since he was a member of Grassroots, he was a potential threat, and should be watched.

But whoever this man was working for, they'd succeeded in their aim. He was well and truly rattled, constantly and obsessively checking that no one was outside watching his flat.

One evening, driven by these persecutory feelings, he decided to make an unannounced visit to Nixie, hoping she might say something which would give him a clue who it could be. After a final check to see if anyone was hanging around outside, he left his flat, slamming the front door behind him and driven by nervous energy walked rapidly along towards Nixie's block of flats.

He took the external stairs two at a time and had reached the beginning of the long corridor running along to Nixie's flat, when he came to a halt. Mike was standing outside. It looked as if he was chatting to her. He took several steps back and stood out of sight, while he reviewed what he should do.

Mike was the last person he wanted to see. Since that first meeting in the pub, he'd disliked him. He didn't like his style, his self-confident aggression and he didn't trust him. He swore softly to himself. He had to avoid him. He looked around. Under every flight of stairs was a stairwell. He'd conceal himself by standing in one of them. Five minutes later, Mike passed. He was whistling and sounded so pleased with himself, Seb felt like punching him. When he was sure he'd gone, he walked back to Nixie's flat, rang the doorbell and stood waiting for her to answer.

She wasn't wearing her usual jeans; instead she wore a short, straight denim skirt and a white linen shirt. It wasn't her usual style.

Her eyes widened. 'What are you doing here?' Without waiting for an answer, she stood to one side and gestured to him to come in. He stood looking at her. Why was she surprised to see him? Was something going on between her and Mike? Maybe they'd had sex. The thought annoyed him.

He walked in, pushed the door behind him with his foot, but remained standing in the small hallway. Folding his arms, he said, 'I saw Mike leave.'

'And?' she said, responding in an equally hostile manner.

'What was he here for?'

'What's it to you? Jealous?'

'Maybe. Maybe not. Maybe just interested.'

'Well, he had an idea he wanted to tell me about – to do with Langhithe.'

'What was it?'

She turned and walked into the kitchen. 'I'll tell you, if you take that scowl off your face. You could help. It's right up your street.' He didn't answer. She laughed. 'Hey, you are jealous, aren't you?' He stared at her, and then looked away. 'Well, you needn't be.'

She walked over and standing close, she looked up at him. The top two buttons of her shirt were undone. She smiled. It was intimate, a knowing smile, as if she knew exactly what he was thinking. He felt a flash of annoyance. She was behaving like Carol used to when she wanted to seduce him – coyly. He'd rather not have been reminded of her and his past sexual experiences.

'You remind me of somebody.'

'Someone nice?'

'No. Someone who got in my face.'

'That's fighting talk. An ex?'

'Yeah. How did you guess?'

'Great. Thanks.' She took a step back. She wasn't smiling now.

He backtracked. 'It was only for a split second. You're nothing like her actually.'

'Tell me about her.'

'Not now. Tell me about Langhithe.'

'After.'

'After? After what?'

'What do you think?'

She turned away and began examining her fingernails. She glanced at him. He took a step towards her, she smiled again. 'I've missed you.'

'Have you?'

'Have you missed me?'

'A bit.'

'Only a bit?'

Her gaze was challenging, direct, provocative. He took a step back. Could he trust her? He felt unsure, uncertain, and apprehensive. The words of Gimp had come back to him. He'd advised caution. Was she really interested in him, or was she was playing games? How would he know? He glanced at her. In his mind's eye, she was lying next to him in the tent, totally naked, stroking him. The idea aroused him. He moved away and sat down on a chair someone had placed by the fridge.

He looked questioningly at her. 'What's going on?'

'Nothing's going on, except you're playing games.'

'It's one you started.'

'I'm not playing games. It's you. Why move away from me and why sit in that chair? It's like you're hiding something from me.'

He said, 'I'll ignore that. I'll have a coffee please, since you haven't asked.'

'Oh, come on, Seb. Let's just cut the crap and get into bed.'

There was a long silence. Seb continued staring at her, trying to read her. 'Okay, so you want me. Is that all?'

'I do. What do you mean, 'is that all.' What's the problem? Why don't you trust me?'

'Maybe it's Mike. Maybe you're right and I am jealous.'

'Listen Seb, I need to tell you something.'

'Go ahead.'

'I've been waiting for the right moment. But I should tell you. I'm poly-amorous.'

'So? Hardly earth shattering. What about it?'

'Well, it means...'

'I know what it means, you put yourself about. Why make an announcement of it? Do you think I care? It's a posh way of saying you like sex with different people. Most people don't give it a name. They just do it.'

'Don't be angry. It's a bit more than that. Monogamy is for the bourgeoisie and a way of maintaining wealth...'

'Spare me the claptrap. Not interested.'

'Well, you need to know. I have other lovers. Now and again.'

'Good for you. So do I. That explains it.'

'Explains what?'

' That you, like me, know how to operate. You told me a while ago, you like all men.'

'Not to be taken literally.' She came across to him, kissed him lightly. 'You know, I do like you... sometimes I even think I'm in love with you. '

'Really, so what score would you give me? Say compared with Mike?'

'Seb, stop being so fucking cynical. You're jealous, aren't you? That's why you're so uptight. Listen, you've got no competition. Maybe we should test it.'

'Test it? Test what?'

'I would say that's fairly obvious.'

'Fairly obvious? Look, this endless verbal foreplay is pissing me off. I want you. That's obvious. Isn't it? Or haven't you noticed?'

She shrugged. 'How would I know?'

'Well, I'm telling you.' Nixie was silent, the expression on her face watchful. 'What are you thinking?'

She looked at him straight. 'That you're a player, and I don't know why I like you so much, or even whether I can trust you… who knows. The jury's out.' She handed him a mug of instant coffee.

He took a sip, said, 'Why wouldn't you? You know, trust me?'

'Dunno. But I'll do a deal. You tell me about the woman I reminded you of, and I'll tell you about Langhithe.'

'You don't give up, do you? Maybe you're jealous too.'

'Maybe I am, but I still want to know.' She smiled at him. 'Come on, Seb, what happened?'

He sighed. 'Okay. The woman? Carole. She's fifteen years older. She took away my virginity. It's a long story, which I'll tell you about when I have more time. Which isn't now.' He waited for her to respond but she said nothing. 'You asked and now I've told you – so what do you think of it?'

'Not good, exploitation of a young innocent adolescent. Is this why you…?'

He interrupted her. 'Whatever you were going to say or ask, don't, because I can guess. It's the past. She doesn't matter. Not anymore. And it hasn't affected my attitude to women.' He took a sip of coffee. 'I hate this stuff, it's not real.' He glanced at her. He put his coffee down. No matter what games he and Nixie were playing, he still wanted to know about the next project and there was only one way to find out.

'Nixie, you may not be able to be straight but I can be.'

'So tell me.'

'I want you and I'm jealous of Mike.'

'Seb, there's no competitor. I'm in love with you.' She walked across, sat on his lap and wrapped her arms round his neck. He was silent. 'Well, have you got anything to say?'

'I'm surprised.'

'Is that all?'

'I don't understand. Why?'

'Why am I falling in love with you? Surely it's not the first time a woman has said she loved you?'

'Look, let's not talk about it anymore.'

Their latest idea was ambitious, audacious and if it worked, would cause total chaos. The aim was to hack into Langhithe's computer system and create a total breakdown of its functioning. It would be dramatic, catastrophic, and, he'd been asked to contribute.

Initially he'd been enthusiastic, but the more he thought about it, the more problems he could see. It won't work, Nixie, I was around the City long enough and I've studied computer security. All the financial institutions have built a formidable system of firewalls to detect malware. They've been constructed to withstand that kind of attack and even assuming one of them was breached, it wouldn't take long for the software to locate and destroy the virus. Think again. Besides, what's the aim? You need a propaganda point, otherwise we'll be written off as a bunch of destructive anarchists.'

'The aim?' Nixie had said. 'To give publicity to the cause. That huge EU grant – it's way out of order. It'll benefit the construction companies, but no one else, certainly not the consumer and already there's price fixing. They're falling over themselves to get their snouts in the trough.'

The comment reminded him of his father, Fortescue, and Makepeace. It was highly likely that they were involved in some kind of price fixing. The emails in his father's office had made clear the extent of the 'kickbacks' and it was only a matter of time before the police showed their hand. Things had gone quiet since the press had got hold of the copy of the email he'd sent out, but it couldn't and wouldn't last. The potential for a dramatic exposé was too great. He came up with an alternative idea; one that would, unknown to Nixie or anyone else, benefit himself as well as Grassroots.

First, he had to persuade Nixie to put his idea to the Operation's Group. 'This is what we do. You've heard of computer worms. I propose we insert a worm into their system. It'll be programmed to access and change all the emails and invoices relating to building contracts. The figures will be altered, the numbers inflated. But not so it's immediately obvious...'

'And then what?'

'The money will be siphoned off into secret bank accounts, and from there the cash distributed to various anti-capitalist groups of our choice. By the time it's identified, we'll have creamed off considerable sums of money.'

'They'll check the bank accounts.'

'We don't use British banks. We use off-shore accounts.'

'Off-shore? Can't they check those out?'

'Nope. It's a system designed by crooks, for crooks, masquerading as legit.'

'Why's that better than the total black-out? We want to hit the press big time. Your idea is good, but not as good as a nuclear plant black out. Look at the consequences. Chaos and consternation.'

'Not so dramatic, I agree. But there's also a danger it could turn the public against us. The "slow burn" approach, in my view, is more effective in undermining the system. Think about it.'

'Okay, but how? Who's going to do it?'

'You mean the techie bit? The worm's attached to an email or an image. It'll look familiar or attractive in some way, like porn, something funny, or a scandal. It doesn't matter what it is. It just has to catch a person off guard. It's human curiosity. They click it and the floodgates open, security systems are breached and once inside the worm travels through the whole network of computers, breaking into segments as it goes, finding and exploiting every weak point. All the time it's changing, and that makes it difficult to detect.'

'How do you know all this?'

'You've forgotten. My degree was partly about computer security and when I worked in the City, we got updates on the latest scams.'

Nixie looked at him thoughtfully. 'I had forgotten… but don't we need an insider?'

'What for?'

'To get the worm into the system.'

'It doesn't have to be an insider, that's the beauty of it. It's introduced via an external email. Anyone can open it. They won't know or think about the possible implications. That's how computer security systems get compromised.'

'Yes, but surely we need to know a bit about an employee… Mike could help. He has contacts in Langhithe.'

He felt a flash of jealousy. 'Maybe he has. But so what? It's not necessary to know someone who works there. It's a random attack, via someone whose mind is elsewhere. Besides, think about it. Who'll be the first in the police round up?

'I'll tell you. It'll be the usual suspects in Grassroots, and that includes Mike. What we need is someone they don't know about, but who's got the necessary background.'

'Like who? Like you?'

'Like me.'

'You!'

'Don't sound so surprised. I'm not on their radar – as far as I know. The contracts and main players at Langhithe will be documented somewhere. It'll be a public record. Who's paying what to whom. Leave it to me.'

Nixie looked at him intently. 'Okay, but I'll have to persuade the operations group. It's a major change of plan.'

'Go ahead, but don't say too much. For all we know there's a nark already in Grassroots. What clinches it for me, is that once it's started, it can't be shelved, not like the Big Ben project.'

'Don't talk to me about that, it still pisses me off. All that practice. For nothing.'

'What happened, you've never told me.'

'Nobody knew for sure. Mike said there were extra police on duty, too many for it to be normal, so on his advice, at the last minute it was pulled by the operations group.'

'So what's the crack?'

'He thinks there's an informer in the group. We're on high alert.'

'That could be anyone. Someone that's been around a while, who looks as if they're going along with things.'

'Well, that covers about everybody, with the exception, that the "he" might be a "she". It could be a woman.'

'A woman. Is that the kind of thing they'd get involved with?'

'Course they do. What planet do you live on?' She laughed. 'Women are like men. Cross them, and they're out for revenge. Look what's happened to my mum. It was horrible.'

'I'm not sure what you're talking about.'

She looked hard at him and said, 'You do know. I told you. She took a baby when she was young. Well, a few days ago, some nutter had got hold of the baby's favourite toy, a giraffe apparently, broke into the farmhouse and stuck it inside her bed. When she drew her duvet back, it was lying there. She freaked.'

'That's sick.'

'It gets worse. There was a note as well and a poem, and they'd been left on the kitchen table. The poem was a copy of the one my mum had left with the baby when she tried to escape off Jura. She's always said it was the worst decision she's ever made and I should know, I'm her daughter. It's really screwed her up. It broke her heart. And now, because of some sick bastard, it's all been brought back.'

'A poem? What about?'

'Love, it was about love because she did love him.'

'But he wasn't her baby to love.'

She was silent and then she said, 'I know that. But love's a strange thing, isn't it?'

'Love? What do you mean? How's that come into the equation?'

'No, you don't understand, do you?' She gave him a long look. 'It's irrational. Nobody knows why someone loves somebody.'

He stared at her, remembering how she'd said she was falling in love with him. All he'd felt was apprehension and curiosity. He'd felt disconnected from what she was saying. The words were meaningless. They had no emotional content. And neither did he care about her mother's response. He felt no guilt he'd caused her pain. He felt himself withdrawing from Nixie. He could hear her voice, but it was faint, as if she were speaking from a great distance.

'Well, whatever, it's set my mum back. She's having nightmares again. She sleeps with the light on, and she's back on anti-depressants.'

He forced himself back into the present. 'Any idea who could have done it?' He waited apprehensively for her answer, wondering whether she might, after all, suspect him.

'Rose, or Anami, or some random nutter.'

'Rose?'

'Rose was my mum's best friend. She'd started off helping her, but then she copped her to the police.'

'Isn't she the one your mum said she was visiting the other day?'

'Yes. They've made up. Apparently... You've got a good memory.'

'And Anami?'

'My dad's ex.'

He was silent. She didn't appear to be suspicious, but he had to continue playing the game of the concerned outsider.

'I'm really sorry, Nixie. It's a shitty thing to do. But why would either of them want to do this, after all these years?'

'Well, Rose might.'

Again he kept his mouth shut, wondering whether she'd made anything more about his slip-up in the restaurant, but she seemed to have forgotten, or at least she didn't refer to it.

'She has a motive. After the Court Hearing, there was an Order banning them contacting each other. The press were incredibly hostile and they both came in for a lot of stick. After it was over, she went to Canada to do research and they hadn't been in contact for years, but now she's in the UK. So it could be her.'

'But your mum said she was seeing her, when she was in London?'

She shrugged. 'Well, it could still be her. After all, she's let my mum down once, and she'd always blamed her for getting her into trouble. She's capable of anything.'

He kept his mouth shut, avoiding asking the question how she could have got hold of the toy and the letter. That detail seemed to have passed her by. He was safe for the moment.

'And Anami? What about her?'

'Like I said, Anami is my dad's ex, the mother of my half sister. She's called Nami. Anami never liked my mum, for obvious reasons. She blamed her for their break-up.'

'She's the one in Japan?'

'Yes. When my dad goes over to visit, usually he sees her as well as Nami, but this time she wasn't there. No explanation given, so she could have been here, in the UK.'

'But that's not credible.' It was a moment's inattention and the words fell out of his mouth before he could stop himself.

'What's not credible?'

He tried backtracking. 'That she was in the UK and broke into the house. That either of them would do that kind of thing… it just isn't plausible.'

'How would you know? You don't know either of them. There's a motive. Isn't there?'

'I guess so. I suppose if either of them hated your mum, they'd know putting the giraffe in her bed would freak her.'

Nixie gave him an intense look. 'Well, that's what we thought.'

'I'm sorry, Nixie. Is your mum getting any help?'

'She is. She used to see a therapist years ago, but now she's retired, she's starting with a new one. In London.'

'London, why come here?'

'Someone's recommended her. She's going to see her on a monthly basis.'

He said no more. That her mother had had a strong reaction to finding the giraffe and the letter was of little concern. That's what he'd wanted; revenge, to give her mother a dose of her own medicine. The feelings were similar to those stirred up by passing on his father's emails to the press. He felt powerful. He pulled her towards him. 'Nixie, let's forget about all of this.' He knew she'd respond and she did. It always worked – for both of them.

His plan, ironically entitled, 'Fair Shares for All' included what he knew of Makepeace and Fortescue, was passed onto the operational group of Grassroots. He left his father out of it on the grounds his interests were primarily financial and he'd gone as far as he wanted in shopping him. The police could do the rest. The plan was reviewed and two weeks later he was given the green light.

It was the opportunity to redistribute money amongst the various anti-capitalist groups that had won the argument. He was pleased. It would give him the opportunity to screw Makepeace. His own role was kept under wraps. Only a few were in the know and that suited him. It was the way he wanted it. There'd been a feeling of triumph in the meeting which he'd tried to dampen down. He warned them the gravy train wouldn't last and that it was only a matter of time before someone noticed money was going missing. Then the questions would be asked and investigations into the breach of security would begin. He planned not to be around then.

He began his research into Makepeace, trawling through a combination of Grassroots' contacts, the business press and published accounts. He was a big player, involved in various projects, all based on the development of transport to and from the power plant, but the biggest was the proposed construction of an enormous jetty. Materials were to be brought in from the sea, presumably to avoid the roads, where they'd be vulnerable to attack.

He reasoned that there had to be extensive emails and invoices flying back and forth between Makepeace's company and Langhithe, and any one of them could, in theory, be programmed to carry the Trojan into the computer system. To save time, he bought a version of the Trojan malware from the 'dark web' and, working through the night, wrote two plausible emails; either one would tempt a recipient into opening the email.

One promised an easy way to make money; the other was a fee-paying service to access porn sites. Clicking on either was potentially disastrous. It was the computer equivalent to leaving your door wide open and going on holiday. Once in the system, the Trojan would do its work and a steady stream of money would be siphoned off from Makepeace's company into a secret off-shore account of Grassroots. From there it would be further distributed to the favoured few.

He'd felt obliged to tell Gimp something about the plan. He realised that working as an undercover agent, as far as what lawbreaking was permissible and what was not, he was sailing close to the wind. So he focused on saying how key members in Grassroots and others working in anti-capitalist groups in the UK, could be entrapped. He left out the proposal to redistribute the money and his personal vendetta against Makepeace. He justified his actions by pointing out it was a way into the heart of the organisation, that he was supplying valuable information on the various environmental pressure groups for his employer and that this could also be passed on to the Met and MI5. He'd sensed Gimp's disapproval, who'd pointed out what he was doing was illegal and warned him to go no further, but he hadn't actually told him to stop. For Seb, that was the equivalent of giving him the green light.

— 14 —

The following month, Seb pored over the numerous press commentaries. When he wasn't reading, he was glued to the television. The 'three fraudsters' had caught the imagination of the public as well as that of the investigative press. Seb watched, fascinated, as Channel 4 did what they do best – expose the corruption and hypocrisy of the rich and influential.

Fortescue had been at home when the police called. A tall, thin man with an angular, humourless face, his response was initially arrogantly self-confident. He treated the press and the police with disdain, confidently asserting his innocence to whatever was thrown at him, but as the days passed, and rumour and gossip swirled round what the press liked to call the 'Westminster Village', his mask began slipping.

Large numbers of camera men and reporters were shown camping outside his house, which was situated in Pimlico, and within walking distance of the House of Commons. But such was the press' intrusive interest the curtains were kept permanently drawn, and on those occasions when Fortescue was obliged to leave his house, the event took place with military precision. His chauffeur pulled up outside, the front door opened and he and his secretary would make a run for the car, accompanied by a retinue of photographers who ran alongside, snapping as they went.

As for his father, he'd been away on his Norway

cruise when the story first broke, but, Seb thought, he'd guess what was coming to him. A day didn't pass, whether on holiday or not, without him reading the financial press, and since this was particularly bad news, he'd have predicted that, like Fortescue, he'd be given the full treatment by the media. And there was no escape. The only let up being that since he lived outside London in an electronically controlled and gated residence, the press were prevented from getting too close. This hadn't deterred them. They took to camping along the verges of the lane outside the grounds, their vans transmitting the everyday comings and goings, their ladders providing the only means of catching a glimpse of his father as he swept past at high speed. He, however, unlike Fortescue and Makepeace, wasn't a Member of Parliament and therefore, ultimately, was of less interest to the press.

Makepeace, however was of particular interest. As a member of the Energy Committee, as well as being on the Board of a large construction company, it was gently implied, that theoretically, he would have the knowledge and interest in the development of Langhithe Marshes Power Station to provide a possible foundation for financial misappropriation. And since these issues were now in the public domain, questions were raised both inside and outside the House, which with passing of each day became more and more strident and insistent. Makepeace eventually went into hiding, only to emerge, with his solicitor in tow, when the police issued a warrant for his arrest.

There was no let up, because, unfortunately for him, someone in the press corps remembered he'd been attacked at Aldeburgh some weeks before. The photos were unearthed and again reprinted, his bruised face and black eye creating as much speculation and excitement as the attendant financial corruption.

The Mirror was first with the beginnings of an explanation. The attack in the sand dunes at Aldeburgh was recent, but one reporter, Jennie Lee, ran a search going back fifteen years on the paper's powerful computer. She was also creative with the spelling of Makepeace's name. From her experience as an investigative reporter she knew changing even one letter in a name was a way of avoiding discovery. What she uncovered was shocking and enough for the papers to now insert the word 'alleged' into their accounts. That Makepeace had a history of a strong and unhealthy interest in pre-pubescent girls was of no surprise to Seb; after all he'd seen him in action already, his only regret being that he couldn't pass on what he'd seen.

Lee had unearthed an early BBC documentary, and one where Makepeace had been an unwilling participant. The same programme was shown again. The programme claimed that Makepeace was one of several influential and powerful people who had contacts with Social Services' Children's Homes in a north London borough. The children cared for in these homes were angry, confused, vulnerable, the type to be open to sexual exploitation and manipulation by the powerful and moneyed – men such as Makepeace.

At the time, he'd denied all knowledge, claimed it was defamatory and threatened to sue. In the absence of hard evidence the reporter backed down and it all went quiet. But the programme had remained online and it now transpired others also knew of his sexual proclivities. The story was immediately picked up and pursued by the Daily

Mirror and three weeks later the plot between Fortescue, Makepeace and Seb's father began unfolding.

Seb had woken up one particular morning and saw the three had been given front-page prominence. The press were in a state of economic and political ferment. It was an Aegean Stable of financial deception and sexual exploitation, and the press were enthusiastically on hand to clear it up. The hacks, along with their readers, took delight in exposing the corruption of the 'honourable members' although, as they dug deeper, the circumstances of the trio's involvement with each other became increasingly dark. Little by little, the story unfolded of the financial misappropriation. The trio had been snapped eating breakfast together at Harpy's Bazaar which the satirical press dubbed as 'Brunch at the Bizarre'.

That brunch turned out to be an hors d'oevre for what followed; the exposure of blackmail, extortion, and bribery – enough to cause a permanent state of food poisoning. As the evidence stacked up, Jennie Lee, a tireless investigative reporter, had had Makepeace followed, since his denials of involvement were, as far as she was concerned, arrogant hogwash. The result? A series of photographs taken of Makepeace and Fortescue, and one was of particular interest. It showed Makepeace with a young girl on a deserted shingle beach. The girl was Imogen, and although long-distance shots taken in low light, the photos were clear enough to show where Makepeace's interests lay.

The images showed him horse-playing, pretending to fall, pulling the girl on top of him, and pulling up her very short skirt. Others showed the same girl entering a taxi and in an apparent drugged state leaning on Makepeace. According to the gossip on the web, Lee had taken them to her editor, who consulted the paper's lawyer. He'd advised against publication on the grounds of a possible breach of privacy but Lee was not put off. With friends in high places, she was determined not to be silenced, and passed the photos to Freda Arnsberg, the MP well known for her support of the 'Stop the Langhithe Marshes Nuclear Plant' campaign.

She couldn't have chosen a better person. Arnsberg with others had a track record in investigating the development of Langhithe Nuclear Power Plant. The organisation had already exposed the potentially terrifying safety concerns not only for the UK but countries across the Channel. They'd pointed out the costs of building a new reactor and that the government was underwriting its development, fixing costs, and inflation-proofing the price of electricity. The quoted price was double the market value for a period of thirty-five years and the burden of risk and responsibility for this would lie, not with the investors, but with the British tax payer. Furthermore, despite all the criticisms and the possibility of such a contract being illegal under EU law, the government and a certain well-known energy company continued ploughing ahead.

Arnsberg was called to give evidence to the Energy and Climate Change Committee. She argued strongly that the government's commitment to the development of nuclear power was based not on scientific principles but on the size of the potential profit for investors. The costs of building extra roads to and from the site, the management of the increased flow of traffic, the construction costs of a new jetty to bring materials in by sea and the employment of skilled and unskilled labour; all were construction developments which provided profiteering opportunities for the unscrupulous.

She, like Lee, had refused to be silenced. Turning to the Freedom of Information Act and the EU Environmental Information regulatory framework, they continued their investigations. They trawled through the contracts, costs, billing and relevant emails of these early developments and before long before it was blindingly obvious that certain firms were being used over and over again. A closer examination had shown Fortescue and Makepeace were both on the Board of Directors of a large construction company and, in addition, Makepeace just happened to be a large shareholder in a concrete manufacturing firm – a firm consistently used by the developers at Langhithe.

At this point the services of a friendly accountant were called upon. A member of the 'Stop Langhithe Marshes Nuclear Plant Campaign' and a Forensic Auditor, he proved to be of outstanding assistance. Working on a voluntary basis and after a two-month search through the accounts, he was of the view there were sufficient discrepancies to indicate the possibility of 'kickbacks'.

Arnsberg, together with her friends, reviewed the evidence, including the photographic, and concluded it was highly likely the 'kickbacks' were not just financial — there was also a strong possibility they included 'sweeteners': access to vulnerable young girls and possibly boys. She, like Lee, had duly consulted a lawyer and he confirmed what had already been advised. The privacy laws would make publication risky and defending any challenge potentially costly.

But this hadn't stopped Arnsberg. Using the parliamentary right of MPs to legal immunity within the Commons, she made a searing speech which included everything so far known about the financial misappropriation relating to the construction of Langhithe. She also stressed the evidence seemed to indicate, that as part of the package, children were being sexually exploited.

Her speech was met with a shocked silence, followed by uproar. Arnsberg remained implacable. She was, as everyone knew, protected by Parliamentary Privilege and this enabled her to say, more or less, whatever she wanted. The outcome couldn't have been better. The press descended on the evidence like a pack of starving wolves.

Seb followed all the media and press speculations closely. He was on a high and with good reason. The exposure of Fortescue, Makepeace and fellow travellers, which included his father, and the agreement by Grassroots' operational group to hack into the Langhithe computer system – both interventions were working and his father's downfall meant they were quits now. He had no desire to see or contact him. His one regret being that he couldn't show his hand to anyone or share with Nixie that he was the one who'd broken into his father's office, had found the evidence of financial corruption and had posted it on.

He was pleased, very pleased. It was a sophisticated rip-off. For the first time ever, members of Grassroots could print as many leaflets, pamphlets, and attend as many conferences as they wanted. So despite all the press speculation about who might have been the whistleblower, it seemed he'd almost got away with it.

Almost, but not quite, because he was still being stalked. He could hardly ask for help from the police or from Gimp. He was on his own and his paranoia was rising day by day. He'd got in the habit before entering his flat of first standing opposite and checking out whether there was anything untoward. It seemed a wise thing to do, given what was going on.

One particular night something was different. He noticed straightaway that the curtains had been pulled across the windows, and he hadn't left them like that. Somebody must have been inside his flat after dark and for all he knew, could still be there.

He waited for fifteen minutes becoming increasingly jumpy with the passing of each minute. He was no good at this, waiting for persons unknown, and the thought that somebody could be or was going through his personal things made his skin crawl. It began to rain. A steady downpour, the kind of rain that only fell in London, dirty, incessant, polluted by the constant traffic, and he wasn't dressed for it. He moved down the street, and took cover under one of those large trees which border London pavements. It gave some protection but not enough. His view was restricted and the longer he stood waiting, the angrier he got. Quite suddenly, he had had enough. He'd return to his flat, and face up to whoever was there.

He walked back, climbed the front steps and tentatively tried the door to the flats. There was no sign of a break in. He stood and listened. The house seemed empty. He walked stealthily into the hall towards his front door and put the key in the top lock. It was stiff, the key difficult to turn. Something was wrong. He tried the lower lock. It was open. He was sure he'd double locked it. He walked in, glanced around It was immediately obvious. There'd been a break in. Someone had been in his flat and it looked like a professional job.

There was no damage, but whoever it was had been in a hurry and looking for something in particular. Cupboards and drawers were left open, clothes strewn on the floor and the laptop he'd left on the table had gone.

He wasn't too concerned. Everything he wrote, at each and every stage, was encrypted, deleted, before being transferred to a USB and immediately passed onto Gimp. The more important facts were stored in his head. That had been how he wanted it, even though he'd been told it could make him vulnerable if picked up by opposing forces. His mind went back to the man lurking outside his flat and following him. He must have been tracking his movements, waiting for the right time. He systematically began going through his possessions, itemising what was missing but, apart from the laptop, the only other item was his TAG Heuer watch. That pissed him off, but it also reassured him. It was an opportunist break-in after all. His watch had been nicked to sell, along with his laptop.

He glanced around the room again. An A4 sized brown envelope was propped against the television. It had been left. He picked it up carefully, weighing it in his hand. Nothing was written on the outside and it was sealed. From the size and shape, it seems like it might contain photos. He tore the envelope open and pulled out the contents. He was right.

The first image Liverpool Street station. The second, Imogen standing outside the station and getting into a black cab. A wave of disgust passed through him. She looked like a tart. She was heavily made up, her mouth red, her eyes dark, ringed with false eyelashes. She was dressed in a very small, denim jacket, a short, white skirt and ridiculously high heels. He forced himself to look at the third image. Taken on a different occasion, she was entering a building. She was on her own and wearing a skin tight, black satin dress.

He looked closely at the background. He knew exactly where it was. Eaton Square, home to the uber-rich, the millionaires, the profiteers, the hedge funders, the amoral, the immoral, the tax avoiders, the off-shore account holders, the playboys of the world – the type that paid for sex and the younger the better. There were more images: Imogen with Makepeace and Fortescue in a night club, Imogen watching a pole dancer with Makepeace, Imogen dancing with Makepeace. Drunk or drugged, she seemed oblivious to Makepeace, whose hands, octopus like, were everywhere. Imogen being supported from the club, Makepeace with his arms round her, half carrying, half dragging her into a cab. She looked out of it, her top barely covering her breasts, her skirt indecently short.

He'd seen enough. He felt sick. It had happened. Her innocence lost, abandoned by her mother, neglected by her father, corrupted by Makepeace's attention and seduced by his money, she had no idea how to protect herself. Her childhood stolen, she was a lost soul. Her ideas of attending art school now irrelevant, she'd given herself up to Makepeace like a sacrificial lamb. She was being used by the rich and powerful, with Makepeace as her pimp. Seb poured himself a whisky and sat down.

He felt strangely calm. Who had left these photos and for what purpose? They knew where he lived. He'd been stalked and now this; a break in. It could only be Makepeace. He was paying someone to get his own back and to warn him off. It was psychological warfare. He was showing him that he, Makepeace had the upper hand and that he could do just what he liked, regardless of Seb. Motivated by rage and hatred, he'd found out that it was him who'd beaten him up on the beach.

He stood up and, still carrying his glass, walked into the kitchen. The window was open. Who ever had been there had exited through the window. The window lock had been disabled from the inside. It could have been like that all the time but he hadn't noticed. For all he knew, the intruder could be living in a flat in this same house and knew of his movements on an hourly basis. He had to speak to Nixie. He picked up his mobile and rang her. She didn't ask why, but said she'd wait up for him. He stuffed the photos in a holdall and left immediately.

She could tell something was wrong. He must have looked in a state of shock. 'What's going on, Seb? You look as if something's or somebody's got to you big time.'

'My flat's been broken into.'

She took it calmly. 'I thought you shared a flat.'

He remembered, just in time. 'I did, but they moved out, and I stayed on.'

'Well, that's how it is in London. Sorry to sound hard, but it happens.'

'Maybe, but I don't like it. It's not just that... someone's playing head games.'

'Like what?'

He hesitated. How much could he tell her? Certainly not the truth, the words came easily. He was getting good at lying.

'Photos were left of a young girl. Vile photos. But I know who she is.' Nixie didn't say a word. She was looking hard at him. 'I knew her years ago. My parents were friends with a couple who'd adopted a little girl. She'd had it tough. Sometimes I've wondered what she was up to. Well, now I've found out. She's been got at. She's the plaything of Makepeace and Fortescue. It shows her in a night club and she looks drugged. She's been bought, corrupted. She looks out of it. '

Nixie looked attentively at him. 'Got at? What do you mean?'

'She's being used. Sexually.'

'How do you know it's the same girl that you knew?'

'Because I know what she'd look like.'

'You could be mistaken.'

'I'm not mistaken. I knew her well enough. It's her.'

She interrupted him. 'Who do you think it is?'

'Makepeace. He's her pimp. He's in the photos.'

'You don't know that.'

'You haven't seen them.'

'So what are you going to do?'

'Go to the police.'

'Are you fucking crazy? If you do that, everything, all our plans, the hacking – they'll be blown apart. You can't. Don't even think about it.'

'Have you got any better ideas?'

'Nope. You can do nothing, absolutely nothing. Just grin and bear it. She's not your responsibility, and has it occurred to you, whoever it is, might want you to do that? You could be the fall guy, a diversion for something or somebody else. You're panicking, Seb, letting personal stuff get in the way of the cause. And don't give me that look. You're an activist You're one of us, and if you contact the fuzz, they'll crawl all over you and the rest of us.'

'I thought you'd care, about a young girl being used.'

'Fuck off, Seb, maybe I do.' There was a long silence, before she spoke again. 'Show me the photos.'

'I destroyed them.'

'You destroyed them? What for?'

'Why keep them? You think I'd want to keep them? Why do you want to see them? '

Nixie didn't answer immediately. Then she said, 'You're lying. You've still got them. I want to see them.' She moved across to his bag, unzipped it and rummaged inside. Seb watched but didn't stop her. She pulled out the envelope, opened it, and flicked through the photos.

'I see what you mean. Evil bastards. But why you? Why send them to you?'

'It's obvious. Isn't it? Because I care about her, and Makepeace is in the shit. He's looking for who shopped him. Maybe he knows I'm in Grassroots and he's out to get me.'

'That doesn't hang together. There's more to it than that. You know more than you're telling me.' She glanced at him. 'I'm keeping these. That way, I know they're safe and you've got nothing to hand over to the police.'

Seb watched impassively. 'Do whatever. You don't trust me, that's obvious.'

'No, I don't. That girl, why do you care about her so much?'

'Why shouldn't I?'

Nixie shrugged. 'Just didn't know you could be like that.'

'What? That I can care? Not such a bad thing, is it?' She continued staring at him. 'Why are you eyeballing me?'

'You want to know?'

'I'm asking you.'

'I'm thinking it was you who beat Makepeace up.' He looked away. 'Am I right or wrong?'

'You are, but how did you guess?'

'Because the story doesn't stack up... now it does.'

'Okay, so now you know.'

'Yeah I do know, but here's something you should know – when push comes to shove, your heart rules your head and that's not good.'

'Maybe.. but can you keep your mouth shut?'

Yup, so my mouth shut, let's go to bed.' Seb stood up, walked across to the window and looked out into the night. She walked over to him. 'Stuff happens. Forget it. We have to get on with our life.' She put a hand out to him. 'Come on, it's late.'

He glanced at her. 'I'm not sure of my next move.'

'We'll talk about it tomorrow. Okay?'

Hours later, Nixie woke him. It was serious. She'd been listening to the local news. Somewhere in Seven Sisters, the exact address hadn't been given, a house had been torched. Petrol had been poured through the letter box of a large Victorian house. Fire officers said it bore all the signs of an arson attack. Everybody in the flats had been evacuated, except for the occupant in the ground floor flat, who, the residents had said, must be away. The police were trying to track him down

Seb listened in silence. The arson attack on his flat wasn't random, it was meant for him. Nixie stared at him, 'Well, was that your place?' she asked. He'd never taken her to his flat. He'd always said it was a mess, and that he didn't want her to see it. Now he had to say something.

'Yeah, it is, or it was. Somebody's out to get me. Somebody prepared to kill.'

Two days later the operational group of Grassroots met as a matter of urgency. Things were stacking up. First the Big Ben demo had had to be pulled, then the stalking, and now the arson attack; things had got serious. But the group was divided over who it could be. Suspicions had grown that someone, somewhere in Grassroots was an informer, and that he or she was feeding information back to a criminal gang, the police or possibly MI5.

A consensus emerged, one that backed up Seb's view. Somebody, possibly linked with Makepeace and/or Fortescue, or someone acting on their behalf, viewed with extreme hostility the recent investigations. Press reports hinting that young girls and boys might have been procured and used as sweeteners for the rich and powerful and that this was tied up with multi-million pound contracts in the nuclear industry, was now in the public domain, and they didn't like it. In fact, they violently objected to it.

Nixie had argued that Seb's life was in danger. He was a significant member of the inner circle. He'd set up the hacking of Langhithe, and knew so much, he had to be protected. Her proposal was put to the vote and carried. There was no opposition and she was charged with implementing a plan to protect him. The exact details of how this was to be carried out were to be kept secret, known only to the few, and that included Seb. It was for his sake, Nixie had said, since the less that was known, the better, and in the meantime he was to stay with Nixie.

She worked fast, a week later, the plan was underway. Nixie had asked him the previous evening to be ready the next day at seven. Then she disappeared, which gave him just enough time to give an edited version of the whys and wherefores of the arson attack to Gimp. He'd said he'd liaise with the Met and to protect his identity, ask for them not to be too thorough in their search for the missing occupant of the ground floor flat.

Nixie turned up the following day in a hired car. She'd also bought him some clothes. He glanced through them. 'Where d'you get these?'

'Charity shops and Primark.'

'Primark. You must be joking. It's a multinational and it exploits its workers.'

'I know that.'

'I'm really surprised that you...'

'Look, needs must...don't you like them?'

'Well, they're okay. Thanks, they'll do. So where are we off to?'

'Beggars can't be choosers.' She looked briefly at Seb. 'Wales. Home, the farmhouse.'

'Home? Your home?'

'Yeah, I've consulted Dad. He's got the know-how about how to keep you safe.'

'Like what?'

'To keep moving. From one place to the next, never staying long. That way, no one'll be able to keep tabs on you. He's done it before.'

'Doesn't sound great.'

'Maybe not, but you know the score . There's no alternative, that is, if you want to keep alive.'

Seb was silent, and then he said, 'What about you? What will you do?'

'I'll go back to London.' She smiled at him, 'Cheer up, it won't last forever.'

He sighed. 'I'd like to believe you... but I'll miss you. Know that song? I've grown accustomed to your face...He smiled at her. 'Is all this really necessary?'

'I'll come back and yes, it is. We're in this together. The stakes are high.'

'How's it going to end?'

'I dunno. Maybe the police will eventually pick up who ever's behind it.'

'Who do you think?'

She shot a glance at him. 'People known and unknown, the accomplices, the ones who've benefited in one way or another, they'll get their comeuppance. So far they've kept a low profile. They may think they've got away with it, but they'll catch up with them. I can guarantee it. '

'How do you know that?'

'I just do.'

Seb turned to look out of the window. An image of his father's arrest came to him, his mother crying – a rare feeling of guilt for causing her pain passed through him. It made him feel bad. It didn't last long. He switched to thinking about what lay ahead, like living under the same roof as Matt, even if it was for a short time.. Through the course of his research on Nixie and his own background, he'd found out more about him, stuff that Matt wouldn't be too pleased that he knew. He'd been an activist in the local environmental pressure group, a member of Greenpeace, the international environmental pressure group, and a constant thorn in the side of the authorities. He'd passed this onto Gimp. What he hadn't said was that he had suspicions that it was Matt who'd helped Flori get to Scotland. He had no definite proof, so he kept his suspicions to himself, but living under the same roof and accepting his help would be awkward. He decided not to dwell on it.

Three hours later, they arrived in Pembrokeshire. Nixie swung into the farmhouse yard. Matt was working, balanced on a ladder just outside the porch to the front door. He climbed down when they arrived.

Nixie ran forward and hugged her father. Turning to Seb, he said, 'Things are tough, I hear.'

It was more of a statement than a question.

Seb nodded, and side stepping this comment, he said, 'Yes and it looks like you're fixing more security lamps.'

'I am and this one has CCTV. Best to be on the safe side.'

'Nixie told me about the break-in, was anything taken?'

'No, it was some crazy, not a burglar, but whoever it was, might strike again. Maybe someone with a drug problem – nasty, vindictive bastard.'

'Really sorry to hear about it.' There was an awkward silence.

'Well, let's go in, Seb. Coming, Dad?'

'When I've finished, go ahead. I won't be long. You know, mum isn't here?'

'Yeah, she told me. She said she'd be in Cardiff at a conference.' She turned to Seb, 'Okay. Seb, let's have something to eat first.'

He picked up his holdall and followed her into the house.

'What's the conference, the one your mum's going to?'

'The usual...psychopathy.'

'Nice.'

'Don't be sarcastic.' She took a quick glance at him. 'Want something to eat?'

'Please, it's been a long drive. Anything will do.'

'Why don't you go for a quick walk? It's a lovely day, and I'll get something together. I'll be about half an hour.'

'Fine, thanks, Nixie.'

He felt uneasy but her suggestion to go for a walk made things easier. He gave her a perfunctory kiss and taking the by now familiar path, crossed over the fields towards the sea. When he returned,

Nixie and her father were sitting at the table. They looked serious.

'Seb, have a seat.' She pushed across a quiche towards him. 'We've been going through your itinerary, where you're going to be staying, and roughly, for how long. Obviously, we can't tell you. It's better you don't know. They're all safe houses, people we've known over the years, activists in one way or another. They're not all environmentalists, but they know the score.'

'I'd rather know where I'll be.'

'We can't tell you.' She glanced at him, 'What's the problem? I'll be in touch all the time.'

'It's going to be disorientating, nothing will be familiar, all the time knowing someone's out to get me...'

'I understand that, Seb. But you're in danger.'

Matt was looking at him long and hard. His intensity made him feel uncomfortable. 'You're right... look, do you mind, I need some space. Need to chill out.'

Nixie glanced at her father, then sprang up. 'I'll show you upstairs.'

He followed her, uncomfortable and keenly aware that not long ago, in the deep of the night, he'd broken into the farmhouse. He hoped Nixie couldn't mind read or pick up how he felt. He desperately needed to be alone, before he became totally paranoid. She came to a halt outside one of the bedrooms.

'You have a choice, Seb. You can sleep alone, or with me.'

He glanced at her, searching her face, wondering what she was thinking. She seemed unsuspecting, guileless, and she was smiling. She reminded him of the time when he'd first seen her standing at the bottom of the steps in Canary Wharf with her leaflets. There was something sweet about her. He took a step towards her, drew her to him, traced the outline of her mouth, kissed her tenderly and whispered, 'What do you think?'

— 15 —

The constant moves were getting him down. From one day to the next, he didn't know where he might be taken and how long he'd be there. Terraced houses in old mining towns, bed and breakfast accommodation in the faded affluence of traditional Welsh seaside towns, suburban semis on the edge of Cardiff, he'd stayed in them all. Today, he was in Snowdonia on a small windswept sheep farm somewhere near Capel Curig. His hosts were Welsh speakers, and hadn't the slightest interest in talking in English, or so it seemed.

He had to be on his guard 24-7, watch what he was saying every waking minute, all the time listening to the endless conversations of the environmentalists. He'd tried reminding himself they were there to help, but it didn't work. He'd tried contacting Gimp, but it was difficult. It meant disappearing into the wilds of the Welsh countryside and inevitably he was asked where he was going. His hosts' endless curiosity wore him down and only increased his paranoia.

He trusted no one, and that included Nixie, even though using a different mobile each time, she contacted him regularly by phone or text. When he texted her, he had no idea whether someone, somewhere was monitoring him or whether she was the sole recipient, so eventually he'd given up contacting her. It was too unsafe. He only spoke to her if she rang. Today, it felt as if he was reaching some kind of breaking point. He stared moodily out of the window across the valley. It was Autumn, moving towards winter and the weather that day was atrocious. He felt he had to get out into the hills before night fell. Waiting for the weather to change might mean waiting forever. How much longer could he tolerate this isolation?

He pulled on his Gore-Tex and stepped outside. Immediately he felt the cold, biting wind and the rain lashing his face. A narrow lane ran behind the farm, and pushing aside the wet foliage hanging in his path, he headed towards an old drovers' path. Stony and overgrown, it offered little protection. He'd had enough of mountain weather, with its constant low temperatures, swirling mists and low grey skies. He was trapped, he felt claustrophobic, and he was angry. There must be another way of hiding from his enemies.

His mind switched to the past, to the holidays he'd enjoyed on the Greek islands. That's what he wanted; the sun and the warm waters of the Aegean. He wanted to go somewhere where he was unknown and no longer had to watch what he was saying. Moodily he contemplated where that might be. An image of one island in particular came to him. It was Karpathos, a place he'd visited two or three years ago. Mountainous and remote, it was one of the Dodecanese islands, and situated off the coast of Turkey. He'd liked its hidden bays, its simplicity, its stunning harbour, and its lack of commercialisation. Now, as he thought more of it, the idea of escaping and leaving North Wales seemed irresistible. He reached the end of the path, and stopped to take his bearings. Endless clouds of rain drifted across the bleak, grey, wet landscape of the mountains. Even the sheep had taken cover. They sat huddled together along the dry stone walls.

What was stopping him from travelling to Greece? It would be a break and one he desperately needed. He began to walk back, stopping to shelter under a tree, planning how he could do it, until he arrived at a decision. He would go and the next time Nixie rang, he'd tell her. She rang the following morning.

He came straight to the point 'Nixie, I have to get away. This constant moving around, it's getting me down. I've got to get away and I've thought where I could go. Want to hear it?' Silence. She didn't say a word. He continued, 'I've decided to go to Karpathos, a Greek island off the coast of Turkey. I'll be there for a little while. Maybe you can come too.'

'You have to be joking.'

'No. I'm serious.'

'You can't leave. You're crazy.'

'I will be crazy, if I don't get away. I've had enough.' Another silence. 'Well, aren't you going to speak to me?'

'I don't know what to say.'

'Do you know the Greek Islands?'

'Nope.'

'Karpathos. It's remote, but not so remote a newcomer would attract attention. It's beautiful, wild, with steep cliffs and secluded beaches, and it's what I need. The rain is driving me mad. It never stops.'

'It's too sudden.' She was wary. 'It'll disrupt our plans. I'll have to check it out with Dad.'

A flash of irritation passed through him. He was determined to go and no one, and that included Nixie's father, was about to stop him. 'With all due respect, Nixie, while appreciating all your father has done to protect me, I'm responsible for myself.'

'You're also responsible to the cause,' she

snapped. 'Anyway, what about me?'

'What about you? I'd like you to come too.'

'I was planning to visit you in Wales'

'Well you still can, but not Wales. What I want are warm seas, sun, swimming, and making love whenever we want.'

There was a long silence. She said, 'If you go, I'll miss you, Seb. I can't afford the cost and the time.'

'I'll pay. It's my present. Give yourself a break. Go wild with me.'

'You really want me?'

'Doesn't it sound like it?

'I need to think about it.'

'There's nothing to think about. You'd love it... It's a thank you, for how much you've helped me.'

'You mean it?'

'I wouldn't say it if I didn't mean it.'

'I'll think about it.'

'Don't take too long.'

She was pleased, he could tell, and he knew she'd say yes.

He wasted no time. His plan was to disappear, vanish without trace. First, he had to work out a way of getting to Karpathos without being tracked down, and it had to avoid the obvious routes. For this, he would need anonymous access to the internet since if his hosts realised he wanted the use of a computer, they would surely ask what it was he wanted to look up. An internet cafe would be best and after reading through the local press for tourists, he found that Bangor, a university seaside town, a few miles away, had several such cafes.

He told his hosts he wanted to explore the coastline, hired a car, a rather flashy red Toyota to drive to Bangor, and spent most of the day glued in front of a computer screen. The time he spent working out a route was successful; firstly, using the services of a small powerboat company it involved crossing the Channel to mainland Europe. From there he planned to cut across to Eastern Europe, and head down towards Turkey, occasionally double backing and meandering, with no apparent particular aim. Only the last stage, travelling from Turkey by boat to the Dodecanese, followed the traditional tourist routes. It would take days, if not weeks, to reach Karpathos, but time was now of little consequence. He yearned for a period of total anonymity and solitude. A place where he had nothing to do, except enjoy the sun and blue skies in the sole company of Nixie.

He thought about his contacts with Gimp. Since he'd been under constant surveillance by the people he was staying with, the regularity of contact with him had faded. There hadn't been much to tell him. He'd been forced to juggle constantly, with who knew what, what he could say or not say, and the thought of not having to contact him for a time, would give him a break. He'd already told Gimp, he'd gone 'in deep' which gave him almost total freedom to do what he wanted. Gimp apparently had accepted this. He was trusted, as long as, Gimp reminded him, not to 'go native.' But even so, he knew he should pass on that he was about to take time out.

Using a coded message via a work website, he told him he was taking a long holiday, and that he'd be back in touch as soon as possible. One less person to lie to, he thought, and even if it was only a temporary break, it felt good. All in all, it had been a productive day and feeling pleased with himself, he walked back to the harbour where he'd parked the hire car. He rather liked the car, and had left it by a renovated square stone building. The building, a restaurant, stood on the quay side close to the water.

He paused. It looked like a smart restaurant, and good food in a stylish setting seemed very attractive right then. Besides, he deserved it. He strolled across to look at the menu displayed outside. He'd give it a go. He pushed open the door and entered the restaurant. It was half full, the music and lighting low, the ambience good. He was led to a window table and presented with the menu.

He made a quick decision, decided on the halibut. It was a good choice. Prepared by a creative chef, together with a bottle of Sauvignon Blanc from the Loire, it was the best meal he'd had for months. He sat for a further twenty minutes, finishing his wine, thinking how it used to be when he'd worked in the City. Waves of nostalgia passed through him. He'd left all that behind. It was light years away.

He gazed out of the window watching the passers-by, trying to place them by the clothes they wore. Some were obviously students; accompanied by their proud parents, probably about to start their degree. Apart from them were the casually dressed, heavily tanned, possible yacht owners, and a smattering of professionals and businessmen. He glanced back into the restaurant, distracted by loud laughter. A woman stood in the entrance, flirting with one of the waiters. Her manner was easy, informal. She must be a regular. His curiosity was aroused. She was in her mid-thirties, and on her own. Elegant, tall, slim with a tan, she looked well heeled. She wore wide leg, white jeans, a black, long-sleeved tee shirt and gold bangles round her wrist.

The waiter brought her to the table next to his

own and as she passed, he noticed her perfume. It was expensive. She sat down, briefly took a look at the menu, and glanced across at him. 'What do you think of the fish?' She smiled. It was a warm, friendly smile, one that reached her eyes. Her eyes were grey blue, but there was something watchful about her. He was intrigued; a moment's indecision, should he leave or should he answer her question? He'd been around the block enough times to know it was an opening gambit.

'The halibut's good.'

'Yes, the fish here is always fresh. But I've decided. I'll just have a quick snack and drink. I like the ambience and it gets me ashore.' She called the waiter across, and asked for a gin and tonic, then turning again to speak to him, she said, 'These tables have the best view in the restaurant.' Seb nodded. She continued, 'I haven't seen you before. Do you live round here?' She spoke with a slight London, almost estuary accent, reminding him of his city days.

'No, just passing through.'

She gave him another smile. 'I thought so.'

He stood up. He wasn't in the mood to be picked up.

'Going already?'

'That was my plan.'

'What about a drink? It's on me, before you go. A quick one.'

Her forthrightness took him aback; it had been a long time since he'd talked with someone other than an environmentalist, especially an attractive woman. He hesitated, but before he'd given an answer, she'd called over the waiter. 'What would you like?'

He shrugged. She didn't wait. 'Same again, a

Sauvignon, wasn't it? It's for my friend here.'

She pulled a chair out for him. He moved across, watching her carefully.

'Do you smoke?'

'No, used to, packed it in some time ago – with the help of nicotine gum.'

'I've tried that, it didn't work for me. I'm dying for one right now, but I'll have to wait... what are you doing here?'

'Walking in the hills.'

'Thought so. I guessed that you were either a climber or a walker. You have the physique. Mind you, they're not usually the type found in smart restaurants. Where are you from?'

'The south east.'

'Where in south east?'

'London.'

'You're not giving much away, are you?'

'I'm wondering why you're so interested.'

She laughed. 'Well, you know how it is, boredom, primarily. My hubby has business interests around here and he's away for a day or two, leaving me on my own.' She looked him straight in the eye. 'So I thought, being as you're sitting at the table right by me, I'd chat to you.'

'Really? A case of while the cat's away?' She gave a tinkling laugh, and took a sip from her drink. He continued, 'So, are you a local?'

'No, I'm not. We live on a boat. My husband gave up full-time work five years ago and bought a motor yacht. Now we go wherever the fancy takes us.'

'Nice one. Like where?'

'Waters of the UK, Europe, Greece, Spain, France. Wherever the fancy takes us and the sun is.'

'Sounds good.'

'It is. He was brought up in Conwy, but he still has some work round here.'

'Which are?'

'This and that. He started out in the fishing industry, but now he's in tourism. Hotels, apartments, high-end accommodation' She was briefly silent and then asked, 'What's your name?'

'Seb.'

'Seb. As in Sebastian?' He nodded. 'Mine's Ella. Pleased to meet you.'

He stood up, 'Got to go.'

She looked surprised. 'If you wait while I finish this, I won't be long, it's only a snack, I can show you our boat. That's if you're interested.' He gave her a look. She was coming onto him, big time. She was bored and she wanted a diversion, possibly sex. Was he up for it? He mentally undressed her. She was okay, but a little too skinny for his taste. She noticed his scrutiny. 'It's just the boat, I'll show you. That is, if you have time? We're rather proud of it. '

He looked away. He was suspicious. He was being drawn into something. What, he didn't know. On the other hand, why not? No harm would be done. He was tired of living like a monk. Ella would know the score. It wouldn't be her first time and it certainly wasn't his. He said, 'Okay. Lead the way.'

The Marina was a short drive away. She offered him a lift, but he insisted on driving himself. He followed her into the car park, parking his Toyota a little distance away from where was waiting. She led the way along a pontoon, passing through lines of luxury ocean going yachts, all carrying an impressive range of radar equipment. He knew very little about boats but it was obvious; there was some serious money to own any one of these. She came to a stop by a large, white, sleek boat.

'This is it. Tom's pride and joy. A twenty-metre Princess with a flying bridge. He'd always wanted one of these.' She turned to look at him, 'What do you think? Do you know much about boats?'

'Nothing at all. I'm impressed. He'd have to have saved his pennies for that.'

She laughed. 'Well, as he says, you can't take it with you, so if you've got it, spend it. I'll show you inside.'

They walked to the stern. Taking a torch-shaped gadget from her bag, she pressed in a code. The back swung open and after they'd entered, she pressed another button which operated its closure. He followed her up a short flight of stairs into a large saloon. Sleekly designed, the fittings were made of ash. Opulent was the word that came to Seb's mind. He took in the clean lines of the fittings, the cream leather seating, the large windows on all sides, and the wall-mounted, framed photographs of the Welsh National Rugby Union. The only discordant note was a small, untidy, pile of books on a side table. Everything was electronically controlled by a press of a gadget. She put on the light. The blinds on the windows swung down.

'I have to do that,' she said. 'People are nosey. They haven't got enough to do... and there's thieves hanging around the Marina. Won't you sit down?' He sat down. 'Like a drink?'

'No, I'm fine thanks. I've had enough. I have to drive back.'

'Where to?'

'Oh, somewhere in the mountains. I know the way, but not the name.'

She didn't seem to notice his evasive answer. 'Well, I'm having one. I won't be a minute.'

She disappeared. While she was gone, he

wandered over to the books, and picked one up, called *Blessed Unrest*. He flicked through the pages. It was about the environment and the global protest movements. Surprising, he thought, it's the type of book Matt might have on his shelves but not one he'd expect to see on a millionaire's yacht. He sat down to wait for her. She reappeared with two glasses and a bottle of champagne which with a practised gesture, she opened, half filled each glass and pushed one in front of him.

'Champagne. I know you said you didn't want a drink, but I can't drink on my own so I thought maybe you'd like just the one.'

She sat down opposite him and smiled. A version of Carole, he knew what was coming, but right now he didn't care too much. 'Okay. If you twist my arm.'

She watched as he took a sip. 'Like it?'

'Who wouldn't?' He was back at Canary Wharf, remembering how he used to drink champers, always a prelude to bedding a woman. This time he was on the receiving end. 'It's good.'

'Have another.'

He did, and another, and after his third, he leant back. It was time to take the initiative.

'Ella, we both know why you invited me here.'

'What?' She looked surprised.

'So where's the bedroom. I presume there's more than one.' She didn't reply. He continued, 'I haven't got much time. I've got to get back. I prefer not to see the dawn break.'

She stood up, turned her back on him, picked up a book and looked at it closely, before she answered. 'You're nothing if not brutal.'

'Brutal? It's about being straightforward, don't you think?' He looked intently at her, 'You picked me out in the restaurant because, if you excuse the pun, I looked like a ship passing in the night. Nothing more than that.'

'It wasn't quite like that… I was hoping, that at least, you might stay the night.'

'No chance.'

'Don't you have any romance in your soul?'

'No, it's not my nature. Besides, you're a married woman and you're hardly looking for something long term.'

'You seem to know the score.'

'If you mean that I've been propositioned by a married woman before, then you're right. The game's familiar, but the rules don't suit. Not anymore.'

'So why are you here?'

'Curiosity, boredom, the same as you, I presume. Nothing more, nothing less.'

She threw back her remaining drink, walked towards the door, and said, 'Okay, if that's how you want it. I'll be five minutes.'

She was longer than five minutes. In fact, she took so long he had to go and find her. She was sitting up in a double bed, with a sheet wrapped round her, and was smoking, He hesitated before he walked over and removed the cigarette from her mouth. 'If you don't mind,' he said. He walked across to an ashtray, and ground it to a small pulp. 'Why smoke?' he asked. 'It's a disgusting habit.' She shrugged. He slowly took off his clothes.

He went through the motions, but he felt little desire. There was zilch chemistry between them. She was passive, unresponsive, almost like an automaton, and afterwards, she turned away from him, and fell asleep. It must have been the drink but that suited him. It had been a mistake having sex with her. He regretted it. He'd rather have been with Nixie. He lay on his back, his arms behind his head, waited for half an hour until her breathing was deep and slow and then left, climbing down a small ladder he found hanging down the side of the boat.

He'd reached the end of the pontoon when he heard her. She was calling his name. He quickened his pace, didn't look back. He reached the Marina car park, identified where he'd parked his car and walked rapidly towards it, his feet crunching into the loose gravel. He glanced across Two men were sitting in a car, watching him. Coppers. They had to be, even though their car was unmarked. He pretended not to notice them, taking extra care to walk confidently as he passed them, aware he might have had one too many. Being pulled up for drunken driving wouldn't go down too well, not with Gimp or his hosts.

But he felt rattled and sat in his car for a moment, thinking through what he should do to get them off his back. He'd wait. He'd see which way they went and whichever way that was, he'd go in the opposite direction. He took out his mobile and pretended to make calls. He looked up. Fuck, they were still there. Maybe they were monitoring the comings and goings of visitors and had no interest in him. After all, she'd mentioned the thefts from the boats. He was feeling more and more suspicious but if he continued sitting in his car, and they were coppers, there was a good chance they'd get out and ask what he was waiting for.

He pulled the car door open and walked purposely towards the pontoon, as if he'd forgotten something. He was halfway along, when to his horror, he saw Ella. She was in some kind of white dressing gown, standing on the stern, looking out over the Marina and smoking. She hadn't seen him. He did a rapid turnaround, and made his way back, just in time to see the coppers pulling out of the car park. They took a left-hand turn and disappeared down one of the side streets. There was no time to hang around if he wanted to avoid a further meeting with Ella.

He climbed back into his car and turned right heading towards what he thought would be the A5 to Capel Curig. He was wrong, it wasn't. It took a while to find the right way, but after a series of stop signs, traffic lights, wrong turns and roundabouts, he eventually reached the right road. It was almost two a.m.

During the day, especially over the summer period, he'd been told the A5 was usually nose to tail with cars, but he was relieved. At this time of night there was little traffic about. He put his foot down, intending to put the car through its paces, but the A5 wasn't built for speed. Narrow, old, and randomly fenced, it passed by numerous vertiginous drops and through some of the wildest and loneliest landscapes of Snowdonia, including the Ogwen Valley. A mountain area, it was notorious for its foul weather and climbing accidents. He slowed down, half opened the side window, enjoying the stillness of the night. The drive was lonely, the skies dark and the massive bulk of the rock-strewn mountains standing each side of the road seemed to close in on him.

He'd covered three miles when he saw headlights. A car travelling at speed, it soon reached him, but annoyingly, didn't pass. It was so close it was almost tailgating him. He watched its headlights in the mirror; he had no reason to be suspicious. Not at this point. He slowed down assuming it would pass. It didn't pass. It remained behind. He briefly pulled over into a passing place, waiting for the driver to overtake him, but the car slowed right down, and stayed behind. That's when he got suspicious..

He pulled back onto the road, and put his foot down. The driver accelerated behind him, his headlights on full. Seb glanced at the mirror. The headlights were blinding. The intention was clear. No mistake, no error. The driver behind was either drunk, insane, or out to get him. He wasn't about to find out which. Adrenalin kicked in. He reached for his chewing gum, stuffed it into his mouth, spat it out, the wrapping was still on. Putting his foot hard down to the floor, the car surged forward. The car, a GT86, was sleek, fast and responsive, and in its element when driven hard. Like now. Seb moved the mirror so it reflected back onto the driver. He'd outdrive his pursuer.

The two cars raced along the deserted mountain road. Flying over humps, tyres screaming on bends, sometimes driving so close to the edge, it was luck that neither went over. The road stretched ahead into the darkness. A steep hairpin bend lay ahead. On one side, the granite side of the mountain, on the other, rocky moorland. Seb took his foot off the accelerator, pulled hard on the steering, and got round – but the driver behind misjudged the angle. At speed his car flew off the road and glancing in his mirror, Seb saw its headlights as the car bounced across the rough moorland.

Seb laughed. 'Gotcha,' he said. He carried on, keeping his speed, intending to stop as soon as he came across somewhere suitable. Two miles later, the lights of a hotel came into view. He braked sharply, swung off into the car park, switched off his lights. He sat for some minutes gathering his thoughts, waiting for his breathing to return to normal, flexing his fingers which ached from their vice-like grip on the steering wheel.

Should he go into the hotel? His life was in danger. This was no random road rage attack. It was personal. So, it was highly likely that the driver of the car pursuing him, assuming his car was driveable, would get back onto the road and resume the chase. He was out to get him, at any cost, and it was also obvious that the elaborate plans developed by Nixie and her father hadn't worked.

He reversed his car at speed as far as possible away from the road, cursing that the place he'd chosen was so visible. The hotel seemed to have some function on. It looked like a wedding. He opened the window. The noise from the party inside the hotel hit the still night air. A small group of formally dressed men stood outside the side door, smoking, laughing, talking in Welsh. He waited until they'd gone back in and then he jumped out, locked the car doors and walked to some nearby trees for a pee. He was desperate for a cigarette and was just weighing up whether to venture inside the hotel and look for a vending machine, when he saw the car slowly enter the car park.

It was a black BMW with one driver, the same one which had been following him. Seb withdrew further into the trees and watched. The driver stopped, got out, looked around, saw the Toyota and paused. He walked across to it and peered through the windows, possibly weighing up whether to enter the hotel and look for him. He was dressed totally in black, of medium height and in his mid-thirties. He looked exceptionally fit, having the tight, spare body of an athlete. He took out a cigarette, lit it, and tried the doors of the Toyota. He returned to his car, finished his cigarette, which he threw out of the side window, started the engine and drove slowly through the car park, back to the road.

This had to be a hit man, possibly hired by Makepeace or Fortescue. His father was insignificant compared to them, and even he wouldn't hire a killer to kill his own son. After all, there was big money involved, not to mention probable prison sentences when the police caught up with them. They had a perfect motive to hire an assassin. He knew enough about the two of them to put them in jail for years, and there was probably more.

He was under no illusions. The guy would probably be waiting for him further down the road – unless he was staying overnight in some hotel, which was unlikely. Whatever he did was a risk. From now on, somewhere, the killer would be waiting for him. The road offered no place to hide other than getting out of his car and walking out into the mountains, but he didn't know the terrain, wasn't equipped, and had no maps. He'd have to give it a go. He'd wait fifteen minutes, then get back on the road, take a chance.

He drove slowly at first, constantly checking his mirror, scanning the sides of the road for signs of a car parked in the darkness. He'd reached Llyn Ogwen, a long, narrow lake bordering the A5, and one of the starting points for the mountain walk towards the Devil's Kitchen, when the headlights re-appeared. Within a split second, he'd increased his speed to ninety.

His breathing short and shallow, his hands gripping the steering wheel like a vice, he drove like a man possessed, tyres screaming, swinging round bends at an insane speed. He drove over humps in the road so fast it felt as if the car was taking off. This time, there was no throwing his pursuer off.

His mirror caught his headlights. The lights flashed on and then off, on and then off, until suddenly for what seemed no reason, the car dropped behind.

Seb breathed in. Five seconds later, he took another look. It was picking up speed, driving straight for the back of his car. It was so close he could see the driver's eyes in his mirror. He glanced at the road ahead. It was narrow, curving round the lake; it wouldn't take much, just a moment's loss of attention, for his car to be pushed off the road and into the lake.

The un-dipped headlights of a car on the opposite side of the road, and travelling at speed was coming straight towards him. He swore softly. Temporally blinded, he was forced close to the edge of the mountain road and for what seemed minutes, but was in fact seconds, the two cars raced towards each other. There was no barrier to the road. To avoid a collision, Seb swung his car towards the lake. The left side of the car was no longer in contact with the road. Its wheels spun uselessly in the air. Seb braced himself. The car tilted sideways. He felt it fall. He saw the dark waters of the lake rushing towards him. He lost consciousness.

The car had come to a stop at a crazy angle. He was still strapped in, but alive. He peered through the shattered windscreen. He was surrounded by tall fir trees. There was not a breath of wind. The mountains were silent. The road was empty. In the far distance he could see the lights of the outdoor pursuit centre. His head and body bruised, he gingerly undid his seat belt and with difficulty pushed open the door. It was dented and had buckled inwards from the impact. He clambered out, wincing with pain and took a deep breath. The car was pointing down towards the lake, its front wheels jammed on a huge boulder. He looked back towards the road. Nothing. No lights, no sound, no sign of his pursuer. He was alone. He pushed his hand into his pocket, his fingers closed round his mobile, he pulled it out. He slowly texted Gimp, then Nixie on the last number she'd used. Dawn was breaking. He began the long and painful walk towards the lights.

— 16 —

Karpathos, a remote Greek Island. Situated halfway between Crete and Rhodes and the second largest of the Dodecanese Islands, it was reached either by the twice weekly, inter-island ferry from Piraeus or by plane which landed at the tiny airport. Seb first visited the island as a child when sailing with his parents. Its wild beauty entranced him and he'd always intended to spend some time there on his own when he could. Two years previously, he'd taken his then girlfriend, Harriet, for a holiday there, but it was a relationship that hadn't worked out. This time he was with Nixie, and he was hopeful that, things would be different.

He walked across to the balcony, opened the shutters and stepped outside. Even though late autumn, the weather was good. He gazed beyond the harbour towards the small yachts on the horizon, then at the pastel-painted houses, rising in steep tiers away from the harbour. He loved the rasping cacophony of the cicadas in the trees and on the hills, and the sweet, earthy smell of the wild thyme and sage, their fragrance strengthening with the noonday sun. Two days before he and Nixie had walked along one of the cobbled paths winding away through the village. They'd stopped at an abandoned village to gaze at the expensive yachts moored way down in the harbour.

He leant on the balcony rail, his mind drifting back to the car chase in the Welsh mountains. It was over a month ago, but the memory still haunted him. He'd spoken of it to no one, other than to Gimp and Nixie. Gimp had been spectacularly unhelpful. If anything, he'd been indifferent and barely reacted when he'd said it was necessary for him to disappear for the time being. He'd said he thought it a good idea.

Since arriving in Karpathos, he'd had plenty of time to think – in particular about Nixie. She'd arrived a week ago. He glanced across at her. She was still asleep, curled up in bed with the sheet wrapped round her. Before she came, he'd missed her and when he'd met her off the ferry, she'd said the first night they were together that she loved him. This wasn't the first time a woman had told him she loved him, but this felt different. He'd become preoccupied with wondering what she meant by love and whether she meant what she'd said. Whatever love was, ultimately, he thought, he didn't believe in it. It implied commitment and permanency, and he valued neither. But, even so, he recognised there was something powerful between them. It was a strong, almost primal attraction, which drew them together.

'Seb, I'm awake, what you doing?'

He turned round. She was smiling, sitting up in bed.

'I'm checking out the harbour.'

'Come here.'

He walked across and sat down on the bed. 'Like a coffee?'

'Yes, but not now. What about breakfast at that coffee place by the water?'

'Which one?'

'The one at the far end of the harbour. The one where I asked the waiter to take a piccie of us. It's got a blue striped awning, it's smaller than the others, with fewer people.'

'And then what?'

'A swim?'

'Great, suits me. We can go back to that small one through the village.' He smiled at her, stroking her arm. 'You skin feels warm.' She didn't reply. He pulled the sheet away from her.

'You've got nothing on.'

'I got hot in the night. What are you thinking about?'

'Sex on the beach.'

'The drink?'

'No, the real thing.'

She looked at him with a half smile. 'Later.'

'Why not now?'

'Why not now?'

Afterwards, he felt a deep sadness. She'd asked if he loved her, but he couldn't say. He'd picked up something intangible between them, as if the end of their relationship was in sight. It had made him feel so bad, he'd held her tight, until with his arms wrapped round her, they fell into an exhausted sleep.

'Seb.'

He opened his eyes. She was awake, propped up on one elbow, gazing at him, looking serious. 'What time is it?'

'It doesn't matter. We've got all the time in the world.'

'Do you think my stomach's fat?'

He laughed, pulling her warm body towards him. 'What are you talking about?'

'I just wondered, you know, why your belly is flat and mine isn't.'

'That's because, you must have noticed, men and women are built differently.'

'You haven't answered my question.'

'You're being silly.'

She pulled his hand onto her stomach and said, 'Go on, tell me the truth, is it fat?'

He sighed. 'No. It's round but even if it was, I'd still...' He stopped.

'What were you going to say?'

'I'd still like it.'

She sat up and stared down at him, looking disappointed. 'I thought you were going to say that you loved me.'

He paused, wondering how to answer. 'You asked me about that before. I'm not sure what love is.'

'You want me to show you?'

She became playful, stroking and kissing his body.

He ruffled her hair. 'Maybe it's the heat, but you always turn me on.'

'It's not me. It's you. You've changed, Seb.'

'Changed? How have I changed?'

'The way... the way you make love to me – you're tender now.'

'Isn't that how I've always been?'

'No... It was all technique once.'

'What do you mean?'

She clasped her arms round her knees. 'A poem I read ages ago called *Sex without Love*, has always stuck in my head, especially this line, 'How do they do it, the ones who make love without love.'

'Is that what you thought about me?'

'I did, but not now... I know you've been with lots of women.'

'How do you know?'

'It's obvious.' She laughed.

'Because I know how to turn you on?'

'You do.'

'Well, it works both ways.'

'I fancied you the first time I saw you. It was like love at first sight. Superficially, you seemed arrogant, too self-assured, but it didn't put me off. You had a certain look in your eyes when I gave you that leaflet. I knew then, I wanted you like no one else I'd ever met.'

His mind went on alert. 'The first time? When was that?'

'In Canada Square.'

He stared at her. What was she talking about?

'Canada Square? We didn't meet there. We first met in Starbucks,... after the demo outside the bank. Don't you remember?'

'No. It was Canada Square.'

'You're wrong. The first time I saw you was after the bank demo.'

The atmosphere had changed. She glared at him. 'Don't lie to me.'

'Lie to you? I've no idea what you're talking about.' He raised his voice slightly.

She paused and, looking directly at him, said in a low voice, 'I know who you are.' 'For Christ's sake. What's this about?'

'It's about you, Seb. You've lied to me.'

'Really? How? How have I lied?' He'd bluff it out. It had worked once and it could work again. She didn't answer. 'What are you accusing me of? I want chapter and verse.'

'You're not one of us. You're a plant. You're working undercover.'

He leapt out of bed and stood looking down at her, his eyes cold, hostile. Breathing heavily, he said, 'What are you accusing me of?'

Nixie turned away and, avoiding his eyes,

looked at the wall. He took a step towards her and pulled her roughly round. 'What evidence do you have for that?'

She glared at him, shifted her gaze, but said nothing.

'Answer me. What evidence do you have?'

'Don't shout… I have… I have evidence. I have enough evidence.'

'Like what?'

She was silent.

He walked across to the balcony and stood, seeming to be looking at the boats in the harbour. Nixie said nothing. After five minutes he returned and stared down at her. 'Go on then, let's hear it.'

This time, she answered. 'I'm not stupid. When I gave you that leaflet, in Canary Wharf, I noticed your really expensive watch. Not many of those about, I thought. I saw it again. You were wearing it when I was with my mother in the restaurant off Tottenham Court Road. You must have forgotten to take it off. It could have been a coincidence, but I don't think so.'

Seb stared. 'Is that it?' He'd easily blag his way out of that.

'No, it isn't it? The same evening – you knew my mum had worked in Harrods. How did you know? You must have done some background research, and there's more. You left the restaurant early. I didn't see you until the next morning. It was the morning after the farmhouse was broken into. It was you. It had to be. You'd had enough time. You left the giraffe in my mother's bed knowing how much it would upset her. The only one other person who would know that, was Rose, and that's not the type of thing she'd do. You had a motive. Revenge. You're the baby my mother stole all those years ago.

The one she called Owain.'

There was a long silence before Seb spoke again.

'You're so fucking sympathetic to your mother. Have you ever stopped to think of the effect her action has had on me? Your mother was crazy. She snatched me and carried me to a remote Scottish island?'

'I'm sorry.'

'Sorry, is that all you can say?'

'I can't say or do anymore. It's the past.'

He moved away from her, folded his arms across his chest and was silent. When he spoke, he stayed where he was, his eyes seeming to bore through her. His voice was clipped, harsh, and he spoke slowly, each word articulated with precision.

'So, all this time, you've been spying on me, and I thought I could trust you. Sex without love, you said. What a joke. You know all about that.'

She leapt out of bed, pulled the sheet round her body, walked over to him and looking into his eyes, said, 'I had to do it. For the cause, for Grassroots.'

He took a step backwards. 'Are you saying… are you saying what it sounds like? That you only slept with me to get information?'

'No, that's not what I'm saying. What I'm saying is, we had to see what was going on. Mike suspected you from the start. He went into your background and all the stuff you told us, and it didn't add up. I wanted to tell you, but I had to keep my mouth shut…

'Seb, right from the start, you've been special to me, you must know that. But we had to test you. It's been really difficult for me.'

'Shut the fuck up. You're talking crap.' Keeping his eyes on her, he walked across to his clothes and pulled them on. He stared at her and breathing heavily, said, 'Who else knows?'

'Mike and one or two of the others. He's always said not to trust you, but we could use you.'

'You bitch, you two-faced duplicitous bitch. '

'What do you think we should do? We had to check you out. We're not kids playing games. The stakes are too high.'

'We, who's the "we", who's the fucking royal "we"? You fucking bastards... someone's been watching me, following me, trying to kill me, and all the time it was you lot, and that arse hole.'

'It wasn't. We're not into that... You need to get real, Seb. You're in it up to your neck now. MI5, the Met, security at Langhithe, it could be any of them.'

'You know what? I don't believe a word you're saying.'

She moved close to him and hissed, 'That's the name of the game. That's how it is. You betrayed us first, remember. Didn't you sleep with me to get info?'

'A job I'm paid to do. Which is why I don't give a toss about you or any of your so-called comrades. Get that into your stupid head.'

'Stupid? Why am I stupid?' she shouted.

'Because you do it for free. For what? You think you're saving the world, but most of the population don't give a damn.' He walked angrily to the door, 'I'm going.'

She ran over to him. 'Going where?'

'I don't know where, but get out of my face.' He turned away so she couldn't see him, and banged his fist into his hand.

She hesitated, her eyes filling with tears. 'Don't go. I'm sorry. I don't know what else to say... A few minutes ago we were going to make love... can't we... '

'Unbelievable! You're all the same... a fuck. That's what you want, isn't it? You think that'll make it alright? I wouldn't demean myself.'

He bent down, picked up her bra and pants from the floor and threw them across the room. 'And put some clothes on. Game-Set-Match. It's over. Finis. Our history stops here. I'm going.'

He stormed out into the hall, followed by her, and angrily stood fumbling with the door to let himself out.

She stood watching, 'Before you go... I know about the woman.' It was designed to be a final slap in his face.

He stopped, turned to face her. 'What woman?'

'The one in Bangor, the one you screwed.'

'Really? Well, isn't life full surprises? What you and your comrades wouldn't know, is that she was a great fuck.'

He left, slamming the door behind him and, oblivious to the fierce heat, walked rapidly through the labyrinth of small white-washed houses, towards the steps leading away from the village. Taking them with long, loping steps until he reached the top, he continued along the old donkey track which wound through ancient olive and fig trees.

He stopped when he reached the deserted village and sat down, took out his water bottle and, lifting it to his mouth, almost drained the water. The cicadas were deafening and the heated air was heavy with the chocolaty smell of the carob and the fragrance of the thyme and sage bushes. He felt calm, even reflective as he considered their row. How things could change in a short space of time. Only two days ago he and Nixie had sat in the shadows of the crumbling ruins of an old house and shared the fresh figs they'd picked from the trees. It was the first time she'd tasted a fresh fig and she'd been entranced with the delicate taste

But then anger took hold of him, so powerful it was like a vice. There was no escape. It was monumental, not just with her, but with himself. Nixie had betrayed him. That she had spied on him cut through his guts like a sharp knife. She'd been the first woman he'd trusted. How stupid could he be? What had gone wrong? Had he been targeted by Grassroots? Had she been specially chosen and had waited for him at the bottom of the steps in Canada Square before giving him a leaflet?

He went over the conversations they'd had, seeking to justify his own spying. His work as an undercover agent was legitimate. He'd been trained for it. It was essential; he was on the side of law and order, protecting the economy and the government. She, on the other hand, was an amateur. Their aim to smash the state was infantile. He'd seen her as an innocent, an ingénue, but how wrong he'd been. She was far from that. She was an operator. She'd used sex to deceive and exploit him. His mind went back to Porth Clais, to when she'd fallen from the cliff, how he'd rescued her and how later, meeting her parents, the atmosphere had become strained. She'd been checking him out and he'd fallen for it. Walking back with him to his tent and having sex with him, it had all been a put up.

Gimp had been right all along. He'd warned him about becoming involved with Nixie. He should have believed him. She was like everybody else. Unreliable, a liar and out for herself. An image of Flori came to him. Like mother, like daughter, he thought bitterly. He'd been used by them both. He tried pushing these thoughts away. It was a long time ago when she'd snatched him. He couldn't remember it, but he could imagine it and he could feel it. This time it was Flori's daughter who'd deceived him. When she'd said he was special, whether it was the truth or not, that was the end for him. Their relationship couldn't survive this betrayal. Nothing could ever be the same.

He stood up decisively. It was over. He'd thought enough about her. It was a waste of time. There was no other choice. He had to leave her. He'd done it before with other women, countless times. He'd tell her he was leaving.

He walked slowly back to the villa they'd shared, stopping only for a glass of iced water with lemon. He followed that with two large white wines, while picking at some olives left out on the table. He didn't feel like eating, and drinking alcohol in the heat on an empty stomach wasn't such a good idea, but he no longer cared what he did or how he felt. His anger had turned to indifference.

He was slightly tipsy when he tried the villa door. It was unlocked. That wasn't unusual. It was usually left that way. He pushed it open and walked into the cavernous tiled entrance hall. In comparison to the heat outside, it was cool. He stood for a moment, wondering if Nixie was asleep and how he was going to tell her it was all over. He glanced at his watch. It was new, not the one that had betrayed his affluent background. He walked into the bedroom, expecting to see her, but the bed was made up. The shutters were closed. The room had been left neat and tidy.

Where was she? Her absence and how he felt about that, surprised him. Her suitcase, lying on the floor, was packed, but left partially open. Feelings of regret and sadness swept through him. He was confused. He hadn't wanted her to go. He'd miss her.

He walked into the bathroom and glanced around. The towel she used for swimming was missing. He returned to her suitcase, and one by one took out her clothes, checking to see what she'd taken and what she'd left. The red bikini she usually wore wasn't there. So she must have gone swimming; probably to the bay through the olive groves.

It would be the one they'd discovered on their first day, and where they would have gone to today, but for the row. She'd gone, even though she would know swimming wasn't a good idea in the ferocious heat of the mid-afternoon. It dawned on him then. She was planning to leave, and before she left, she must have decided to go for a final swim. He had to see her. He didn't know why or what he'd say, but he didn't want to part from her, not like this.

It was a fifteen-minute walk to the beach. He walked quickly and by the time he'd got there and climbed down through the trees to the water's edge, he was covered with a film of sweat. He'd been right Her towel, her hat and the loose top she wore as protection from the sun had been left under one of the scrubby trees standing back from the water. Shading his eyes against the sun's glare, he looked out to sea. He could see her standing on flat rocks, some distance away from the beach. She looked as if she was about to dive into the sea. She hadn't noticed him. He watched until she disappeared into the water.

What should he do? Nothing seemed more attractive at that moment than swimming. However warm the water was, it would feel cool compared to the mid-afternoon heat of the Greek sun. He hadn't brought his swimming gear with him, but that was of little consequence. He took a quick look around. It was siesta time; the bay was deserted, there was no one around other than Nixie and she was already swimming. He stripped off, and within a minute he'd entered the water and swum out to the rocks to where she'd been standing. The water felt deliciously cool. Treading water, he waited for her to emerge. She came up out of the water right by him and glanced at him. She must have known he was there because she didn't seem surprised.

'I had to see you, Nixie.'

She didn't reply, but dived under the water, and pulled away strongly from him. The water shimmered in the heat, but it was so clear, so translucent, he could see her swimming along the bottom. Kicking his legs, he pointed his body down through the water and followed. He swam until he caught up with her and for a brief moment they circled one another, before they both rose to the surface. He grabbed hold of the rock and looked at her. She was a couple of feet away and treading water. She looked inscrutable. He couldn't make out what she was feeling, what her thoughts were.

'Won't you speak to me?'

'What is there to say?'

He hadn't intended to apologise, but he heard himself say, 'I'm sorry.'

'For what?'

'For what I said to you.'

'Maybe I deserved it. I have betrayed you.'

'You're leaving me?'

'Of course. We can't continue now. It would be impossible.'

'I suppose so.'

'I'm going back.'

He watched as she swam away, pulled herself out of the water, and walked back to the beach. He followed, expecting her to leave as soon as he sat by her. But she didn't. She pulled out her towel, dried her hair and, arranging the towel in a straight line, sat down and looked out to sea. He was unsure what he should say to her. He waited to see where she was in her head. She glanced at him, but she didn't seem angry, more resigned.

'I forgot to bring my towel.' He didn't know what else to say.

'And your trunks, I see.' She moved over, made a place for him to sit by her. 'Shouldn't you put your shorts on?'

'There's no one around. I will, when I'm dry. Let's get some shade.'

He put out his hand to pull her up and they walked silently towards a clump of trees. She didn't speak but lay on her back, shielding her face from the sun with her hat. That way he couldn't see her face, but then, neither could she see his.

'Are you really leaving?'

'I am.'

'Will you forgive me?'

'I might. In time.'

'What do I have to do?'

'Sort yourself out.'

'Don't I have a right to be angry?'

'Yes, it's not what you said, but how you said it. You have a cruel side… like what you did to my mother.'

'I'm sorry, Nixie. But I was so angry.'

'I know that. But it doesn't excuse it.'

'We might have worked something out.'

'Like what?'

'I don't know, but something.'

'Seb, I don't want to argue any more, but I'm going to tell you, and this is whether you want to hear it or not, or whether you believe it or not, I have feelings for you. It wasn't a case of me using you, like you said. It wasn't like that.'

'You have feelings? What kind of feelings?'

She pulled her hat away from her face and looked directly at him. 'Love. I love you, Seb. I've said it before. I love you – despite everything.'

'I don't believe you. How can you? I'm a bastard.'

'Maybe. Maybe you have cause to be, but I think you don't know what it is.'

'You mean love?'

'Love is what I mean.'

She looked at him. Their eyes met. She smiled. Her eyes said everything and against his better judgement he leant over and, taking her face gently in his hands, kissed her. It was long and slow and her mouth was warm and receptive to his tongue. She pulled away from him.

'Seb, I don't want it to end. Not like this.'

'What are you saying? How do you want it to end?'

She looked away. 'I think you know, I need you just one more time,' she said, still without looking at him.

'Are you sure?'

She didn't reply.

'It'll make it more difficult.'

'Maybe. But you always make me feel good.'

She gave him the smile, the one that reminded him of the time when they first met, pulled off her bikini and closed her eyes. He touched her. He'd never desired a woman as much. She was responsive, sensuous, her body warm, inviting. They made love, slept, and swam until exhausted and hungry, they returned to the villa, driven away by the sound of visitors clambering down to the bay.

Her ferry left at eight. He accompanied her

down to the harbour but just as she left, she gave him a note. 'Open it after I've gone,' she said, 'but before I go, I'd like a photo of you.'

It took him aback, and he said, 'What for?'

'To remember you by... we may never meet again.'

He stared at her, 'If you must,' he said and forced a smile.

'Do you want one of me?'

'No.' He turned away and walked back to the villa. His mood low, it was some time before he could open her note. It said,

> Dearest Seb,
>
> Soon it's going to come out that you've been working undercover, so you have to leave Karpathos, and go some place off the map, where you can't be found. You've got to keep on the move and you've got to live like that for months, possibly longer.
>
> I do truly love you even though neither of us has been straight with each other. I think that after what's been said and what's been done, the trust has gone between us and there is no going back. Please don't try to get back in touch with me because I won't answer. It has to be that way and I've no idea when or if it's ever going to be okay.
>
> But whatever happens, I won't ever forget you. I've said before, love is a strange thing and I don't understand it, but it's happened and you were and always will be special to me.
>
> With all my love,
>
> Nixie.

He read it several times. It was poignant, sad, but she was right. He had to disappear. The word would soon get round that he'd been an agent working undercover. He began packing the same evening, took the next ferry and for months travelled round the Islands, stopping randomly, anywhere convenient, anywhere that appealed. He cut himself off from his previous life. Gimp contacted him several times, but he ignored him. Occasionally he read an English newspaper. He thought a lot about politics, the economy, the protest movements, what he'd observed, what he'd experienced over the past three years, and the discussions he'd had with Nixie and the others.

He was hardly aware that he was changing. He'd been in a night club, when he heard an old jazz number. It was a mournful love song, sung by Chet Baker and it depressed him. He'd heard it first years ago and it had stayed with him. 'You don't know what love is, until you know the blues.' Maybe he had loved her because she was always on his mind. He had a couple of short-term relationships, but they weren't the same as with Nixie. No one interested him or turned him on in the way she had.

The shock waves from the 2008 crash meanwhile continued reverberating across the world. Its impact was particularly destructive to the Greek economy, but the Greeks had a different political history from the Brits. They fought against the restrictions of the EU and IMF. For a while Seb stood on the side lines and watched but the rise of Syriza interested him. In 2011 he moved to Athens. He'd decided to stay on in Greece.

PART TWO

— 17 —

Nixie came through to the Arrival lounge. Mike was waiting for her and walked forward to greet her, his eyes searching her face.

'So did you tell him?'

'Yeah.'

'And his reaction?'

'What do you think?'

Mike didn't answer, but picked up her holdall, and said, 'I'm in the short stay.' They walked in silence to the car park. 'You're not very talkative.'

'Not surprising is it, we've worked together. We've been close, and I liked him. A lot.'

'Great. He's a copper's nark, but you liked him. That's what's important.'

'Cut the sarcasm. No one's perfect.'

'I know you. It's the sex you liked, not him.'

Nixie stopped, glared at him, then she said, 'None of your business.'

'Just joking.' Mike opened the boot of the car, and placed the holdall inside. He turned to look at Nixie and looked grim. 'I need to tell you something... but get in first.' Nixie didn't respond. She sat in the front seat and stared straight ahead. 'The police are onto us. They know about Langhithe and the hacking. We have a problem.'

'Okay, but don't hang about here. How long have you had this car?'

'It's not mine. Borrowed. Are you listening?'

'I will be, when you move off.'

'I've been pulled in. No idea how they traced it to us. So far, I've said I know nothing but if we spill the beans, Seb'll be nicked, and, he's hardly gonna keep his mouth shut, is he? He knows too much and he could bring the whole organisation down.'

'What's the alternative?'

'We keep schtum, deny everything, in which case, he might get off, but they'll be monitoring us for years after, and that'll seriously cramp our style.' Nixie was silent. 'So... what do you reckon?'

'It seems obvious to me, we keep schtum, like you said... unless you want to take revenge. Besides, Seb's going into hiding. Where are we going, by the way.'

'Not your place or mine, they're sure to be bugged. To a new member.'

'Who?'

'You don't know her.'

Nixie glanced at him. So this woman must be his latest. She silently wished her good luck.

'Let's hope she's safe.'

'That's a good one, coming from you... She's okay. She's been checked out... So what more do you know?'

'About Seb, you mean?'

'Who else would I be talking about?'

'Okay, I'll run though the situation. He's been followed, and there was the arson attack – that much you know. But there's another incident, really hard core. Someone ran him off the road in Wales. He doesn't know who did what, and he's paranoid. Not surprising. He thinks we did the lot.'

'Does he know we set up the woman?'

'We? You mean 'you'... He does now–because I

told him.'

Mike laughed. 'Well, he certainly knows how to operate... when it comes to women. Jealous?'

'As I was saying... the arson and being driven off the road could have been anyone, in theory. But attempted murder isn't usually in the Met's bag of tricks, and as for hacking into Langhithe, he's not important enough to be bumped off by Security or MI5. That leaves Fortescue, Makepeace and Melbury in the frame...Melbury's a small player, using and selling his connections to make a little something on the side, Fortescue's a fraudster, so far, so predictable, but Makepeace is something else. Weird. A piece of shit. He deserves everything coming to him, and he's got a lot to hide.'

'So what's your point?'

'With Seb out of the UK, we may be the next target. It could get heavy.'

'You think I hadn't got that?' Mike turned off the A4 flyover and began negotiating a way through the heavy traffic towards Camden.

'Where are you taking me?'

'You'll see when I stop. Don't write it down. I'll see you there tomorrow night.'

He turned off the main road, drove down a side road, and came to stop just by a narrow passage way. He turned to look at Nixie.

'We've been dropped right in it, by your lover-boy. You realise that, don't you?'

'You agreed to the plan. What do you want to do? Hang, draw and quarter him?'

'Something like that.'

'He's made us thousands.'

'At a cost.'

'We'll work something out.'

'Yeah, well, in the meantime, watch your back.

This is your stop. Got some stuff to pick up. See you here tomorrow. Four Potters Mews...Oh and by the way, if you miss lover boy, you know where I am.' He leant over and opened the door for her.

'What are you talking about?'

'For old times sake...if you miss him...I'm still here.' Nixie glowered at him. 'You're an attractive woman Nixie, even if you do fall for unsuitable men.'

'That includes you, so fuck off,' she said, and jumping out, she slammed the door and made the V sign through the window. Mike wound the window down, and shouted as she walked rapidly away, 'You know you want me, Nixie. We can make music together, baby.'

Her flatmate was out. She glanced at herself in the mirror. Nice tan, but so what, she already missed Seb. She dumped her bag on the sofa, made herself a coffee and sat down. Her mind went into overdrive as she obsessively went over their row. Why did it have to end like this? She stood up and began going through her post. Her mobile rang. She picked it up. It was her mother.

'Nixie, welcome back, sweetie. I had a premonition that you might be back. I tried to phone you in Greece, but there was no answer. Are you okay? You're back sooner than you said.'

Nixie did a mental run through of how much she was willing to tell her mother. 'You're right. I am back earlier. We quarrelled.'

Her mother sighed, 'I'm sorry. I know how fond of him you were.'

'Fond... I loved him.'

'You've said that before about other men.'

'Maybe I have. This time it's the real thing. Or it was.'

'So it's serious.'

'As it gets.'

'I thought you two got on so well.'

'Well, we did, especially in bed. That always worked, but not this time.'

'Do I need to know that?'

'Just telling you how it is, or was... Mum, I'm tired. I'll give you a ring tomorrow.'

'I'd like you to come home for a few days. There's someone I want you to meet.'

'Who?'

'Rose.'

'Did you say Rose? The Rose? Rose from your past...? But you only saw her a few months ago.'

'Yes, but it wasn't for long. I'd said she could visit when next she's in the UK, so she called me up. She's at a conference. I'm pleased, Nixie. More than pleased and I'd like you to meet her.'

'Mum, I can't take that in. I've only just got back. It's been hard and I need to sleep. I'll ring later. Sorry.'

'Well, come home soon, it's been a while since I saw you.'

Nixie sighed. 'Okay. I'll be in touch.'

She put the phone down. She felt drained. The thought that her mother and Rose were re-establishing contact after all these years was more than she could comprehend. She'd hoped the brief meeting she and Rose had had in London would be enough, but apparently not. She distrusted Rose. She'd been her mother's joint accomplice. She'd helped her to hide the baby after she'd snatched him, and a good friend would surely have talked her out of it.

Now, on top of everything, she'd have to deal with meeting her, whereas what she felt now was devastation. She had nothing to give. The breakdown of her relationship with Seb was all consuming. Everything reminded her of him. She walked into the bedroom and burst into tears, when she saw his tee shirt he'd left behind. She brought it up to her face, then put it down and stared into the distance. Rose was sure to bring back the past for her mother – how she snatched the baby and how she'd kept him with Rose's help.

Had they thought about the impact it must have had on Seb? The whole experience must have been a major disruption in his life. She'd read once that early trauma could permanently damage people even if as adults they had no conscious memory. Maybe that was why he'd broken into their farmhouse at the dead of night. It was as if he wanted revenge and to pay her back, he'd left the giraffe in her mother's bed to frighten her. It was weird. It was horrible

She moodily made herself a coffee, sat down, and prayed her flatmate wouldn't be coming home tonight. The thought of sitting idly chatting about Greece was the last thing on her mind. She pulled off her clothes and threw herself on the bed. Her mobile rang. Irrationally, she hoped it was Seb, but it wasn't. It was an unknown number. She didn't pick up. It was likely to be Bill, and she didn't have the energy right then to speak to him. It went onto voicemail. 'Nixie, it's Bill, call me. a.s.a.p.' Nixie sighed, too late, too tired. She'd call him tomorrow. She fell into a deep sleep, a sleep punctuated by fragments of the row and images of Seb.

She was woken at eight by her mobile was ringing. She grabbed the phone. Bill — again.

'Nixie. Where the fuck have you been? I know you're back. Been trying to get hold of you. Need to see you. Today. Get your arse round her a.s.a.p. The usual place.'

'What's it about?'

'You think I'm going to tell you? If I want it broadcasted, I'll put it out as a news bulletin.'

'It's Langhithe, isn't it?'

He rang off without answering.

She dragged herself out of bed, walked across to a desktop computer, and unscrewed the front fascia. It was an old machine, stripped of its electronics, she used as a convenient hiding place for sensitive documents. She removed the photos, the ones sent anonymously to Seb which she'd taken from him and the ones passed onto her by Freda Arnsberg. Then she showered, flung on some clothes, and joined the morning commuters fighting their way across London.

The 'usual place' was a safe house just off Shoreditch High Street. She knew the score. The coffee was awful and she'd had no breakfast, so she bought herself a cappuccino and a cream-cheese bagel from the nearby cafe. Only then, balancing the coffee and bagel in one hand, did she ring the door bell. The door swung open. She walked to the room at the back of the house. Bill was waiting for her and he wasn't smiling.

'Sit down... So, our weary traveller returns.' She didn't answer. 'You've been off the radar. Where were you?'

'I told you. I was going abroad.'

'Abroad. That could be anywhere. Where's abroad?' He eyeballed her. Watching her every response, he said, 'Actually, we know where you were. You were with a certain Sebastian Melbury, also known as Seb Harvey. He's of significant interest to us.' He paused, but since she made no response, he continued, 'I'm not going to waste time.

We have reason to believe that at some point he gained unauthorised access to computer material, with intent to commit or facilitate further offences, namely to insert into the said computer, malware, in the form of viruses, worms and Trojans. We'll charge him once we catch up with him.'

'I know nothing.'

'You're lying.' Nixie pulled off a piece of her bagel, dipped it into her coffee and looked thoughtfully at him. He continued, 'You have no choice. Tell us what you know. That's what you get paid for.' She took a sip of her coffee, her gaze focused on the window but remained silent. 'Look... your silence is pissing me off, well and truly. We have certain rules in this game and you're not playing by them.'

'I haven't been up long. I'm thinking.'

'There's nothing to think about. You're screwing Melbury and by definition, we know from past experience, yours, and others, he'll be telling you stuff, stuff that would be of import to us. Stuff we want to know.'

'He's one of us. Did you know that?' Bill's face was inscrutable. 'Okay, you're not saying. Well, I will. He works for a private security firm. It's a big one. International.' He eyeballed her. 'What precisely do you want to know?'

'Where he is, for a start.'

She shrugged, 'Dunno.'

'Another lie. You do.'

'I'll tell you as much as I do know, if you tell me the score. What's going on? Give me a clue.'

'Fuck you, Nixie. Stop playing hard ball.'

'That's the name of the game. Look, I'm prepared to consider a deal. But before I lay my cards on the table, I have to know more.'

He tapped his biro irritably on the table, then

leant across towards her. 'We've been contacted by security at Langhithe. Thousands have disappeared, they don't know where, and they don't like it. A Trojan was inserted into the invoicing system by a person or persons unknown. We've done our homework. We've come to a conclusion that most probably, it was yours truly. His profile fits.'

Nixie sniggered. 'Looked in cyberspace?'

'It's not funny. As well as that, certain Members of Parliament aren't pleased, like Makepeace, whose invoices, in particular, have been doctored. In fact, he's more than not pleased, he's going to have our guts for garters... so we have to solve it. Otherwise. Cut.' He drew his hand across his throat. 'Which has implications for you.'

'Like what?'

'We won't be able to afford you.'

'Why?'

'Because. Work it out for yourself. We've been watching our little public-school renegade for some time. We've got his number. He's playing both sides against the middle. He can't be trusted. He did a Masters in Computer Security. He's angry. He's out for revenge. He has attitude problems.'

'What's that got to do with it? Is that all?'

'That's enough for us to get the thumbscrews out.'

Nixie stood up and using her hand, swept the crumbs from her bagel onto the floor. 'I've finished breakfast.'

'Good. Pleased to hear it. What about it?'

'I've got to go.'

'You know more than you're letting on.'

'Too right, I do... Are you interested in a deal? Yes or no?'

'Depends on what's on offer.'

‘I need your word first.’

‘Okay. I’ll rephrase it. If I give you this info and you go back on your word, I go to the press. I tell them everything. How the Met operates, the truth, the lies, all blown apart. You’ll be exposed, eaten alive. I can guarantee it.’

He smiled. ‘You’re frightening me. Not. Okay. The info. Let’s hear it, and sit down, you’re making my room untidy.’

‘Right, this is the score. I want you to lay off Seb. I don’t know where he is. Besides there’s other fish to fry. Melbury’s the middleman, the other two, Makepeace and Fortescue, are Honourable Members of Parliament but they use their office and contacts to instigate fraud on a grand scale. Money is being siphoned off in shed loads from Langhithe Nuclear Power contracts and that’s where you need to look.’

‘How do you know this?’

‘I know it, I have contacts, but to continue, that’s government money, taxpayers’ money as the Tory press never tire of telling us. But financial corruption is one thing, bribery another, and, where’s there’s bribery, blackmail is not far behind.’

‘Bribery?’

‘Sweeteners.’

‘Like what?’

‘Like the sexual use of young girls as part payment for contracts.’

‘Evidence?’

Nixie picked up her backpack, drew out the A4 envelope and handed it over to Bill. ‘Photos. I can’t say where they’re from, or who they were sent to, but, take a look.’

He opened the envelope, took out the photographs, and silently flicked through them:

Fortescue with Makepeace dining together in a London restaurant, Fortescue in a pole-dancing club, and entering a flat in the Barbican, a place known to the police for the adherents of sexual-masochism. Finally, a series of images: Makepeace with a very young girl.

Bill placed them face down on the table and looked intently at Nixie. 'These turn my stomach. I've seen enough. How old is the girl?'

'Don't know. She looks early teens to me.'

'Same as my daughter. And he's how old?'

'Sixties, I'd say.'

'Bastard... Where did you get them?'

'I said person or persons unknown.'

'Who?'

'I don't know, but if I did, I still wouldn't say. They came from two different sources, with two different motives, for all I know. The press know about them. Copies were sent to various investigative journalists. But they can't be used. They've been gagged.'

'How come?'

'When Fortescue and Makepeace got to know of them, they immediately went to Court. Counsel argued publication wasn't in the public interest, and it was a "breach of their privacy". The application was successful. Based on that famous case... you know the one, where a well-known businessman liked pretending he'd been a naughty boy at school before he had sex with the matron.'

'Who's the girl?'

'Her name's Imogen. Known to Makepeace since she was twelve. She lives somewhere near Aldeburgh, or did, until he got his hands on her. Suffolk Coastal, includes Aldeburgh... You get it?'

'I don't need a geography lesson. I do, but who's

the source of this info?'

'I just said. The answer's the same. Person or persons unknown.'

'Seb Melbury?'

'I didn't say that.'

'We know that lover boy's home is in Lavenham, and that Aldeburgh happens to be within driving distance. Also, there's an outstanding assault perpetrated on Makepeace at Aldeburgh. Assailant unknown, or was. Coincidence, isn't it? Maybe our Seb could help with the inquiry.'

'You gave me your word.'

He stared intently at her. 'So I did.'

'I've given you enough information to give them the run around.'

He smiled. 'Well, all that remains is for me to say, thank you. Your money will be in your account.'

'So, you can afford me, after all.'

'A joke, Nixie.'

'What's your next step?'

'You'll see. The photos, please.' He put his hand out.

'I'll get you copies.'

'No copies. I want the ones you just showed me. Pass them over.'

'Don't lose them.'

'As if. They'll come in useful.'

'How?'

'I'll decide later.' He stood up, winked, and said,'Off you go and don't work too hard.'

Nixie remained sitting, then she said. 'That comment is worthy of a complaint.'

'For what?"

'You know "for what". You're a sexist pig.'

'Fuck off, have you lost your sense of humour?' He grinned at her.

She stood up, gave him a look, gestured with her two fingers, and left.

She'd got to the end of the road when she realised her mistake; Bill would have no conscience in releasing the photos to all and any social media platforms if he thought that would help the case. She sighed, it was too late to take them back, but since she'd aimed to protect Seb from prosecution in any way she could, that had been achieved, and for the moment, that pleased her.

— 18 —

Flori was impatiently waiting in the farmhouse for Rose's visit, an event to which Nixie felt increasingly hostile. Watching her mother's excitement rise until she could bear it no longer, she'd eventually told her mother she was going out.

She'd been sitting outside the pub for what seemed hours, watching the tide creep in. It was as its highest now, the boats gently moving back and forth with the water's rhythmic flow. Preoccupied with thoughts about how she'd handle Rose's visit, her mind returned to what she knew about her mother's friendship with her. Over the years her mother had found it difficult to talk about what had driven her to take the baby, and she was still prone to get upset.

When she'd applied to work undercover in the Met, she hadn't been able to keep her mother's past from her employers. She'd been naive; it hadn't occurred to her that her parents would be checked out. But they were, and though they knew her father was an environmental activist, she was still taken on. She'd been given a hard time, asked how she could square working undercover with having had a radical upbringing. She'd said that her father was secretive, but her mother seemed to blot out the reality of her past. It wasn't a proper answer but the questioning went no further.

Today she had to face up to the reality of her mother's friendship with Rose and for whatever reason had come back into her mother's life. There was no avoiding that. It was real and present and she had to deal with it.

'Nixie, what are you doing here?'

Her father's voice. She spun round, her eyes filled with apprehension. She might have guessed he could drop by. It was near to the farmhouse and he often liked a pint before going home.

'What's going on? You look upset.'

'I am,' she said, speaking quickly, driven by anxiety. 'It's Rose. I don't want her here. I'm frightened of what she might do and say to Mum, and what they might do together. She was a bad influence.'

'Nixie, what happened was years ago, when they were still kids.'

'No, that doesn't explain it. Not totally, anyway. I'm about the same age as Mum was when she took that baby, and you wouldn't call me a kid, would you?'

Matt looked serious. 'I'm getting a drink. We need to talk. What can I get you? '

'Nothing.'

Matt gave her a look. 'Okay. I won't be long. Wait here.'

She'd moved along the sea wall by the time he came back, and was staring at the tide as it began flowing out from the harbour and into the sea. 'It's more private here,' she said.

Matt passed her a fruit juice. 'I know you said you didn't want anything, but you might like this. You don't have to drink it.' He smiled. 'It's not compulsory.'

He sat down next to her. 'Okay, tell me what's going on.'

'Have you seen her?'

'Rose? Not yet.'

‘Do you know what’s she like?’

‘Flori said she’s attractive, good sense of humour, off beat.’

‘Off beat. What’s that mean?’

‘Well apparently, she dresses in a particular way. Oh, I don’t know. It’s only what your mother has told me. She’s an anthropologist so, you know, she’s unusual.’

‘How can you earn a living doing that?’

‘She teaches.’

‘Where?’

‘Look, Nixie. This will be the first time I’ve met her and I... ’

Nixie interrupted him, ‘First time... I thought you knew her already.’

‘Nope, never met her before. But what’s bugging you?’

‘I’m scared... that she and Mum will do something stupid, out of order, like they did before.’

‘Like what?’ Nixie didn’t answer. She looked down at her glass and turned it round and round in her hands.

‘You’re being irrational. She sounds totally normal and they plan to just spend time talking, and going for walks.’

‘What will they talk about?’

He sighed. ‘I guess, the usual things women talk about, plus work stuff. I think she’s helping your mother with the paper she’s giving on psychopathy.’

‘How would she know about psychopathy?’

‘She’s an academic, she knows the score...how to give conference papers.’ Nixie stared out to sea. ‘You’re going to have to meet her at some point, Nixie. Face up to your fears.’

‘Why did she want to see mum after all these years?’

'I have absolutely no idea and I'm answering no more questions.' He glanced at her. She was silent. They both stared out at sea. 'Did you know your mother and I met here?'

Nixie turned to look at him. 'You're changing the subject. But I did know, Mum told me years ago. You spent an afternoon by the harbour talking until the weather turned, and then you drove her back to the caravan and stayed the night.'

'She told you that?'

'Yes. Love at first sight, that's what she said.'

'It was.' He fell silent, before he said, 'But it wasn't all straightforward. It took a while before I realised I loved her, and I still do.'

'You're both romantics at heart.'

'Aren't you the same? What's happened to Seb?

'Seb? Surely Mum told you? We split up. In Greece.'

'She did mention it, but not what it was about.'

'He's difficult, too difficult. Personality issues. He could be brutal.'

'I'm not surprised. There was something about him I didn't trust. Not sure what it was. He could be glib and his charm didn't always ring true.'

'No law against charm, is there?'

He sighed. 'No, no law. But I always suspect charm. But I could see in your eyes and his,for that matter, there was something between you. Still... it's a shame, but maybe it wouldn't have worked.'

'It wouldn't have worked. I know that.'

'You sound sure. Give yourself some time. See how you feel after a few months.'

'Too late, Dad. It's over.'

'How's work?'

'Same as, same as.'

'Isn't it time you did a proper job?'

'You know I have a proper job.'

Matt was silent. 'Do I? You've never said what. In fact, if you don't mind my saying, you've always been a tad evasive

'You don't want to know and I don't want to tell you.'

'It's more like you don't want me to know. Actually, I'm intrigued.'

'I'm a carer. It's a career of sorts. I can come and go as I want, and that suits me fine.'

'There's more to your work than that.'

'Like I say, it suits me. You know yourself, some things can't be spoken of.'

'Well, if I can be of any help.' He stood up, ruffled her hair. 'Before you go, what about walking with me up to the headland. We might see an early seal pup.'

'What about your own work?'

'I've done enough for today. Testing sea water can wait.'

Nixie sat in the car for a few minutes before she got out. She walked into the hall, called out she was back, but was met with silence. Her mother must have gone to pick up Rose. The thought put Nixie into a bad mood.

She walked upstairs to the spare bedroom and looked around. Her mother had put a vase of flowers out for her and by her bed she'd placed a selection of magazines, presumably specially chosen. She picked them up, National Geographic, Psychology Today and even Vogue, which filled Nixie with disgust.

She walked across to the window and stood looking out. A car pulled into the driveway. Her mother and a tall, slim woman got out. Nixie pulled away from the window. Her father had said Rose was 'offbeat' but to her eyes, she looked anything but offbeat. If anything, dressed in jeans and navy blue sweater, she looked boringly normal. However, for her mother's sake she decided she'd try to be friendly.

She forced herself to walk downstairs to meet her mother and Rose. Her mother greeted her with a hug and then said, 'This is Rose.'

Rose was smiling and holding out an outstretched hand, she said, 'So you're Nixie. I've heard so much about you from your mother. It's a pleasure to meet you.'

'Thanks, I thought we'd meet one day. It was kind of inevitable.'

Rose ignored her dig. 'I saw Flori when she was pregnant with you, but circumstances intervened.'

'By circumstances, I suppose you mean the Court Hearing and the Court Order?'

There was an awkward silence. She'd embarrassed them, in one fell swoop. Not that that bothered her too much.

'How long have you been here?'

'A week. I'm giving some lectures at my old uni and decided on an impulse I could meet up with Flori. When we met in London a while ago, there wasn't enough time. It's been so long. I phoned your mother, with some trepidation, I have to say, and suggested we met up. She was delighted.'

'Are you allowed to meet each other?'

Rose didn't miss a beat. She gave a tinkling laugh. 'Oh, you mean, because of the unfortunate event in our past? That was years ago. We're both law-abiding citizens now. Wouldn't you say so, Flori?'

'I'd say it was more than unfortunate.'

Her mother spoke sharply. 'Nixie, please.'

Nixie's voice was cold. 'I was merely referring to the truth. Has it occurred to either of you the after effects of what you call the "unfortunate event" might have had on others?'

Rose said, 'Whom did you have in mind?'

Nixie silently observed her posh accent. 'The baby.'

'Nixie, please.' Her mother was looking at her imploringly. 'Let's go into the kitchen and I'll make some tea. Rose, did you bring that cake out of the car?'

'No, I'll get it. I left it on the back seat.' She turned and left the room.

Flori stared at Nixie and said in a low voice, 'What's got into you? Why so rude?'

'I don't want her here. She's trouble.'

'Nixie. This isn't like you at all.'

'How long is she staying?'

'She goes the day after tomorrow.'

Nixie turned away from her mother's gaze. 'I'm going up to my room. I'm tired and I need to sleep.'

'Will you come down later and be sociable?'

'I'll try. When Dad's back, I'll come down.'

'I don't know when he'll be back.'

'I do. I saw him. At Solva.'

'Solva? What was he doing there?'

'Talking to me.'

Her mother tightened her lips, said, 'Have your sleep Nixie, and then come down. Maybe by then you'll be in a better mood.'

Nixie shrugged her shoulders and left the room.

She was determined to make the minimum effort to talk with Rose. She would ignore Rose's attempts to be friendly. She felt resentful that Rose and her mother would, most probably, spend hours together in her study talking about the paper she planned to present at the Cardiff Conference. It made her feel excluded and jealous. Fortunately Rose didn't stay long, so after she'd left, Nixie, still preoccupied with thoughts of Seb decided to walk to the cliff path.

She chose the same way across the fields when, three years ago, she'd accompanied Seb back to his campsite. Her mind returned to the row they'd had in Greece. It had been Mike who'd insisted she confront him with their suspicions. He wanted him out of Grassroots, and her arguments that he'd helped Grassroots with his knowledge of computer hacking had got nowhere. She'd agreed in the end, but all the time she'd hoped he'd deny it.

She'd since wondered, if, at some point, she could recruit him to work for the Met. It would be a way of keeping in touch with him, but realistically, Seb's response to her accusations made all thoughts of further work together impossible. How naive she'd been, she thought, to think they could carry on as before. It was true their final afternoon on Karpathos had been tender and sweet, and she was pleased she'd left the note for him, but she had to accept it was over.

Her mother was reading when she returned and looked up as she entered the lounge. 'Are you okay, Nixie? What's wrong? You look upset.' Nixie went across and sat down by her. She unconsciously began to twirl her hair round her finger, a gesture that her mother also did when she was distracted and uncertain.

Her mother said, 'I prefer your hair now it's longer.' Nixie made no comment. 'Would you like something to drink? Coffee or tea?'

Nixie sighed. 'No thanks. Not for the moment.'

'Are you missing Seb?'

'Of course I am.'

Her mother continued to scrutinise her, then she put her book down and said, 'Tell me about it, what happened between the two of you. It was difficult to talk when Rose was here.'

'I was aware of that.'

'You didn't like her, did you?'

There was a long silence until Nixie said, 'Not exactly. It wasn't the right time for me to meet her. I've got a lot on my mind.'

'I'm sorry. It was arranged before I knew you and Seb had split up.'

'You could have cancelled.'

'Hardly. She'd offered to look through my paper, the one I'm reading at the conference. Besides, over the years, I've missed her.'

'I'd have thought you wouldn't want to see her again.'

'Why do you say that?'

'Because... she aided and abetted you when you took the baby and a true friend would have talked you out of it.'

'You're still dwelling on that.' Flori stared at Nixie intensely. 'I had no idea you felt so hostile towards what happened.'

'"What happened." You talk as if it was all outside your hands and you were guided by some invisible force.'

'That's how it felt.'

'You're talking bollocks. You were totally responsible for all your actions.'

'I know that, Nixie. Why so angry? It happened years ago, not yesterday.'

For a split second, Nixie was at the point of spilling out all her thoughts and feelings about her mother's past and its effects on Seb. His moods, his anger, his deceptions, and how he might have been if he'd had a normal upbringing. She stood up and, forcing herself to speak calmly, said, 'I don't know why I'm angry. Maybe it's because I feel ashamed.'

'Ashamed? Of me?'

'Yes, of you, and your past. When I was a child people had heard about you, and they'd stare at me, as if I was a freak like you. All my life I've had to lie because of you.'

Her mother was silent, then she said, 'Nixie, that's one of the most hurtful things you've ever said to me.'

'Well, it's the truth and I'm tired of all the lies.'

'You don't have to repeat yourself. I got it the first time… I just wish you'd told me before how you felt. We could have talked.'

'Talk. You've always been wrapped up in yourself and your books. There's never been space for me.'

'That's not true, Nixie. I'm sorry.' She stood up and walked towards the door.

Nixie ran across and caught her mother by the arm. 'Where are you going?'

'To work. I've got work to do.'

Nixie stared at her mother, her eyes furious, her body tense. 'How can you stand there so calmly, after what I've told you and just say you're going to work?'

'What more is there to say?'

'Your work has always come before me.'

Flori didn't reply. She paused at the door and looked at her daughter. 'Nixie. You're angry, and you're in no mood for us to sort things out. I'm sorry.'

'Yes, you're busy, you've got your work to do.' Nixie's tone was contemptuous. 'What's so important about it?' Silence. 'What you were talking about with Rose?' Flori turned away. 'Well, go on, tell me.'

Flori sighed, 'It's for the conference.'

'And?'

'I've written up certain case studies.'

'Case studies? What case studies?'

'You're bullying me, Nixie. Stop it.'

'I just want to know.'

'It's confidential.'

Nixie turned on her heel and left the room. She pulled on her Gore-Tex and walking boots, and set off towards the sea. She was monumentally angry. She reached the cliff path and walking parallel to the sea, stopped to watch the movement of the water. She continued to a place where the path curved down into a hollow. It was one of her favourite places and as a child she'd sit unseen watching the waves crash in fury against the high cliffs, scattering the sea birds into a grey sky.

Today it was calm, the water moving with the gentlest of swells. She slid down into the hollow and, closing her eyes, listened to the sound of the wind, the sea and the call of the seabirds. This had always soothed her and it still had that effect. She lay for some time thinking about the past few months. She wondered how Seb was and where he was living. Maybe he'd left Greece now. He could be anywhere. What would he do now with his life? He'd been 'outed' as an undercover agent and every protest group would know of him. He'd become an outcast.

Yet, it could happen to her. Normally, she rarely thought about this but since she'd been with Seb, and observed his slips, she'd become aware that she too only had to make one mistake, or be seen somewhere she shouldn't be, and the whole pack of cards would collapse.

Not only did she have to conceal her work from Grassroots, but also her parents and that had always been hard. Her mother had shown little interest, but her father was more inquisitive. She wondered how much he suspected. Sometimes she caught him looking at her intently, but he'd never asked directly. The nearest he'd got to that, was the other day, the chance meeting in Solva. But in the end, he hadn't pushed her for more information, so she could maintain the deception that she worked as a carer.

Why had she taken the opposite view to his politics? She hadn't thought about it until she'd applied to the Met, but they'd focused on this from the start and grilled her at every interview. Their questions put her on the spot. She'd said she didn't agree with her father's ideas or his activism, and that she disapproved of lawbreaking, but she was also curious about the other side and why they held different views. It was easy to pretend to be one of them, she'd said, she'd been brought up in an atmosphere of secrecy so she knew how and when to lie. She'd added it was part of life and everyone did it.

Since then, she realised that some, and she included herself and Seb here, could play both sides at once. But it didn't bother her too much, because whichever way she looked at it, whether working for the State or Grassroots, it was all for a good cause. She glanced at her mobile; it was time to go. She pushed herself up, and began the walk back.

She felt in a better mood. Perhaps she'd been hard on her mother, blaming her for how she felt. It was the break up with Seb that had really upset her. It was still light when she reached home. Her mother's car was in the drive but there was no sign of her, so she must be working. She walked to her office, and stood at the door. Her mother had her back to her and was staring at the screen.

'I'm back.' Flori swung round and gave her a big smile. 'Mum, I'm sorry I said the things I did. I was upset. You know, about me and Seb. The truth is, I'm gutted.'

'I understand, Nixie. It's alright. Do you want to talk it over? I know I asked you before, but maybe that was the wrong time.'

Nixie sat down in the nearest armchair, twirled her hair round her finger and looked thoughtful. 'Thanks, but I don't think so. What will be, will be. It was just one of those things.'

'Nixie, every couple has their ups and downs. Maybe it'll blow over.'

'It was too fundamental for that.'

There was a silence as mother and daughter gazed at each other. 'I'm really sorry, Nixie, for what's happened and I can see how upset you are, but you know, and I can say it now, I didn't really take to him.'

'Why not?'

'He seemed evasive and well, maybe I shouldn't say this, but I suspected his charm.'

'That's what Dad said. But I liked his charm, although he could be moody, that's for sure.'

'I suppose we all can.' Her mother paused, then said, 'Mmm. You know, I've been researching the psychopathic personality? Well, he did have some of those characteristics. It was…'

'Mum, you're pissing me off. I don't want to hear anymore. I'll see you later.'

Nixie stood up and left the room. Once again her mother had angered her. She heard her father's

Land Rover come into the drive. He was the last person she wanted to see. She wasn't in the mood for any further discussions. She went up to her bedroom and flung herself down in her favourite chair. She wanted to leave. All these intrusive comments meant she had to be on her guard all the time. She was tired of having to lie to protect herself and Seb. And if her mother ever found out it had been him who'd broken into the farmhouse, it would for sure, confirm her views that he was psychopathic.

Well, was he a psychopath? The break in was a weird thing to do, by anybody's standards. She'd assumed it was because of his anger with her mother, of being snatched. She didn't doubt her mother would have cared for him to the best of her ability, but even so... her mind drifted away as she thought of what he must have gone through.

Seb had rarely spoken of his own parents. She wished she knew more. Suddenly she felt very irritable with herself; why should she care? It was over between them and she'd never see him again. She stayed in her room, restlessly picking up and reading random books, until she was called down to eat.

She felt preoccupied and disconnected, and although they tried to draw her out, she refused to open up.

'Look, I don't feel like talking. I've just broken up with Seb and it's kind of playing on my mind. That, and other things.'

'Can't you tell us? Maybe we can help.'

'It's best if I sort things out myself. I've decided to go back to London tomorrow.'

'Nixie, I'm worried about you. Why don't you stay a little longer?'

'Well, don't worry. I'll be fine. Give yourself a

break, I'll be back as soon as I've got some stuff sorted.'

The truth was she wanted to escape. For the first time ever she felt claustrophobic in her own home.

— 19 —

The press were in melt down. As the weeks had passed it became increasingly clear the tentacles of financial corruption had spread throughout the government, so much so the Serious Fraud Office had been called in to investigate. But despite the alleged offenders having gone to considerable trouble to cover their tracks, it hadn't been enough. The financial dealings of Makepeace, Fortescue and Melbury were now subject to close scrutiny. Contacting possible witnesses and experts for the prosecution from a range of sources, including the House of Commons, the press, the various administrative offices of the Nuclear Industry, and the financial sector, was, it had been found, time consuming and complex.

The SFO with their staff of lawyers, forensic accountants and computer security personnel had a long and extensive history in scything a path through the thicket of financial obfuscations. They knew the email tip offs from Fortescue, the trail of inflated invoices drawn up by Makepeace, the orchestration by Melbury as bribery-broker in chief, for what they were — fraud, bribery and corruption. But even so, it took months of intensive investigation before enough evidence had been gathered of the collusion, the kickbacks, and the illicit exchange of money and sexual services, for the SFO to make public their intent to prosecute.

Behind the big players were the hangers-on; these were the small fry who, like the remoras clinging for sustenance to the sharks in the high seas, had attached themselves to the principal financial predators. They too realised, it was time to go it alone. But there was no escape; they, like everyone else, had been dragged into the financial dragnet before the SFO moved on to the next stage.

Witnesses and experts for the prosecution were contacted. The photographs posted to Seb, shown by him to Nixie, who passed them onto Bill, from whence they were released to the press, were just part of the SFO's case. The SFO was also following the paper chase between Makepeace, Fortescue, various construction companies and certain other government departments. As for Melbury, it was by now common knowledge that his particular contribution lay in lining up bribes and sweeteners.

Nixie followed all these developments from a distance. It was obvious to her that Bill had ignored her strictures not to release the photos; but he'd got away with it without some outraged MP threatening court action for breach of privacy. Probably, she thought, because it suited somebody high up, but she was under no illusion. At some point, her relationship with Seb would put her in the frame and it was only a matter of time before she was contacted.

She didn't wait long. It was a mid-afternoon when she received the call, but it wasn't from the SFO, as expected, but from Bill. She'd just attended a Grassroots' operational meeting and had returned to her flat, when he rang. He wanted to see her immediately, but the address he gave was different from the usual one.

Situated near the Houses of Parliament in Victoria, it was a flat in one of the old Peabody

Estates and, as with the other safe places she'd visited, it merged in with the rest of the properties surrounding it. Only the metal strip running round the fortified, exterior door, indicated it might be different; its use more typical of areas of high deprivation, rather than the affluence of South West London. She rang the bell and while waiting for the door to be opened, looked round for the hidden security cameras. She couldn't see any, but that didn't mean they weren't there.

Bill opened the door and after a cursory greeting led the way to a room at the back of the flat. He gestured for her to sit down. Two folders lay on the table in front of him. He looked serious. There were none of his usual pleasantries. She glanced around. The room was painted white, pot plants had been placed on the balcony, and it was furnished sparsely with Ikea type furniture.

She looked with at him with some curiosity. 'So what's with the new venue?'

'It's convenient.'

'There's more to it than that. What's going on?'

'I'll come straight to the point. You're aware of the SFO's investigation into Makepeace et al?'

'I am. It's all over the papers like an outbreak of measles.'

'What I'm about to say is highly confidential. There's a witness missing. The young girl in the photos you gave me, we need to speak to her. We have no idea where she is, but it's essential she's found.'

'How am I supposed to know where she is?'

'Through your lover boy, Seb Harvey.'

'Ex lover. He's an ex. Anyway, putting that aside, how would he know?'

'We know Makepeace was with the girl in the

dunes at Aldeburgh and it was highly likely Seb who gave him a good kicking. We have two separate witness accounts. One, he was seen walking away with her. Two, he was with her in his car... then it goes cold. We're assuming he knew her and that it wasn't a random attack. What do you know?'

Nixie silently took this in. She hadn't known for sure about Seb's role in the attack, but it made sense. 'All I know is what he told me, which was very little, that he knew her, and that she was an adopted daughter of friends of his parents.'

'And?'

'He felt sorry for her.'

'Did he give a name?'

'Nope... he just said, she'd been got at by Makepeace.'

'We've got plans for Makepeace – we've got him on the fraud, but not the sexual exploitation. For that, we need a witness... like the girl. All possible leads have been followed up, but Makepeace has been advised by some smart-arsed lawyer to keep his mouth shut. We also know several girls have gone missing in Aldeburgh the last year, including her. So something is going on. The Suffolk coastline is right opposite mainland Europe. We suspect traffickers. It's under surveillance, but if Seb knows anything more about the girl, which might help us... we'd be back in business.'

'What do you expect me to do?'

'We want you to track him down.'

'I've told you. It's all over between us. I haven't seen or heard from him for a long time.'

'That's your problem.'

'It's also yours, because I haven't the faintest idea where he is.'

'He owes us.'

'For what?'

'For not leaning on him. The hacking. Remember?'

'I'm sure that suited you. The Met does no favours, unless there's something in it for them. Anyway, it makes no difference, since I don't know where he is.'

'That's because you don't want to know. Where did you last see him?'

'Greece.'

'Where in Greece?'

'An island.'

'Well, start there.'

'Do you realise there's hundreds of Greek islands, many totally uninhabited and besides, it was some time ago – like a year or so.'

'I don't give a shit. I know you well enough, Nixie. If you put your mind to it, you'll find him.'

'Maybe, but what if I don't want to?'

'Your problem. Get over it. You have a job to do.'

They sat in silence, eyeballing each other. Bill leant forward, opened one of the folders lying in front of him, pulled out several photos, lined them up neatly, and then pushed them across the table to Nixie. 'Maybe these will help.'

Nixie took the photos and looked at each one closely.

They showed a riot, a large, angry, crowd, out of control. Cars had been turned over, some torched, and lay burning and abandoned along the road. Windows of official-looking buildings had been smashed with bricks and anything else that came to hand. More images showed tear gas and water cannons directed at the protestors, who in an effort to hide their identity, had wrapped scarves round their faces.

In a series of dramatic close ups, the camera focused on one man in particular. With his arm raised high, he was pictured throwing a Molotov cocktail at a government-building window. Then he ran, pursued by two police officers dressed in full riot gear, one of whom grabbed him round the legs, pushed him onto the ground and in the grip of the two police, subjected him to what looked like a brutal assault.

Other demonstrators piled in to defend him, while others attacked the police. The man struggled free, staggered to his feet, pulled off his scarf, and with his eyes streaming from tear gas, noticed the camera. He gave the V sign.

Nixie put the photo down. 'Impressive. Okay. Yeah, that's Seb. Where were these taken?'

'Impressive. I don't think so. Try being a member of the riot squad in the middle of that mob. Where do you think it is?'

She shrugged. 'By the look of the city and the riot police, I'd guess Athens?'

'Right. The Greek debt crisis and the subsequent anti-austerity demonstrations, and, as you can see, the Greek police, unlike ourselves, don't pussy foot around.'

'Who took them?'

'Can't say.'

'Who's Seb working for now?'

'No idea, but that's not what we're interested in. What we want from him is some contact with the girl, and any information she can give about Makepeace – which means a trip to Athens.'

'I don't speak Greek.'

'Neither does he, but it hasn't stopped him getting involved.'

'One small problem... he doesn't know I work

for you.'

'He doesn't need to know.'

'Really... so how am I supposed to explain why I'm there?' She stared at Bill, before she spoke again. 'I can't do it.'

'Why not?'

'Because, if I find him, I'll have to say I want us to get back together again, otherwise why would I be in Athens –that's the only thing I can say if that's where he is – and it's a lie.'

'Lying isn't usually a problem for you, so what's with your reluctance with the truth, that you work for the Met?'

'Don't want to. He'll hate me forever.'

Bill stared at her thoughtfully, then tapping his pen on the table, he said, 'I'll make a coffee.' He disappeared into the kitchen.

Nixie walked across to the window. It overlooked the corridor running outside the flats and was made with one-way glass. She knew this because a woman passing by didn't appear to see her, even though she was standing close. She returned to where she'd been sitting, just as Bill placed a coffee in front of her.

He sat down, and looked questioningly at her. 'Well?' he said.

'I don't know. I'm not sure the best way to go about it, and there's also the small matter of what I say to Grassroots. I can't just up and go to Greece without giving some kind of explanation.'

'If you want my opinion, which admittedly you haven't asked for, I think the love angle is the best.'

'Love angle? What love angle?'

'Right, everyone knew you two were running around together, so it would be no surprise if you said you wanted to get back together again, and went to find him. It's what women do.'

'Spare me the stereotyping.' She paused, then said, 'I have another idea... I could use the personal angle for Grassroots, but as far as Seb goes, I could tell him who I'm working for, and then ask whether he'd be up to working undercover for the Met.'

'Are you having me on?'

'Nope, I'm serious.'

'Don't see the point.'

'Everything's above board and he'll know the score.'

'He wouldn't have a snowball's chance in hell of being taken on. He's virtually gone AWOL.'

'I couldn't care less. It's not whether he might or might not be taken on, that's not the point, it's more about getting his trust by making a case for why I'm there.'

'I'm not interested in that. All I need to know is what he knows about the girl and Makepeace.'

'You have no idea do you?'

'Of what?'

'Of how to get somebody to open up.'

'I'll leave that to you, Nixie. You can do and say what you like, as long as you get your arse into gear and move. We want to know who she is and where she is. End of story.'

Nixie stood up. 'Okay. I'm going. You get the money into my account. I'll be on a plane to Athens.' She'd got to the door when she had another thought. 'What if he won't play ball?'

Bill smiled. 'He has no choice. If he obstructs police investigations I, personally, will make his life hell.'

'How?'

'Wouldn't you like to know?'

'Well, yeah, I would. It'll also help to make

him see some sense – in the event he refuses to cooperate.'

'Considering he's your ex lover, your hardness is impressive.'

'It's my job. I've learnt to develop it. So to continue... what's the crack?'

'Melbury is Seb's father and there's no love lost between them. It was Seb who posted on the emails, thus dropping his own father well and truly into the shite.'

'Melbury is Seb's father?' Nixie's voice rose with surprise.

'That's what I said.'

'Incredible. How do you know?'

'Courtesy of the SFO. They investigated who'd posted the emails. They figured it had to be someone with a major grudge, and whoever it was, would have more info pertaining to the fraud. They discovered it was him.'

'How did they work that out?'

'Forensic evidence – the envelope, matching the saliva, and the handwriting. The rest followed, logically. Melbury lives in Lavenham. Aldeburgh is fairly close by. Seb spent the weekend in Lavenham while Melbury was away with his missus. It was the same weekend the emails were posted and Makepeace was attacked in Aldeburgh. We liaised with Seb's company and they confirmed what we suspected. Melbury is his father.'

'Christ. Seb must hate his father.'

'That's bleeding obvious.'

'So, in the event of non-compliance, what do you plan to do?'

'Tip off the press. They'll have a field day. I can see the headlines already. "Rich kid cops father".'

'That's evil. It's psychological warfare.'

Bill shrugged. 'The means justify the ends. Not so evil as the game Makepeace is playing... so see what you can do.'

Nixie had been in Athens for just over a week and had spent the first few days getting to know her way round. She irritably opened the international edition of the Guardian and looked up the temperature: thirty degrees plus in Athens, twenty-two degrees London, eighteen in Pembrokeshire. She sighed. How did the Athenians survive this heat? It was stifling. It was unbearable. Her clothes stuck to her. It felt like she was living in an open oven.

Today, she was in the locality of Exarchia. She reasoned that if Seb lived anywhere, it would be here. Known for its history of opposition to the conventional, political system, its multiculturalism, its anarchic politics, its militancy and its street art, it was a no-go area for the establishment. In 2008, following the crash, and the subsequent street protests, its fame spread world-wide. A fifteen-year-old protester by the name of Alexander Grigoropoulou was shot dead by the police. It was an event which triggered days of violent and destructive rioting and his name and identity were now permanently commemorated on many of the buildings. Today, however, the streets were quiet, possibly due to the visible presence of the police, many dressed in full riot gear and apparently ready for the first sign of trouble.

Sitting in one of the casual pavement coffee shops, just off Exarchia Square, she'd spent some time reflecting on what was known about Makepeace, Melbury and Fortescue. She'd concluded it was safe to assume they all three were crooks and fraudsters, but Makepeace's twisted interest in the sexual exploitation of young girls, so far, had been kept under wraps. She was under age, so the press, ostensibly, had conformed to the legislation to keep her out of the public eye which meant that as far as the general public went, she was unknown. But what Seb would know about her, or where she was, remained to be seen.

She had no idea how she could track him down. The memories of their last bitter row and their final hours together before they parted was as vivid as if it had happened yesterday. Until she actually met him, she wasn't sure what she would say. She glanced up; a young woman had squeezed past her and sat down at the next table. Dressed in jeans and carrying a couple of books which she placed on the table in front of her, she began reading a typed, written paper, drinking her coffee at the same time. Nixie quickly assessed her as a student.

This was the type of opportunity Nixie had been trained for, namely how to make contact with the locals. Wasting no time, she smiled, and said, 'Excuse me, but do you speak English?' The girl looked up and nodded. 'I'm looking for the Quinta Hostel. Would you mind pointing me in the right direction?'

'Do you have a map?'

'I've lost it, I need to buy another.'

'You don't need to do that. It's not far.'

'Thank you. I haven't yet got my head round your alphabet.'

'It takes a while. Are you from the UK?'

'Yeah.'

'London?'

'Yes, ever been there?'

'Yes, I was at the LSE on an Erasmus exchange. I loved it. I want to go back.'

'Well, your English is good.'

'Thanks. I practise whenever I can. The hostel isn't far. If you wait, I'll take you.'

'You're very kind.'

She laughed. 'Not really, I just want to use my English.'

'That's fine by me. I'll go and pay for the coffees, while you finish. My name's Nixie, by the way.'

'I'm Kloe, spelt K.L.O.E, not the English way.'

The girl was waiting for Nixie when she came out, and led the way past the secondhand bookshops, the cooperative cafes advertising meeting rooms, and shops selling new and secondhand CDs. Many of the walls were painted with the bold, stark colours of street art, the graffiti of protest, which seemed to visually shout with the energy and the spirit of resistance.

'Exarchia must be an exciting place to live.'

'It is. Exciting at its best, but dangerous at its worst. Everyone has a story to tell about riots and protests. But things can blow up at any moment. It's like living in a powder keg, particularly since 2008. You know, after the virtual collapse of the global economy. Since then, the locality has attracted all the politicos and the anarchists, and they're really militant.'

'Really.'

'Yeah.' Kloe stopped and looked at her. 'Do you mind telling me why you're here? You're well off the tourist trail and, if you don't mind me saying, you don't look the type.'

'Type?'

'A politico.'

'Well, actually I am political, and I'm looking for someone in particular.'

Kloe looked wary. 'Who? Who are you looking for?'

‘A Brit by the name of Seb... he was in trouble with the police in the UK. Political stuff, not crime, and he’s on the run. I need to find him. He’s likely to belong to one of the anti-austerity groups, which is why I’m here, not that that’s the main reason, I’m...’

Kloe interrupted her. ‘For all I know, you could be the police.’

Nixie glanced quickly at her. She was astute and she’d have to be careful.

‘If that were true, I’d use the usual cross-border channels of communication between the police, instead of hanging around here looking for him. No, this is strictly personal. I met him at a demo, the one outside the bank in the City of London. It was part of an international day of protests. You must have heard of it. We were activists and became lovers, but we fell out. It was over a year ago now, and it sounds stupid, but I’m still in love with him and, well, I want to see if we can get it together again. That’s why I’m here. So having heard of Exarchia, I thought there was a good chance he might be here.’

Kloe seemed to relax and looked sympathetically at her. ‘I know what you mean. We’ve all been there and done that. Do you have a photo of him?’

‘I do. I keep them in a little wallet. I’ll show you. Let’s sit down there.’ She pointed to a randomly placed bench on the street, took out two photos and passed them to Kloe. ‘These were taken in Karpathos. It was our first day together, and taken at the sea front, and this was after the huge row we’d had. I was about to catch the ferry. I was gutted and it suddenly occurred to me I might never see him again. I asked him if I could take a photo. He said yes, but I could see he wasn’t too keen.’ Nixie looked into the distance. ‘The row we had... it was about lying. I felt I couldn't trust him, but I didn't want to split up, but he said it wasn't possible after what I'd said. That was the last time I saw him.'

Kloe stared closely at the photos, then handed them back. 'Maybe it was for the best. He looks familiar, so perhaps I have seen him before, but where, I have no idea.'

'Is there anyone you could ask?'

'Sure, plenty. There can't be that many Brits in Exarchia who live round here and are also politically active. Does he speak Greek?'

'Not as far as I know.'

'Okay, look, I'm going to have to go. I've a tutorial. Can I get in touch with you, if I hear anything?'

'Thanks. I'd really appreciate your help. Here's my number.'

'I'll do my best. Ciao, Nixie, but take care and watch who you speak with. The place swarms with informers. Some of them are undercover cops.' She walked off, but immediately turned round and said, 'I forgot. Keep going down this side of the Square, turn left and you'll get to the Quinta.'

Three days later, Kloe called her. She had some information and asked to meet her at the same coffee shop where they'd first met. Nixie arrived early and waited with some trepidation for her to arrive. She was late, in fact so late Nixie was beginning to give up on her, but when Kloe did arrive, she was accompanied by another woman. She flung herself down next to Nixie.

'Sorry we're late, Nixie. This is Lydia. She's lived here for five years and works in the Community Cafe down the road. She knows the score and if anyone's new in the area, she's the first to know.'

Lydia smiled at Nixie. She had a broad, friendly smile, long brown wavy hair, deep brown eyes and well defined eyebrows. She held out her hand to Nixie. 'Hi, Nixie, good to meet you. Kloe tells me you're looking for someone by the name of Seb. Well, I might be able to help.'

'If you can, that would be great.'

'No worries. Let's have a look at the photos that you showed Kloe.' Nixie handed them over. 'Yeah, I know him. Seb Elliot.'

'Elliot? Are you sure? Not Harvey?'

'Elliot was what he was known as round here. He's definitely the one I know. He took up with some rich girl called Zanthe, a student at the university. An architecture student. She's leftist, with anarchistic sympathies. I heard she came from a rich family on Spetses, and they met at a political meeting run by Syriza. She's good. Fiery, militant, but also very beautiful.'

Nixie felt sick in the stomach. She looked down at her hands. Kloe noticed. 'Hey, Nixie, don't look like that. It may just be a fling.' Turning to Lydia, she said, 'Seb was her lover. They fell out, but she'd been hoping they'd get it back together again.'

Lydia said, 'Well, you win some and you lose some. Sorry to bring bad news.'

Nixie shrugged. 'I'll get over it. When did you last see him?'

'Maybe four months ago? He was with Zanthe, and I heard on the grapevine she was going to introduce him to her family.'

Nixie stood up. 'I really appreciate your help, but I've got to go.'

'So soon. Where are you off to?'

'Dunno, think I might walk around a bit. See the sites.'

'You look upset. Why don't you meet up with us later? Don't let it get you down. He's just a man, after all.'

Nixie hesitated, then smiled. 'You're right, but he was special to me. I need to walk, get my head straight. Where shall we meet?'

'What about somewhere different? Like City Zen, they make good coffee. Say, this evening, round about eight?'

'Okay. See you there, and thanks.'

Nixie walked away. She was devastated. She reminded herself she was in Athens for work and that, despite how she felt, she still had to find Seb. Knowing he'd hooked up with a beautiful young woman, and it was serious, hurt. Maybe his relationship would be temporary and just a holiday romance. Except he wasn't in Athens on a holiday, he was here because he was on the run. So why was he using his Elliot name, instead of Harvey, as he did back in the UK? None of it made sense.

She continued walking, oblivious to the traffic noise and her surroundings, her head down, deep in thought. The stuff Bill told her about Seb being the whistleblower; must have been him. He must hate his father and felt let down not only by him but by both his parents, so it made sense he'd been the one who'd released the incriminating documents to the press. He'd have known where to look for them and he had the perfect motive, revenge. Revenge because his parents had been negligent the night he'd been snatched.

It also made sense what he'd said about Imogen, the girl in the photos. She might have been the adopted daughter of friends of his hated parents, but maybe he identified with her. He felt like him, she didn't belong, and that made him feel protective. She wondered how much of this Bill knew, but she'd take a bet on it, even if he did, he'd have no interest whatsoever in understanding him or his motives.

She walked randomly through the city streets, until she came across a travel agency, which brought her to a halt. Lydia had said Zanthe came from Spetses, so wherever Zanthe was, it was likely Seb would be too. That's where she should go next. Spetses would be her next port of call. She swung in and booked a ferry ticket to Spetses, before returning later to meet Kloe and Lydia at City Zen. She said nothing of her plans to them. The following day, she caught a bus to the port of Piraeus and took the ferry to Spetses.

— 20 —

Spetses, a picturesque island, was much favoured by the Athenians because of its closeness to the mainland, had once been the residence of the British author John Fowles. It had also been the setting for his novel The Magus, but apart from this and the startling absence of vehicles, which for the sake of preserving its aesthetic appearance, had been banned, Nixie knew very little about the island.

After leaving the hydrofoil, she took a look around. The island's affluence was immediately apparent. Neo-Classical mansions lined the harbour and facing them an impressive array of luxurious super-yachts. Each of them equipped with every technological aid possible, including the presumably essential ocean-going marine radar. By way of contrast, moored close by and bobbing on the water, were the small wooden painted boats of the local fishermen.

Sitting on a harbour wall, she pulled out the instructions she'd downloaded off the net and after orientating herself, she walked away from the harbour and into the narrow pebbled passageways towards the small apartment she'd rented.

Part of a larger house, it was owned by two artists. It had been advertised as having wi-fi, views of the bay and as being suitable for an independent traveller, which suited Nixie fine. She'd understood by that she'd be left alone. Simple and rustic, the courtyard was painted white, the windows picked out in an azure blue. Plants tumbled out of urns, cascaded and wound round the walls and windows, generally showing a total disregard for any difference between the inside and the outside. This also applied to the little geckos, one of which, she subsequently discovered, had taken up residence in the shower room.

The owners had been out when she arrived, but had left the key under a small plant pot by the front door. Conveniently and thoughtfully they'd also left a bottle of the local white wine chilling in the fridge. After unpacking what little she'd brought with her, she opened the bottle, poured herself a large glass, and sat down at the small table and considered her next move.

Before she'd left Athens, Lydia and Kloe told her they'd further discovered that Zanthe's father headed up an architectural practice, which was based somewhere near the harbour. This meant it would be comparatively easy to hang around close by and watch the comings and goings and at some point, Nixie reasoned, she might see Zanthe and Seb. It was, after all, a small island and since Zanthe was also an architectural student and presumably in the same line of business as her father, it was highly likely she would drop into his office – hopefully accompanied by Seb.

Just as she thought this, her mobile rang. She sighed, it could only be Bill. She picked it up. 'You don't have to ring me every day. I've told you, when and if I find him, you'll be first to know.'

'I'm giving you moral support.'

'Thanks, but I don't need it.'

'What's your accommodation like?'

'Great. Love it but look, I've just arrived. I'll be in touch.'

She put the phone down, picked it up again, and

switched it off. She'd walk down to the front by the old harbour.

The harbour was buzzing. Noisy, lined with outdoor tavernas and restaurants, it was full of tourists and residents. She chose a smaller and quieter taverna, further away from the main area, ordered a coffee and baklava, and glanced again at the address of Zanthe's father's practice. Although in English, she had no idea where to start looking, but he had to have a website, which would give directions as to how to get there. She'd wait until she got back to her accommodation to check that out, but in the meantime explore the area, get a feel for the place and how the streets connected.

She looked up. An older man was sitting fairly close by. He was tanned, dressed in chinos and a navy tee shirt. He seemed to be staring at her. She was immediately wary and looked away to avoid his gaze, and as soon as she'd finished her coffee and baklava, she stood up, paid, and left. Glancing frequently over her shoulder, to make sure she wasn't being followed, she walked randomly into the small town and spent the next hour looking at the highly expensive gold and silver jewellery displayed in the brightly lit shops.

While she'd been out, the owners had left a note, saying they'd drop by tomorrow late afternoon to check everything was okay, but not to stay in especially for them. This gave her enough time to check out Zanthe's father's address beforehand, but if she couldn't find it, she'd ring them on the number they'd given her. Meanwhile she'd start some preliminary research. She tapped in his name on her mobile and immediately a website address in English appeared. Nikos Mataxas advertised himself as specialising in the design of non-commercial properties and the renovation of the old. Suitably arty black-and-white photographs illustrated some of the projects he and his associates had completed, but there was also a map of how to find his office.

So far, so good. Nixie felt a rush of excitement. She had to find out there and then where his office was situated. Again she left her apartment and, following the map she'd downloaded, she eventually found it. It was situated in one of the narrow, cobbled streets off the old harbour, with a convenient outdoor coffee shop close by, which she'd use as a base to watch the comings and goings.

It wasn't going well. Five days later, despite hanging around in the coffee shop in the vicinity of his architectural practice and observing the numerous visitors to his office, there had been no sign of Seb, or of anyone who might have been Zanthe, and she was bored. She was also sick of drinking coffee. She rang Bill for advice.

'I can't believe I'm hearing this. You know the score. Be pro-active, use your imagination, take some risks.'

'Any ideas?'

'Nope, that's your call but time's running out. I'll ring you later, but get on with it. You're not on holiday.'

This last comment annoyed her. But the following day, swallowing her irritation and in a mood of defiance, she walked into Zanthe's father's office. There was no sign of a receptionist. A pile of brochures had been left out on the desk and after waiting five minutes for someone to appear, she took the liberty of helping herself to one of them to take back to her accommodation. There she'd go through it carefully.

One project, in particular, stood out. Stunningly beautiful, it showed a newly built, long, white building, combined with what was described as the 'vernacular' of the old. It stood on one of the Spetsion headlands; and had uninterrupted views over the Saronic sea. It was so different from anything she'd ever seen before, she was fascinated. She looked at it again and again, wondering whether it was Zanthe's father who had overseen this particular renovation. It was atmospheric, a triumph of the best of modernist sculpture. The stark black-and-white photography, focused on the interplay between the shadows of the building and the brilliant white light of its walls. She had to see it, and gradually it came to her how she could use her curiosity with this house to locate Seb. She formulated a plan. It was simple and straightforward, and she'd execute it the following day.

It was midday, and searingly hot as always, and she'd just finished her usual coffee at the usual taverna. She paid her bill, walked across the square, and entered the cool, air-conditioned offices of Nikos Mataxas. This time there was a receptionist. She was sitting behind her desk, staring at her computer screen. She looked up and, in English, she said, 'Can I help you?'

'Good morning. Yes, I was wondering if you could help me. My parents have been visitors to this island for some years and they're about to retire. They've always wanted to buy an old property, and do it up. So they've asked me if I could check out some properties. I'm a kind of advance guard.'

'What kind of property are they interested in?'

'Something in a village, or even along the coast... they're open to ideas.'

'Do you know what kind of budget they have?'

Nixie shrugged. 'Sorry, they haven't said. It all depends on the property. If they fell in love with it, then they'd find whatever was necessary… Sorry to be so vague.'

'Are they here now?'

'No. They had some business to finish in the UK. That's why I'm here. I offered to help. I'm not sure where to start, to tell you the truth. I did look at your website…' Her voice trailed away and she smiled expectantly at the receptionist.

The receptionist paused, as if she wasn't quite sure how to respond, then she said, 'Just a minute. Nikos is in, I'll ask if he'll see you.'

She stood up and disappeared. While she was gone, Nixie idly looked at the photographs of Greek island architecture displayed against the white-washed rough wall. They were dramatic in the simplicity of their design, but apart from these, mounted on a small table at waist height, was the tiny replica of a building. It showed the intended finished project of work in progress. Nixie bent over it, fascinated, and for the moment was lost in admiration at the architectural detail.

'Nikos suggested they take a look at this.' Nixie turned round. The receptionist was standing right by her and handed her a copy of the brochure she had picked up earlier. 'This might give them a better idea of what they want. Then if they're still interested, they can get back in touch and I can make an appointment for them to see him.' She smiled. 'As you'll see, there's a range of styles.'

'Thank you very much.'

She stood waiting as Nixie began flicking over the pages. She came to a stop. It was the villa she'd noticed before, the one set on the headland, with views over the sea. 'Oh, a friend of mine told me about this place. It's so beautiful. Any chance of seeing it? My parents would love it. Would that be possible?'

The receptionist peered over her shoulder. 'Yes, it is beautiful. It's Nikos's present to his daughter.'

'A present...?' She looked at the receptionist with amazement. 'Wow, lucky for some.'

'He's been working off and on it for years now, ever since she was tiny. It's a hobby of his. It was almost derelict when he took it on, but he wanted to pass on something to her, something of his work, and of his passion for renovating and preserving the Spetsion design. When it's finished, he'll enter it in the inter-island architectural competition.'

'It's almost finished then.'

'Just about. What I love is the central courtyard. He's had pebble mosaics laid down. The style goes back centuries, but we still have a few people on the island that can do this. Their designs are all different. Zanthe insisted that one was of Bouboulina. She's a big fan.'

'Zanthe. Is that his daughter?'

'Yes, his daughter. She takes after her father. She's going to be an architect.'

'So I'm guessing Boulboulina is a woman?'

'Yes, she lived on the island in the nineteenth century. She's our heroine. She inspired the men to fight against the Ottomans. You can visit the museum about her. It's fascinating.' She laughed. 'Zanthe should have been named after her.'

'She sounds like a feminist.'

'She is, she says, I'm keeping her spirit alive in my own way. She's political. She's involved in the anti-austerity movements, you know after the crash. It hit us really hard.'

'Tell me about it. We have our own protests,

especially in the City of London, but you Greeks are more political and militant than the average Brit. But good for Zanthe, I say.'

'It's true, probably because of our history of invasion, but funny you mention Brits because she's met one. He's just like her.'

'And he's a Brit?'

'Yes, they come to the office now and again to see her father. He's as militant as she is. They met on a demo in Athens. They seem very much in love.'

Nixie was silent. She didn't want to know anymore. She felt close to tears. She pulled herself together. 'Well, thank you for all your help. I must go. I'll pass on this information to my parents and I'm sure we'll be back in touch… By the way, your English is very good. You must have lived in the UK for a while.'

'Thank you. I did, I lived in London for years. I was in love with someone, but it didn't work out.'

'English?'

'Yes, he came from Wanstead.'

'I'm sorry about that…but you do have a really good accent.'

'Thanks, I'm over it now.'

By the way, where did you say the house was? You know, the one Nikos has given his daughter. I might take a look at some point.'

'I can ask Nikos if he'd show your parents round, that is, if they're serious about their plans.'

'That's a kind offer. We'll certainly bear it in mind, but it's too soon to say. I was thinking that maybe I could have a look around the area before I speak to them about it.'

'Well, go to the harbour and get one of the water taxis. Ask for the Zogeria beach. It's the other side of the island. It has no tavernas, so take some water.

When you get there, you'll see a path through the pine trees and that takes you very near the villa. You can't miss it.'

'Thanks again. You've been so much help.'

'My pleasure. What's your name – for my records.'

'Ehr. It's Elly. Elly Sanders.'

'Well, maybe see you again, Elly.'

Nixie smiled, shook her hand. Returning to the furnace-like heat outside, she walked back to her apartment. She now knew more, but she didn't want to know about Seb and Zanthe being in love. Could that be true?

A wave of exhaustion passed over her. She lay down on her bed to sleep, but it was impossible. Tortured by images of Seb laughing with Zanthe, she tossed back and forth, until eventually she fell into a fitful sleep. Hours later she was woken from a dream. She was back on Karpathos with Seb. They were in the hills and he was picking fresh figs for her. It had been so real, it took her a minute or two before she was fully awake, and to realise it was a dream. She made herself a coffee and walked down to the harbour to organise a water taxi for the following day. The side streets were thronged with tourists, shopping, talking, and deciding on which tavernas for their next meal. She stopped outside the taverna she'd visited on her first day. The same man she'd seen before was there. He recognised her and greeted her in a friendly way, but she didn't respond and instead looked through him as if he didn't exist. She didn't feel sociable. She sat alone, picking at her food, preoccupied with thoughts of the following day, whether she'd finally meet Seb and if she did, what she might say.

Nixie stood and watched the water taxi disappear from the bay, then turned to look at the beach. Zogeria was one of the most beautiful coves she'd ever seen. It was gloriously remote and peaceful, horse shoe shaped, edged with large rocks which tumbled into the turquoise deep waters. There were few people and most of these lay under the shade of the fir trees, reading, listening to music, or staring into the distance. Only the occasional raucous chatter of the cicadas disturbed the silence.

She walked over towards the trees set back from the water, sat down in the shade and considered her next move. Her first priority was to swim, even before she looked for the path through the woods. Her mind constantly played with what she might say or do, when and if she met Seb. She was under no illusions. Even if she did meet him, she wouldn't say anything about the real purpose as to why she was there. All she wanted him to know at this stage was she was on the island, but what her next step would then be, she had no idea.

How much did Zanthe know? Would she suspect he was working undercover? Was he deceiving Zanthe, the way he'd deceived her? Was he pretending to be somebody he wasn't; a militant politico, opposed to global capitalism, and an environmentalist? Whereas, in actual fact, he was a financial mercenary, with no commitments to any organisation, a free agent, motivated by money to spy on whichever organisation he was asked to investigate.

She glanced towards the water. It was too inviting for her to be brooding on a past relationship. She decisively stood up and, pulling off the white shirt covering her bikini, she ran across the hot sands and plunged into the water. Compared with the heated air of the beach the water was deliciously cool. She swam towards a group of flat rocks she'd seen as the boat had come in and, pulling herself out of the water, lay down on one of them. From there she could see the whole beach.

It was lunchtime and a few people carrying food and drink, looking as if they'd be there for the day, appeared from amongst the trees and settled in the shade. She remembered what the receptionist had said; there was no taverna. All she had was a bottle of water. So either she'd have to look for a taverna up on the headland or wait for the next water taxi to take her back to the harbour. She stood up, plunged back into the water to cool off and then returned to her place on the rock. The rock felt warm on her belly, but the strength of the sun meant it was safe to lie there for only five minutes. She stared out to sea and tired after her bad night, gradually drifted off into a deep sleep.

'You shouldn't lie in the sun. It's bad for you.'

She opened her eyes. His face was close to hers. He was holding onto a rock, and treading water, and smiling. She gathered her thoughts. Her face flushed, she sat up.

'How did you know it was me?'

'The bikini... how could I forget?'

'It's been a long time.'

He pulled himself out of the water and sat by her, his legs dangling in the water.

'So Seb, what are you doing now?'

'I think you know what I'm doing now.' Nixie was silent. 'You need to cover your tracks better, Nixie. Or is it Elly?' He smiled. 'I knew you were on the island. I knew you were looking for me, and I knew at some point our paths would cross.' Still she said nothing. 'So, why are you here? I assume it's not to get back together again.'

'No. I've heard about Zanthe.'

'So you also know it's a committed relationship.'

'Yes, I'd heard.'

'So, why are you here?'

'I'll tell you, soon, but not right now.'

'Don't play games, Nixie... We had something, once, but it's over. I'm determined... history isn't going to repeat itself.'

'What does that mean?'

'No more lies.'

'Lies? Not sure I'm following you.'

'It means being truthful. I'm with a woman I love, and politically, I've changed sides.'

'Can I believe that?'

'I've had a lot of time to think. I've read widely and I've come to the conclusion, I no longer want to be part of this system.'

'So what system is that?'

'The one supporting the privileged few. The one skewed to maintain the status quo. Once I understood how it works, it was simple. I want to fight inequality and global capitalism.'

'Big deal, you've learnt the words but it doesn't ring true.'

'Your prerogative. You taught me a lot, for which I have only gratitude.'

'Why are you telling me this?'

'Why not? I've changed. I thought you'd like to know.'

'If you weren't with Zanthe, I'd be thinking you want us to get back together.'

'I'm in love with Zanthe.'

'Really?'

'Yes really.'

Nixie slowly smiled. 'Sweet.'

‘You’re jealous.’

‘Probably. What of it? I loved you once.’

‘So you said, but a long time ago, you told me you were polyamorous. Remember? So, I assumed, wrongly, it seems, that if that was true, jealousy would be an alien emotion.’

‘Well, there you go, you learn something new every day.’

‘What about you? Are you still with Mike? We were always contenders for your affection.’

‘You always came first.’

‘My turn to say “really?”’ He stood up and stretched his arms above his head. ‘Well, it’s been good to see you. I have to go back. I told Zanthe I was going for a quick dip. She’ll be waiting. Like to swim with me back to the beach?’

‘No, I don’t, but thanks for the offer.’

He looked at her closely, and said, ‘Well, see you around.’ He slid back down into the water, and hanging on to the rock, looked up at her. ‘You know I’ve always fancied you, don’t you? It was good, wasn’t it? What we had once.’

She said nothing. She stood up and, choosing the same rock as he’d used, let herself down in the water and said, ‘At some point, I have to meet up with you. It’s about work and it’s important. When can we fix a time?’

‘What’s it about?’

‘I can’t say. Not now. Give me a time and place.’

He paused, scrutinising her face. ‘Tomorrow. Lunchtime. There’s a taverna called Aptora, it’s where the ferry comes in. It’s popular with tourists and crowded, so it’s easy to blend in.’

‘That’s no good. We could be overheard. I still don’t trust you, whatever you say. You could still be on my case. My apartment’s better. Say tomorrow evening? Nineish? Do you know where it is?'

'I do.'

'Will Zanthe allow you off the hook?'

'Leave it out. She's not like that. I'll see you there.'

He pushed himself off the rock and lay paddling the water on his back, looking across at her. Then switching himself round, he swam rapidly back to the beach. She watched him pick up his towel, wave in her direction, and disappear into the fir trees.

— 21 —

Seb was early, but Nixie made no comment, other than greeting him. She led him through to the courtyard. The table had been placed exactly in the centre primarily because when the long shadows of the evening touched the white walls, the fragrance of the surrounding flowers hung heavy in the air, and she liked that. They sat facing each other.

He glanced round. 'Very attractive. Where did you find it?'

'It was an advertisement.'

She looked across at him, wondering what he was expecting of the meeting and whether he'd told Zanthe he was coming to see her. An image of the two of them swimming naked and then lying on the flat rock came into her head. She felt herself flush.

'What are you thinking?'

'Oh, this and that. Nothing much. Why do you ask?'

'Because you look embarrassed.'

'Well, I'm not, I'm just wondering how and what to say.'

She couldn't say that for the past hour she'd been pacing back and forth and that she had no idea how the meeting would play out, or how she could ask for information on the girl without revealing that she too, was a double agent. Had he really changed sides, because if so, his response would be an unknown quantity? Would he want to support who he'd now see as the enemy? But whatever side he supported, the proposal she'd been tasked to execute meant, for him, there was little room for manoeuvre.

He had to come up with the information on the girl, or face the consequences of his assault on Makepeace, and hacking into Langhithe. If all else failed, she was prepared to play the psychological card. She'd refer to the probable impact on his parents when they were told the whistleblower was their son.

'So why have you asked me here? What's it about?'

His directness took her aback. 'Give me a break, Seb. I will tell you, but... it's a long time since we last met... and it feels a little strange.' He didn't respond. He was closely scrutinising her. 'And don't stare at me, it's making me uncomfortable.' She looked away, aware of the rising background chorus of the cicadas, which competed with the chatter of tourists passing outside.

'My apologies, I was thinking how much a tan suits you.'

She looked at him, unsmiling. 'I'm not interested.'

'In what?'

'Your chat-up lines.' She stood up. 'It's hot. I'm going to get a glass of cold, white wine. Like one?'

'Please.'

She disappeared, returning a few minutes later with an opened bottle and two glasses. She placed them on the table between them, poured out the wine but remained standing a little distance away, nursing her glass, occasionally catching his eye. Right now, she wished she was anywhere, rather than where she was.

'Who else lives here?' He seemed oblivious to her edginess.

'A couple of artists. They live in the main house. I haven't seen them yet.'

'So you have the place to yourself.'

She nodded, took a sip of wine. 'How did you know I was on the island?'

'What do you think?'

'No idea.'

'If you don't know, I'm not telling you.'

'I'm not in the mood for banter' She walked over to a climbing plant, pulled away a tendril pushing its way through a window and turned round to face him. 'I have a gecko in the bathroom.'

He smiled. 'Does that bother you?'

'No, I like it... Did you tell Zanthe you'd be coming here?'

'Not in so many words... I just said I had an old friend to see... Look, I don't want to pressure you, but you said you had a proposition to make. When do you plan to tell me, because, at some point, I have to get back.' Nixie gave him a long, hard look, but was silent. Seb stood up and walked across to her. 'What's so difficult?'

She tapped the side of her glass with her forefinger, waited for it to ping, which it didn't and then said, 'I guess I'm wondering how to tell you, or rather how to ask you.'

'Ask me what?'

She shrugged. He was standing so close to her she thought he was about to make a pass. It crossed her mind she'd feel better if he did, but she pushed the thought away as quickly as it came.

'Shall I tell you what I think it might be?' He put his arm round her and pulled her gently towards him, but she jumped away like a scalded cat. 'Get off me.'

He backed off. 'I see. Well, no problem, Nixie.'

'I thought you were in a commited relationship.'

'That's right. I am.'

She sighed. 'You haven't totally changed.'

'Maybe not, as far as you and I go. We went through a lot together, but leaving that aside, I'll make it easy for you. I'll tell you why I think you want to see me, and it's not about our relationship.'

'Please do.'

He paused. 'After we split up, I got in touch with my handler. I had to. He wanted to know what was going on. I told him everything. I said you knew now I worked undercover. He was concerned. Not about me, but for the consequences – its implications for other agents and projects. He was going to liaise with the Met, tell them my cover was blown... He came back to me, a day later.' He took a step closer and, looking directly at her, said, 'He had something important to tell me.'

She guessed what was coming. She waited, still nursing her glass, her gaze inscrutable, her eyes fixed on him.

'I think you know what that is.' She turned her head away and stared at the vines trailing along the walls. 'He told me you worked undercover.'

There was a total silence, except for the the dying chatter of the cicadas and the muffled, excited talk of the tourists passing the apartment.

'I was surprised, and that's putting it mildly. I was also angry, very angry. I felt betrayed. I'd trusted you. Unfair, irrational, because I'd done the same. But it didn't last... I knew I'd get over it. You have to. Besides, being away from London and living here, in Greece... has put things in perspective.'

He walked over to her and put his arm round her shoulders. 'You look upset...What's wrong?'

She said, 'Is that why you changed sides?'

'Not really. I was thinking, after we'd split up, how much longer could I put up with working undercover? The deception, the lies, watching my step all the time, wondering when there'd be another attempt to kill me. I didn't want to go back. I'd become sick of it.'

'So what did you do?'

'I'd been told I was for the chop. I'd gone AWOL after all, and that's when I decided to stay on in Greece. It was an easy decision.'

'Why didn't you go back into finance?'

'I couldn't stomach it. Finance, the unregulated market – it creates inequality and I'm not talking relatively, I'm talking about absolute poverty. Homelessness, crap education, bad diet, high mortality; scale that up five or ten times in the southern hemisphere and throw in war, for good measure.'

'But it's never going to change. It's human nature.'

'I can't believe you're saying that.'

'I'm a realist.'

'So, does that make me an idealist? What I'm saying is, the rules are fixed to benefit the few. But you know that already...Ironic isn't it? I was employed to spy on the opposition, but they're right. Before, I hadn't connected things. I'd assumed it was inevitable. Then it slowly dawned on me, it's not at all inevitable. Once I realised that, I had to leave.'

'So then what?'

'I gave my notice in. I was called for a debrief, but I ignored it. But knowing as much as I do about the security forces, and with my financial background, I knew I could still be useful. The Greek government is in a mess. The IMF and the EU wants a fall guy, and blame and shame is the name of the game. So I moved to Athens. I took up with the opposition and allied myself with Syriza. It's led by Tsipras and I have the utmost admiration for him.'

'I know very little about Greek politics. Does Zanthe share your views?'

'Yeah, she does. Her family have a history of political involvement.'

'Is that why you were spying on me? For Syriza?'

'What do you think? Put yourself in my position. I knew you were working for the Met. You know and I know the Security Forces work across the European borders.'

'How did you know I was looking for you in Athens?'

'I was tipped off. I was intrigued. There were three possible reasons. I was still useful to the security services, I was wanted for questioning, or it was strictly personal.'

'Was it Kloe and Lydia who tipped you off? Or the receptionist?'

'No, She isn't an informer. It was a chance conversation she'd had with Zanthe. She said a young Englishwoman had come into the office, on behalf of her parents who were looking for property to renovate. She described you, and I put two and two together.'

'Does Zanthe know?'

'About you? A little'.

'Does that include that I'm here?'

'What's it matter? Why do you ask?'

'No reason.'

They were silent for some time. Seb was first to speak. 'So why are you here? You said you had a proposition to make. Does what I've just told you make a difference to that?'

'Not really.'

'"Not really." I'm surprised. I thought you might ask me to join the Met and work for them.'

'Well, you're partly right, but not in the way you probably think.'

'So what is it?'

She stood up suddenly. 'It's almost dark. I'm going to get some candles.'

'I'd like a beer. Have you got any?'

'I haven't, but I can get some. There's a supermarket close by.'

'I'll go.' He stood up and left.

She felt alone, weighted down with responsibility and, to distract herself, she lit some candles, and placed them along the sides of the courtyard. The light glowed through the darkness and tiny insects whirled about attracted by the light.

He returned and glanced round. 'Very pretty,' he said and sat down. He poured Nixie a glass of wine, opened a can of lager for himself, and waited. She was silent, and looked away from him.

Eventually he said, 'So let's hear it. I'm assuming it's still relevant.'

Nixie said, 'I've got nothing to lose. You know all about me now.'

'Yes, I do. You're a game player-and a thief.'

'That sounds hard, what do you mean?'

'You steal identities, hide behind a mask, because without a mask, life's hell – do you get what I'm saying?'

'I do. But that applies to you too.' She paused, took a sip of wine, examined her fingers, stood up and walked over to one of the vines. She pulled away a tendril pushing its way into the bathroom and turning to look at him, said, 'So what do I do?'

'Be authentic. Be true to yourself.'

'I don't know what that means.'

'That's the point.'

There was a long silence. Nixie walked slowly round the small courtyard and came to a stop close to Seb. 'Okay, this is the score.' Her confidence was returning. Her voice steadied and her gaze met Seb's curious eyes. She was on familiar territory, persuading somebody to do something, or be somebody, for another's benefit.

'The fraud case involving Makepeace, Melbury and Fortescue was passed onto the Serious Fraud Office. They've spent the last year unravelling it. They know everything. They know you were the whistleblower, they know about the sweeteners, the bribes, and the rest of the crap that motivates these loathsome bastards to get out of bed every morning… but there's one piece of the jigsaw still missing. It's the use of children as "sweeteners". Namely, rape and other sexual offence against children.'

'You're talking about Makepeace?'

'None other.'

'So where do I come into this?'

'Not the fraud. Counsel is appointed, and there's a date fixed for the hearing, but the criminal case is at a standstill. One potential witness is missing. We're talking about Imogen, the young girl, the one in the photos you showed me, and the one of her with Makepeace on the beach. It was you who assaulted Makepeace. I don't need to spell it out. You saw what was going on and you beat him up.'

'How do you know I beat him up?'

'Supposition.'

'There has to be more than that.'

'There is more to it than that. When those photos hit the press, there was a call for witnesses.

Potential witnesses came forward. The public was obliging. The police now have a timeline of your movements. The weekend in question: starts in London, then you drive to Lavenham, then you take a trip to Aldeburgh, and then come back to London.'

'So it was you – you took those photos from me and passed them on to the press. Thanks.'

'Not guilty. It was my handler.'

'Right. I get it. It's all coming together now. '

'What's coming together?'

Seb looked grim. 'I'll tell you, but not right now. Anything else?'

'They want everything you know about her. It's important, Seb.'

'Whose they?'

'The Met, the Crown Prosecution Service. The girl could be an important witness for the prosecution. So you have to tell.'

'I'm not sure I want to.'

Flori gave him a long, hard look. 'What's your problem?'

He paused. 'The publicity primarily. She's a vulnerable child.'

'Maybe she is, but wouldn't she want to put that bastard behind bars?'

Seb stood up and walked away from where he'd been sitting. He leant with his back against a wall, and stared at her. His face was inscrutable. 'Nixie, what you're asking me to do, is heavy duty. I can't do it. Not right now.'

'Why not...? Okay, I'll put it another way. You have no choice.'

'So... it's tough talk now.'

'Yeah, it has to be, because if you remain schtum, I can guarantee you'll get subpoenaed for both trials. The criminal trial of Makepeace, and separately for the fraud. They're connected. And remember I know all about you. Running and hiding? Forget it. Because Zanthe and her family can't or won't. That'll be the end of your beautiful love affair.'

'You're a real bitch, Nixie.'

'Yeah. A female version of you. A thief you said. But be authentic, you also said. So that's exactly what I'm doing. What do you know?'

'I don't take kindly to being threatened – especially by you, Nixie. It makes me more stubborn. You should know that.'

'You're pissing me off, Seb. If it's protecting the girl that's holding you back, surely you know in this type of case, the child's anonymity is protected.'

'I didn't know that, but it doesn't change my decision. There's a bit more to it than that.'

'Okay, maybe this'll change your mind. If you refuse, you'll also be charged with grievous bodily harm of Makepeace and with breaking and entering your father's office at Lavenham, plus any other stuff the creative minds of the Met can come up with and, I hate to say this, but daddy and mummy won't take kindly to knowing it was their son who dropped him in the shit. Not forgetting, of course, hacking into Langhithe computer system.'

'Fine. Pile it on, Nixie. As far as my father goes, there's no love lost between us, so I couldn't care less. Besides, it's only a matter of time until he knows that I was the whistleblower. As for my mother, I'm expecting her to take my side so I can make my peace with her as and when... assuming of course, when it does all come out, she chooses divorce rather than the marital trap of money.

'Your threat of criminal proceedings – hasn't it occurred to you, since you also work undercover, that's hardly going to happen, is it? Because, in the process of bringing me to book, your role will be blown apart. I can guarantee I won't keep my mouth shut, and what would your Mike say to that? Not to mention the whole of Grassroots. No one would be pleased.'

'There's ways round it. So what do you say?'

'I say that your work is particularly nasty.'

'Couldn't agree more. Yours too. Nasty, but necessary.'

'It takes a certain type…'

'That's right, and I'm that type. You know that. I know that. So what about it?'

'Let me think about it.'

'How long will you take?'

'I've no idea, but I'm not coming to a decision right now.'

'Okay. What about tomorrow?'

Seb shrugged, 'Can't say for sure.'

'So when?'

'Soon.'

'Christ, what's the problem?'

'Because it's serious stuff, Nixie. More than you know.' There was a long silence as they contemplated each other. 'I've got to go. It's late.' He glanced at his mobile, stood up.

'Where are you going?'

'Where do think…? The house on the headland, the one you're so fucking interested in.'

'To see Zanthe. How are you getting there?'

'Dunno. I came by car, but I've had too much to drink… the water taxis stop after one.'

'Do you want to stay here?'

'That's not a good idea.'

'Maybe not. But neither is driving down precipitous coastal roads in the early hours, while under the influence, if that's what you were thinking... You should stay, but it's up to you.'

'Yeah, it is up to me...' He walked over to her and looked straight at her. 'What's your game, Nixie? We're not an item any longer.'

'I know that. No game. But, I still care about you.'

'Really...don't make me laugh... after what you've just been threatening me with?'

'It's my work. It's how we operate, as you know. Nothing personal. It's what we do. You understand that.'

'Life according to Nixie. The personal and the professional. Unrelated. I don't buy it anymore. But whatever, I'm assuming you have a spare bed?'

'I don't.'

There was a long silence. 'What's going on? '

'Who knows?'

'Okay. You always did know your own mind. Fuck it.'

'I'm not sure what you mean but...'

' Nixie You have to know that my relationship with Zanthe... It's important. I need to text her. Give me five minutes, and I'll be with you.'

She woke alone. Distraught, half asleep, she stumbled into the courtyard. There was a note on the table. She picked it up. 'Nixie, meet me today, about four. Go down to the ferry terminal, ask for Andreas and he'll take you to a beach where we can talk. He's totally trustworthy. The swimming is superb, by the way. See you later, Seb.'

— 22 —

Andreas swung the boat into the bay, and brought the boat to a halt by a large, flat rock. It had taken twenty exhilarating minutes from the harbour to reach there. Nixie watched as he tethered the boat to a bollard alongside a speed boat already moored there, and a moment later he jumped out, and holding out his hand, he steadied Nixie as she stepped from the boat onto the rock.

She glanced around, her attention immediately caught by someone swimming strongly across the bay towards them. It was Seb. He pulled himself out of the water, said a quick hello and dripping, picked up the towel lying flat on the rock, and after wrapping it round himself, shook hands with Andreas. There was a short but animated conversation in Greek which involved Andreas raising his voice, and banging his fist down onto his other hand but just as she thought this had to be a serious argument, they burst into laughter and Andreas left. They were on their own.

Seb smiled, said, 'Hello, you. You're looking unusually shy.'

'I feel shy.'

She was unsure after their conversation the previous night what decision he might have come to and she regretted offering him her bed. It had been madness. It had awakened all the strong feelings she'd thought she'd got under control. She forced herself to speak.

'You understand Greek, then.'

'Just a little.'

'Is this place safe, can we talk?'

'Yes, if that's okay.'

'I prefer somewhere with shade.'

'Well, we can go up there.' He pointed to a narrow path leading into the trees. 'There's a tamarisk tree. It has shade, a view of the sea and it's private.'

'Good. Is this bay near where you live?'

'It's not far. But you can only get here by boat – that keeps most of the tourists away.'

'Is that yours?' Nixie pointed to the speedboat.

'No, it belongs to Nikos… Let's go. We have to talk.'

He picked up his backpack, slipped his feet into flip flops, and looking at her expectantly, waited for her to follow him up the rough track. The path curved through the trees and away from the water. Eventually he came to a stop and pushing his way past some shrubby bushes, they came to a small clearing.

'This is it.' He pulled out a towel from his backpack, cleared some stones away, and laid it flat under the tree. 'Okay? '

Nixie glanced around, 'Thanks, but I prefer to sit on that rock. It looks like a seat, but thanks anyway.'

'You seem jumpy.'

'I am. I want to know what's going on.'

'Okay.' He paused. 'Right… What I'm about to say is to go no further.'

'That's not possible. I have to report back. You know that.'

'I'm talking about the press. You've let me down once.' She didn't answer. He eyeballed her. 'Are you wired? That back pack you've brought with you, empty it, please. And your bikini? Is that concealing anything?'

'Seb, this isn't necessary.'

'If it wasn't, I wouldn't be asking. Do you have a mobile?'

'No mobile.' Nixie picked up her backpack and emptied out the contents. It contained a towel, sunscreen and a bottle of water. Seb put his hands in the bag's pockets. Empty. He gave her a hard look. 'What about your bikini?'

She glared. 'Don't be stupid. You have my word for it. I'm not wired.'

'Okay. But there's a reason for my paranoia. The photos of Imogen that got plastered all over the press were seen by certain people. Thugs, I'd call them. They didn't like them and they didn't like me. It was bad enough before they cottoned on I was the whistleblower and I beat up Makepeace... I can do without a repeat situation.'

'Who are you talking about?'

'Some arseholes...I'm about to tell you, but those photos...I can't trust you.'

'I told my handler not to pass the photos on. He ignored me. I'm sorry about that.'

'So, it was your handler. Well, great, thanks to him my life's been threatened.' Nixie was silent. 'I'd assumed it was Makepeace behind the arson and being run off the road, and that's partly true. He is involved – but not in the way I thought. He's a consumer, if I can put it that way, of sexual services supplied by a gang of human traffickers. They import young women from Eastern Europe. Gullible and desperate women, hoping for a better life. They think they're going to proper jobs. They want to send money back to their family. The reality is they're forced into prostitution.'

'So how does Imogen come into this?'

'Imogen is part of the supply chain.'

'How do you mean?'

'I'm talking about sex for the so-called civilised members of society; the effete, landed gentry, the wheelers and dealers of industry, the rich, and the stupid. The service was unknown, they operated in the shadows… until this hit the press.'

'You sound angry, Seb.'

'I am fucking angry. Anyone with a modicum of humanity would be, wouldn't they? They fuck up lives. And somewhere, somehow, my father's involved with them.'

'How?'

'He operates in those grey areas, the ones where people say, "I didn't know, I didn't see, I can't say, I can't help."'

Nixie glanced at him. There was no way now she could get him to cooperate. Guilt just wouldn't work. He actually didn't give a fuck about maintaining a relationship with his father, but he cared about the young girl. That was obvious.

'I still don't understand how Imogen is involved.' Seb glared at her, but didn't answer. She tried another tack. 'How did you find out about all this?'

'I'll tell you. Those photos, the ones left after the break-in. I recognised the buildings in some of them, so I did some detective work. I went back to London. It wasn't difficult. I hung around the square. I observed what was going on. I watched the cabs, the chauffeur-driven cars, the comings and goings, the men, the girls. It's big business. And there's tie-ins with restaurants and night clubs.'

'When did you go back to the UK ?'

'A month or two after we split up. I felt a total mess so I had to do something. I missed you and the buzz of the work.' He looked out over the sea, then turned to face Nixie. 'Losing you, and everything that you said you valued, was one motive, but besides that, Imogen's face haunted me. I remembered her as she was, a sweet, serious child. I wanted to speak to her but then an idea came to me. One that could help her breakaway from the shit she's got herself into.'

'Why didn't her adoptive parents help her?'

'Her parents?'

'Yes, you'd told me she'd been adopted.'

'Oh, that wasn't true. I first met her on the beach at Aldeburgh. She was about eleven or twelve and I was fed up with my life. I'd walked along the beach and I came across the Shell. It's a piece of sculpture. Do you know it?' Nixie shook her head. 'So I was standing there looking at it and this small girl walks up to me and she starts talking to me as if we knew each other and we just clicked.

'I met her later, again by chance, I was on the beach walking towards Thorpeness and I saw that prick, Makepeace, having a pop-shot at her. I just lost it. I wanted to kick the shit out of him. Then I took her back to her father. Another useless specimen of humanity. I realised then that she'd had a bad start in life and it was only a matter of time before some arse hole would take advantage of that. And how right I was.'

'So where are you going with all this?'

'I'm about to tell you.'

'When I first met her, she'd told me she wanted to go to art school and be an artist. Like the sculptor, she said, who'd created the Shell. But she'd been told it was too expensive. So there I was, a rich kid with the best of education and I'd been left some money in my half brother's will.

'I had no need for it so I went to a solicitor

specialising in missing persons and I said, find her, and tell her, if she leaves prostitution, I'll pay her fees if she gets herself into art school. He employed a private detective. He found her. She said, thanks, but no thanks. She wanted to be independent, she said and she'd use her own earnings for education... It'd be funny if it wasn't so tragic.'

'Did you believe her?'

'No. I didn't. I insisted on meeting her. We met in the solicitor's office. She looked wasted.'

'Did she tell you what was going on?'

'Yeah. She did.'

'And did she mention Makepeace?'

'She's one smart cookie. She told me the whole shebang. Makepeace confides in her. He uses this gang to supply sweeteners for potential government contracts, which includes Langhithe. He tells her, "the girls oil the wheels."'

'What does she make of that?'

'She can't stand him, even though, whatever she wants, he gets for her. But she's under no illusion. He'll move on. He likes young girls but she's almost past her "sell by date".'

'So how did you leave it with her?'

'I was straight. I gave her an ultimatum. She quits. I pay her fees.'

'Surely, that won't work. She can't just walk away.'

'True. But she hates what she's doing, and she's seen what happens to girls who continue with drugs and prostitution.'

'So where is she now?'

'Some place in London. I think she'd quit, but she's frightened of the thugs that run the gang. And like I say, she's dependent on Makepeace. He gives her attention, sweet talks her, buys her presents, and she has her friendships with the girls. She likes them, she helps them with their English, and she tells them about England. That's her life.'

'It's awful. Does he pimp her?'

'I don't want to know. Probably not in an obvious way, after all, he has a reputation to consider.'

'It's sad.'

'It is sad. She's sad. She's been on this track from childhood. I've told her she'll have other friendships, if she starts art school.'

'Wouldn't she have to have a portfolio?'

'That's no problem. She has a sketchpad; she carries it around with her. I've seen some of her drawings and she's good, or to my untrained eye, she's good. I've got to find some way of getting her out.'

'Have you been to the police?'

'Not yet, but I will. I'm giving her a little more time to think things over.'

'But what about you? They'll be down on you like a ton of bricks.'

'I don't care about myself too much.'

'They know you were behind the hacking.'

'So what? If I go to the police with information about this gang, maybe a deal can be stitched up'

Nixie looked directly at Seb. 'Yes, you're right, a deal could be worked out. I was asked to find you and I have found you, and you know enough about Imogen and Makepeace for the SFO and the Met to put the final nail in the coffin of the Langhithe bribery and corruption investigation. Providing you're prepared to pass on your information.'

Seb raised his eyebrows. 'What's the catch?'

'No catch. This is the deal. It's simple, straightforward. All you and Imogen have to do is cooperate with the police. You tell them everything you know. In exchange, we ask for all charges to be put on hold, and we'd ask that both of you go into the Witness Protection Scheme.'

'The Witness Protection Scheme?'

'Yeah. You must have heard of it. You're relocated and given a new identity. It's run by the police.'

'What if I don't want that?'

'Your choice. Maybe staying in Greece will be enough to maintain your anonymity.'

'And Imogen?'

'Same applies. She does whatever suits, more or less.'

'Sounds good, but I'd like her to get to an art school in London.'

'London isn't the only place. The Witness Protection Scheme is international. The States, Europe, or wherever, it's a new beginning.'

'Maybe she could come to Athens.'

'Athens? You really do care about her.'

'Yeah, I do. I don't have a track record of treating women right and I was born lucky – financially speaking – so this would be one way of making amends.'

'So what's your thinking?'

'About the deal? Great, if it works. But do you have the authority to carry it through?'

'No, not personally, but I can work on my handler. He has the contacts and this case has been going on for too long. He's sick of it, and he has a teenage daughter, which means he has zero tolerance for the sexual exploitation of young women, and he likes me.'

'He likes you?'

'Yeah. He likes me.' Seb was smiling. 'Not in the way you think. Not in a sexual way. Or at least I don't think so.'

'And what about me?'

'Do I think you like me? I'm pretty sure you like me.'

'Well, you're right, I'd say I like you a lot. Let's swim.'

'I'm up for that. It's too hot now, even in the shade.'

'What's so funny? Why are you laughing?'

'If you don't know, I'm not telling you. Let's go for it.'

They gathered up their belongings and walked back through the trees until they reached the bay. Nixie walked along the flat rocks until she came to deep water, then pulling off her flip flops, she briefly hesitated, before jumping in. The water was warm, its colour, turquoise, reflecting the sky, and looking up, she saw the sun's light splitting into a thousand fragments as it entered the water.

She swam to the surface, took a deep breath and, curving her hands away from her body, kicked her feet and headed down towards the bottom. It was so clear she could see the shoals of tiny fish darting around underwater. She glanced up. Seb had followed her and for a brief moment, he circled round, before he grabbed her hand, and pulled her up to the surface. Holding onto a rock with one hand, he drew her towards him and kissed her. It was a kiss that seemed to last so long, time and place had little meaning.

— 23 —

Nixie glanced round. The waiting room was full. She'd rather be anywhere than where she was right now. Surgeries... she hated them. She took her place in the queue for the receptionist and waited her turn.

'Have you got an appointment?'

'Yes, I rang.'

'Your name?'

'Nixie Morgan.'

'Take a seat. The doctor will be with you soon.'

She walked across and flicked through the pile of magazines. Most of them were old, well thumbed, a random selection of Hello, Country Life, Hair Dressing Journal, Vogue and the Observer Weekend Magazine. Something for everyone. An elderly man coughed incessantly. A baby cried. His mother picked him up and, holding him in her arms, carried him round the waiting room. The loud beat of music through someone's head phones. She sighed, crossed her legs, irritably swinging one leg back and forth, hoping she didn't have to wait long. She had to see Bill later.

A disembodied voice came over the intercom. 'Nixie Morgan. Room five.'

The doctor was attractive, in her thirties, and had her eyes fixed on the computer screen. She glanced up as Nixie entered the room and smiled. 'Sit down, Nixie. How can I help?'

'I think I'm pregnant.'

'You sound unsure. When was your last period?'

'Three months ago.'

'Do you have any other changes in your body?'

'Like what? What kind of changes?'

'Sore breasts, tiredness, back ache, morning sickness.'

'Actually yes, I have noticed sore breasts and some sickness. I did think I might be pregnant, but I wanted to be sure.'

'When did you last have sex with your partner?'

'My partner? I wouldn't say I have a partner. Not really.'

'Assuming you are pregnant, you must have had sex with someone, whether partner or not. Do you remember when that was?'

'Yes. I can remember very well. I was on a Greek island. We'd been lovers, but we split up and he got involved with someone else, but then we met again, and we spent an afternoon together, you know, making love... by the sea.'

Nixie smiled engagingly at the doctor.

The doctor paused, looked searchingly at Nixie's face and pressed on, 'And did you use contraception?'

'No, no contraception. We didn't have any on us.'

'So it's likely, don't you think, you are pregnant.'

'I suppose so.'

'And that he's the father.'

'I don't know whether he is or not... everything I say ... it's confidential, isn't it?'

'Of course.'

'Because there was another time, with someone else. That was an earlier occasion, but it could be him, you know, if you think about the timing. I only did it because, well, I suppose I was upset, because, I missed him, and I was trying to pretend I didn't care, and I was angry as well, but really I did care. It didn't work anyway... because all the time I was thinking about him. So he could be the father, couldn't he? I mean it's possible either of them, could, you know, be the father.'

The doctor took a quick look at her, her face showed considerable disbelief. She sighed. 'Yes, theoretically, either could be.'

'So how will I know which one it is?'

'You can't tell until the baby's born. There are ways before, while you're still pregnant, but it involves taking a blood sample, and that puts the baby's life at risk. It's not done, for that reason.'

'And what about after the baby's born?'

'Apart from the obvious – does the baby look like the father and share any distinguishing features – there are DNA tests that can be undertaken.'

Nixie stared at her. 'I see. Okay, well thanks for the info. I'll be off now.'

'Before you go, I presume you would like to know, more definitely, if you are pregnant?'

'Oh, yes, I suppose so.'

'Well, take off your clothes, pop yourself on the couch, and I'll take a look at your tummy.'

Nixie stared at the ceiling as the doctor examined her.

'Thank you, Nixie, you can get dressed now.'

She pulled on her clothes and stood hesitantly by the desk. 'Take a seat. This is your first visit, isn't it?' Nixie nodded. 'Yes, you are pregnant so we need to keep an eye on you and the baby. You'll need an ultrasound. I'm assuming you want to keep the baby, but if you don't...'

'I definitely want the baby.'

'It maybe, after your ultrasound, and dependent on the baby's size, we can tell more precisely when you got pregnant, and that will allay your fears about who the father is.'

'I don't have any fears. I don't need to know. I know already. The baby's father is Seb, the one on the Greek island'

'Seb? But you mentioned someone else. Wouldn't you like to know for sure?'

'I do know for sure. I've just thought about it. I want Seb to be the father... I want him, whereas if it was the other one... well, I don't want him... Does that sound awful?' Her voice petered out.

'Do you still see him? Or was it a one-off? I'm referring to the one you call, "the other one".'

'Mike? We're in the same group, I know him alright. I see him all the time.'

'Why so?'

'It's an environmental pressure group. We work together. We're activists.'

'What about the baby – when he or she grows up, they'll want to know for sure who their father is.'

'They will know for sure. It'll be Seb.' The doctor silently scrutinised her face. 'Okay, Nixie, please make another appointment before you leave. I need to keep an eye on you.'

Nixie left and immediately made her way to her favourite coffee shop. That she was pregnant didn't surprise her. Her mind drifted back to Spetses, the long afternoon of love making, the heat, the water, the swimming, Seb's caresses. At the time, she'd had no thought she'd get pregnant. It hadn't crossed her mind that there could be consequences. She'd assumed that, as before, she could take risks and get away with it. But later, she had thought about it. She'd wondered what she'd do if she got pregnant, but she knew the answer now.

That Mike could be the father, wasn't part of her plan. He wasn't and never would be a permanent part of her life. She'd always loved Seb. She didn't know why. She just did. Besides, he'd be a good father. Zanthe wouldn't need to know, nor her mother. She'd spin her mother the same line she'd told the doctor, she didn't know who the father was. Whether her mother believed her or not was immaterial. Whether she disapproved of her or not, was also immaterial.

She caught the tube to Bethnal Green and made her way to the safe house. Bill had asked to see her, why, she didn't know, but probably to give her an update about the Fortescue, Makepeace case. She got to the house, rang the bell and waited for Bill to open it, her mind filled with the excitement of her pregnancy.

'You look like the cat that got the cream.'

'You could say that.'

'Well, come in. Talking of which, I've been down to the deli and bought some French pastries to have with our coffee.'

'No thanks. I have to think about my diet now – for the baby.'

He glanced at her, his mind clearly elsewhere. 'What baby?'

'He's not born yet.'

Bill did a double take. She had his full and undivided attention. 'Is this your way of telling me you're pregnant?'

'It is and I am.'

Bill sat down and stared at her. 'Fucking hell... who's the father?'

'I dunno.'

Bill paused, and then roared with laughter. 'Pull the other one. It has to be Seb Melbury.'

'I told you, I don't know.'

'Nixie, you may get away with lying to other

people, but not with me. How many months are you?'

She paused; if she told him, he could work it out, but he'd know soon enough. All he had to do was a quick calculation, but he could never prove it. She'd tell him.

'Nearly four months.'

'Three to four months... now let's see, that would be about the time you left that Greek island to return to the UK. Well, it was a productive meeting, in more ways than one, it seems.' He grinned.

'Two and two make five. What did you want to see me about?'

'And one and one make three. If I put a bet on the father, I'd say it was Seb.'

'And you'd be wrong, because I don't know who the father is.'

'Do you think I believe that?'

Nixie sighed. 'Tell me what you want to see me about?'

'Well, good luck, whoever the father is... We've got a date for the trial. Everything's set up. Seb Melbury has been informed and it won't be long before those bastards, Makepeace, Fortescue and Melbury, get their comeuppance. We've had to negotiate around the dates a little as Seb is getting married in the next six months.' Bill's face was deadpan. 'But I expect you knew that.'

'I didn't, not about the proposed marriage. Is it to a Greek woman, called Zanthe?'

'I believe so.'

'And Imogen? What about her?'

'She's our star witness. Revenge is sweet. She hates the bastards and is well and truly sticking the knife in. She's in hiding and that's where she'll stay for the interim.'

'Is Seb helping her? He said he'd get her to art school.'

'That's the deal. She wants to be like the woman who made the sculpture on a beach in Suffolk – which is, ironically, where she first met that odious character, Makepeace.'

'It's like a shell. I've not seen it myself, but I've seen Gormley's work near Liverpool.'

'Gormley. Who's he?'

'Anthony Gormley, another sculptor. He's put copies of himself all along the beach. '

'That's weird. Haven't seen either of them, but then I'm a philistine.'

'Is that it?'

'It is.' He paused. 'And thanks for all the work you've done. Does this pregnancy mean you're giving up working?'

'Don't know. Maybe. Maybe not.' Nixie stood up to go.

'I hope not. You know how to take your work to the next level, when it's something you want.' He smiled seductively.

Nixie paused. 'Fuck off. I'll tell you something… If I do leave, I won't miss your dirty little innuendos.'

'Just joking, Nixie.'

Nixie had had to go into hospital for the birth. Necessary, she'd been told, given the possible dangers to the baby who initially was laying the wrong way. But the baby finally arrived safely, and all her fears had now been forgotten. Looking at the baby, she felt she'd burst with pride. She was fascinated by her tiny face, her fine, dark, straight hair, her miniature hands and her large serious eyes. When the nurse had first put her into her arms, she'd said her eyes reminded her of the baby's father, and there and then she'd decided to call her Dora. She'd said this was because the baby's eyes, were like her father's, adorable. She was careful not to say his name.

She looked out of the hospital window for the tenth time, apprehensively waiting for her mother's car to swing into the hospital car park. It would be her mother's first visit to see the baby – and she was late. She sighed. She hoped her mother wouldn't again bring up the question of Dora's father. They'd had a disagreement about her not knowing; when she'd first told her she was pregnant. She remembered the conversation well. Her mother's first question had been to ask about the baby's father. She'd told her she didn't know.

Her mother had said, 'What do you mean, you don't know?'

She'd snapped back, 'It means what it says, I don't know.'

Her mother had pursed her lips and fixed her eyes on her as if struggling to make sense of what she'd just heard. 'Surely you know who you've slept with?'

She'd given her mother one of her looks and had said, still irritably, 'Yes, but not precisely when... look, it happens. You're behaving as if you never slept with anyone other than Dad, and I don't believe that either.'

Her mother stared at her, and then she'd smiled, 'Maybe that's true. But you've been seeing Seb for quite a while, so why couldn't he be the father?'

She'd fired back, 'You hate him.'

There was a short pause, before she answered. 'I don't hate him. I just wouldn't want him as the father of my granddaughter.'

'Well, that's what I thought, but fortunately,

he's going to be the father of someone else's child.' That response had come out of the blue, but it was enough to throw her mother off the scent. 'What do you mean?'

She'd said, 'He's getting married.'

Her mother looked disconcerted. 'So his bride is pregnant?'

'I have no idea. She could be for all I know. I was just talking theoretically.' By this time, she just wanted her mother to shut up, but she didn't shut up. She went right on with her questions. 'But I'd assumed you and Seb had made up.'

'What gave you that idea?'

'You went to Greece not long ago. Didn't you?'

'Not to see him. I was in Athens, doing the tourist bit.'

'Well, surely you must have some idea of who the father is? It's unbelievable.'

'Stop nagging. You're getting on my nerves.'

'So when's the baby due?'

'In five months, give or take a couple of weeks. I thought you'd be pleased.'

'I'd be even more pleased if there was a father around.'

'So you keep saying. Isn't this a case of history repeating itself?'

'And what's that mean?'

'It means that at the time you had me, there was no sign of my father. You told me. Remember? He tracked you down after I was born.'

'That's because he didn't know I was pregnant, because I hadn't told him. I knew he was the father.' Her mother sounded defensive. They glared at each other. 'Look, Nixie, I am a little upset, for the baby's sake, but I'm also pleased for you. When will you know whether it's a boy or a girl?'

'At the next ultrasound.'

'Do you have a preference?'

'No. Boy or girl. I really don't mind.' And with that, she'd refused to discuss the subject any longer, even when her mother tried to broach the issue again.

She glanced out of the window. There was still no sign of her mother. But waiting around for her was making her edgy. If she did ask any further questions, she'd say the situation was as before, she had no idea, and what's more she wasn't concerned. She was pleased she'd had a healthy, beautiful baby and that was enough. She walked over to Dora and gazed down at her.

Seb didn't yet know about the baby's birth. She'd tell him after her mother had gone. That had been another awkward conversation. When she'd told him she was pregnant with a little girl and that he was the father, his reaction unsettled her almost as much as her mother's response. For a start, he'd taken the news so calmly, it was as if he expected it. Either that or he didn't care. She'd asked him if he was shocked.

'Shocked?' He'd said, 'No, why should I be, we weren't exactly careful, were we?'

She'd paused thinking maybe he'd split up with Zanthe, perhaps hoping he'd say no, but that's when he'd told her they were getting married.' She'd said, 'Really? How sweet. You getting married – are you having me on?'

'It's what she wants and what her parents want.'

When she'd asked, 'So what about the baby?' he hadn't answered and for one awful moment, she thought he'd put the phone down. But he hadn't gone. He said he was thinking. He'd told her that he loved Zanthe but he wanted to do the right thing.

He'd said, 'I'll come and visit when the baby's born.'

A flash of anger passed through her, but she restrained herself, enough to sound calm and said mildly, 'Is that all?'

'What else can I do?'

That was when she pointed out that he had responsibilities. His answer angered her even more. He said, 'I want you to keep our relationship and the baby a secret, for the sake of Zanthe and her family. Can you do that?'

Still keeping her temper, she'd replied, 'Keeping a secret –so what's new. But for you, anything.'

'You sound bitter.'

'Why wouldn't I be?'

'What are you saying?'

She'd given it to him straight, 'I'm thinking of the baby's future, and you as the father.'

'And...?'

'You have financial responsibilities for a start.'

'I can accept that. It's not a problem. But my condition remains. What's gone on between the two of us, has to be secret.'

'So I can never tell her who her father is? Is that what you really want?'

'Well, that's harsh, but I'll face that problem when and if it comes. People and circumstances change, so who knows what the future will bring?'

That reference to their relationship had both upset and intrigued her. She'd said, 'What about us?' and he'd answered, 'It remains as it is.'

'Which is?'

'You know exactly what it is, Nixie.'

'I don't.'

'And neither do I and that's about it and how it's always been. But... now and again, maybe we can meet up, don't you think?'

'Do you care about me, Seb?'

'I do, more than you'll ever understand and...I'm pleased about the baby. In fact, if we were together, I'd make love to you.'

'But soon you'll be married man...'

'So what,' he'd said, 'I'm still the same.'

'You need the excitement of the forbidden.'

'Always, and who better than you to give me that.'

That had been the end of their conversation. It had left her totally stirred up. As she stood thinking back to that, Dora's eyes opened, her face reddened and puckered, and waving her small fists in the air, she began wailing. It grew stronger and louder by each second. Nixie walked across and held her close, before sitting down to feed her. The baby's eyes closed with satisfaction. Her small hands clenched Nixie's finger. Nixie idly separated each of her fingers as she lay in her arms.

The little finger on both hands had a noticeable curve. Where had she seen that before? It reminded her of something said to her. She paused; it had been the doctor. The one she'd seen when she'd first thought she was pregnant. She'd asked how she would know who the father was. Dredging back into her memory, the conversation gradually filtered back into her consciousness. The doctor had said that if the baby shared any distinguishing features with someone else, that could indicate who the father was.

She went cold. The only person she knew with a curved little finger, was Mike. That could mean only one thing. Mike was the father of Dora – not Seb. She took a deep breath. She willed herself to stay calm. She stared into space. She was shocked, unsure how she could cope. Maybe she'd got it wrong, maybe she'd misheard what the doctor had said, maybe the doctor was wrong.

She waited until Dora finished feeding then put her down in her crib and walked across to the window. She prayed her mother hadn't arrived. She needed time to think things through, but she was there, in the car park, standing by her car, holding a large bouquet of flowers. She had to pull herself together. She was sure to ask her again; can you remember now? Who is Dora's father?

She'd planned to say, it's the same as before, I don't know, but now the words would stick in her throat. She did know, but she couldn't tell the truth – the father of Dora was Mike. She had to say something, something convincing. What could she say? What should she say? She sat down, tweaking a lock of hair through her fingers thinking through the implications.

The truth was hard. A lie was easy. She came to a decision. She would say things were just the same, she didn't know. Lies had always come easily to her. It was what she did. It would be one of many. She'd lived long enough in the parallel universe of truth and lies to know the territory well. She was good at it.

Seb would carry on thinking that Dora was conceived on Spetses. Zanthe would never know that she, Nixie had had a daughter, and that Seb believed he was the father. Mike would always assume Seb was the father. And she'd tell her mother, as she'd said before, I don't know who the father is.

Each of them would know a partial truth, based on what she wanted them to believe, or what they thought they knew. But only she knew the whole truth, and if she chose to lie about that, it wasn't really a lie. It was what she wanted, so she was being true to herself. She was being authentic, just as Seb had said. The truth would be a secret she'd carry with her for as long as it suited her and for as long as her luck held out. But what of Dora? She smiled to herself, and whispered to the baby, 'One day, I'll take you to meet your daddy.'

Acknowledgements

My thanks to all who continue to show an interest in my writing, especially Richard Grove for my website, the formatting and cover of 'Truth and Lies', to Richard Pearce for his invaluable advice on the political references to the UK and Greece, and to Anne Russell on issues of continuity. Jay Dixon's work as editor was, as ever, superb and any mistakes that might remain are wholly my own.

Also by Marguerite Valentine

'Between the Shadow and the Soul'

A story about the conflicts of love and friendship, Flori is an attractive, successful young woman living in London when in a moment of madness, she steals a tiny baby. Calling for help from her best friend, Rose is forced to face the consequences of Flori's traumatic history.

'It was very gripping. The main character and her state of mind was particularly well developed, in a way that I still have a clear image of her. Looking forward for the next books!'

(Amazon customer)

'My name is Echo'

Echo is growing up. She's sharp, quirky and funny but life is a problem, especially her relationships with men.. Written in her own words, this is a magical tale of desire, fantasy and revenge.

'Echo is the compelling and exciting story of a young girl with a troubled relationship with her mother, and an absent father ,who gradually learns to recognise and accept love. Highly recommended!'

(Amazon customer)

If you enjoyed reading my books please consider writing a review on Amazon or Good Reads. You may also be interested in visiting my website www. margueritev.org which I endeavour to regularly update and where you can also sign up to receive news about my forthcoming writing. .

Made in the USA
Columbia, SC
30 December 2017